$5.00

IMPASSE

ALLISON CREWS

IMPASSE

ALLISON CREWS

Tilda Bogue Publishing
Post Office Box 414
Canton, Mississippi 39046
www.tbpublishing.net

First Edition: November 2010

Summary: Elliott Marks is sure that her dreams have come true when the love of her life moves into her neighborhood. At the same time, she wonders whether her attraction to him is a gift, a cruel twist of fate, or prelude to greater things to come.

ISBN (Hardcover) 0-9841692-1-0
1. Horses – Fiction 2. College – Fiction 3. Schools – Fiction 4. Mississippi - Fiction

Printed in the United States of America

To my grandmothers,
Mother – Marjorie Bullard Turner and
Granny – Elfie Bigby Grogan

Thank you for your wisdom, love, and instruction that remain alive in my mind to this day, whether I want it to or not.

CONTENTS

A list of characters and foxhunting terms are included at the back of this book.

Receive my instruction, and not silver; and knowledge rather than choice gold.
~ Proverbs 8:9-11

PREFACE

I'd never given much thought about the one with whom I'd spend my life. That never really interested me – until now. For me, the choice had always been easy. My horse. I'd worry about dating and marriage and family after college. Education and career first...focus.

It wasn't after college. I'm in college. And that's too soon for such final choices. But when I look into his eyes I see hope, a future, real promise for eternal happiness in the arms of this one – the one I love.

Somewhere deep in his eyes, though, I could see that his anger, uncertainty, and love for me were driving him away – from commitment, from happiness, from hope.

There was nothing I could do to change him. Did I even want to? Of course I'm not going to willingly choose a life of emotional volatility – I never have had to deal with that; well, not counting growing up with two older sisters. I love him, but Mother and Grand say love isn't enough. What do I know about love? Attraction is obvious, at least, with him. But love? Day to day love? My parents make it look so easy.

Just how much anger smolders behind those green eyes? And would he ever direct it at me? Surely not, but...what if he did? After all, his father made him an orphan in one fiery instant. How can I be so sure he's safe if he doesn't even know if he is himself?

Today I trust him, about most things. As long as trust remains, I remain. We have years before we have to make drastic decisions, so, for now, I'm in…just putting a little distance between us. After all, isn't that why we date? But we have to date more than one person to be sure. Don't we? We can be friends and date other people, can't we? Just to be sure…

So, what is he going to do with his uncertainty? The choice was his. He was saying something to me that I couldn't catch...he loves me… yes, yes, he always says that, but did he just say something about… leaving…starting today? Where's he going? What have I done?

He reached over and touched my chin with his fingertip. "I do love you, Elliott. Never forget it."

Then he walked to his truck…and drove away.

BACK IN THE SADDLE

Chapter 1

"Foxhunting provides those fleeting moments of total abandonment – of wind in your hair, bugs in your teeth kind of living. At its best, it is totally out of control. Hounds are screaming, hooves are thundering, the horn is blasting as you race and jump across country to die for, often in weather not fit for man or beast. It is the original extreme sport..."

~ *Carla M. Hawkinson, MFH*

Black hooves pummeling the frozen field, Viva whirled across the sage. I asked for more speed, twisting a bit of her mane in my right fingers to steady myself should she leave me behind with her response. She didn't, and I leaned forward ever so slightly to compensate – doing my best not to upset her balance at this blistering pace.

At the edge of the field, menacing thorn bushes impaired our progress, and we slowed just enough to negotiate. Bouncing, dodging, jumping, leaping through razor sharp branches, she at last stretched down and long when we reached the field beyond – her strides now pulling maximum speed. I sat as if riding a missile, glorying in her fluid motion. No time to check for holes, can't even see the ground, can't see through my wind born tears...have to get across this field before the hounds, their music was getting louder, the orchestra in full crescendo...

"Split pack! Stop the ones going south!" William's voice cracked over my radio. Although he was shouting, I barely heard him over the wind's roar. We were already going that direction at top speed since the pack of foxhounds had suddenly turned and headed our way. Behind me, I heard more thunderous rumbling.

Stretched along Viva's neck, I glanced over my right shoulder to see Griffen and Jet approaching like wingmen closing the gap. Griffen signaled for me to continue south while they turned towards where hounds were likely to appear. The unspoken gesture meant that he wanted me to keep going south to get ahead of the pack should he be unable to stop them.

I was not familiar with this part of our hunt country, for I had never ventured this far south. Although we had only been galloping a few minutes, Thoroughbreds and foxhounds at top speed could cover several miles. A barbed wire fence loomed, and my heart sank. I had no idea whether or not there were jumps or gates in this fence. Precious time would be lost looking, so we kept going – straight for the fence. Hounds were behind us, but we had to get to the other side...just in case. Beyond this pasture was a dangerous interstate, and the hounds had to be protected.

Griffen's whip cracked behind me, and he yelled at the hounds trying to generate enough noise to make them lift their heads and stop hunting. Maybe he would be able to stop them in time. *Where is a good place to cross this fence? It's barbed wire – No safe place to jump...why had I not taken the time to teach Viva to jump wire?!*

At last, I found a spot with no bushes or trees on either side, dropped Viva's reins, laid my hunting whip across my saddle, snatched off my red coat, and tossed it toward the fence – Viva impatiently dancing and prancing all the while – and rapidly losing precious seconds as the hounds continued to gain on us. I planned to jump my coat since wire is hard for a horse to see. Viva and I had done this before, the tattered lining of my coat all the worse for our improvisions. Viva's prancing was irritating me now…it was hard to manage this with her incessant impatience.

"Whoa! You and I have to cross this together, Viva!" I said, exasperated as she continued to prance.

The coat flew through the air and crumpled to the ground. Missed. Swinging off Viva and thinking unladylike thoughts, I picked it up and flung it over the wire. Jet's hooves rattled the earth behind me again, and I glanced around Viva in time to see Jet and Griffen shoot over the fence like a comet just three feet away – *I guess they showed us. My heavens what a pair! Incredible at a distance, dangerous up close. If only I could ride like that some day…what a site. My heart skipped three beats –*

"Concentrate, Elliott! Yes, he's quite a sight! But you have a job to do!" my long dead but very much alive in my mind grandmother, Grand, cackled.

Hounds were screaming across the field, but I had not seen what they were chasing. It looked like there were only six in this group, but they were racing hard on the line. I tried to steady Viva to get back on, but she continued to prance.

"Whoa!" I barked and tightened her reins reprovingly.

Still at last, Viva blew a deep, impatient breath while she waited for me to climb on. I swear she rolled her eyes. Once mounted, I circled her back a few paces to prepare to jump the wire. Griffen fired his pistol, and at the shot the hounds lifted their heads and stopped hunting.

He gathered all six and directed them away from the interstate. When they heard William's horn, they ran to him. I heaved a sigh of relief and frustration, for now I had to get back down, collect my coat, and prepare for the onslaught of abuse about "girls being slow in the field." He would give me unmitigated grief about being left behind, but I welcomed his good-natured abuse. I was proud to be able to keep up with him most of the time, since I had only been riding for a few years. He and Jet had been doing this a lot longer than I had.

Viva started, and I turned so I could see what had caused her reaction. She was still keyed up from the long gallop, but I had not expected anyone else to be in this area.

"Elliott!" Addy called urgently as she and Harley trotted over to us. "Our radio's not working. Ben asked me to swipe yours since you and Griffen are riding together." She glanced around for Griffen, but he was not in sight.

"Take it," I said, plucking my radio from its harness and handing it to her. "Griffen's just on the other side of this fence, and I have my cell phone. Go on!" I added when her denim eyes narrowed.

"All we need is for something *else* to happen to you," she teased. "I don't want Griffen breathing down my neck, at least not for that reason!"

I glared at her. "And what am I supposed to think about that remark from none other than you, my best friend? I'm supposed to just let you get *away* with that?"

"Ah, well, no harm in looking," she grinned and cantered back to Ben before I could pop her with my hunting whip.

Everyone was surprised that I had at last admitted that there was something between Griffen and me, especially Addy. I was lucky to have her as a friend. And Ben, too. He'd finally gotten over hating Griffen and had invited him to stay with him this weekend in Oxford. *Male bonding, I guess. After they beat up two men together last week that had threatened the hunt, or more specifically, me. Boys can be so primitive.*

Griffen and I met foxhunting when I was a senior in high school, but he never paid me much attention. Then one day he appeared at a hunt in all his glory and said he was crazy about me. In almost the same breath, he told me that his father had killed his mother…on purpose…in a drunken rage. Combined with his mood swings, he was someone with whom I chose to proceed cautiously…my head did, that is. My heart was hopelessly lost the first time I saw him.

My friends had no idea about his background, but they noticed his mood swings. My parents knew but were leaving the decision to me…more confident in my strict, Southern moral upbringing than I was. Now that I was in college, they acted more like coaches than parents. Part of me wished to be told what to do, but they refused. And my parents liked him…a lot. Mother was glad I had finally shown interest in something other than my horse. She had previously lost hope and conceded she would have to rely on my sisters for grandchildren.

Addy and Harley disappeared down the trail where the hounds had gone to get back to William. Viva pranced wanting to go with her or do something, but I held her in place…waiting for Griffen and Jet.

It had been a week since the foxhunt near Clarksdale, Mississippi, for the New Year's weekend. I was now in our home country outside of Memphis, and Griffen had driven from Nashville again to foxhunt with us, or rather, me. He had grown up with this hunt but had recently volunteered as staff, or a whipper-in, for one of the Nashville hunts, the Cantata Hounds. While at Vanderbilt, he had hunted with several hunts in that area, but for the last two years had been serving as a whipper-in for the Cantata Hounds.

We had a hard time concentrating on anything except each other when we were together, but still wanted to foxhunt. So Griffen had told his hunt in Nashville that he would be spending the rest of the season in Memphis, and William welcomed him back as staff with open arms. The thought made me smile.

The main purpose of the whippers-in is to protect the hounds and ensure their safety, and that is what we had just done – protected them from getting out onto a busy interstate. We are also to report to the huntsman anything we see of relevance to him, or her in some cases. Usually, that meant telling the huntsman what the game was doing and which hounds were leading the pack. We communicate with radios as little as possible, but they are critical when hunting the ever present and very fast coyotes that frequented this spot, or fixture.

This morning, there were about thirty riders out, with eight serving as staff. After the holidays, most everyone was ready to get back to the Saturday foxhunting routine. We were no exception.

Griffen had radioed in to William, the huntsman, and one of our hunt's Masters, that the hounds were heading back to him. Even though I had never been this far south of our hunt country, this general area was my favorite side to cover when I whipped-in, and my favorite place to jump my lovely horse. She floated over the coops as if lifting me on angel's wings. I felt safe riding her no matter how high the jumps or how fast the chase.

Griffen and Jet popped back over the four-foot wire fence like it was a two-foot log. *Boy, are they splendid.* I always get goose bumps just looking at them…especially when they are looking at us.

"How do you *do* that?" I asked, admiration unmistakable in my voice.

"Forget about the wire and jump the posts," he said. "Nothing to it."

"Right," I said riding towards them. Those posts were well over four feet high. There was most certainly *something* to it, but I let it go. I stopped at a "safe" distance from them…close enough to speak in low tones, but too far for any physical contact.

"Addy said Ben needs my radio. His died," I said. "So here we are."

"Marvelous," Griffen said and flashed his glorious smile. "Any excuse to keep you closer to me is just fine. That is, *if* you can keep up."

I shivered but pretended to ignore the compliment and jab at my riding prowess and looked across the field, feigning interest in whatever game I might see. After all, we *did* have a job. With any encouragement, Griffen would move closer, and that wouldn't do – not now. Being near him on a horse shot my heart into overdrive, and I needed to stay focused…for now.

"We had you on the speed part," I said.

"Hardly. You had a head start."

"I don't think so! You just can't admit that *I* have the faster horse."

"You *wimped* at the fence. Useless girl whipper-in. No wonder William needs someone to ride with you."

"Did you see anything come out on this side?" I asked, changing the subject, for he was partly right, and I hated to admit it...although no one else in this hunt would have dared jump wire like that dead on I was sure. "Surely you were focusing on the pack."

"Not anything in front of those puppies, but you may have clouded my vision – since you were in the way."

"Not in the way, just in front of you. Faster horse, remember?"

"So what did you see while you were being *left*?"

"Nothing. I just heard them coming our way and started moving when they turned south."

He smiled at me, and I shuddered again. "Before we took off, I did see four deer going in another direction, two raccoons, and a rabbit. Oh, and two red-tailed hawks. At least one of us was paying attention."

"Busy day," I said with a smile, then abruptly looked back to the woods when a hound spoke. "I think that's Rufus."

The other hounds opened, and William's excited voice cracked on Griffen's radio.

"Elliott, they're coming back your way," William said. "If you can keep Griffen from watching you, I'd appreciate a report."

"She's lost her radio again," Griffen said with way too much enjoyment, "but I'm of course keeping an eye on her. You may or may not get a full report on the pack."

How embarrassing. Endless abuse for couples in the hunt field. And it was now all too obvious that we were exactly that.

"Give me that radio!" I snapped. But Griffen used my lunge for his radio as an excuse to grab my hand and pull me over to him for a kiss, nearly unseating me from Viva.

"Now who's being the problem?" he grinned. "You're shamelessly attacking me in the hunt field in broad daylight. Where *are* your manners?"

I smacked him playfully with my hunting whip and turned Viva toward the woods where the hounds were working. "We had better watch that covert, or we'll catch more abuse," I said, referring to the woods where the hounds were hunting.

"Bring it on," he said. "They're just jealous."

"You're going to get me fired," I said even though we were all volunteers.

"Not likely."

Sounder's and Spice's cries joined Rufus's baritone voice. They were getting closer, and Griffen and I crept to the edge of the covert to hide behind some trees. From this point, we could see anything that either ran out into the field or along the edges.

Viva's heart pounded beneath my knees and mine, too, raced. Hounds were together as a pack or "all on" and coming very hard right at us. Their lovely chorus filled the woods and echoed through my soul. Seconds passed seeming like minutes, and we stared with our peripheral vision watching for movement. So many times, game is harder to see when looking intently at a specific spot. Over the years I had learned to take in the whole landscape watching more for movement than forms.

A flash of something…there it was – no, there *they* were – first a gray-brown streak, then a jet black spot – black standing out like an exclamation point in the gray landscape. Two heartbeats later, Rufus was behind them, then Sounder and Spice. By that time, we were galloping parallel to the pack, keeping up with the coyotes and encouraging them to remain on their current, safe, course.

Griffen and Jet galloped alongside us, Griffen reporting the two coyotes and the pack's order after them. We were moving blindingly fast and relished the exhilaration, speed, freedom, and elation from these moments. Coyotes were running together – glorious!

Suddenly, things changed, and the black coyote stopped, turned toward the pack, and darted straight for us. Griffen was on it first and tried to send it back to the other one. With a yell and crack of his whip, Griffen startled the coyote into returning to its original course, for now. At this speed, another split pack would be difficult to remedy, so we had to do all we could to keep them together.

The coyotes turned east, but we had to go north to jump out of the pasture. We spurred our horses to gallop as fast as they could to the coop, slowed ever so slightly for balance, and shot over, Griffen ahead acting as my pilot. *I love it when he does things like that. Even better than opening doors for me. Such the gentleman.*

We flew across the pasture, and the coyotes had remained true to their path…or so it seemed. The gray-brown one appeared, and we waited…one second…two…hounds singing, still moving east – not as far north as we had traveled – nothing behind him. We galloped over to his line, or the place where he came out of the woods, and waited, no hounds on him – all must be on the black. Griffen reported to William, and we dashed north of the pack, still going east.

One more coop, and we were out on a gravel road – flying floating – some shacks appeared – people on the porch – I smiled and waved to them as we sped by – they gaped at us and cheered us on – little yappy dogs barking in indignation as we blew past – hooves clattering on the gravel. I stayed well behind and to one side of Griffen, avoiding the many rocks that fired like bullets from Jet's hooves. Occasionally one would spark – I never tired of noticing things like that at a gallop. *Wonder if a galloping horse ever set a pasture on fire?*

We heard the hounds but paused to listen and get a bearing on their course. Too much radio chatter…Lydia was snapping at Stephen, typical Lydia, and Susan said they were approaching her. Griffen and

I were way north of the action, so we remained in place. We were in a good position should the hounds turn but were of no use at this point until they did.

His interpretation of the situation was like mine, so of course, he rode over to Viva and me to take advantage of some rare alone time. Steam rose from Jet's heaving sides, and his black coat shimmered with sweat. Jet impatiently turned his head toward the hounds' distant cries, but Griffen gently urged him toward us.

"I love doing that with you, Elliott," he said as they moved in place beside us, "almost as much as I love doing this…" He doffed his cap and leaned in to kiss me ever so softly on the lips.

I was always glad to be sitting when he did that. My body went limp – I never knew if he was going to grab me and yank me over to him with a jolt or surprise me with a soft one. Either way was fine, but I could never tell. He kept me off balance…all the time.

Viva pranced, and he leaned in for another gentle kiss and sat back on Jet, assessing the damage. His green eyes glowed with mischief as he smugly watched my expression clear.

"Like that?" he asked, his voice a low growl.

"A little," I said, my voice catching. I cleared it to recover some composure. "I hear Rufus again."

"Oh, that's *great. Perfect* timing."

Jet had already started trotting toward the approaching pack, and we stopped at the next pasture. This time, we were very near the north line of this section of the property and would need to turn the coyote back into the hunt country or stop the pack if they came this far. We watched and listened as they approached. The voices were loud but indistinguishable in the wind. As if on cue, the black coyote sprinted out – not even looking tired – and headed straight north.

I can never get enough of seeing these magnificent, arrogant, aloof creatures, and my heart skipped a beat. Griffen, too, was transfixed by his appearance but only for a moment.

At that instant, we bolted toward where the coyote was running – we would have only seconds to get to him in time to turn him – if he would allow it. Jet flew past the black missile with his head lowered and ears back as if he would tear the coyote to pieces if he dared to pass. The coyote did not hesitate as he fled north. Griffen and Jet were on him – Viva and I two lengths behind.

The coyote paused just long enough for Jet to overrun and realize his mistake. Viva stretched to cover the gap, but we were too late, and the black coyote passed between us. Rufus and the pack were not far behind, so our full attention was now on them.

"Hold up!" Griffen yelled and cracked his whip. His whip sounded like a gun, and the hounds lifted their heads.

"Hounds hold up!" I said with him and cracked mine too, but with not nearly as much panache. Mine sounded like a pitiful hiss compared to his.

Miraculously, we were able to stop the pack. To ensure they would not continue after the coyote, Griffen had dismounted and snapped couples, or leather leash-like ties, on Rufus and the other lead hounds to make it difficult for them to charge off. Now the main hounds were connected to other hounds in pairs, so they could not leave on their own.

William rode up, delighted to see us with the pack.

"Well done, you two," he beamed. "I'm very impressed, Griffen, that you stayed focused."

"That's quite enough, William!" I said, feeling the blush rise, and trying to sound more piqued than I was. This was all so embarrassing and not at all helping the situation with Lydia. I didn't care what Lydia thought, but I disliked tension between anyone with whom I shared this pastime. She had never liked me, even before Griffen came along. In spite of my efforts at making peace, our already tense relationship was teetering tentatively toward disaster. Lydia, the lanky, gorgeous blonde, had never failed in her efforts to snare whatever guy she wanted…until she met Griffen. Griffen had made a point to ignore her for years, and his recent attention toward a plain brunette like me that she never liked in the first place was more than she could handle.

With William present, the hounds were not likely to stray, so Griffen unsnapped the couples, and we roaded, or took them back to the hunt house for the hunt breakfast. My friends, Ashley and Leslie, had come today and had already laid out the food. Although Ashley rarely hunted, and Leslie never rode, they loved to be around for the Saturday parties… and to check out any new guys.

Ashley was on the prowl again, and I was certain she would find a target this afternoon with so many riders present. I had not noticed anything except Griffen, so she'll be on her own with that. Leslie was just along for the ride. She had no serious boyfriend but was not at all as concerned with that as Ashley. She just went with the flow. Ashley always had a plan.

"Elliott, take Jet, please," Griffen said, snapping me out of my musings. "I'll take care of the hound chores if you'll fix me a plate."

The hunt members always brought an impressive spread of potluck items for the breakfast. A few loyal souls often took it upon themselves to prepare quite a repast. Most of the time, however, staff like Griffen and me got shorted on the best dishes, for we had to spend extra time caring not only for our horses, but also the hounds.

I took Jet's reins from Griffen and led him over to the trailer. When Viva and I reached our spot, I dismounted and slipped Viva's halter over her bridle and flipped Jet's reins back over his neck. While I got Viva organized, Jet walked to his place and waited for me to bring him his apple. Jet was ridiculously smart and usually told me what he wanted.

Before securing Jet to the trailer, I let Panzer, Griffen's grizzly-sized Chesapeake Bay Retriever, out of the trailer's tack room, grabbed the apples, and put the horses' hay nets within their reach. Panzer was glad to be free but way too dignified to bound around in glee. He yawned and stretched and gently "held" my hand in his mouth in appreciation.

"You smell so fine," Griffen said into my neck, and I almost kicked him in surprise.

"How do you *do* that?!" I snapped but leaned back into his arms after restarting my heart. *Why bother? He's just going to stop it again.*

He chuckled and spun me around to face him. "All the hounds were in and the others had everything else under control. Let's make this quick, shall we?" he said and pulled me toward the clubhouse where everyone was gathered. My heart did a little flutter at his double meaning – exactly *what* did he want to make quick? Unfortunately, his intentions were grabbing a quick lunch and not, well, some alone time. "I have plans for us this afternoon that don't involve thirty people."

"Well, and what if *I* have plans?" I said to stall him, not ready to go to the clubhouse to chatter with the masses and stood my ground. We were, after all, hidden behind his trailer for the moment in a little cove of privacy. I wanted a kiss right here – now, not later. *Who knows how long I'd have to wait once he started eating, and I'm sure everyone would want to talk about the day, and…*

"Cancel them," he said in his distinctive growl, turned back to me, and leaned in closer, eyes sparkling.

Ha! That stopped him. Oh my goodness, those eyes.

"And if I don't want to?" I pouted and looked up at him under my eyelashes and blinked. *Surely that will do it.*

"You will," he said and kissed my neck.

Even better. My whole body shuddered. "You're right," I said and smiled to myself. *Worked* him *like a charm…for once…*

"I want to take you shooting this afternoon," he said as he loaded Panzer back into his box. "We can leave the horses here in the paddock. The sporting clays range is twenty minutes away. What do you say?"

"Sure," I said, not having any idea what else *to* say.

"It won't take long," he said, reading my indecision. "And I think you'll like it. I brought you a gun if you want to shoot."

"Me? Shoot?" I asked, stunned. "I really don't think I'm ready to kill anything, Griffen. Even *if* we eat it."

"We're not killing anything, just clay targets – it's fun. You'll see," he said.

"I don't have a change of clothes."

"You look fine," he said. "I promise it will not matter. You brought your Barbour, and you can wear that instead of your red coat."

I never got used to being given wardrobe advice, but he'd not steered me wrong yet. We passed through the clubhouse gathering food we could transport and saying our polite "goodbyes." Addy had returned my radio to William, and she tried to corral me into a double date with her and Ben that evening. I agreed to lunch after church the next day, but begged off on evening accompaniment. These couples that were together all the time had it made. Griffen and I lived nearly four hours apart, so we treasured our solitude.

As I was leaving, I caught Lydia's eye, and she glared. Somehow, I thought that was funny and laughed as I hugged Leslie goodbye. Over Leslie's shoulder I saw Ashley being cornered by a distinguished-looking guy, or maybe even a *man. I'll get the details on* that *adventure later.* I waved at her, and she winked.

Griffen had already unhooked the trailer, untacked both horses, and turned them out into the paddock. They rolled with pleasure, feet flying up and bodies flailing around on the ground. Each stood and shook with delight, and they pranced around to inspect their spot. They nibbled the hay Griffen put out for them and grazed nose-to-nose as content in each other's company as we were.

"You ready for this?" he asked, smiling down at me as he helped me into his truck.

"As long as I'm with you," I said and beamed at him, truly happy to be escaping the crowd.

"You *are* too good to be true," he said and touched my cheek lightly with his finger.

SPORTING CLAYS

Chapter 2

Well oiled leather, waxed cotton jackets, dirty dog, cold fried chicken, hot chocolate, Delta mud – even a tidy horse owner's truck never truly masks the smells of fun.

On the way to the sporting clays range, Griffen held my hand and rubbed his thumb absent mindedly over and around my fingers. I leaned against the seat relishing his company, his smell, and the next adventure we'd have together.

"I'm going to have to think of something to surprise *you* with," I said, closing my eyes and smiling at the thought. "You're always coming up with adventures for me."

"*You* are my adventure," Griffen said, squeezing my hand. "I love to see how you react to new things."

"Still," I said, relaxing against the seat. "I'll have to come up with something."

"Why don't you give me some more of that chicken while you're thinking? I'm still hungry."

I wrapped the chicken in a paper napkin and handed it to him.

"So what's the plan for today?" I asked when he had his mouth full.

He smiled, swallowed, and got that mischievous glint in his eye. "Well, if you're going to duck hunt with me, which I do hope you will do again, you'll have more fun if you can shoot," he said. "This is a better way to learn than just having you try when you are wrapped up in all the duck gear with Panzer soaking you and all the other stuff going on. At least you can see if you like it at all."

"Does it hurt?"

"Not if you shoot right," he said. "I've got a gun that you'll like. It's a Beretta tewnty gauge over-and-under. You saw several guns like it in Scotland."

"I told you last week I trust you, so, here's my chance to prove it."

"You're too trusting, Elliott."

"Well, all or nothing with me," I said and leaned over to kiss his cheek. "So where are you taking me tonight?"

"Get back to your seat, or I'm not taking you anywhere except to the side of the road," he said with a wonderful growl and a gleam in his eye.

I obeyed, wishing he'd do just that than try to come up with things for us to do all the time. I'd rather sit and look at him…listen to him talk…run my fingers through his hair…

"You're right handed, aren't you?" he asked, breaking me out of my daydream.

"Yes, why?"

"I want to make sure I start you off correctly on shooting."

We pulled into the range and, to my surprise, it was crowded on a Saturday afternoon in January. There were all-too-familiar trucks everywhere and people hanging around with shotguns cracked over their shoulders. Although there were not many, a few ladies were there – some with and some without guns. Black, brown, and yellow Labrador Retrievers wandered around sniffing posts and marking their territories. Griffen parked, and we walked to the office, leaving Panzer happy in his box in the back of the truck.

"Griffen Case!" a man behind the desk bellowed. "Been a while since you've been in. How's your uncle?"

"Fine, Jim. I'll tell him you asked. This is Elliott Marks. She's going to shoot for the first time today. Will you help me get her started?"

"Nice to meet you, Elliott. I'm Jim Black, and this is Charles Johnson," he said, and he beamed a welcoming smile towards me that made me forget about being nervous. "I'll be honored to assist. First, look at me straight in the eyes. Don't worry, I have a shooting reason for doing this."

I smiled conscientiously and stared. He had nice blue-green eyes, but I had no idea why he needed me to look at him this way.

"Now, put your hands in front of you, like this," he said, reaching forward and making a triangle with his fingertips and thumbs, "and keep looking at me."

I did as instructed, feeling ridiculous.

"Ok, close in the triangle until you can only see my nose," he said. "Good. You are right-eyed."

"How do you know that?" I asked.

"Because I'm looking at your right eye. If you are right-handed, all the better. With rifles, you aim and close an eye. With shotguns, both eyes stay open when you look at your target, and you use your reflexes," he said.

"How do I aim?" I asked, getting more confused.

"You'll see – I just wanted to see what we were working with."

"Don't mind him, Elliott, he's harmless," Charles said with a grin. "Although when you are ready to really learn how to shoot, call me."

"Of course I'm harmless, Charles. I'm happily married as you well know. But with the likes of you and Griffen around, even the nicest girls need to know to shoot."

"I hardly think I'll be shooting anyone today," I said. "At least, not on purpose."

"All the more reason to teach you the right way to do this," Griffen said as he collected some orange foam earplugs, three bottles of water, and shooting glasses.

"Just let me know if they give you any trouble," Charles said, laughing at us as we gathered our shooting supplies.

We walked back to the truck to let Panzer out of his box. Although he bristled and stalked around the other dogs, he behaved. The shotgun Griffen handed me was…elegant. I had never thought about weapons being pretty until I had visited Scotland and witnessed undisguised lust in the eyes of many of the shooters when they admired a nice gun. This one, too, was pretty even though it had no gold or fancy engravings on it. It felt awkward in my hands, but I said nothing. The gun was cracked open with its barrel pointed down, and I rested it over the crook of my right arm.

"Just remember to act like it is always loaded, Elliott, and keep it pointed in a safe direction," he said. "Down or up – never towards anyone."

"Got it," I said with much more confidence than I felt. "Have you always done this?"

"Shot? Well, no. I didn't start shooting until I moved in with my uncle, if that's what you mean."

"I just wondered if you and your father did things like this," I said, unsure of this topic. Griffen's family life before his uncle adopted him had been troubled, to say the least. He had witnessed his father strangle his mother and burn her body when he was fifteen, so family topics were… touchy. I had come from the "perfect" family – so hearing about his fascinated me. I wanted to know all about Griffen…this too…but I knew to tread carefully. His concern that he would follow in his father's footsteps was the only real hindrance to our relationship – but a hindrance nonetheless. Griffen thought he would end up like his father if he ever married and had his own family, but I found that harder to believe the more that I got to know him. Before we met, he had chosen not to marry to ensure that would not happen. But I had changed all that. Still, his concern loomed...

"No, he wasn't a hunter. He worked all the time. He had some guns, but I don't remember him ever using them. I don't know what happened to them, now that you mention it. I guess my uncle has them," he said.

Jim joined us at the shooting range. He suggested that we practice a few times on fixed targets before moving to flying objects. I wholeheartedly agreed. Griffen stood back and let Jim take over. I felt him watching me but tried to focus on what Jim was saying.

"Hold the gun like this," Jim demonstrated as he raised his gun in one fluid motion to his right cheek. "Then, look downrange along the barrel at the target. Focus on the target and keep your face against the gun. Be sure to hold the gun tight against your right shoulder. Your body will be able to take the recoil without a problem. You'll see. Just be sure you're holding it against you. You try."

I raised the heavy gun to my cheek and looked at the target. I could only hold the gun up for a few seconds before my arms shook.

"That's it," Jim said. "You can lower it now. See, nothing to it. Now, make sure your earplugs are in, and we'll shoot this time."

He handed me one shell, and I dropped it in the lower hole of the barrel. Like I'd seen Griffen do so many times before, I closed the barrel, keeping the gun pointed toward the target, or downrange as Jim instructed.

"Now, Elliott, all you have to do is move the tab this way, and the safety will be off. After you do that, pull the trigger. Just barely squeeze, and it will fire. Keep the gun close."

My heart was pounding, and I started to shake. I took a deep breath and fought back the nerves. I really did not want to look stupid in front of either of them.

"Take your time," Jim said, and his voice calmed me.

"You can do it, Elliott," Griffen said. His voice made things worse. I started to shake again and lowered the gun.

"Here, let me show you," Griffen said and gently took the gun from my hands. His being so close was definitely *not* helping and part of me wanted him to leave. I looked over at him a little embarrassed and something else…frustrated.

"Just watch," he said with unabashed confidence. "Stand back a little."

He raised the gun and fired in one motion. The sound made me jump, because I was not expecting it to happen so quickly…and I was definitely on edge watching him shoot. *He is just so…confident…and, well, so…*

"Give it back," I said, clearing my head and trying to sound brave.

"I want to do it."

He reloaded a shell, handed me the gun, and stood way too close again. My heart pounded, and the shakes returned. *This is so embarrassing.*

"Take your time," Jim said. "Griffen, why don't you sit over there?" He indicated a seat a few yards away behind the pavilion.

As soon as Griffen left, I was much calmer. I raised the gun and pulled the trigger. The explosion was not as bad as I thought, but it surprised me, and I jumped. Miraculously, I hit the target.

"Good job!" Jim and Griffen said together. "Let's do a few more," Jim said. Griffen got up, but Jim indicated for him to stay where he was. *I'll have to find a way to thank Jim.*

I shot ten more times and each time the gun was less and less a factor. I was no longer scared of the sound and was ready to try moving targets. I still felt like I was all thumbs, but things were definitely improving.

"Now, to the course," Jim said and released Griffen from his spot. "Griffen will shoot first so you can see how the targets fly. Then, I'll help you with yours."

Butterflies reappeared, those inside me, that is, as we moved along the pretty trail. I tried to concentrate on anything but thoughts of shooting in front of Griffen. As we walked, I focused on the huge hardwoods lining our path. Their bark was so distinct, and many of the trees in this range must have been here for centuries. The cedars and pines stood out this time of year. I could even see abandoned bird nests in the barren bushes.

Griffen walked ahead with a confident swagger. His gun was draped over his arm, and he looked ridiculously handsome in his element. Panzer stayed close to Griffen as if he were on a leash – but he wasn't.

He stayed on Griffen's left side and matched his pace no matter where or how fast they walked. It was as if a magic cord kept him in place, and I marveled at their unity. When Griffen stopped, Panzer sat. When he moved, Panzer moved with him silently, but as alert as I have ever seen him. As I walked with them, I felt awkward carrying the gun in these unfamiliar surroundings and was glad Jim stayed beside me. They both offered to carry my gun, but I wanted to get used to handling it.

The first station on the course was called Overhead Doves. Jim picked up a long electric cord and glanced over at a big machine nestled almost out of sight. Although I heard a lot of shooting at the range, there was no one else at this station. Griffen was already loaded and in position.

"Pull!" he said.

Bright orange and black dots shot from the machine and zipped toward us, straight overhead. He shot both with ease. Two shots… two broken targets.

"Pull!" he said again.

Two more over, two more broken.

"Pull!" he said.

Two more over, two more broken. He turned to me with a wide grin – so glorious and cocky. "Your turn," he said, and his eyes glinted.

I'm going to get *him for this.* Jim walked with me to the station and put only one shell in my gun.

"How do I shoot two with one shell?" I protested.

"One at a time, Elliott," he said. "Just concentrate on the single bird, or target, rather."

One target. Concentrate.

"Watch the target and bring the gun up. Don't think about the gun, Elliott. Just focus on the target and shoot where it's going, not where it is. The rest will come…in time," Jim said.

"Ready," I said.

I heard the sound of the target being released and looked for it. Before I could even see it, it was gone. *Oh dear.*

"That's ok, Elliott. Try again." Jim said.

Griffen chuckled. I felt myself blush, but I turned around and glared at him. He laughed.

"Griffen, either you be quiet, or I'm sending you on without us," Jim snapped, not too good-naturedly this time, and I noticed that he was a good bit larger than Griffen. "You're not helping things here."

He had no idea how right he was. I grinned smugly back at Griffen but said nothing. My nerves were shot, and I didn't want him to know how awkward I felt.

"You ready to try again, Elliott?" Jim asked.

"Ready," I said.

The same sound, eyes on the target, *focus*, pull the gun up and shoot.

"Click!"

The target escaped again, and Griffen could not contain himself.

"Go on!" Jim barked. "I've had enough of you! We'll meet you at the next station."

Griffen walked by me, grin barely contained, and I glared at him so he could not tell how embarrassed I was. *This was terrible. Only a day and a half with him and now he's being banished. And I wanted him to go. I'll pick the activities next time. Let's see how cocky he is at, well, let me see, maybe I can teach him something new so he can feel awkward…for five minutes…Scrabble? Probably not. Water skiing? Oh yes. I'll definitely set that up this summer.*

"Elliott, you just forgot to take off the safety," Jim said, snapping me out of my deliberations. "Tell me when you're ready."

"Make sure Griffen's gone, or I may have to shoot him," I sulked. "*If* I can remember to take off the safety."

"Don't worry about this. Most of the time I take students alone. This is more common than you can imagine. Fathers bringing their sons or daughters, people bringing their friends for the first time, and especially cases like yours – boy brings girlfriend or husband brings the little wife – all fraught with disaster. You have enough to think about without all those pressures, too," Jim said.

"Thanks," I said and really meant it. "Ready!"

The machine thunked, target out, safety off, *focus*, trigger BOOM!

No target. I actually HIT it!

"Attagirl!" Jim beamed, and I whooped with delight.

"Do that again!" I said.

"Say when."

"Ready!" I said when I reloaded and clamped the barrels shut.

Target out – safety off, *focus*, trigger, boom!

I hit it AGAIN!

"Try for three!" Jim said. "Say 'pull' this time."

"Pull!"

Target out – safety off, *focus*, trigger, boom!

A third dead target. *I wanted to fly! How fun was this! I could do this all day! And that time I didn't even hear the 'boom.'* We continued on that station until I had shot ten in a row. I missed number eleven, but fired at the rest until I had hit fifteen.

"Let's find Griffen," I said, feeling very confident now. "I want to show him."

"Ok, but remember to focus. And don't get mad at yourself if another station doesn't work as well," Jim said.

We walked past four more stations and found Griffen at number five with a group of three guys and a girl. She had already shot, but I wanted to watch them – maybe later. Griffen was up and broke five of the six at this "Decoying Mallards" station. He grinned at me, and I beamed back barely able to contain myself.

"Well?" he asked, walking toward me.

"I hit some!" I said. "I can do this!" I tried to contain my enthusiasm, but it was hard.

"Show me then," he said, indicating to the station.

"One shell or two?" I asked Jim, hopefully.

"One," he said. "Don't get ahead of yourself. Say 'when.'"

"Pull!"

Target out – safety off, *focus*, trigger, boom! The target flew overhead, unscathed.

Silence. The woods were closing in – wrapping me up in a blanket of noiselessness...but there was nothing comfortable about it. I felt like I would be smothered if I did not shoot my way out.

"Pull!" I said, determined to concentrate.

Target out – safety off, *focus*, trigger, boom! The target exploded!

"Perfect!" Griffen said and winked at me.

"Pull!"

Target out – safety off, *focus*, trigger, boom! Another dead target.

"Even better!" Griffen said, truly relieved at the turn of events.

We kept shooting, and Jim finally issued me two shells at a time. More escaped than were shot, but there was definitely improvement as the day went on. I got Jim's card and was going to make sure to send him something for being such a wise instructor. M*aybe I'd come* *back for lessons without Griffen and surprise him when we hunted again…where does a girl find a shotgun?*

"Where do you want to eat?" Griffen asked as we left the range.

"Let's get some drive-by food and eat at the barn," I said. "I'm ready to have you all to myself for a while."

"I have an idea," he said. "Want me to surprise you?"

"Sure," I said. "But I get to plan tomorrow."

"Deal," he said and brought my fingers to his lips.

In no time, we pulled into the clubhouse to retrieve the trailer and horses. As we rounded the corner, my heart sank. The paddock gate was open…Viva and Jet were gone.

SNAPSHOTS

Chapter 3

And God took a handful of southerly wind, blew His breath over it, and created the horse...

~ Bedouin Legend

"Griffen!" I said, trying hard not to scream as the panic welled up inside me. Viva was gone. *Was she hurt? Would she get hit by a car? How does anyone find a horse? We need to call the police!*

"I see," he said calmly, maddeningly calm.

"What's happened? Where's Viva?" I shrieked, wanting to leap out of the truck.

"Hang on, don't panic, Elliott," he said. "Jet's good at opening gates. Someone probably didn't close it well, and they just wandered off."

He backed up to the trailer, and I exploded from the truck, running on air to the paddock to make sure they were really gone. The area was open, but woods were not far away…and the highway – so close. *Had someone taken them or had they really just wandered off?* It was getting late, and darkness would be upon us soon. I wanted Griffen to hurry – *why was he so calm?*

"Griffen!" I yelled, just to yell. I wanted to choke him. His calm demeanor inflamed my anger.

"You're so calm when people are trying to kill you, but lose your horse and you go to pieces." He smiled indulgently, referring to my unexpected overnight incident in the Delta woods at our last foxhunt where I'd been attacked by thugs.

I wanted to punch him. "Hurry up! It's getting dark, and we'll never find them. What if a car hits them? What if they've tried to go home? Should we call the police?"

"Go let Panzer out of his box," Griffen said.

"Panzer is fine! We've got to start looking for the horses!" I yelled, trying hard to keep from smacking him.

"Elliott, let Panzer out, and put a handful of horse food in a bucket – just get it out of the trailer," Griffen said when I shot him another impatient glare. He was still ridiculously calm and…amused…as he finished hooking up everything.

I stormed over to the trailer, released his beast, and yanked open the door to get a bucket and food. I was so angry by now that I had nothing left to say. I wanted to fling everything out of the trailer in exasperation but resisted. He looked at me, almost said something, then looked away, still calm, but controlling his…*was that a smirk? I'm going to slap that smirk off his face…*

"Panzer," he said in a low, calm tone.

Panzer bounded over to him adoringly. *Why is he playing with the dog* now *of all times? Where is my horse? He and his precious uncle may have all the money in the world to just get another horse, but if I lost Viva, I'd want to die. Where is my horse? Oh why won't he* do *something?*

"Get Jet," he said to Panzer.

My mouth dropped. *No way.*

Panzer charged to the paddock and circled the place where the gate had been left open, nose to the ground. He then took off across the field and bolted into the woods. A few minutes later, I heard him bark, and Jet and Viva burst from the woods galloping directly at us, Panzer running at their heels. Their tails were held high, and they bucked and kicked exuding joy in their freedom. It looked like something out of a Lassie movie.

"You'll probably need that bucket for Viva," he said. I still wanted to punch him – especially now.

"You could have *told* me, Griffen!" I stammered, trying to resolve my anger and relief and overwhelming sense of awe at the things I kept finding out about him. "I…I…you have no idea what it feels like to think…"

He stopped me in mid-rant with one of his uninvited fly-bys on my lips. I, of course, melted – nothing more to say. "Go collect your horse," he whispered as Jet nudged him in the back. "I'm hungry."

Back in Oxford, I wanted to pick up some fast food, but no, Griffen insisted on making a grocery run. He got a baked chicken, some drinks, potato salad, slaw, bread, two kinds of cookies, apples, and three kinds of cheese…always cheese. All we needed was a picnic basket…but he settled for some paper plates and napkins. I also noticed he grabbed fire starters, lighter fluid, and matches.

We drove the horses to the barn, unloaded them and the gear, and unhooked his trailer. After feeding them and checking them over for any injuries from their day's adventure, they were free to charge around in their paddock. We kept Viva in the paddock with Jet to keep him company. This weekend routine was working out nicely, so far. They danced and pranced in the waning sunlight, beautiful in their perfection. Panzer couldn't resist chasing them, and he whipped them into a whirling frenzy.

The air started to get much colder as the sun lowered into the earth. The sunset was breathtaking, and I was delighted we'd turned Ben and Addy down on their dinner invitation. Griffen started a fire in the huge cast iron fire pit, and I retrieved our makeshift feast from the truck. There was no one at the barn – we had the place to ourselves. *Perfect.*

In spite of his dubious upbringing, ever since Griffen had told me he intended to marry me someday, my grandmother's and mother's voices in my head had been silent; when before, they had barked at me around every corner where Griffen was concerned. Even here, alone with him in such a picturesque setting, there were no warnings or retributions from them. I had yet to change out of my filthy foxhunting clothes and was longing for a bath, but no reprimands from Grand or even the Southernmothers who loved to "guide" me with their manners, moral, and other motherly missives. *Strange.* Instinctively, however, I had rearranged my hair to an acceptable tangle and made sure I kept a little gloss or something on my lips.

I arranged the food near the fire. If it had been up to me, I would snack on it and watch the horses play and kiss Griffen. But I knew that for Griffen, meals were a celebration, so I did what I could with the minimal accoutrements and arranged what I thought was a lovely presentation. At least I was able to take everything out of its plastic packaging and display it so it looked home cooked.

Griffen was in the barn, so I admired my handiwork, threw a few more sticks on the fire, and went to collect him. The fire was burning perfectly, and the sun's brilliant exit was getting even more breathtaking each moment. I had never had a sunset picnic – the natural scenery alone was stunning.

"Griffen, come see!" I called, as I headed toward the barn. He turned the corner just in time to see Panzer explode from the paddock after chasing the horses one more time and head directly toward my perfectly presented picnic.

"No Panzer!" I said, but of course, he ignored me. There is no creature that makes a person feel more ridiculous than someone *else's* highly trained dog. I might as well have been yelling at a charging lion. Even so, I ran back to the fire just in time to collide with him, knocking him off the chicken. By this time, Griffen realized what was happening.

"Panzer, heel!" he said, and Panzer, of course, obeyed *him*… dashing immediately to his side.

"Bad dog," he said, rubbing his ears and trying not to show me how hard he was laughing, then trapped him back in his box. Panzer gazed at him adoringly, and I wanted to kick both of them. This was *not* my day.

"Griffen!" I wailed in exasperation, looking at the picnic disaster. "I tried to set this up for you, but *that dog*!"

"I always said dirt becomes you, Elliott dear," he grinned and sat down carefully beside me wrapping me up in his magnificent arms. He pulled me against his chest, then leaned back and looked at me. He ran his fingers along my cheek and brushed some of Panzer's spooge off my face.

"I do love you so much, Elliott," he said. "You are such a treasure, and I hope we can do this forever."

All anger and frustration gone, I closed my eyes and let his words wash over me. The warmth from the fire barely reached us and kept the cool night air at bay. We sat together, picking at what was left of the remaining food and watching the sun retract its final rays from the sky.

"I hate that you have to leave tomorrow," I said. "It seems like we only get snapshots of time with each other, and they go by so quickly."

"It will not be like this forever," he said and pulled his fingers through my hair. "I've been doing a lot of thinking about you…and being closer to you…on a more permanent basis."

"I'm all ears," I said and leaned against him.

"First, I plan to wrap up the work in Argentina this fall. Three weeks away from you would be torture, and I'm sure they can do fine without me; they always have," he said.

"But, are you *sure*?" I asked. "I know how much those kids mean to you."

"Elliott, they do, but there are kids everywhere that need help, and I will still do that or something like it, just not on the other side of the world now that you're a factor," he said.

"A factor?" I asked, nestling closer into his arms. "That makes me sound like a complication."

"More like a force to be reckoned with, I should say. At least, for me," he said and tousled my hair. "You are a powerful presence – and one I'm not willing to ignore…any more…as you can see."

"I've spent a lot of time considering this. When I'm away from you, all I have is time," he said. "I'm going to stay in school a little while longer, too, like my uncle suggested, and get a law degree. After all, I don't want to live off his generosity forever, and the insurance money will only go so far. It may have worked for my original plans, but when you happened, a lot of things changed."

"A lawyer, then?" I asked. "You'll probably have to start studying if you do that."

"I'm not worried about that," he said. "It's a great general education, or so I've heard. I may not practice law, but you never know. I do know that my radar is up now for gainful employment. I want to take care of you – and give you the kind of life you deserve as well as help kids."

"All I want is *you*, Griffen," I said.

"Yeah, that'll last about a month. You and I were created to live largely – I can see that in you already. So, I'm sure you'll be needing more horses, more land, more places to foxhunt, more adventures… you know you have expensive taste…we both do. And you'll be wanting your own shotgun – probably a matched pair…your own hunting dog, a bigger horse trailer, maybe even some kids of your own…then you'll want to be able to help all the needy causes that touch your heart, too…the list will be endless." He smiled and kissed my neck.

"Just keep that up," I said, trying to remember to breathe and glad we were sitting beside the fire so I didn't need my knees to work. "That will do…just fine…for now."

I stared into the fire then closed my eyes – basking in its warmth and reveling in these wondrous feelings coursing through my soul.

"When will you start applying to law schools?" I asked, hoping he'd be thinking locally…and that my voice still worked.

"I already have."

"Which ones?"

"Only the best, of course," he said, a little smugness or smile in his voice. I couldn't really tell since it was dark, and I was watching the fire, avoiding his eyes. I wouldn't beg him to move closer, and I knew I couldn't follow him – Southernmothers' and Grand's combined fits at *that* would cause a minor earthquake, and I didn't want him to ask. I didn't trust myself to remember my upbringing. Watching the fire rather than him gave me some distance, and maybe, a slight advantage. Otherwise, I knew he'd read my thoughts.

"I know that, Griffen," I said, a little worried. "But how long will you be in school? How long does law school last?"

"Three years," he said. He was quiet for a while, but he kept running his fingers through my hair, and I tried not to show how disappointed I was that we would probably not be in the same state any sooner than I had dreamed. He was graduating from Vanderbilt in May, and I had hoped, well...

"*Elliott, don't you even think about following him!*" At last! Grand was starting to talk in my head. This felt much more normal.

"So, have you decided what you're going to do?" he asked, switching the topic away from him.

"I'll major in biology and minor in business," I said. "I still have two more years you know."

"How well I do," he said. "I just hope you won't get tired of me being so close to you."

"What are you talking about? Close? Do you already know where you're going to school?"

"I told you, the best law school in the South," he said. I could hear his smile this time, so I turned and looked at him. His wide grin was so unexpected, and I finally understood what he was saying.

"Griffen! That's wonderful! Ole Miss? Here? When will you

know for sure?"

"You'll be the first to know, I promise. I'm glad that sits well with you."

"Of course it does, you idiot," I said. "I just wish you could graduate this weekend and get here sooner. This summer is going to last a lifetime. Oh, I can hardly wait until the fall! Can you start this summer if you're accepted?"

"Slow down, I'll find out about all this, but for now, let's look at the stars and enjoy this," he said and pulled me close to him. "Wait, I have a better idea."

He disappeared.

"I don't like that idea at all," I said into the darkness.

"Just wait a minute – I'll be *right* back," he said. He went to his trailer and retrieved one of Jet's blankets. "Come over here where it's darker." *And that remark didn't even get a rise out of Grand.*

He laid the blanket in the pasture and pulled me down beside him. The night sky was moonless, so the stars glowed.

"There's Orion, and the Big Dipper, you see?" he said, pointing across the sky. "This is one of my favorite things to do. I've loved doing this since I was a kid."

"Were you able to see stars like this where you lived?"

"Sometimes." He was quiet…too quiet. And too still. His mood had definitely changed. He lay next to me, very close, very still, and very very…distant.

"Griffen?" I asked after a long time.

"Yes."

"I love you, too, you know. Just exactly like you are."

"I hope so," he said. "I hope I can be good enough for you…that the monster's not there."

I rolled over onto my elbow and looked at his worried green eyes. "Griffen, you sound like a little boy trying to please a parent. I love you like you are. You don't have to prove anything to me. You already have. I trust you, and I love you. What more do I need to tell you?"

He sat up, too, and looked at me then. "Elliott, I hope you're right," he said. "But only time will tell. Spending time with you and making sure I can do this…be someone worthy of you, your love, your trust. If I'm not, then you can kick me out and move on with your life."

"Enough," I said and silenced him with a kiss. He pulled me close to him and held me there – so long I thought my body would explode. He was so still, but so powerful, so strong, so solid, so *here* with me. So completely here…under the stars in the dark. I wanted to lie beside him all night – forever.

"Time for me to take you home," he said softly and nuzzled my neck. I lay back on the blanket and looked up at the stars one more time to clear my head. As soon as I did, he was kissing me, his hands beside me, holding himself above me so he wouldn't crush me, but I *so* wanted him to crush me, and I reached up to pull him down on the blanket.

He sat up with a start, almost jerking me upright.

"Time to go," he said. "And don't do that again."

"Kiss you?" I asked innocently.

"No," he said. "You know what you did. You've got to help me here a little bit, or I'll need to stay in Nashville or be sure we're always surrounded by witnesses."

I'm sure I blushed, but I really didn't know what he was talking about.

"Really, Griffen," I said, hesitantly. "What did I do to…provoke this?"

"Don't play with me, Elliott," he said, and his eyes had a dangerous threatening glint in them. "You *have* to know exactly what you're doing."

"I don't know what you mean," I said, really confused. "I've told you before that this, well, you…feeling like this about someone…*is* a first for me, too."

"Lying back on that blanket, looking at the stars," he said. "It was like the day you were looking at the fox…the day I kissed you for the first time. So beautiful and so absorbed in what you were seeing – that, my dear, is irresistible to me. Dangerously so."

"I just need to keep my eyes on you, and not other things?" I asked, repeating this ridiculous revelation back to him.

"Exactly."

"So, I'm in danger whenever I'm *not* watching you," I said. "That's interesting."

"And it's definitely time to go," he said. "We have a breakfast date. I want to see as much of you as possible in the daylight before I have to drive to Nashville. I have a much clearer head around you when the sun's up."

We gathered everything, put out the fire, and walked to his truck. For a while, we drove in silence listening to random songs on his iPod through the stereo. I loved the music he chose – he always found the best songs – so many sounded like they were written just for us. I relished the things they could say that I couldn't. I held his hand and enjoyed having him with me…even if it was only for a few more miles. This time I kissed *his* hand gently and scratched his forearm with my fingernails, gently tickling the skin on his soft, but oh so strong arms.

"Elliott, will you let me come back down next weekend?" he asked as a song ended. He reached up and turned the music down to hear my reply.

"If you didn't, then Viva and I would come get you," I said. "I hope to see you *at least* every weekend for the rest of my life!"

"Demanding, aren't you?" he said. "The rest of the world has been put on notice that I'm yours first."

"How did they take it?"

"With shock and awe," he said. "But they do want to meet you sometime. I can arrange for you to come to Nashville one weekend if you like. There's plenty to do in that town."

"What made you choose Vanderbilt?"

"That's where my mother and uncle went," he said. "My father, too, actually. They met there."

He didn't turn the music back up, but he was silent. I didn't know if he wanted to keep talking about this, so I looked out the window at the stars. I knew thinking about how he was raised pained and frightened him. Although Griffen managed to escape the day his mother was murdered, the scars remained. He feared that he'd follow his father's path, and a small part of me did, too. We just didn't know. I, on the other hand, had no idea what growing up like that would be like. My parents were happy, loved my sisters and me with abandon, and made the perfect life look effortless. He pulled my hand to his lips and kissed my fingers.

"See, there," he said playfully. "You weren't paying attention. You looked out the window, and here I am about to whip off the road and attack you…again."

"You're just changing the subject."

"No, little vixen, you did that – switched me off onto another line," he said. "Don't tell me any more that you don't know how that works on me."

We drove into the sorority house parking lot, and he walked me to the door. Then he leaned down and brushed his lips softly against mine.

"Goodnight, my Elliott," he said. "I'll pick you up at 7:00."

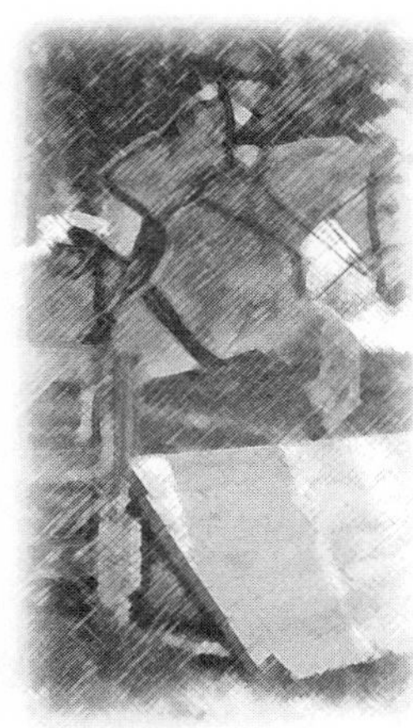

SUNDAY

Chapter 4

We attended stables, as we attended church, in our best clothes, no doubt showing the degree of respect due to horses, no less than to the deity.

~ *Sir Osbert Sitwell*

Leslie was wide-awake when I floated into the room. So was everyone else on the hall since it was only 10:00. Everyone flocked to our beds wanting details details details of Griffen and our day. No secrets in the sorority house.

"Spill all, Elliott!" she hissed. "You're not getting away without details this time! You have been gone *all* day and are *still* in your riding clothes. *Whatever* would your mother say?"

"She has already said, 'it's about time you kissed something besides your horse!'" I laughed, and the room exploded in giggles.

"Where have you been?" Leslie persisted.

"We hunted this morning…together for once…I might add. Viva was perfect. She was so…" I smiled and paused dramatically when they rolled their eyes in unison.

"*Griffen*, Elliott, we want to hear about *him,* not your *horse*!" Tracy Sullivan, a sophomore who lived down the hall, said.

I grinned. "Ok, well, we hunted, then he took me…shooting," I said and let that hang in the air for a minute. Once again, not what they expected.

"Why did you do that? And…what did you shoot?" Missy Cole, Tracy's roommate asked.

"He likes to hunt and wanted to see if I would like to shoot a shotgun. So…I did," I said triumphantly.

"Is that where you've been all day?" Leslie asked suspiciously.

"Then we went back to get the horses and went to the barn and had a picnic," I said.

"Now, we're getting somewhere!" Tracy said.

"Oh yes," I said. "Perfect sunset picnic, all alone, just cold enough… awesome stars."

"Tell me you did *not* just look at the stars," Leslie said.

"Well, not the whole time," I said and blushed.

"Come *on*, Elliott," Tracy said. "You're killing us!"

"He told me he loved me, kissed me until I nearly collapsed, and brought me home," I said in a rush. "What else is there to tell?"

"Is he a good kisser?" Missy asked.

"Missy, have you *seen* him?" Leslie said. "It wouldn't matter if he could kiss or not. He's gorgeous."

"Let her talk, Leslie," Tracy snapped.

"Well?" she asked. "Is he?"

I sat for a minute looking at their eager faces wondering how much to tell them. This was fun…up to a point. Then it was way too personal.

"Yes," is all I said. By the look on my face, they knew that was all they were getting. I felt a pillow in my face.

"*You!* I guess you finally deserve a thunderbolt," Missy said. "You've got that *look*!"

"Pitiful! It takes her until she's a sophomore in college before she gets it!" Leslie laughed. "I'm with her mother…its about time!"

"Enough for tonight – I have a breakfast date with him…and church!" I defended myself from flying pillows, and Leslie ran them out and locked the door. After I had a chance to shower and get into my pajamas, she crawled up on my bed and sat beside me.

"So, are you still in the *club*?" she asked, smiling mischievously.

"Oh yes," I smiled. "Charter membership still holding strong… and prospects are looking very very good."

"Have you said anything to *him*…yet?" she asked.

"He knows. But he brought it up first…I never had to say anything," I said.

Leslie's eyes grew wide. "No way! It was *his* idea? That has to be a first. Are you sure he's not gay?"

"Ab-so-lutely," I said. "He's holding out for marriage…like us." I didn't tell her that not only did he share the way we thought about this, his disastrous childhood had him avoiding women, or relationships with them, at least. He had never planned to get that close to anyone for fear of being as mean as his father, so he had decided to remove that factor from his life…so far.

"Ohhh. He *is* too good to be true!" Leslie gasped. "That sounds like something that's so far away, but it isn't really, is it?"

"Not in the big picture, no," I said. "He's so guarded about so many things I wonder if I'll ever really know him."

"What difference does it make when you're on the same page,

Elliott?" she said. "It sounds like you are off to a perfect start with him. I really am happy for you. It must be great to be able to be with him without having to constantly brandish a sword."

"The lines are there, for sure, but they scream to be crossed already," I said. "And we've just started dating. No wonder everyone talks about how hard it is. I feel, well, almost helpless sometimes when he kisses me." I looked down and felt myself blush…again. That was enough detail. I sounded weak and didn't like to admit that. *Enough about me.*

"Your turn…any details for me?" I asked.

"No, just the same old wanting the milk without the cow routine," she said, tossing her hair over her shoulders. "Plenty of dates and proposals even, but nothing that *I* want to go anywhere…yet. There's something about letting guys know that you're holding out for marriage that either has them running away screaming or falling to their knees with a ring!" We giggled at the absurdity and truth of this and gathered the stuffed animals around us on my bed.

"Oh, I meant to ask you about Ashley," I said. "Where is she?"

"I can't believe I didn't tell you!" Leslie sat up and beamed. "She and Shannon are on a date with two guys from Memphis. Ashley said she met one at the hunt today."

"That was fast! I saw her talking to a guy, but I didn't get a good look at him," I said. "Where were they going?"

"Dinner and a movie, I think," she said. "Ashley's a *machine*, now. She's working on being engaged by the end of next year. Her senior year goal is to have a ring and a date handed to her with her diploma."

"That's no surprise," I said. "Are you going to church in the morning?"

"Yes," she said and yawned. "Elaine's going with me."

"Griffen and I are going to breakfast, then the late service, then lunch with Ben and Addy. Are they still out?"

"Yes, I haven't heard her come in. They went with two other couples somewhere."

She walked back to her bed, and we turned out the lights after saying goodnight. I closed my eyes and thought about our conversation and about Griffen.

Even Leslie didn't know about his upbringing, but my parents did. It wasn't my secret to share. My parents had learned about him on their own…Mother has an intelligence network better than most branches of the military. I was relieved when they learned about him, but they did not forbid me to date him…much to my surprise and concern. They thought this should be my decision. Oh dear. *Would I ever really know Griffen? Will that past of his come back to haunt me…or us? Just how important is the way a person is raised?* Finally, the day caught up with me, and I surrendered to a dreamless sleep.

I was waiting downstairs when Griffen arrived. Leslie wasn't getting up until later, so I dressed as quickly and quietly as I could and left the room. He looked stunning in Sunday clothes. Like me, he dressed on the formal side for church.

He had on a crisp white button-down shirt, khakis, and penny loafers. He caught me eyeing him appraisingly and misread the scrutiny.

"I have a jacket and a tie in the car if you think I should wear them," he said.

"No, you look perfect. I was admiring you, not being critical. A jacket in this little church may be a bit too much. But you can wear it if you like. Overdressing is always fine with me."

"That's what I thought," he said and pulled me close for a quick kiss. He smelled fabulous – so clean – a little bit of some cologne or something, and it was nice. Civilized. But not as good as he smelled at the end of the day. Like he did last night. All *him* mixed up with the smell of the fire and the horse blanket. This was a clean smell, but not *his* smell.

"Remember, I'm feeding you," he said when I did not make a move. I wanted to stay right here wrapped up in his arms…in my thoughts about him.

"Oh, yes," I stammered. "To the Square."

"You look lovely," he said, smiling down at me and stroking my chin with his hand. My knees tried to lock, and I bent them ever so slightly. No need to collapse in the foyer. "No dirt, but lovely nonetheless."

He took me to Smitty's on the Square. I was looking forward to a leisurely morning with him – in a public place – so we could talk without complications. There was so much I wanted to know about him and never enough time.

"Are you going to order breakfast for me?" I asked playfully.

"Only if you'd like me to, of course."

"Since I, or rather, Panzer, destroyed the picnic last night, why don't you take over the food plan for today?"

He ordered the standard Southern breakfast, and I couldn't complain. We had hardly eaten last night, and I was starved. The biscuits, grits, eggs, bacon, and toast arrived almost instantly, and we ate for a while in silence.

"I had a great time last night," I said. "Those constellations were glorious."

"I'll have to remember that. Much better than the movies," he said. "So, tell me about this church. What made you pick the one that we're going to this morning?"

"My uncle preached here a long time ago, so I thought it would be a good place to start. I tried a few others, but this one felt the most like a family, and they seemed to still have respect for worship – you know – the midday worship style that I grew up with. Not the modern casual deal. Those churches feel too much like a fad to me. The people here, they still dress up. The choir wears robes and sounds like angels. They even bring in a violinist – it's lovely."

"Oh, and there are five little ladies who make me feel like I'm their special granddaughter. They're always so glad to see me. They make a big fuss over all of us, my friends, I mean, and, well, it's…nice. And my Sunday school class is fun. My teacher's great – really wise. You'll have to meet her sometime. We do service projects in the community from time to time – you wouldn't believe all the needs out there even in a relatively wealthy college town. The sermons always give me something to think about; they're really interesting. It's just…well, a good place. It's small, and it feels like a second home," I trailed off, embarrassed that I'd rambled so much. After all, I was here to find out about him but had been prattling nonstop.

"That's what matters the most," he said. "Church should be a good place to go – where you feel loved and welcome no matter what. That's how it was for me growing up, and that's what I remember…what finally drew me back. The love. A safe place. People really caring about you. The right kind of family."

"Do you have a church in Nashville?" I asked, surprised that he had been listening to all my chatter.

"Not really. My Memphis church is the one I like the most. I never found one that I settled on in Nashville. You're lucky to find a good one here," he said.

"Do you go to church?"

"When I'm in Memphis, I go with my uncle. In Nashville, I went some, but not to any one consistently. I do like visiting random churches whenever I travel to see how other people worship...especially little old ones. While I've been in Nashville, though, I worked on getting support for the Argentina branch of the orphan project by going around to the larger churches and speaking to Sunday school classes. I never put the time in to get much of a connection to one church, but the people I worked with on the orphan project in Nashville became my extended church family. They're part of a national missions board. It's an impressive network and incredible what they do for so many kids here and around the world."

"And you think you're going to stop doing it," I said skeptically. "Just like that."

"Yes and no," he said. "There are seasons of life, Elliott, and what I can do one day may not work with what's supposed to be my job in a different phase. That's another thing my uncle taught me to watch for…change…and pay attention to what I'm supposed to do – get direction on that. Not just blaze away doing the same thing and tuning out everything else. I didn't believe him until you…happened to me. He was the one knocking me in the head telling me to go after you. I didn't even have to tell him about you. He just…knew."

"If I'm a divine thunderbolt," I said, "then let's leave this place and ride around for a while."

"As long as we make it to church," he said. "I'd hate to disappoint the One who shot you into my life."

“That’s *really* not playing fair.”

He paid for breakfast, and we drove to a nearby reservoir and parked in a spot that overlooked the lake. We had about two hours before church, and I didn’t want to share him with my Sunday school class, or anyone, for that matter. He played some music – a really cool selection of Sunday music that ranged from old hymns, to country, to rock – and everything in between. His taste in music was so varied. I wondered where he found all this.

We walked over to a picnic table where we could hear the music but sit a lot more comfortably together. There was no one else around this early on a Sunday morning, and the weather was perfect.

“When do you have to leave?” I asked, not wanting to bring it up, but I did want to hear him talk.

“Around 3:00,” he said. “I have some things that I need to get done before tomorrow, so I’ll have to get on the road.”

“I can’t wait until you’re here all the time,” I said and leaned back into his arms. He kissed the top of my head and let me lie against his chest.

“Me, too.”

He was quiet but so comfortably close. We sat for a long time enjoying the cool air and watching the bright winter sunlight sparkle across the water like diamonds.

“There’s so much I want to know about you, Griffen,” I said. “But I don’t want to talk about things you don’t want to tell me.”

“Elliott, there should be no secrets between us,” he said. “You ask me anything, and I’ll try to answer.”

“You told me about your father…what he did,” I said and hesitated. “But you never said much about your mother…except that you loved her a lot. What was she like?"

He stayed quiet for a long time, and I knew I had already crossed a line that I probably should not have. I waited, hoping he'd answer, but not daring to change the subject.

"She was perfect," he said. "Just perfect. But she made a really bad choice when she picked my father."

"If she had not done that, then I would not have you," I said. "So it wasn't all bad."

"She was not bad, but *he* was," Griffen said and stiffened. "He would hurt her, and she would try to hide it. She always took up for him, and I never understood why. I still don't. I wanted to do something, but I always felt powerless. After he'd rage at her, he'd turn on me."

I sat quietly for a while feeling his anger and frustration emanating from inside. He was holding me tighter now, and I was afraid to move – not afraid of him, just afraid he would stop talking, and I wanted to hear more. It was so sad, but fascinating, because I was looking with him into his past.

"He was a sick person, Griffen," I said. "You're describing someone with a lot of deep problems."

"Yes, but he *chose* to drink himself into a stupor, *chose* to marry her, *chose* to have me, and *chose* to let his anger get out of hand," he said getting more agitated with each word.

"You are right," I said, calmly. "And *you* can choose now to let it go. You don't have to stay mad at him. He's gone."

"But he's *not* gone," he said. "I see him every time I look in the mirror. He haunts me – the memories – the rage. I don't touch alcohol because I'm *afraid*...afraid of what would happen if I did. Why did *he* not choose to stay away from it if it caused so many bad things to happen?

She *loved* him! Why did he kill her? Why did he hate me so much?"

I turned to face him and put his magnificent, anguished, angry face between my hands. "I don't know the answers to those questions, Griffen, but I do know that *you* don't have to stay angry at who he was. Turn your energy away from that and *pity* him. He was your father, and the gift he gave you was life and a healthy respect for boundaries. What if you never knew he was a crazed alcoholic and got trapped by an alcohol addiction as a teenager? Then you might have fallen into his same trap. Don't you see? You have some things you can be grateful for about how you were raised and even what you saw."

"That's a high price to pay," he said, but he was calmer.

"Shhh," I said and kissed him softly. "You're getting *me*, Griffen. Every minute I spend with you I fall more in love with everything about you. The more I know you, the more I love who you have chosen to be."

His face looked unconvinced, but he kissed me back. For that, at least, I was glad.

"We're going to church, now, remember?" he whispered into my neck as he brushed the hair away from my face and looked into my eyes.

"I need all the spiritual strength possible when you're in town." My throat had gone dry, and the words caught as I reluctantly leaned away from him.

When we walked back to his truck, he stopped me at my door. "Thank you, Elliott," he said. "Thank you for helping me make some sense out of things I've never talked about…with anyone. You've given me a lot to consider."

I didn't reply, just hugged him and held him. I wanted to keep him here with me – not let him drive so far away – not have to share him. I loved hearing him talk – and we wouldn't be able to be alone like this for who knows how long. The telephone was not the same – text and e-mail too impersonal – letters too slow.

"We've really got to go now," he said and pried my arms from his sides. "I hate it when you make me do that."

The church was packed. January sunshine held the cold at bay, and everyone lingered outside. When we finally walked into the sanctuary, the five little ladies were lined up in their regular pew right behind where my friends and I always sat.

Leslie and Elaine were already seated, and they had saved two spots for us. I introduced my five "grandmothers" to Griffen and they gave *him* the peppermints they brought for me. They also were not bashful about hugging on him and winking their approval. It was so nice to have him here beside me in another piece of my little world. Once we were seen at lunch, the town would deem us engaged with marriage plans for the fall. This town was so similar to mine even though it did house a major university. You could always find the small town atmosphere if you looked for it.

The service closed with one of my all-time favorite hymns, *How Great Thou Art*, and we walked out with Leslie and Elaine.

"You're welcome to join us for lunch," I said. "Ben and Addy are meeting us at the Beacon.

"We're going back to the House," Elaine said. "Leslie's parents are in town, and she needs moral support."

I looked at Leslie, and she rolled her eyes.

"The inquisition," Leslie said. "Why don't you let me borrow Griffen and pretend he's my boyfriend? That would get Mama off my back."

"Not a chance," I hissed.

"Come on, Elliott, I only need him for an hour," Leslie said and batted her eyes at Griffen. "You'd look so good draped on my arm, and Mama would quit being unmercifully persistent about this dating thing."

"She's appealing to my chivalrous side, Elliott," Griffen said and put his magnificent arm around *her*. I bristled, but only for effect. "I do need to help your friends out when I can so they'll put in a good word for me when *I* need it."

"In that case," Elaine brightened, "I need a date for the game Saturday, Griffen. Could you just *stand in*..."

"You both are *crazy* if you think I'd let him out of my sight for a microsecond when I only get him on the weekends!" I roared, frightening two little girls dashing by in their Sunday best. "Now go away – forget that I even asked you to lunch!"

They laughed and ran dramatically to their car. Griffen lightly held my hand as he pulled me to his truck – nothing too obvious, but oh, so sweet. The church bells pealed noon in the background as the January wind blew leftover leaves into the street. Such a beautiful college town...a place it looked like I might be able to enjoy with him for many years to come.

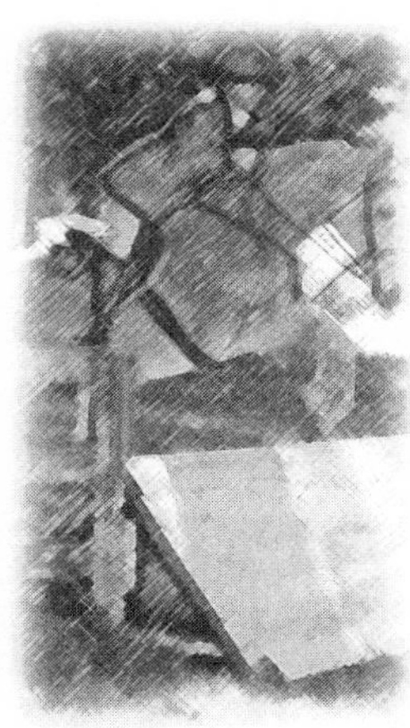

LUNCH

Chapter 5

Sensitive, opinionated, elegant, effervescent – like well-bred Southern ladies, Thoroughbreds have an abundance of these distinctions and much more.

Ben and Addy already had a table since their church finished before ours. In small towns, many of the churches staggered their worship times to help the restaurants from getting over crowded at once. I was glad they were there, for the line was backing up fast.

"Hey Griffen," Ben said as we approached the table. "She didn't shoot you, then?"

"You knew he was taking me shooting?" I asked, surprised.

"Of course," he said. "I'm taking Addy next week. I think it's a great idea. Addy knows how to shoot, but practice is always good."

"You shoot, Addy?" I asked, stunned that she had actually wielded a shotgun.

"Since I was eleven," she said. "I just haven't had a lot of incentive to go. But I liked it then, and I'm sure it will be a fun way to spend the afternoon."

"You'll all have to come to my camp to duck hunt some time," Griffen said.

"You just say the word," Ben said. "I'll be there."

We piled the buffet food on our plates and returned to our seats. The food was great, but I was still full from breakfast. And this new friendship between Ben and Griffen was taking some getting used to. Ben was my neighbor in my hometown of Canton and had decidedly disapproved of Griffen's interest in me until recently. Now they acted like the best of friends. He was like an overprotective big brother in spite of being smitten with my best friend, Addy.

"Have you talked to Ashley?" Addy asked quietly.

"No, why?" I asked. Ashley was Ben's former girlfriend, but there was no animosity between them…we were all close friends.

"I don't think her date went very well last night."

"What do you mean?" I asked, concerned at the look Addy was giving me.

"She and Shannon double-dated, thank goodness, but I don't think they were prepared for those guys," she said. Ben and Griffen bristled; I felt the air around me charge and resisted the urge to duck and run as if a bolt of lightning were about to strike.

"Maybe we should talk about this later," I said, feeling the tension mount.

"What happened?" Griffen asked Ben.

"Addy," Ben asked, "were they hurt?"

"No, just surprised, I think," she said, avoiding my gaze. "The guys had a little more in mind than dinner and a movie."

"Who were they?" Griffen asked Addy. He was tense, but calm… concerned, probably. But, I could feel him…his intensity…building.

And Ben was not far behind. *I thought Ben was overprotective. Now we have two to deal with.*

"She said she met one of them yesterday at the hunt. I saw them talking and didn't realize they had just met," she said, uneasily. "It looked like she'd known him before. Anyway, she agreed to a double date as long as she could bring one of her friends, and Shannon was game."

"Everything was fine until they left the movie and drove to the reservoir. The guys got a little too…friendly, and, well, nothing happened, but I think it shook them both up," Addy said.

"They better not show up here again," Ben said.

"Ben, you don't like anyone that has an interest in any of us," I said, trying to lighten the mood. "Remember you said Griffen was arrogant. I think you just want to keep us *all* to yourself."

"He *is* arrogant, and what's wrong with having all of you to myself?" Ben laughed, glancing at Addy to make sure she was still laughing. "But he has reason to be arrogant – he's a black belt."

"Like that makes a difference!" I said but was surprised. *I didn't know that about Griffen, either. How did Ben?*

"He made it crystal clear to me that his intentions with you were not, well, never mind. Just know he passed my inspection, and he can be as arrogant as he wants," he said, laughing at my obvious surprise at this revelation.

"Did you get their names?" Griffen quietly asked Addy, ignoring Ben.

"Yes," she said softly.

"I'd like to have them, if you don't mind," Griffen said, and his icy words burned.

She told him, and I felt very sorry for them…even though I was sure they deserved what was coming.

"Griffen is going to be in law school here this fall," I said, changing the subject.

"Oh, that reminds me, Griffen, I want to hunt in Nashville before you graduate. Why don't we make plans for a weekend trip there?" Ben said.

"I've thought about that, too, for some time. Maybe we can have a joint meet…next month. You talk to William, and I'll work on the guys in Nashville," he said. "Even though the fixture cards are probably set, we may be able to convince them to do something like this for us."

"I'm not ready to hunt again behind the Levee," Ben said. "I'm sure William will say things are fine, but we need to give that place some time to settle down."

Ben was referring to our hunt in the Mississippi Delta earlier in the season. Some people in the area were not as enthused as others that we were hunting on their property. They had threatened Griffen and given me a good scare at another time.

"I agree," I said. "A lot of those people do not want us around, and I still don't understand how it all got so out of hand. I hope William gets to the bottom of it before we go back…if we go back."

"Well, *you're* not hunting there without me," Griffen said. "I don't care if we're the *only* staff that show up – I'm not letting you out of my sight."

"We have papers to work on this afternoon, so we're off," Addy said. "Griffen, always great to see you. Elliott, I'll come by later this afternoon."

We said our mutual goodbyes, and Griffen drove me back to the sorority house. He had a few minutes before he had to go, so we stayed in the truck – the House had absolutely no privacy. What little time alone we had remaining, I certainly did not want to share.

"I like the idea of hunting in Nashville," I said. "Do you think your *former* hunt will agree to it?"

"I do," he said. "Especially if we can put together two days – that's easier to do this time of year. That way we can hunt one pack Saturday and the other on Sunday. It'll be up to the Masters to decide, but I'm sure they could work something out. And there would be plenty of parties – not a lot of time just for us, though."

"Let's not worry about the parties," I said. "I would like to hunt in another place as long as we can ride together. That would be a treat – in your home country."

"If you want to do this, it *will* happen," he said, "whether or not we can get the hunts together. In fact, if you want to hunt with me Saturday, just come on. I'll find a place for you and Viva to stay. Better yet, I'll find a horse for you to ride there. That will be better than you taking your trailer all that way alone."

"Whatever happens, just make sure you're kissing me Friday night somewhere," I said, smiling at him.

He leaned in close to me and rubbed his fingers along my jaw line, traced my neck, then brushed my hair behind my shoulders. I shivered and wished it was not broad daylight in the sorority house parking lot. His eyes had me spellbound, and there were no words to express how much I wanted him not to leave. Every time he drove away, a piece of my heart went with him.

Then he moved closer and kissed me softly, an attempt at a gentle, parting, peck. I wasn't going to let him get away with just that and pulled him into much more of a kiss – a week's worth of kisses – but he backed away. My head spun, and I blinked to clear my vision.

"Let's get you back to your room before I have to kidnap you," he grinned. "I'll go with you in case you forget to look both ways when you cross the street."

He walked me to the door where people constantly were in and out. So very very public. His kisses made me want to dance pirouettes across the street, but that would be embarrassing. I was glad I had his arm to contain myself.

"I'll call you tonight," he said and kissed me on the cheek.

My euphoric mood evaporated as soon as I stepped into our hall. Ashley and Shannon were screaming at each other, and Addy was attempting to mediate.

"...your fault we went in the first place!" Shannon said. "We could have been killed, or worse! They know where we *live*!"

"Hey, Shannon, Ashley, what's going on?" I said.

"Stay out of this, Elliott," Ashley said.

"I'm in it now," I said. "What's going on, Addy?"

"The guy that went out with Shannon last night was in the parking lot this morning," she said. "It was really kind of...freaky. Shannon saw him and called the guard."

"Ashley will go out with anyone as long as he's cute and looks like he has money!" Shannon screeched. "I'm *so* embarrassed by this whole thing, and now they know where we *live*!"

"Shannon, that's crazy," I said. "Ashley had no idea, and going together *was* a good idea. No one was hurt, and the guy's not coming back since we have security all over this place."

"Yeah, *whatever,* Elliott," Shannon said. "You didn't have to break out pepper spray to get a guy to drive you home."

"Did you get to use it?" I asked, fascinated.

"No, but you should have seen the guy's face when she whipped out *her* pink menace," Ashley said and started to giggle. *This must have really upset her – she never giggles.*

The image first of the horror of two strange guys coming on unexpectedly too strong and then of Shannon wielding terror with pink pepper spray took us all by surprise, and we could not control the spasms of laughter that exploded from us. The tension was gone, and Shannon actually hugged Ashley when it was all over. *Hormonal, for sure.*

"So, what's the weekend plan?" Addy asked.

"I don't know yet," I said. "Griffen said he'd check on the Nashville thing, but he also asked me to go up there this weekend and hunt with him."

"I want to go!" Addy said. "You know Ben does, too. Let me know what he says. That would be fun even if it were not a joint meet."

"We can't take all of William's help away," I said. "Let's see what happens. Either way, he'll be here, or I'll be there."

"Oh, and Ashley," Addy said. "If either of those guys show up here again, I think Ben and Griffen plan to rip them up and burn the pieces. I told them their names."

"Oh no!" Ashley said. "I've heard what they did to those men in the Delta. More bad boys eating liquids for a while. Oh dear – but I can't say that makes me feel bad…I like being so, defended."

"Ashley, you are ridiculous," Shannon said. "All we need is another brawl that gets them kicked off more hunt country. Didn't that guy say he was some kind of landowner?"

"Who cares?" Ashley said.

"I think it will matter a lot to everyone else," she said. "Even *I* know you can't foxhunt without land."

"We need a change of location," I declared. "Addy, see if Ben can to go to Nashville this weekend. It's time for a road trip. I'll make this happen with Griffen and William."

"We're in, too," Ashley said for herself and Shannon. "We need to get out of town…just to see the sights. We don't want to ride, just go, if that's ok."

"Good, then we can split a hotel room four ways. That will be a lot better. And we can take your trailer, Addy, and Ben's truck, and split the gas. This makes sense all around," I said. "Ben can stay with Griffen or something like that."

The rest of the afternoon was spent handling a flurry of details. I hoped Griffen would be up to all of this. It was getting out of hand, but William was fine with us taking a road trip and abandoning him. He said he thought he'd have plenty of staff for the next weekend since the fixture was at home. He also thought the joint-meet was a good idea and for us to work on developing that when we were there.

That evening, my cell phone buzzed – Griffen's 615 number. My heart sped up, still, every time he called.

"Miss me?" I said when I answered his call.

"You have no idea."

"I came up with my surprise for you," I said, wishing I could see his face.

"You are always a surprise," he said, big smiles in his voice.

"I'm hunting with you Saturday."

"Oh, you are? William's ok with that?" he asked, sounding very pleased.

"Yes. And he's also fine with Ben and Addy coming, too," I said and waited.

"That was fast – did you already arrange a joint meet?"

"No, but Ashley and Shannon want to come too, but not ride," I said in a rush. "We'll stay in a hotel, and Ben can stay with you…if that's ok."

"That will be fine. I will make sure there's room for three horses and a bed for Ben. Anything else, dear Elliott?" he asked, amused.

"Are you sure you're all right with this?"

"Why in the world would I be upset that you are bringing your lovely self and most of your friends into my domain? No pressure at all, really," he said, and I think he was still smiling. Only one way to tell.

"I love you, Griffen," I said with as much syrup as possible over the phone.

"That is very good to know," Griffen said, purposefully hiding his tone, I could tell now.

"Griffen?"

"Yes, Elliott."

"What are you doing…right now?" I asked as softly as I could, as I recovered from hearing him say my name over the phone…like that.

He sighed, and I so wanted to have my head lying across his chest – feeling it rise up and down – so warm – so secure and close.

"I'm talking to you, Elliott," he said in his most wonderful deep lazy telephone voice.

"And?"

"Wishing you were sitting here in my room," he said, and I blushed. *Blushing over the phone!*

"Me, too."

"I'll see you this weekend, then? Friday afternoon?" he asked.

"As soon as we can figure out when we can all get away, I'll let you know. We'll probably skip Friday classes if we can. I wish I could leave now."

"The sooner the better, love. I'll call you tomorrow. Goodnight."

NASHVILLE

Chapter 6

We are in for a gallop – away! away!
I told them my beauty could fly;
And we'll lead them a dance ere they catch us today,
For we mean it, my lass and I!
She skims the fences, she scours the plain,
Like a creature winged, I swear,
With a snort and strain, on the yielding rein;
For I'm bound to humour the mare.

~ *G. J. Whyte-Melville, "The Good Grey Mare"*

Griffen's instructions all week were ringing in my ears as we traveled over the breathtaking Nashville countryside. *Be sure to wear breastplates, you will need them for the hills. Take your time pulling the horses, the roads to where you are staying are hard to navigate with a trailer; make sure you get here before dark.*

I was glad Ben agreed to drive, because Griffen texted me every ten miles. I had never seen him so excited about anything. The drive was lovely but tricky. Ben drove carefully with three horses, and it gave us time to enjoy the scenery.

Griffen met us at the barn looking glorious. His place was almost as beautiful as the barn where I used to board Viva in Canton. The Oxford accommodations were good, but basic, for all my parents could afford with college was pasture board. That suited me fine as long as I had Viva with me. Here, though, was a different story. Many of the horses were in the pastures, for it was late in the evening, and they spent nights out and days inside when the nights were not too cold. This helped them keep their coats looking rich and true to their colors, not bleached by too much sunlight. I was glad we had bathed our horses and refreshed their clips. They would look gorgeous, too, in spite of their basic care. We had polished them and all their tack until everything gleamed.

I jumped out of the truck and into Griffen's arms. He caught me but backed away, surprised, and a little embarrassed, so I refrained from planting a kiss on him in front of everyone. It was priceless to see him blush.

"I'll show you where the horses go," he said after he had recovered. "This is the barn manager, Raphael Lavalle. Let him know what you need for the horses. He's taking care of them for you this weekend."

After introductions around, I pulled Griffen aside and said, "This place is glorious!" Stone accented everything, and the fixtures were made from cast iron. The cobblestone barn isles, wooden panels, and large stalls gave the barn a clean and welcoming feel.

"I'm glad you like it," he said. "Come over here so I can show you where Viva's going."

Every stall was immaculate, so I could not wait to see what special place he had for my girl. They all looked the same, but he led her proudly into one on the end that overlooked the pasture. The sun's residue painted a glowing purple, orange, and red canvas backdrop to her window. I stared out the window in awe and felt him grab me and pin me to the wall. He kissed me so hard I was sure I'd have bruises, but I didn't mind. I smiled to myself remembering that I'd looked away…

"I'm so glad you're here," he whispered in a low rumble. "But don't pounce on me like that in front of everyone. Do you *want* me to ravish you in public? You underestimate my self control."

"I don't care *where* you ravish me *as long as* you ravish me!" I said, laughing quietly so the others wouldn't hear.

The others were approaching with their horses as they admired the barn. "So, whose idea was it to bring all this company?" he asked wryly.

"Sorry."

We reluctantly left our sanctuary and settled the horses in for the night. They had racks filled with fresh hay, and the shavings were piled so high that the horses had dropped and rolled as soon as they circled their stalls. Viva reveled in the thick bedding and nuzzled me as if she was thanking me for her great room. She was clean, but I could see that we would need to make time to brush the shavings out of their tails in the morning. We had drenched their tails, legs, and coats with special silicone spray to help keep the dirt from sticking, but they would need some attention before we showed up at the hunt.

I rode with Griffen to where we would be staying, and Ben followed with everyone else in his truck. After changing clothes, we left for a nearby restaurant. Griffen's choice was excellent as usual, and we ate until we couldn't move. He drove me back to our cabin, and we found a place on the property where we could be alone – even if it was only for a little while.

"I'm so glad you came," he said. "I may not let you leave. You can finish the semester here you know."

"Don't tempt me," I said. "This place is so pretty; the land is breathtaking. It looked like we were riding through a coffee table book."

"Wait 'till you see the country from Viva's back," he said. "I don't think there's a prettier place on earth." He leaned down and kissed me softly. I flinched a little, and he sat back in alarm.

"Surely I didn't *hurt* you when I kissed you?" he asked, worried.

"No…well, just a little, but it's no big deal," I said and pulled him to me. "Something to remember you by. *Please* don't stop."

He kissed me senseless, then gathered me into his arms as he stood to go.

"I'll be back at 8:00 to collect you tomorrow," he said, looking down at me, his arms resting on my lower back holding me so wonderfully close to him. "Call me if you need anything."

The next morning came way too soon since Ashley, Shannon, Addy, and I had laughed and talked well past any reasonable bedtime. For the first time in my hunting career, I was way behind schedule. When Griffen and Ben arrived, I gobbled breakfast and drank two cups of hot tea to get going. Unfortunately, the rest of the girls were no better off than I was, but they were hardly trying. By the time the female portion of our operation was ready to move, both guys were starting to behave badly.

"Wait, Griffen," I said. "I forgot my hair net."

He glared at me in front of everyone, but I ignored him. His stare penetrated and was embarrassing to endure, especially in front of my friends. Ben, too, was nervous and edgy, but at his suggestion, they had already collected and tacked up Harley and Viva. Even with that out of the way, we were running late. Griffen barked orders at us like a sergeant, and we were soon on the road. He visibly relaxed once underway, but I wasn't ready to warm up to his icy countenance towards me in spite of us finally being alone.

We rode most of the way in silence, then he turned on his iPod. It was eerie listening to classical music in silence as we traveled over the gorgeous land. He reached for my hand, and I gave it to him, still looking out the window and not at him. I was hurt at how impatient he was this morning but didn't want to be. I wished my heart would respond, but it wasn't ready to, just yet.

After twenty minutes or so it looked like Griffen was no longer visibly irritated. When we reached the meet site, trailers were parked everywhere. This was a much bigger turnout than I had expected.

By whipper-in standards, we were quite late. The hunt was scheduled to move off at 10:00 and it was already 9:45. Typically as staff, we arrived one hour and a half early, and as visitors, we would have planned to be there at least an hour early to have time to make introductions, saddle our horses, and relax. Thankfully, he and Ben had not only tacked our horses for us, but had also brushed them down, and Griffen had handled our paperwork before we arrived. Visitors typically have to provide release forms, pay capping, or guest hunting fees, and show current Coggins or health papers for the horse they ride, and that can take some time to organize.

He pulled into the guest parking area, the only place left to park two trucks and trailers. Mountains, definitely not hills, stretched to the sky around the trailers. They filled me with awe...such marvelous, majestic monuments to the wonder and variety of our country...and of the many different places in our world where people celebrated the chase.

Although I felt so comfortable with this sport, being in such unfamiliar surroundings with strangers was exciting, if not unsettling, especially since we were being so keenly observed. I could feel curious eyes of the members upon us. It felt like walking into a restaurant in Canton or Oxford where everyone expected to recognize you, or categorize you, in one quick glance. I kept expecting Grand to hiss in my ear, but she was silent. She and my Southernmothers should be telling me to "keep a pleasant look on your face, don't let them see you looking rushed, don't you ever appear too busy for pleasantries. Remind yourself, Miss Elliott, you're a Lady!" But for once, there were no voices in my head.

"I'm going to get Ben and Addy settled with Ron Jenkins, the first flight field master. You'll ride with me," Griffen said and got out of the truck. I wasn't sure whether he wanted me to stay put or unload, but I knew we were in a hurry, so I decided to be helpful and unload Viva. As I got out and walked to the back of the trailer, several people welcomed me with their smiles, and I returned the gesture. They knew we were late and were in a hurry, so they kept their distance.

"Elliott, what *are* you doing?" Griffen roared from Ben's truck.

Silence. A horse jangled its bit and another stamped its feet; maybe it was the same one. Who could know? But all conversation within earshot had stopped, and time stood still. When I looked up, all eyes, some familiar, most not, were on me. I wanted to crawl under the trailer.

"Unloading the horses," I said, chin up, dignity intact.

"Don't let him see you cringe, honey. But, oh, he's not to ever do that again," Grand said. God bless her. She's back…that must mean trouble.

"*I'll* do that," he snapped. "Just get back in the truck."

Oh I will. And oh, will he pay for this. We *don't talk to* me *like that.* I met the strangers' eyes that were staring, lifted my chin, and got back into the truck. The longer I sat, the angrier I got. By the time Griffen returned, I was ready for him.

"They're settled. You're riding with me," he said, like nothing happened. "We're going to unload over here with the staff. I want you to meet Bob, the huntsman. He's going to love you."

"I will *not* meet *anyone* right now, Griffen," I spat.

He looked at me like I'd slapped him.

"Don't think that I will *ever* go with you *anywhere* if what you just did *ever* happens again," I hissed. "You just made me look like a *complete fool* in front of not only my friends, but also heaven knows who out there that I'm supposed to meet. *I* will be riding with Ben and Addy only because it would look even worse if I sat in this truck and pouted. I'll not let you *ruin* the whole weekend after all we've done to get here and hunt with you!"

Griffen had not moved. He sat, shocked, on his side of the truck. After a few minutes, he regained his composure, but his response did nothing to diffuse the situation.

"*You* will be riding with me," he said, his jaw clenched tightly, "or I will take you back right now."

My heart was pounding, but definitely not in a way that was healthy for him. I had a number of murderous thoughts flash across my mind and banished them since we were in an entirely too public place and under a deadline to be ready – thirty minutes ago. *Impasse.*

"All right," I said through clenched teeth. His jaw relaxed a little and he turned towards me slightly. Before he could speak, I finished my sentence. "If you're going to be like that, take me back."

"Elliott, we don't have *time* for this," he said, trying to keep his words under control. His carefully calculated attempt at composure made me even angrier.

"I have all the time in the world," I said. "I'll be riding with Ben and Addy. Right now, I really don't want to be anywhere *near* you."

"I'm sorry I snapped at you, Elliott," he said. "Please ride with me. I've been looking forward to this all week."

"Griffen, you can snap at me all you want in private. I may even deserve it from time to time. But in public? On what *planet* would you *ever* think that would be acceptable? I have not been here three minutes and you humiliated me," I said, in a much more even tone.

"I am sorry for that, Elliott," he said, but he was not looking very sorry. He was actually looking angry and impatient…again.

I sat very still. I could see his patience leaving like sand from the last seconds in an hourglass. I envisioned an explosion when the sand disappeared…three…two…one…

"Fine," he said. No explosion…yet. "I'll see you at the breakfast."

My throat constricted, but I couldn't let him see how much this hurt. I felt like the explosion happened in my heart. *No one could know… but Grand. She had her big, floppy arms around me and was holding me. I had to keep from crying. He's breaking my heart, just like she said he would. The raindrops…they came all at once this time…and rolled right into a hurricane. She tried to tell me….*

He unloaded Viva and Jet beside Ben and Addy's trailer rather than drive over to the staff area. His composure was impressive…

no one would ever know we had just had a row in the front seat from they way he carried himself. I wanted so badly to knock him off his horse and prayed silently that, for once, Jet would pitch him headlong into the crowd. Once I mounted Viva, we trotted over to Ben and Addy like nothing ever happened. They were already situated in first flight and were talking to the other riders who were, thankfully, still waiting for the huntsman. We were not really late as guests, just late had we been expected to help with the hounds.

"What are you doing?" Addy asked when she saw me approach.

"Viva's a little off, so I thought I'd better ride in the field rather than whip-in," I lied, my pitiful excuse sounding ridiculous even to me. "I don't want to slow Griffen down; he said they need him and Jet today to help and that they really didn't like whippers-in to ride in pairs here."

Ben bought it, but Addy didn't. I'm sure she saw it in my eyes. My heart had exploded, and the world just kept on going.

The galloping, jumping, flying, climbing, scrambling, uproarious, beautiful, rocky, mountainous woodland madness moments kept me well occupied for the next four hours. This felt like rollerblading on horseback, and the danger and uncertainty of whirling up and around trails I had never seen had adrenaline surging through my veins. I had braved the first few minutes at this hunt stoically, but with charm that would have made my Southernmothers proud as Griffen introduced us. Some members made brief comments to us, and others admired our horses. Ashley and Shannon had found a place to ride with car-followers, and I had not had to look at Griffen again.

Ben placed us in the back of first flight, the proper place for guests.

Since Addy and I had never had the chance to hunt together, this, too, was a treat. Harley was handy over the stone walls and had only a little problem with the mountains. Viva floated flawlessly over everything, and I was so glad to be with her, my constant companion, my forever friend. I knew her as well as myself and was grateful for the ride she was giving me today, of all days.

So concentrated I'd been on my own riding that I had had little chance to notice how many riders this hunt had. There were about forty in first flight, and second flight, as far as I could tell, had almost as many. There were four or five trucks following the pack, for we would see them every time we jumped onto a road. I did not notice how many whippers-in they had, since I was trying hard not to look for Griffen, but I would guess about eight.

Beside the glorious mountains and stone jumps, my favorite thing that this hunt had was kids. There were kids and ponies everywhere, and we rode among them in the back of the flight. I heard that this huntsman and his whipper-in wife had three young boys. Between those boys and their friends, the whole atmosphere was kicked up a notch. They were perfectly polite but fearless and highly competitive over the obstacles although they had enough manners to be subtle. Their ponies climbed these "hills" like mountain goats.

I laughed watching them all morning; it was miraculous what they did to lift my spirits. One little girl had braids flying behind her, and I longed to be her age again. She had bright red ribbons in her pigtails and braided into her pony's tail. Red ribbons indicate that a pony or horse kicks, and I thought about putting them in my hair – to warn Griffen that I was still mad. *But he deserved to be kicked...again...if he did not work this out. I had already warned him.*

In the back of first flight, I had to pay much more attention to our neighboring riders. Some adults were not as well mannered as the kids and tended to stop suddenly or crash in front of us with no advance notice, or cut us off at the jumps. Ben and Blazer did their best to keep Addy and me from colliding with them; more than once, I had to bite my tongue when we were buffeted in the tight turns. The anger and shock I felt at being hit by a horse at full gallop was actually, fun. This was a whole new feeling I had not yet experienced in the hunt field. Viva was not daunted either and welcomed the challenge.

"Mercy, child, the thoughts going through your mind would make a sailor blush. Keep a check on 'em honey," Grand scolded. "Thank the Lord for good breeding and your mother's nagging."

Addy glanced back at me after one particularly tight, twisting, run and grinned. I gave her a "thumbs up" and grinned back. Although I had not seen anything but Harley's or Blazer's rump for hours, I could hear the hounds' music heralding these excellent runs. It was also unusual for me not to know what was happening with the hounds and staff since I didn't have a radio. For all I knew, we could be chasing deer. Members of the field weren't issued this equipment, so my "take" on the day was like being tied to the tail of a tiger and hoping for the best.

There were no wide-open vistas here like in our home country, so I wasn't able to see much of the other riders once we really got going in the mountains. I could see for miles when we reached the top of some of the trails, but all that was below were trees and rocks. I shuddered at the thought of falling from these heights and patted Viva gratefully for her agility.

"So, the Mississippi group's still on top?" a sultry voice said as she rode back to us when the hounds paused from their chase, or checked. She had been riding at the front of first flight and was on an elegant bay horse with no markings, probably more than 17 hands, or a little over five and one half feet tall at its withers, or shoulders. As she approached, something about her countenance made me bristle.

"We…yes," Ben said, agreeably of course. I was certain he didn't notice anything past her lean perfect form, storm gray eyes, and bright smile directed at him.

"So, you're all from…Cantonville, or something?" she purred.

"Canton, yes," Ben said. "But Addy's from Memphis."

"I know a *rider* from there, Ashley something. She and I show together. Is she here today?" Miss Big Horse said.

"Ashley Woods," Ben corrected. "She's riding with the car followers. Her horse isn't really suited for this activity."

"Oh, well. I don't hunt my show horses, either. I have this one for the field. By the way, my name is Meredith Stanley," she said to Ben only.

"Nice to meet you, Meredith," he said. "I'm Ben Allen, and this is Addy…"

"There are the hounds," she said and spun away, splattering me with mud. *Did she just do that on purpose? Surely not…I think so. What was up with that?*

Addy and I exchanged glances as we galloped after the hounds. I had forgotten how much more difficult in many ways it was to ride in the field than whip-in, but I was enjoying this. All my frustration with Griffen was forgotten for now, since I was focusing solely on survival. Now this Amazon had piqued my curiosity. Fortunately, Viva was manageable in the Pelham bit I'd chosen for this day…just in case I needed "yes ma'am" brakes. So far, I had needed it a number of times already.

At the next stop, our new friend returned, or rather, Ben's new friend came back to check on him. She had purposefully been riding at the rear of first flight, now, I suppose, to show off her perfect physique. Since Addy and I were flanking him, she had to acknowledge us this time.

"That's a nice *pony*," she gushed, looking down at Viva and me making a point to stare at the mud she'd flung. "I didn't know *gaited horses* jumped."

"She's a Thoroughbred," I said, struggling to check my already jangled nerves. Her comment confirmed she was baiting me. There is no way Viva would ever be mistaken for a gaited horse by anyone who knew horses…she was casting the first stone to gauge my reaction. I wasn't in the mood to be baited, especially not by some*thing* like her.

"I thought most people had gaited horses down in Mississippi," she said, syrupy sweet. "You know, to ride on the farms and stuff."

"Actually, there are lots of them in Mississippi, but seeing as the Tennessee Walking Horse originated in this state, I would have expected to see more of them here. Oh, but I think they're owned mostly by those with Old Money…the genteel landowner types," I said, refraining from adding "The ones with manners"… only by Grand's insistence that I didn't start a cat fight in the hunt field. The barb hit home, and she stiffened.

"You're quite right," a new female voice said. "My grandfather has a whole stable of them and hunts twice a week with us, doesn't he, Meredith?"

"In the hilltopper group. It takes horses with a lot of leg here to hunt in first flight," she said, looking down her nose at Viva and me – really, she did that…it was a first for me. As she trotted away, she called airily over her shoulder, "See you at the breakfast."

"I'm Jill Post," the new voice said to me. "Don't mind Meredith. She can be a real pill, but her bark is much more impressive than her bite. You must be Elliott since she directed most of her snarls at you."

"Yes, Jill, nice to meet you. And this is Addy Falls and Ben Allen. We're Griffen's friends from Mississippi.

"How well I know that. Your visit is big news here. Meredith and the rest of the single female crowd are astonished that Griffen not only showed up with you, but three other women. They'd long given him up for a hopeless cause. Your visit's caused quite a stir," she laughed.

I felt myself blush, and, to her credit, Jill smiled.

"They're just beside themselves with jealousy," she said. "Don't think we're all like her, though. Jealous, yes, but not all nasty about it. I rode over when I saw her circling to make sure you didn't leave here thinking we're all a bunch of harpies!"

"I had no idea," I said.

"Yeah, well, we were all hoping you had three eyes, a hidden horn, and couldn't ride, but you're doing an impressive job keeping up like you are on a day like today…in this country."

"It certainly hasn't been easy," I said. "But this land is gorgeous! I do hope we can come back sometime and that some of you will come hunt with us, too."

"We'll miss Griffen, well, looking at him of course, since he never really pays much attention to us. He's always focused on the kids…and they follow him around like a litter of puppies," she said. "Especially the huntsman's and his wife's kids. They spent a lot of time together."

As usual, the hounds interrupted our conversation with their mighty chorus, and we dashed around for another thirty minutes without checking. Half the first flight "fell out" at this straight-up-the-mountain dash, Meredith and Jill being the first pair. I hated to see Jill go, but Meredith, well, it couldn't have happened at a better time. My *little gaited pony* and I passed her with relish, and I wished we were in the Delta where you could fling real mud that stuck…for weeks. All I could send her way was scorn.

Way too soon, the hunt was over, and we were back at the trailers. This hunt had started from one of the Master's homes, so the setting for our breakfast feast took my breath away. Since I was certain Griffen would still be out with the hounds, and I wasn't expected to help with hound chores, I could take my time untacking Viva, cooling her down, and wiping off her surprisingly clean tack. There was so little mud here that it almost looked as clean as it did when we started. *That's a nice perk about the mountains, too.* Viva was tied to Griffen's trailer, and I hesitated a moment…considering whether to move her to Ben's trailer so I wouldn't have to deal with Griffen right now or wait around on him if he had to stay out and find lost hounds…

"Elliott," he said. My stomach clinched. *I'm not up to this, not yet.*

I was holding Viva's saddle still trying to decide which trailer to put it in, and made no move to set it down. My hard hat was still on… and I turned to look – giving him my best exasperated blank stare – at him – nothing inviting about my stance or gaze…at all.

"Griffen."

He made his customary move toward me, and I took a step back. "Keep your distance."

"Let me take your saddle," he said, grabbing it and taking it to his trailer before I could protest. Now I had no prop. *Disarmed. What now? Think fast; he's coming back.*

"Keep your eyes on him, Elliott, don't look away, or he'll find a way to get *to you…and you won't be able to stand your ground," Grand coached. "What you do in the next few minutes is very important, dear."*

Yes, I know, but what to do? I reached over and untied Viva and picked up a bucket. I could take her to get water – good reason to escape without looking like I was running away.

"Where are you going?"

"Taking her to get some water," I said as casually as I could muster.

"This way," he said and took her lead rope from my hands.

Now I was following him…I had to…I had the bucket…he had my horse. *How ridiculous.* He walked Viva behind a barn and out of sight of the other people. As soon as he turned the corner, he rounded on me. I didn't see that coming, so I ran into him. He took advantage of my misstep and pulled me close, planting another uninvited kiss on my outraged lips.

"Stop it!" I hissed and stepped back, barely resisting the urge to crash the bucket into his thick skull. "Griffen!" I stammered, because my heart was now hammering in anger *and* longing and that would *not* do. *Not* now.

"I didn't mean to hurt you, Elliott," he said, carefully watching my eyes. "You are my whole world, and I would never do anything to hurt you, or embarrass you, on purpose. Please forgive me. I love you. I was completely out of line."

He took my silence as acquiescence. Maybe it was, because I could think of nothing to say and couldn't move. His green eyes may have well as belonged to a cobra – they had me completely mesmerized. Like a defenseless rodent, I was paralyzed by the eyes of the one who was going to kill me – and could do nothing about it.

He moved closer, leaned down, and kissed me…so so softly. For a moment, I couldn't move or get my bearings. I dropped the bucket, and the world started to spin. My knees buckled, and I would have collapsed had he not pulled me next to him. He held me close and kept kissing me…gently, so softly…then I reached up and grabbed as much of his hair as I could and pulled. He released his hold on me, and his hands flew to the back of his head as he gasped in pain.

"Ouch! What the…?"

"You are not…being…fair," I hissed and backed away.

"Have you lost your mind?" he asked, truly confused now, still rubbing the back of his head. "What is *wrong* with you?"

I sat on the overturned bucket and put my head between my knees. I felt faint and certainly did not need to do that…right now. He was immediately by my side.

"Elliott, come on, talk to me," he said, stroking my hair, softly, gently. I calmed down under his touch, listening to his voice; I was acting like a horse acts when he touches it, giving in, relaxing…and it felt so much better to relax.

I looked up, but didn't look at him. Bad idea. I kept my gaze on things near him so I wasn't actually looking away, but stayed away from his pleading eyes.

"Do you understand what you did?"

"Yes, and I truly am sorry," he said.

"Why did you talk to me like that? In front of them?"

"I didn't think, Elliott. I was frustrated and let my words fly. I was irritated at a lot of things and you were the one that got hurt," he said. "It was reprehensible of me to do that to you, to say those things in that way to you."

"Ok," was all I could say. I was really tired from lack of sleep, emotional strain, riding up and down mountains for four hours, and now, hunger.

"Ok?" he asked, wary still.

This time I looked at him…in the eyes. My whole body ached and begged for rest. I had neither the energy nor the desire to fight, not here, not today. "Ok. Really," I said. "Let's go get some food. Then, I want a nap."

When we walked in the house, they pounced. Meredith first.

"Griffen, welcome home," she purred. "I was just telling Carol here how nice it was to ride with your friends today. I see *Eunice* made it back."

"Meredith, why don't you hop back on the broom you flew in on and leave my guests alone?"

"Why Griffen, I just…"

"I'm sure you just…" he said and led me out of her path.

"Griffen? That was rude!" I said, smiling appreciatively at him.

"You have no idea."

"Enlighten me."

"Later. I want you to meet…"

"Hey Griffen," another female voice said. "Do I get to meet this lovely girl of yours?"

"Ginger Richards, meet Elliott Marks," he said smiling widely and gave her a…kiss…yes, a real kiss…on the cheek. I was shocked speechless. This was so unlike the aloof-with-all-women Griffen I thought I knew. "I was just heading your way. Ginger's my favorite redhead and the best whipper-in in Nashville."

"Hardly, but thanks. Nice to meet you, Elliott," Ginger said. "Griffen's been bragging about you for quite some time. I'm so glad to meet you, but I was hoping to get to see you ride. He's told me so much about you and Viva that I feel like I already know you both."

I was surprised that my anti-women-in-his-life Griffen I thought I knew so well had told this one so much. Even if it was about me. And, she was beautiful…no rings on her hands, either…but, then again, less is the norm regarding jewelry at a foxhunt. Typically, traditionalists wear only their stock pins and no jewelry, although some wear small gold, pearl, or diamond stud earrings. No *bling.* Rings sometimes interfered with gloves, so that may not mean anything. I couldn't get an idea of her age, but was helped when two rowdy boys assailed Griffen right in front of her, then blushed when they saw me.

"Oops, sorry, Mom. Didn't mean to butt in…"

"Boys, this is Elliott Marks," Griffen said before Ginger could react and cuff them.

"We know, I mean, nice to meet you…again, Miss Marks," they said over each other.

"You, too, guys. I had a ball watching both of you ride today. Your mother should be really proud," I said.

They beamed and dashed away to torment some other people. "They are excellent riders, Ginger," I said. "You and your husband must have started young…I mean…teaching them to ride."

Oh my. I can't believe I just said that…what a blubbering idiot!

She laughed knowingly at my flushed face, putting me instantly at ease. "They have always ridden, but it wasn't until Griffen got here and inspired them that they really turned around. It helps to have "cool" guys for them to emulate, other than their father.

"Well, Ginger, I don't know about Griffen here being much of a role model for them," a man said in a rough British accent. "He's not bloody around anymore. Seems to've gone to ground with some little vixen in Mississippi."

His warm smile felt like an embrace as he directed his charismatic grin at me. He looked tired but elated, filthy yet gorgeous.

"Hey Bob, back off," Griffen warned. "Too much of that will overwhelm an unsuspecting girl like Elliott. Don't make me remind you that you've already found your vixen; and if you don't keep a close eye on her, well, I can't make any promises."

"You said you'd bring her right to me, and I've had to seek her out myself. So, Elliott, what did you think about my hounds?"

I wasn't prepared at all for this, for him, and I stuttered, in spite of Griffen's ridiculous description of my being a poor little girl. I found, to my astonishment, that I *was* a bit...overwhelmed...by Bob. "Well, um, they sounded great." My voice seemed weak, and I was glad when Griffen put a Coke in my hands.

"That all?"

"I...I was in the back of the flight, so, well, it was hard to see... anything."

"Next time you come, you ride with me so you can see something besides the back of the horse in front of you. I would have thought Griffen would have taken care of that," he said.

"Not a chance," he growled. "Leave her alone with you? For four hours? I'd never be able to look her father in the eyes again."

"Surprised you can now."

"That's enough," Griffen rumbled.

"I'm just getting started," Bob said and winked at me. Ginger rolled her eyes.

"Elliott, I *do* hope you don't think we're all ill-mannered rogues. We are both delighted to have finally met you and can see that Griffen's in good hands," she said gripping my fingers and indicating her head towards Griffin conspiratorially. "I wish you the best of luck with *that* one!"

"No kidding. Thanks," I said, trying not to blush…again. These two made me feel self-conscious even though I sensed genuine good wishes from them. I felt so insignificant and that their confidence in me was misplaced. I had taken him away and they were being so gracious. He was planning to leave all this for…me? Our situation was tenuous at best, especially today. So why was he leaving all this? This, too, was his family, just like the Memphis hunt. They needed him here, and he was leaving…was really already gone.

No sooner than these thoughts floated through my mind than a great crashing sound erupted from the kitchen. The room fell silent as each person's mouth formed a perfect O. A huge white sphere exploded from the kitchen, crashed into the centerpiece via the shrimp cocktail, bounced onto the floor, and rolled to a stop at Bob's feet. Simultaneously, the youngest Richards boy appeared, sheepishly, in the dining room… and made a beeline for whom I guessed was the owner of this elegant home.

"Mrs. Turnipseed, I'm so, so sorry. I don't know what happened… I just, I, well…I'm so sorry about your window," he said, visibly shaken and struggling hard to form his words. He caught Bob's eye, dropped his chin to the floor, and stood by Ginger and Griffen as if comforted by their presence.

"Oh my Dear, I don't know what I'd do without your wonderful energy and your soccer ball! Don't you worry about that old window. It's not every day that a lady can claim that a world-class soccer player was the reason she got to remodel her kitchen!" Mrs. Turnipseed said, leaning down to embrace the little redheaded boy. He relaxed, some, but stayed huddled between Griffen and Ginger.

He looked up at her, and she shooed him and his filthy soccer ball back outside with the others, smiling the whole time.

"Eleanor, I will certainly pay whatever is necessary to replace that window," Bob said.

"Nonsense! I was wondering when to get started on that project, and now I have some incentive. You just keep bringing them around and keeping this hunt lively," she said.

"You are too kind," he said, kissing her proffered cheek. "At least let me have him work off some of his energy in your flowerbeds.

"All right then. He can come over tomorrow, and we'll plant some bulbs," she agreed.

After being introduced to the world and telling Ben and the others goodbye, Griffen led me back to his truck. Our friends had plans of their own this afternoon leaving Griffen and me with the rest of the weekend to ourselves.

"See what we have to look forward to someday? Who would have ever thought we'd see a soccer ball in *that* dining room?" he laughed.

"I can only imagine that one of yours would probably rope a deer and *ride* it into the dining room…if he gets your gift with animals," I said.

"Actually, I'm surprised the soccer ball didn't hit you between the eyes and flatten you, Miss Disaster-waiting-to-happen."

"Yeah, well, sorry to disappoint. But, Griffen?" I asked, stopping on my side of the truck.

"Yes."

"Why would you leave this place…all these great people…all this…to, well, I mean, you have so much here. Such a great hunt and people who love you and, well, need you. Are you sure about Oxford?"

"Positive. Now, it's time for me to show you around Nashville...while I still have some roots here. You game?"

"Nap first, remember?"

"Nap. Yes. How could I forget?" He grinned, helped me in his truck and shut the door behind me.

SUMMERTIME

Chapter 7

In how many other sports does one don a tweed jacket, velvet cap, breeches, long-sleeved shirt, wool vest, silk tie, and leather gloves before exercising?

I pulled on my boots after a very short hour-long nap in a stifling hot cabin with no air conditioning. Eight teenage girls shared this luxury with me this summer in the mountains of Alabama. On this steamy afternoon, I am a riding counselor at an all-girl's camp, a summer job I had accepted long before I met Griffen Case.

Summertime was here in full force, and the camp was heaven – except that I was only allowed to see Griffen during the very short three day break in the middle. And that break was two days away.

Griffen graduated with honors from Vanderbilt in spite of visiting me every weekend. We never were able to get the joint-meet organized since the Nashville visit had not gone exactly as planned. We had recovered from that disaster and not had an argument since. I must have made quite an impression, but we had not spent more than two or three days together at a time since we started dating, for we lived so far apart.

We foxhunted through March, visiting hunts farther north that had later season endings than ours. In April, I took a hunter safety course with him that actually ended up being fun and spent time with his uncle at the duck camp – transformed for the spring into his turkey hunting headquarters.

Having exposed me successfully to the madness of duck hunters, Griffen got a kick out of my reaction to the Eastern wild turkey. Now *that* had been a Worthy Opponent. Turkey hunting was like playing chess – outside – with a much more difficult adversary than a human. Every time I heard a gobble, I shook. I was sure my thundering heartbeats always gave us away. They had to have been moving my shirt. That adrenaline rush had been so addictive that I had wanted to stay out all day to hunt them when we spent the weekend at his uncle's camp. Calling, or rather, listening to Griffen call, and pursuing something that wary in the woods had been ridiculously addictive.

And the naps we took in the afternoon under the bright green budding trees after a picnic lunch were heavenly. Sometimes we would go shooting at the club's clay range, and I had continued to improve. He helped me pick out my own shotgun one weekend, and I smiled thinking about how strange it was that I now owned and could shoot a real weapon. Grand was scandalized that I could shoot, ran around in the woods for hours on end, and even owned a gun but was pleased I remembered to pack lipstick and wear gloves to protect my nails – as much as possible. Mother rolled her eyes and laughed at both of us.

Griffen was accepted at Ole Miss Law School for the fall. He had also taken a job as a stunt rider for a steeplechase movie that was being filmed in Virginia, so he, too, had a busy summer in store. He made the contact at the Nashville hunt, the Cantata Hounds, where some of the people in the following cars happened to be talent scouts. Who would have thought that could ever happen? One look at Griffen and Jet was all it took to seal the deal. Of course, Ashley and Shannon helped as well. Few people could resist the charms of Ole Miss girls as beautiful as they, even those in the movie business. They assured the scouts that Griffen could ride and were offered summer jobs as extras in the film. Two days from now, I would be flying out to meet them. He described movie making as watching water boil, but I could hardly wait to see that and him.

Right now, though, I had lessons to teach. I slipped quietly from the cabin so I would not disturb the girls before the bell rang. We had mail call right after rest time, and I hoped to get a letter from Griffen. Cell phone service didn't work well in these mountains and neither of us had much access to land line phones, so we had resorted to writing letters. It was fun to write them and get them, but it made me a slave to mail call each day.

I could hear the girls shuffling inside the cabin. When the bell rang, we bolted from the door to line up for snacks and letters. The mail girls made a production about calling my name, and it made me feel like a kid at Christmas. I snatched the envelope, and my heart leapt when I saw the distinct handwriting – Griffen!

"Who's it from?" squealed Pamela, one of the girls in my cabin.

"Griffen," I said with a huge grin.

"Ooohhh! Read it to us tonight!" she begged.

"We'll see – go away so I can read what he's doing!"

The girls in my cabin loved romantic drama, and they were all ears about Griffen. They could never get enough of hearing about him, the kinds of things we did on dates, the way he treated me, the things he said to me, and in general, what a great guy he was. It was like we were on a prolonged first date since we had to spend so much time apart. He gave them hope that there were still good guys out there – *me, too. How ironic, Griffen would think, that he was universally considered a* good *guy. I certainly did. And treasured him.*

I finally got the letter open and found a semi-private place to read it. His neat handwriting was almost as fun to see as his beautiful face.

Dear Elliott,

I am counting the hours until you get here. We have finally started filming, so I will not be able to meet you at the airport. Of course, I will text you Friday and let you know if that changes. For now, plan to rent a car at the airport and drive out. I will be watching for you.

The stunt riding is not difficult. We have to jump around a course all bunched up, which is no problem. The horse they are letting me use is great. He behaves well, and so far has been a lot of fun to ride. I have not met the actor that I'm playing. He's some new guy that I have never heard of, but I've met a lot of other interesting people. They're going to love you.

It hurts me to be so far away from you, and I can hardly wait to be with you every day this fall. Counting the days until I can hold you, my little vixen.

Love,

Griffen

Short, but wonderful. I read it ten times before I headed to lessons. Twenty horses awaited us five counselors, and I had the trail-riding shift first. When I reached the arena, eight girls surrounded me eagerly awaiting their lesson.

"Do I get Appleseed today, Elliott?" Jennifer asked.

"I want Jeremiah…or Trigger if you think I can handle him," Melissa said.

"But Appleseed is *my* favorite…oh, and DeSoto, too. How are they doing today, Elliott? Did you take them an apple from me this morning?" Chrissy asked.

It was constant…and wonderful…to have these young faces following me around all the time. We counselors were here to love on them and treat them like spoiled little sisters. It was a real honor to be given the responsibility to help them grow and understand more about who they were and what their purpose was on this earth. We were there to encourage them to grow up and become who they were created to be without the distraction of dealing with boys. It was normally heaven for me, too, before Griffen.

I felt like a rock star…riding counselors at month-long camps developed "groupies" of little girls that dreamed only of horses. I had no privacy, but I didn't mind. I could certainly relate and did all I could to accommodate their every horse related whim. Even a few adults and other counselors still had "the bug," and I took them riding every morning at 6:00 before camp began to let them get some time on the back of a horse and see the gorgeous mountain trails.

Early morning rides kept me centered. It was a great way for me to celebrate being alive and focus on what matters – my mission in life – showing these little souls God's love and listening for God's answers to which choices presented to me daily were the right ones for me to make. This summer, I really needed to practice this, for everything about Griffen pointed to permanence. I wanted to be sure my compass was pointing in the proper place and wasn't being misdirected by glimmering green eyes.

I reached into the nearby storage building to get a raincoat since the sky was darkening. Rain, to me, was welcome. I told the other counselors and kids that we rode rain or shine. They had never done that before and were surprised at how much they enjoyed it. I never understood the aversion to riding in "bad" weather. I would rather be wet any day than sweat under a scorching sun. Of course we didn't ride if there was a chance of lightning, but that threat was rare. Most of the time, we were treated to afternoon showers that warded off the oppressive heat. After two rounds of lessons and putting the horses up for the night, I headed back to my cabin to change before supper.

"Any letters?" Elaine asked. I had walked right past her and not even noticed, so lost I had been in thought.

"Yes!" I said, beaming.

"How's the movie going?"

"He said they were filming now. Are you going to go with me to see them?"

"If you don't mind, I will," Elaine said. "Shannon's out there now with Ashley for the crowd scene. I really would love to see how all that movie stuff works."

"Good. I'd like the company," I said and gave her the flight information I could remember off the top of my head. Hopefully she could get a ticket on such short notice.

"See you at supper," she said.

Elaine was teaching crafts. There were lots of girls and guys from Ole Miss that were working here, or at the boys' camp this summer. Most of them, like me, had been campers as kids. I didn't think camp could be more fun…until I was a counselor. If only Griffen were here…or at least at the neighboring boys' camp…

Our flight to Virginia was on time, but rough. Storms were everywhere, and I hated the thought of bouncing around dodging lightning bolts. In spite of the bumps and delays, we landed safely and on time. Since we didn't have to collect luggage, we went straight to the rental car area. No text yet from Griffen.

"Ashley says they're not filming any more today," Elaine said, reading her iPhone. "It's pouring right now, and they've called it off."

"Oh well, maybe tomorrow," I said, a little disappointed, but glad that I would probably get a lot more time with Griffen than I expected, so I brightened at the thought. As soon as I walked out of the terminal, there he was. I learned in Nashville that he didn't like to be assaulted in public, so I restrained myself.

"Elliott!" he grinned and lifted me in a huge hug and kissed me on the top of my head. "I'm so glad to see you! Elaine, you too," and gave her a welcoming hug with his free arm.

"I'll get the car; you two go on," Elaine smiled.

"No way, Elaine," Griffen said. "I'll handle this, and you can follow us to where you're both staying. Ashley and Shannon are free for the rest of the day, too, and staying in the same place. I'll get you settled with them and *then* swipe Elliott."

"So, how are all the little horse crazy girls?" Griffen asked.

"A *few* like crafts!" Elaine protested but laughed when she said it.

"I'll have to admit, I don't have a throng of groupies like *she* does."

"They are precious," I said. "I just wish I could grant them all their pony wishes. I *so* know how they feel."

"You're going to love these horses here and the people," he said. "They'll film the crowd scene tomorrow, so there should be more action than usual. I'm supposed to ride a runaway horse and knock over some bystanders. The actor guy will be here tomorrow, too, so you'll probably get to meet him. He's supposedly some big deal."

"What about the leading lady?" I asked.

"She doesn't come until later," he said. "I doubt she'll be here this weekend."

"Who is it?" Elaine asked.

"Another new person that I've never heard of," he said. "But she looks good."

"I would hope so!" I said. "Anyone else I know in this movie?"

"Morgan Freeman, Keira Knightley, and Matthew McConaughey," he said.

"Matthew McConaughey! Will he be here?" Elaine and I asked way too enthusiastically and almost simultaneously.

"Probably, but I don't know," he said.

"That's the big secret Ashley and Shannon have been keeping to themselves," Elaine said. "I bet they've met them all."

"I wouldn't put it past either of them, but I don't think any of them are here yet," he said.

Elaine's phone buzzed and she glanced town at the text message.

"There's a party tonight for the cast and crew and their friends," she said. "Shannon says we're invited, too. They've made the arrangements."

"I would rather just be with you," I whispered to Griffen while

Elaine walked to the rental counter.

"We'll go for a little while," he said under his breath in his lovely growl. "It's not every day that you get to meet people in this field. But I promise, we'll have plenty of time – just you and me. I have a plan."

I trembled and took a deep breath. He walked over to help Elaine and my head was already whirling. *Would I ever get used to being close to him? This could be really inconvenient.*

Outside, the storm raged. I had never been so grateful for rain. Ashley and Shannon met us at the hotel, and Griffen spirited me away immediately once Elaine was with them.

"Where are we going?" I asked.

"To my place," he said. "And to see the barn, then to eat, then to the party."

"Wait," I said before we left the hotel. "What are we supposed to wear to the party tonight?"

"You look fine. It's not a dress up thing. And you look your best in those jeans," he said appreciatively.

"If you insist," I said but didn't argue. He was the only one I wanted to impress anyway. Jeans it would be.

"His" place was an old log cabin nestled in the woods along a lake. It was breathtakingly beautiful and immaculately clean. There were fishing rods, a johnboat, canoes, kayaks, and even a ski boat hanging in a covered dock.

"How did you find this place?"

"It's being rented for the guy I'm playing, but he's not coming for a while. He has somewhere else he had to be this week, so he's supposedly flying in tomorrow morning and leaving the same day," he said. "So, they're letting me use it all summer. He may have to use it occasionally, but they said they would let me know. But for now, it's all mine."

"Wow!" is all I could think to say. "And we *have* to go to that party?"

"Not until much later," he said into my neck. He pushed me gently into the enormous hammock on the porch, lay down beside me, and kissed me until my stomach growled so loudly that we could ignore it no longer.

"That's some serious background noise," he said. "I'll make us a snack. Don't go anywhere."

"Don't worry," I said and lay back in the hammock. The pillow smelled like him, and I rolled over and inhaled, swinging gently and admiring the view.

After a few minutes, the rain stopped. Griffen was busy in the kitchen, so I got up and walked barefoot to the dock. I rolled up my jeans and dangled my feet into the water. From the pier, I could see people in other places heading out to their docks to take advantage of the break in the rain.

Steam rose from the lake and despite the recent rain, the air was warm. I was tempted to suggest that we go for a swim, but remembered I had not brought a swimsuit. And...well...we were a little *too* alone here, even if Griffen was ridiculously trustworthy. That could be too much temptation for either of us. I felt my face flush and was glad I didn't have to explain those thoughts to Griffen.

I looked up when I heard a faint splash – like a paddle slicing through the water. A red kayak had started towards me, and I examined it with interest wondering who would be bold enough to paddle over to a complete stranger. The pilot, or whatever you call a guy operating a kayak, looked young, about my age, and his bare chest and arms were well proportioned. I didn't sense any menace in his intent gaze, but as he got closer, I noticed he was eyeing me suspiciously.

"What are you doing here?" he asked in an almost rude tone as he floated within earshot. *Wonderful. Hostile locals in Virginia, too. That is all that I need.*

"Putting my feet in the water, why?" I asked, taken aback by his abrupt question.

"I didn't think anyone was staying here, I mean, at that cabin, this weekend," he said. "I'm sorry, what's your name?

"You first," I said, nonplussed at his lack of manners, despite his impressive physique.

"That's not something I give out to just anyone," he said, clearly irritated now, but curious. He acted like I was supposed to dive in after him or something. *Really cocky. I liked it. Two can play at that game.*

"And why would you think *I* would identify myself to a complete stranger?" I said. "You're not the first guy that has begged to know *my* name. I've been invited here by a guest of this cabin's owner, and that, sir, is all you need to know about me."

I stood to leave and he let out a low whistle.

"Nice," he said.

I tossed my hair hoping he couldn't see me blush and returned to the cabin. *Let him chew on that a while. Cocky guys. Just because he's somewhat cute he thinks he can get whatever he wants from any woman.* Griffen was halfway down the lawn coming to collect me. *Now,* that's *gorgeous!*

"Food's in the kitchen," he said and wrapped his arms around me. "I can't have you starving on my watch."

"Are you sure we can't just stay here for the whole weekend?" I begged as I gobbled the delicious sandwich momentarily assuaging the snarling beast within.

"Yes, but we can stay here for hours…and I *plan* to," he said. "You are desiccating that sandwich!"

"Sorry," I said. "I would rather get this over with and get back to the hammock."

"You eat like Panzer," he said. "But I'm not arguing. Back to the hammock…"

His phone buzzed – text. He glanced at it, then looked at me apologetically.

"I've got to go make a call; slow down and eat. We have *almost* all day," he said.

I took the sandwich to the screen porch and could no longer see the red kayak. Other boats and swimmers were now out in full force. The rain seemed to have left for good. *Maybe they'll film something today after all. I hope not.*

"We have to leave in an hour," he said. "They are rearranging some scenes because of the weather and are trying to get the actor-guy to come in today. They have to get the place ready. He'll be on site tomorrow, so you'll probably get to meet him," he said.

"Where will you stay?"

"The same hotel you're in," he said. "Just for the weekend. The guy will be gone Sunday afternoon."

"That's not all bad."

"Neither is this," he whispered into my neck and pushed me back in the hammock to make the most of the time we had in this beautiful little cabin.

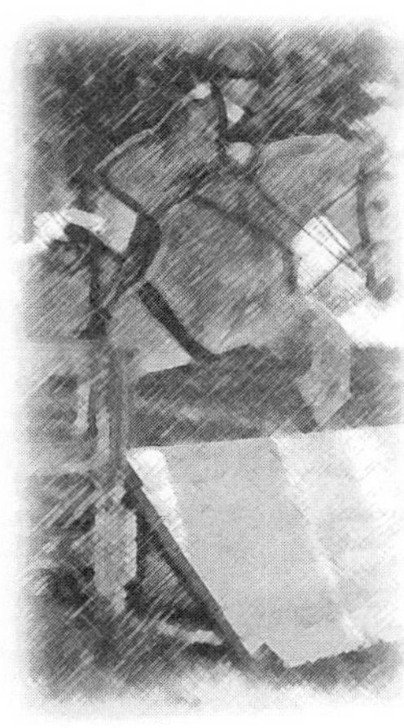

ACTORS

Chapter 8

"As in a theatre, the eyes of men, after a well-graced actor leaves...are idly bent on him that enters next, thinking his prattle to be tedious."

~ William Shakespeare King Richard II Act V Scene II

The party was packed. Ashley, Shannon, and Elaine were already there and spun Griffen and me around to meet everyone as soon as they found us. I had at last been able to change out of my travel clothes since we had been evicted from the perfect cabin, but I wore jeans at Griffen's request.

We had spent the afternoon at the magnificent barn that contained the movie horses. Griffen's bright chestnut gelding gobbled the apples and carrots we brought, and I patted his soft muzzle. His eager affection made me homesick for Viva. Griffen showed me how they painted a star on his forehead to make him look more like the horse he was playing. The actor's horse looked like this one but was much older and gentler. He would not be filming his own jumping scenes, or moving scenes, for that matter. His agents said he was too valuable to risk, but

Griffen and I thought he probably didn't know how to *really* ride.

Riding ability is not something a person can fake. It takes time to learn, and this movie called for excellent horsemanship. Griffen said he would have a lot more screen time in this movie than his counterpart, but that it was not too unusual in movies with lots of action.

"Elliott!" Elaine whispered discreetly, but urgently, in my ear. "It's Morgan Freeman!"

I had to go all the way to Virginia to meet another Mississippian, but it was still really cool to shake his hand. He was gracious and polite and very handsome in his mysterious way. He had always been one of my favorite actors, and his welcoming handshake and willingness to meet us only made him more impressive. I discovered that he was coming to talk to Griffen, having discovered that he was the actor's stunt double. Mr. Freeman, too, owned horses, so we had fun telling stories about our foxhunting adventures near his Delta home. We were so engrossed in his stories and listening to his mesmerizing voice, that we didn't notice another person until he was already in our circle.

Ashley and Shannon looked like they had seen a ghost. They, for once, could not speak. I saw their faces before I could see at what they were gaping. *Matthew McConnoughey, I guessed, was probably standing right behind me.*

I turned slightly to follow their gaze and nearly dropped my drink. Fully clothed, he could have been Griffen's twin, not as handsome, but ten times as cocky. *Not Matthew McConnoughey.*

"I guess you've figured out my name," he said, to me…only… completely ignoring everyone in my circle, including Mr. Freeman. "But I still don't know yours or why you were sitting on my pier this morning." He pushed himself between Griffen and me, and I was shocked, again, at his manners…or lack thereof.

"No, actually, I don't have any idea *who* you are and could care less. You, in fact, are quite rude and just interrupted a conversation with Mr. Freeman here that we were enjoying immensely."

His face reddened, and he stepped back like he'd been punched. It was a good thing, because Griffen didn't take kindly to being brushed aside…not at all.

"Mr. Reed, we need you over here for a photo op," some random busyperson said and tugged on his arm.

"One minute," he said swatting away the offending man like he was a mosquito. "I'm Sean Reed," he said extending his hand. I had not extended mine and noticed that he didn't realize that his pitiful attempt at manners was actually *all wrong.*

"I'm sure he wasn't Raised Right; give him some slack, dear," Grand said. "You, after all, do have manners, therefore no excuse."

As I reached for his hand to keep him from looking like an idiot, Griffen came to my rescue, as always.

"Mr. Reed, this is Elliott Marks," he said and continued the introductions around the circle ending with his own name.

"Oh, my stunt double," he said with a hint of condescension that did not go unnoticed by Griffen. *Here we go again, marking their territories like a pack of dogs.* "I tell these people I can do my own riding, but they insist *I'm* too valuable to risk."

I made no remark, but Ashley didn't miss the chance to flash her blue eyes at him.

"Mr. Reed, I can't *wait* to see you in *this* movie," Ashley said. "You were great in *The Rescue.*"

"Thanks," he smiled and returned her gaze. She blinked, and I thought she'd pass out if he did that again. Then he turned to me, took my hand, and kissed it. "I'll be looking for you later, Elliott."

Thank goodness someone pulled him away or Griffen would have knocked him into the next room. He was so angry that he was shaking. I thought it was quite amusing and would have continued to think this had Griffen not remained so angry. The others had wandered off to socialize, so Griffen and I stood alone.

"When did he see *you*?" he snapped.

"This morning, when you went to make my sandwich, and I walked out onto the pier. He paddled over in a red kayak," I said, calmly.

"Why didn't you tell me?" he said.

"Why would I need to?" I said, getting angry myself, now.

"Because that's who's staying in the cabin; I told you that!" he said.

"I didn't know who he was, Griffen," I said, getting impatient with his inquisition.

"Some Hollywood superstar paddles over, you chat him up, and he makes a beeline for you at a party," he said, jaw clenched. "And you don't think it is any of *my* business?"

"Not at all," I said, puzzled at his reaction.

"Fine. Just fine. I'm going to get another drink."

Now I was standing alone – surrounded by people but totally alone. Griffen just left. *Maddening. Would I ever figure out his strange moods? Was this just jealousy or something else? Overprotectiveness? Why would he ever be jealous? RRRR!*

I walked outside to think and get away from everyone. Grand was not in my head, yet, but I still had to think…away from Griffen. I'd have to watch this, too, like the incident in Nashville. Jealousy wasn't good, but I'd never seen him act jealous before. Maybe this was an isolated incident. But I'd hardly ever been around guys by whom he felt in the least bit intimidated. Most we were ever around were our friends.

Griffen was really gorgeous when he was angry…silly stupid me. That wasn't a good train of thought. Jealousy's not something with which to trifle…especially with his checkered past. Why did that one little thing set him off so? Was there something I should have done differently?

The huge moon hovered in the sky, its eerie luminescence unnaturally bright. I looked at it for a long time trying to organize my thoughts. I was so glad to be here, finally, with Griffen, and I wanted to block all of this out and be with him somewhere that we could pick out the faded constellations, well, no stars with a moon like this, but what a moon! Maybe we could go walking somewhere – anywhere – in this lovely light. I had no desire to meet anyone or any of these people right now. All I wanted was to be in his arms, feel him hold me…

"I told you I'd be looking for you," a male voice said, and I jumped.

He, too, had escaped the throngs, and we were alone on the porch. It was dark, but I could see the moonlight reflecting in his eyes, and they were glowing with satisfaction that he had found me…alone.

"Mr. Reed," I said, as I backed away from him. "I really don't think…"

"Sean," he said, slithering uninvited into *the space* and putting his finger to my lips. "And it's not thinking that I want you to do right now..."

Before I could react, Griffen had him in an iron hold and had slammed him against the wall.

"Get off me, you…idiot!" Sean screamed, but I could see the fear in his formerly way-too-confident eyes.

Ten people were immediately on the porch when they heard Sean's screech. Two took Griffen by the arms and hauled him to the parking lot. I followed demanding that they release him, but to no avail. He was fuming, but he allowed himself to be carried off the property.

"Don't set foot back in there, man," one guard said, not unkindly. "Or we'll have to hurt you. Just go on home."

"I'm going to tell Elaine we're leaving," I said. "I'll be right back."

"Don't you dare go back in there," Griffen growled. "Just text her and let's go…now," he added menacingly when I hesitated.

He walked me to his truck, and I sent Elaine a message that we were going back to the hotel and to not worry about us. *But I was worried about us. He could really pull some stunts. I guess he's fired now.*

"Thanks, Griffen," I said, trying to ease the tension in the car.

"Thanks?" he asked through clenched teeth. "Have you completely lost your mind? I'm sure your little stunt just cost me my job."

"Little stunt?" I said, not believing my ears.

"I saw you sneak out by yourself – like you didn't know he'd be right behind you. He just told you he would be looking for you," he hissed.

"Griffen, *that* was no stunt! I wanted to get some air – to think," I said.

"Think? Right!" he snapped.

"Just take me to my room."

"That's the plan."

We rode the whole way in a very uncomfortable, angry silence. My phone buzzed a few times, and I replied to Elaine's texts and assured her we were fine. *But we weren't. I wasn't. This was not working…will not ever work…if he jumps to conclusions like this.*

He pulled up to the hotel, and I let myself out of the truck before he could move. He came around to my side and stopped me, pinning me against his truck. I turned my face away, looking down so I wouldn't meet his hypnotic gaze. This was neither the time nor place for me to lose my head.

He touched my chin with his fingertip and raised my face to his. I still wouldn't look at him.

"Elliott," he said. "I…well…I'm so sorry."

I looked at him then…and melted. He kissed me and pulled me to him, and I leaned back against his truck and forgot all his unreasonable anger and jealousy and floated with him back to the place I loved the most.

"Girl, you better watch yourself, now. This is serious stuff, this jealousy," Grand said.

I shoved Grand as far away as possible and kissed him back.

"Come inside," I said, "Just for a little while."

Grand was beating down the door of my consciousness, but I ignored her.

"Are you sure?" he said, voice very low and husky.

"Absolutely," I said.

Once inside the tiny room, he was everywhere, surrounding me, holding me, kissing me, and I felt so safe, so complete. I had missed him terribly over the past few weeks, and these kisses were not at all like those from this afternoon on the hammock or in the barn. They were stronger, more forceful. I had to make myself remember to breathe. I couldn't get him close enough to me, and I pulled him, all of him, next to me down on the bed. He stopped me and pushed away gently, but with great effort.

"I'll see you tomorrow," he said.

I couldn't speak, so I just nodded. This was way too much for either of us – no one else around – no one else *would* be around for hours.

"Do you want to watch a movie?" I mumbled when my head finally cleared, and my limbs were acting a little more normal.

"Not tonight," he said. "I'll call you."

I flipped through the channels more interested than usual since I had not seen a television for weeks. Not that I missed it, but it was entertaining. I had not brought the book I was reading since the plane ride was short, and I didn't intend to have any down time when I was so close to Griffen.

My phone buzzed – 615.

"Hey," I said.

"Hey back," he said.

"Do you still have a job?" I asked.

"Probably not, but I'm going to show up anyway. I have to be there at 5:00. Do you want to go that early?" he asked.

"Definitely," I said. "I don't want to miss a minute with you."

"About tonight…"

"Don't worry about it."

"Elliott, I told you I'm new at this," he ignored me and continued. "I was…jealous…of him…or something. Everyone makes such a big deal over him, and I couldn't believe you were not like all the others. I've never felt it like that before. There was a real monster in me… and I'm sorry for how I acted. I should never have behaved like that."

"I don't know why you would ever be jealous, Griffen," I said. "How many times do I have to tell you that I love you until you believe me?"

"Just once more," he said.

"I love you, you thick brained maniac," I said. "What were you going to do to him?"

"Nothing, only because I've had *a lot* of training to *keep* me from doing anything," he said. "Without that, I would have probably killed him on the spot. Martial arts is more discipline training than anything else. Also, it kept me from fearing what would happen if my father ever came back."

"I thought he was dead. You watched him kill your mother and he's still…alive? I thought people were put to death for doing things… like that." I stammered, truly surprised.

"Oh no," he said. "Dead to me, yes, but in prison for life."

A chill went down my spine at the thought of that man, Griffen's father, alive, and in prison. Somehow, that was more unnerving than if he had been…well…killed or something. Death was, in a way, clean. But this? I shuddered, then put those thoughts away…far away. No need to think about that. But I was spooked now and did not want to sit here alone.

"It's only 9:00, Griffen. Why don't you come over here so we can talk in person. I promise I'll behave," I said.

"I can't promise the same for me."

"Come on, Mr. Discipline, I trust you," I said.

"You need to seriously rethink that, Elliott, but I'm coming," he said. "It *is* crazy to be talking on the phone when we're just two floors away."

Elaine arrived around 11:00 with Ashley and Shannon in tow. They weren't too surprised to find Griffen with me, but they offered to come back.

"No, tell us both about the party," I said. "What happened after we got thrown out?"

"It was *unbelievable!* You should have *seen* Sean when they brought him back in the room!" Elaine said. "He looked like he'd seen a ghost! You must have scared him to *death*!"

Griffen blushed, but I couldn't resist.

"I wish he'd punched him," I said. "That *jerk* followed me outside and started to kiss me – unasked – I might add!" I glanced over to Griffen to see how he was taking it.

"So, do you still have a job?" Ashley asked Griffen.

"Who knows? I'm still showing up. Did either of you do anything to get fired tonight?" he asked Shannon and Ashley and smiled his gorgeous, mischievous smile. *Looks like he's recovering nicely.*

"No," Shannon said. "But we did meet some really nice – and cute – guys.

"I'm sure you did," Griffen said and pulled me closer to him on the bed. *Glad we had witnesses. That's an unusual amount of affection in public for him.*

"If we have to be there at 5:00, when are you coming to get me?" I asked.

"4:00 – the dreaded hour," he said.

"That's worse than turkey hunting," I groaned.

"Yes, but at least you'll be riding in my truck and not walking in the dark for an hour," he said as he got up to leave. Shannon and Ashley followed him. "I'll see you in the morning."

When the three of them disappeared together, Elaine gave me

an astonished look.

"Why did you let him get away without…you know?" Elaine asked. "I wouldn't do that to him."

"He's had plenty," I said and hid under the covers.

"Have you been…here…all this time?" Elaine asked, astounded.

"Not the whole time, but most of it," I blushed.

"Still in the club?" she asked.

"Yes indeed!" I said. "I told you about him. It's tough but not impossible since this is his idea as much as mine."

"Hmmh," she said contemplating my remark. Then she looked at me sideways. "Did Sean Reed really…try to kiss you?"

"Yes! And he was a *total* jerk about it. He may have even succeeded had Griffen not seen it. I think he knew it before I did," I said. "I was so naïve, but what guy would just waltz up and think he could kiss a girl he'd never met? And *why me* of all the glamorous people in that room – including you, Ashley, and Shannon!"

"Oh, well, let's see," Elaine smiled. "Someone who makes about a million dollars a minute, looks like him, and has had his face plastered all over television and magazines for the past year. And don't sell yourself short, Elliott. You hold your own in spite of not trying to. That itself to some guys is irresistible. And, even if you didn't notice, Griffen made it quite clear with his body language that you were his. Maybe Sean's one of those guys that gets off on grabbing a girl who's already attached."

"Thanks, Elaine. That's sweet of you to say. To me, Griffen seems to almost avoid me whenever we're in public," I said.

"Oh, but he makes it quite clear to everyone else that you're his," Elaine laughed. "He never takes his eyes off you."

I was surprised and more pleased than I wanted to admit to hear her say that and felt myself blush. "Well, Sean is an idiot. I'd like to think people like him have manners, but I guess you're right about the cocky actor thing. But Morgan Freeman has excellent manners. He was great to talk to."

"Yes, but he's also from the South. He is so cool," Elaine said.

"Surely people from other places have manners," I said.

"Of course they do, but maybe it's not as common as it is where we're from," Elaine said. "You know that."

"I guess I was just stupid," I said.

"I can't wait to see what happens tomorrow," she said.

"Neither can I," I said, fighting the image of Griffen's father behind bars that had reappeared and pulling the covers over my head. It was a long time before I drifted off to sleep. But sometime in the night – or in the early hours of the morning – I saw my own father behind bars…and screamed.

THE SET

Chapter 9

What can be better than a long, lovely, leisurely day lounging around and admiring the horses?

Even though the hour was insanely early, people flew around everywhere preparing for the day. From our spot above the action, tents for the "extras", or miscellaneous unnamed actors, look like billowing blankets, and the air was electric.

Sean Reed's first scenes in this movie would be filmed today. Morgan Freeman and Matthew McConaughey would be here in the afternoon with Kiera Knightley. Security was everywhere, and the day promised to be perfect.

"I still have a job," Griffen said as he walked over to kiss me goodbye. "It seems my gift for riding like a fool on that horse saved me. No one else could shoot the scene they're doing today…especially not that jerk they picked for this part."

"Try not to kill him, Griffen," I teased.

"I hope I don't have to deal with him at all," he growled.

Elaine arrived an hour later still sleepy and chewed on me about my midnight outburst. "Leslie said you talked in your sleep some, but screaming! That curled my hair. Are you sure you don't want to talk about it?"

"Definitely. I told you, it was nothing. Just a stupid nightmare about Sean attacking me on the porch," I lied.

"That wouldn't make me scream…at least, not like that," Elaine said, trying to make me smile.

It didn't work. We wandered around and found a place where we could watch the steeplechase scenes. The horses and jockeys were glorious in their riding silks. Griffen seemed large to me for a jockey, but the story called for it, and he was exactly Sean's size.

The people working on the set were friendly and had gotten a *huge* kick about Griffen getting thrown out the night before. They all liked him and hated Sean. Some were even hoping Sean wouldn't show up. I was with them.

Griffen appeared looking much more agitated than usual. "I'm about to go on, but they want me to say some lines. I may not see you for a long time," he said. "Just keep your phone close by, and I'll let you know when I can see you."

"You'll be great!" I said and kissed him on the cheek. He blushed, smiled sheepishly, and disappeared.

"They should use him," Elaine mused as she watched him leave. "Do you *know* how fine he is?"

"Yes, thanks," I said. "You don't have to remind me. I still think he's a mirage. Wait 'till you see him on a horse – I don't think the world is ready for that!"

We found Ashley and Shannon in their pretty outfits in the grandstands parading around looking lovely and carefree. The crew showed us to a place where we could safely watch the scene. After what seemed like an eternity, things started to happen.

The horses exploded from the gates, barreling around the track. Griffen was easy to spot in the hero's bright green silks. *Those are going to look great with his eyes. Too bad he won't be in the close-ups.* He guided the horse flawlessly over the jumps and into the crowd. The people panicked and screamed way too believably. I gripped the bleachers worried about how Griffen would contain that beautiful horse in a carefully calculated crash. *Did those people have any idea how hard this was to do? What if the horse veered at all? So many people, Griffen included, could be killed!* I was not at all sure about the logistics of this scene.

As soon as it started, it was over. And then they did it again – three more times that morning. No word from Griffen. Elaine and I ate lunch, and the buzz around the crew was that Sean was a no-show. He had supposedly eaten something that had not agreed with him. *Could not have happened to a better guy.*

A few hours later, the mood on the set changed. As soon as she arrived, the whole place started to hustle. Keira Knightly was here to film her scene but was also on her way to another place, so there was no chance to meet her. We watched her move in the crowd for about an hour while they filmed her shots, then she was gone. Morgan Freeman, too, came and went. Still no word from Griffen.

Elaine and I wished we had a book, but we didn't know whether or not we would be able to get back in if we left. Elaine attempted to download one on her iPhone, but she felt bad that I wouldn't be able to read, too, and changed her mind. So, we were stuck. Finally Ashley and Shannon showed up, but still no word from Griffen. We ate at the crew table and Ashley made sure that it was all right if Elaine and I ate as well. We had lamb chops and feasted on some of the finest food I had ever had in a pasture. I couldn't believe how well everyone ate.

The afternoon dragged on into early evening. We had talked to everyone around us ten times and understood now why this had been described as watching water boil. The crew started taking down the equipment and most everyone was preparing to leave. Still no word from Griffen.

"Elaine, you can go on with Ashley and Shannon if you want," I said.

"You sure?" Elaine asked, grateful to escape.

"Yes," I said. "I'll let you know what happens here…if anything."

They left me, and I walked around the set for a little while, then decided to risk it and go to Griffen's truck. At last, my phone buzzed…615.

"Hey!" I said, glad to finally hear from him.

"I don't have much time, Elliott. Please listen carefully," he said, all business.

"What's wrong?"

"Nothing. Go back to the hotel and get my bag. Check out for me, please. I've already paid for the room, and the staff is expecting you. Bring the bag back to me and hurry. They're waiting, and I don't have much time."

"Where are you?" I asked.

"I'll find you," he said. "Just park the truck where it is now. There's a key in my toolbox on the driver's side, and the extra room key is above my visor. When you get back, call me, and I'll come to you."

"Griffen?"

"Hurry, I've got to go. I can't say anything else right now," he said.

The line went dead. *Strange.*

Thank goodness the hotel wasn't far away. I found the keys and did what he asked. I was back in less than thirty minutes.

"Pulling into the parking lot," I said when he answered on the first ring.

"On my way." And he hung up. Again.

I waited, and a dark car pulled up. I couldn't tell how many people were inside, but Griffen stepped out of the back seat, and I walked toward him with his bag.

"Thanks," he said, but his face was stern. He looked exhausted. I wanted to reach up and hold him, but he remained at a distance.

"Are you going to tell me what this is about?" I asked, eyeing him suspiciously.

"No…I can't," he said.

"Can't or won't?" I asked, getting angry now. *Here we go again.*

"Can't," he said. "Please, Elliott, don't start with me now. I have to leave…you too. We're finished here. Go back to Alabama." He clenched his jaw, and he looked at me…not asking, but *telling.* I had been here all day hanging around for a simple phone call. And now he's leaving with no explanation.

"Fine," I said. "Here's your bag."

He turned around and left – without a word. Not even a conspiratory wink. Nothing. *What was I supposed to do with his truck? Is he even coming back? Was he in trouble?*

I drove back to the hotel and found Elaine sitting in our room. After recounting my strange meeting with Griffen, we changed tomorrow's afternoon flight to the morning. Ashley and Shannon said they were not filming at this location any more and that they had been told to go home, too.

"At least someone communicated something to *you*," I snapped, when she gave me the news. "I can't believe I've come all the way out here, dragged you with me, Elaine, and he just takes off, with not even a phone call – just delivery service! He's making me crazy!"

"Elliott, you're overreacting," Shannon said. "Look, you know Griffen has mood swings, but I think something else is going on. Maybe something happened to the horse he was riding or someone is trying to sue the movie company – who knows? He'll call and explain everything, I'm sure."

"He'd better," I said. It was already 9:00 pm, and I had still not heard from him. "He's probably having dinner with Kiera Knightley or something."

"Look, we can sit around here wondering…but I'd rather go do something fun," Ashley said. "I say we go to the movies."

"I'm in," I said. Anything to get my mind off Griffen.

In the middle of the movie, my phone buzzed…at 11:00 pm… Griffen. I let it go to voice mail. *He'd just have to wait. I'm busy.* It buzzed again – text message.

> Please call me as soon as possible. I can explain some things. Griffen

I left the movie right as things were getting really good and went to the restroom to call him. *I'm such a sucker – kissing up to him like this. But, what if something really was wrong?*

"This better be good," I said when he answered the phone.

"I'm sorry I cannot see you," he said formally and quite distant. My heart skipped a beat. *Was he breaking up with me? Already? Over the… phone? At least it wasn't a text…I'd kill him for that.* "Where's my truck?"

He's breaking my heart over the telephone and wants to know where I put his truck? Oh, he'll pay for this! I took a deep breath and tried to stay calm, aloof. This can't be happening. "It's at the hotel," I said.

"Just leave the keys where they were," he said.

I'd like to put those keys somewhere else, but you're who knows where! "Ok," I said, trying to stay calm – focused. It was so much easier to remain in control with him when we were on the phone.

"I'll call you as soon as I can, but I don't know when that will be," he said voice flat.

"I don't understand. Are you safe?" I asked not able to read anything into his tone except…distance.

"Of course I'm safe," he said. "You're being melodramatic."

"You're being a jerk," I said. "What am I supposed to think?" The hurt was just under the surface, and it exploded before I could stop it.

"I'll explain everything as soon as I can. I can't talk now. Good-night, Elliott."

"Don't hang up on me…Griffen!"

The line went dead.

I did not hear from him again until late Sunday evening. I was already back at camp and still fuming from our last conversation. As far as I was concerned, between his jealousy and now this, well, he could just wonder what I was doing for three more weeks.

Please call me as soon as possible. I can explain some things. Griffen

That text showed up at 9:00 pm. I wasn't sure whether or not it was accidentally sent since it was the same message he had sent me Saturday evening. I texted him that I would call tomorrow, at exactly 12:45 pm – when we had cabin rest time – and hoped that the text would go through. I knew I could get to a real telephone then.

The next day flew by, but I was still frustrated with him. I called at 12:45 and got his voice mail. I left him a voice message telling him that I would try again tomorrow at 1:30. While I was at a landline, I checked my cell phone messages. No messages. No texts had come through, either.

Now, was it my phone, this crazy unpredictable mountain service, or…that he just didn't care about me enough any more to call? That thought made me angry; no…that thought terrified me. The idea that he no longer cared enough to call speared a shock of pain through my heart. Thank goodness I was too busy here to think about that for long.

At mail the next day, I got a letter…

Dear Elliott,

I am sorry I had to leave you the way I did. I cannot tell you where I am or when I'll return, but I can tell you that I love you. And I miss you terribly. These people will pay for doing this to me, but I promise it will be all right in the end. This will not last past the summer, and I will be with you – every day – this fall. I am counting the days until I can hold you every day.

Griffen

What? I read the letter ten times, and it made no sense. There was no return address, but the postmark was in California. California? *That* did it. If he was not going to tell me anything, I was going to find out what was going on. I put the letter into my pocket and walked to the head counselor's cabin and dialed Griffen's uncle.

"Mr. Hinton? This is Elliott," I said. "Yes sir, I'm fine. I'm calling to check on Griffen. Did you know he was in California? You did? Is he all right? Are you sure? I got a letter from him today that sounded strange. No, he did not say anything specific, but he won't tell me what's going on. I just want to be sure he's safe. Ok, well, if you're sure. Yes sir, I'll come see you as soon as I can. You have a good summer, too. Thanks. Bye."

I kept getting cryptic texts, calls, and letters all summer. We talked a few times, but there was never any more information than he loved me and missed me and that he was ready to be settled somewhere near me. He did not want me guessing, so we talked about everything else.

At last, I was home, but no Griffen. He was still gone. Classes would begin in a few weeks, so I was busy gathering what I needed and riding Viva. It was so nice to have time to do nothing. I just wished desperately that I had Griffen here to do nothing with. I helped William with hound chores and shot sporting clays with my new shotgun a few times with Addy.

Finally, when I was lying in the pasture with Viva, my phone displayed my favorite 615 number.

"I'll be there tomorrow afternoon at 2:00 for good," he said, a definite smile in his voice.

"Really? Do you have a place to stay yet?"

"I hope so," he said. "My real estate agent says I'll love it. Go check out 240 Oak Street and tell me what you think. I hope you'll be spending a lot of time there."

"Will you be able to talk about your summer?"

"I'll spill all! You will not *believe* what I've been doing," he said, definitely happy now.

"Give me a hint," I demanded, not wanting to let him off the phone.

"I can't believe you haven't figured it out."

"You told me not to try," I said, frustrated that he's now all but telling me I could have tried.

"What do your friends think?" he asked, amused.

"That you are psycho, and that I should run away from you and leave you for them to deal with," I smiled. "They *wish*."

"I'll see you tomorrow," he said, "if you will let me get off the phone and get ready."

"Goodbye!"

I leapt up and Viva jumped. She eyed me suspiciously then returned to her grazing. I walked over and put my arms around her letting her wonderful smell surround me. Then, I swung upon her back and lay down, looking up at the clouds. *Tomorrow he'd be here for good. And we'll really see how things will work between us.* I had my reservations, serious ones about him that had begun to settle, but for now, I pushed them way back in my mind. All I could think about was seeing his face and feeling him wrap me all up in his arms.

TOGETHER AT LAST

Chapter 10

Riding alone, such wondrous bliss. How lovely to feel lovely floating and flying through the soft, sensual forest.

So far, I had rearranged my half of the room, reorganized my closet, and visited Viva, twice. I had ridden early in the morning but went back for something to do around noon. Viva looked at me like I was crazy, but she enjoyed the extra attention and carrots. I brushed her again, trimmed her bridle path, cleaned my tack, and swept the barn isle. Those simple tasks calmed me.

I knew things were about to change, a lot. I hoped they would be for the better. Griffen would be here today, for the first time, forever. We had never been together more than a few days, so this would be a real test of how compatible we were. I was a junior in college now, getting to the age to have to start considering permanent companionship options, and all my eggs were in Griffen's basket.

There was so much mystery about him – this whole summer thing had me baffled. He shouldn't keep secrets from me like that, but we weren't married, so I really had no say. Would I have any say with him even if we were?

I finally left the barn and headed back to campus. The August heat was getting to me – even in my truck. I gave up and rolled down the windows capturing my hair into a ponytail while steering with my knee. The humid Mississippi air felt like dragon breath on my neck, but the stereo's sound with the windows down made the burning wind worthwhile. The music pounded through me and pushed the stressful deliberations out of my mind. I was coasting on a romantic, emotional high today and would think about the rest tomorrow.

Crossfade blared from my speakers, their gravelly voices fitting my semi-rebellious romantic mood perfectly. A little Guns 'n Roses, Skillet, Decypher Down, Red Jumpsuit Apparatus, Creed, *thank goodness they were back together*, now the ultimate…AC/DC. Griffen had made this CD for me earlier in the year, and I played it all the time. I pulled into the sorority house parking lot – still an hour before he would arrive.

I liked the companionship of living in the sorority house; it enabled me to keep up with what was going on with everyone without trying. Ashley was still searching and had her sights on another older guy – a law student or maybe a real lawyer; I wasn't sure. It was hard to keep track even living with her. Elaine was out today with some water-ski team guy on the water-ski team that had a magnificent body. I didn't think he was very smart, but he looked great.

Leslie had found a few guys that seemed promising, and Shannon was dating one of the movie people she met in Nashville. For the most part, I liked them all; they were from good families and spoke in complete sentences. Ben and Addy would be married right out of college for sure – they were perfect for each other and still my best of friends.

Christopher was thinking about coming to graduate school here this semester, but I had not heard what he decided. I think he should date Elaine, but what do I know? He's a lot of fun, and it would be nice to have him around more. He'd stopped slouching on a horse, too. Robin, our trainer in Canton, probably took him aside and straightened him up. She'd been taking care of his horse for him since he started foxhunting again.

The clock only said 1:30 pm. I went outside, then thought better of it and returned to my room to stare out the window. After a few minutes, I moved away from the window, my Southernmother training reminding me to never look like I was waiting on any boy.

I checked my phone. No messages. I brushed my teeth and stuffed some peppermints in my jean pockets. Finally, I settled on reading some more about Mitch Rapp. If anyone could get my mind off the clock, Vince Flynn could. Mitch had whacked six terrorists before I realized time had disappeared. I watched for Griffen again outside the window being careful to be far enough away so he could not see me gazing after him. I felt like a princess locked up in her castle waiting for her prince, but not wanting to look desperate – so unbecoming and improper for princesses even in medieval times…silly me.

He walked up the steps precisely at 2:00 pm. I was in his arms at 2:01 pm regardless of how he felt about public displays. He could deal with that later.

He was dressed in a madras short-sleeved shirt that now had a few more wrinkles, khaki shorts, and topsiders. I noticed that his arms and legs were brown and strong and the veins in his arms made distinct little rivers all the way down to his clean, perfect hands that were attempting to lower me to the ground.

"Let's go see my new house," he said peeling me off him gently, but firmly, after reluctantly supplying a welcome home peck on my forehead in front of way too many eager onlookers.

"I'm ready!" I said, turning toward the door. "It's about time you got here! I expected you to be early."

We drove the very short distance to his house, and I was surprised to find it already furnished. "How did you get this done so quickly?" I asked.

"Nothing a little money won't handle," he said, smugly.

"Yours or your uncle's?" I asked rudely before I thought about what I had just suggested.

"Actually, mine," he said. "I was gone all summer, Elliott. They had to pay me a lot to leave you like that."

"Who's 'they' and what was it worth?" I asked, teasing him.

"That's yet to be determined, but…you'll be the first to know, I promise," he said and pulled me down onto the couch.

"Griffen! What will the neighbors think?" I gasped and pulled him even closer to me.

"I don't have neighbors," he said into my neck. "That was part of the deal."

"I *have* to know what you were doing this summer," I said, trying to concentrate, but finding it more difficult the more kisses he placed on my throat, my neck, my lips, in my hair – his hands everywhere holding me close to him.

"All right," he said and sat up on one elbow. "If we *must* talk…"

"I thought I'd be helping you," I said. "I don't want you to jump up and run out on me like you did in Virginia."

"I'm better prepared for you…now that I know I'll see you every day," he said. "Mind over matter."

"Matter! Is that all I am to you?"

"Mmmm…let me see…"

"Summer!" I reminded him.

"You have to promise not to tell anyone," he said. "That was part of my contract."

"Contract?"

"Are you going to let me talk?" he said, "or can we get back to what we were doing before?"

"Both! Talk first…I promise I'll be quiet."

"I was an actor this summer," he said. "And supposedly I was doing a good job. But time will tell."

"Actor? Not stunt double?" I asked, finally realizing what he was saying.

"When that actor boyfriend of yours didn't show up, they asked me to do some of his lines, as a test. So I did. And they liked it…a lot. He didn't have a big part in the movie, just a really visible part. So, since I did most of the visible part for him anyway, they decided to try me with his lines. It worked. Or so they say. The movie won't come out for a few months," he said, looking at me and assessing my reaction.

"You're going to be the *Sean*? Surely they paid you a lot for that!" I said.

"Oh yes," he said flashing his perfect, cocky grin, and my heart melted.

"And I thought you were breaking up with me!" I said, feeling exactly like he had said I was acting – melodramatic and stupid.

"Elliott, that will *never* happen," he said. "How many times do I have to tell you that you *are* my life?"

"Just one more."

"You…are…my…life," he said looking deeply into my eyes. My stomach plunged. The only time I had experienced anything like this was at Disney world riding, rather, free falling, on the Tower of Terror. Overwhelmingly good, but terrifying. *It was so hard to believe – would this work? Could I really have these feelings for someone who loved me back so much? I am the luckiest girl in the world.*

"So, tell me about it," I said. "Did you meet the other actors? What was Keira Knightly like?"

"I suppose you'll find out soon enough, so I better tell you myself," he said, watching me carefully.

My heart skipped a beat. It never occurred to me what this movie was rated. What if?…O*h no...* I just looked at him, not sure I wanted to hear what he was going to tell me. *Surely she doesn't, but oh, what if she does? What if he did?* I felt my face flush and Griffen's eyes still on me. This could change everything.

"I had to kiss her."

I sat for a minute digesting that. But, strangely, it didn't bother me… at all. I was enormously relieved. I hope. I had to know. "Just kiss?"

"That's all. Nothing else or I wouldn't have agreed to it," he said, watching me.

"But you're back here telling me that I am your life, so I guess she wasn't that great," I said.

"I did *not* say that," he said, before he realized how that sounded. His face turned purple, but I laughed at him, so he recovered.

"Is that why you wouldn't say where you were? So I wouldn't charge in and knock her off you?"

"Hey, I was getting *paid* to kiss her," he said, still blushing. "That Sean idiot was taking advantage!"

"Oh, and that's supposed to make everything just fine?" I teased.

"It's not the same," he snapped.

"Settle down. I'm really proud of you and want to hear more about this, later." I pulled him beside me and continued where I'd interrupted before. It was magnificent having him here…I wanted to celebrate this moment with no interruptions…

The front door banged open and Ben and some other person came stomping through the house. "Griffen!" he yelled. "Where are you? Oh, sorry," he said when he saw us and dropped his eyes. Thank goodness we were just on the couch and not, well, in his room. That would have looked, *oh dear…*

"Elliott, this is Sam King," he said, still embarrassed and grasping for something to do to recover. "Griffen, Sam and I wanted to see your new place, but we can come back. I didn't know you *already* had company."

"Good idea," Griffen said glaring at both of them. "You better knock the next time if you don't want your jaw wired shut for the semester."

"We're gone – good to see you, too!" Ben said as he backed away.

"Whatever!" Griffen barked and glared at them.

"Are you going to Memphis Saturday?" Ben asked on his way out the door.

"Get…out!" Griffen snapped and threw a pillow at the back of his head. Ben made some ridiculous gesture at Griffen as he and Sam slammed the door behind him.

"What's in Memphis?" I asked since they had smashed the mood.

"William wants help with the country – paneling and stuff – before the season gets going," he said, distractedly. Instead of continuing where we left off, he stalked to the kitchen and attacked the refrigerator. "Two percent milk? What's *that* about? Oh, grapes…*just fruit and watery milk?"* He opened the freezer and peered in hopefully. "Not a steak in sight. *Lean Cuisine?* Who does he think I am? No ice cream."

He stalked to the pantry and continued his inspection…no good news there, either. "Unbelievable! No chips, crackers, no *cookies.* Wheat bread – oh, peanut butter…*that's* something. Jackson already thinks he can tell me how to eat…we'll see about that…white water my…" he mumbled something I was sure that I wasn't supposed to hear. "Let's go get something to eat. I haven't had time to stock my kitchen...properly."

He was really edgy, and now I understood. Always food – he's so predictable. It was nice knowing we didn't have to rush anything anymore. And he had this great little house – all to himself. No neighbors.

"What are you grinning at?" he asked suspiciously.

"Oh, nothing," I said as we left to start the first day of what I hoped would be the rest of *our* life.

NEW DAYS

Chapter 11

Youth, the circus-rider, fares gaily around the ring, standing with one foot on the bare-backed horse – the Ideal. Presently, at the moment of manhood, Life (exacting ring-master) causes another horse to be brought in who passes under the rider's legs, and ambles on. This is the Real. The young man takes up the reins, places a foot on each animal, and the business now becomes serious.

~ *Sidney Lanier, "Ambling, Ambling Round the Ring"*

William had us working like slaves to get the hunt country ready for the season. Replacing old coops, trimming branches, bush-hogging trails – anything the landowner wanted us to do, we handled.

Griffen and I had fallen into an easy routine, and everything was going better than I had ever dreamed. His class schedule and mine worked where we could almost always play from Friday afternoon through Sunday afternoon. He either fed me or took me out to eat every night on the weekends, and I was ready to treat him to something different.

"You're mine this afternoon," I said one Friday morning when he called to check on me. "Pick me up at 3:00."

"What are we doing?" he asked, knowing I'd never tell.

"Just wear something you can swim in and riding clothes – jeans are fine for the riding clothes," I said. "But, be sure to bring Panzer's box."

I had spent the week thinking about this, so I was able to throw everything together for a sunset picnic quickly. Addy wanted to come, too, but I wanted Griffen all to myself this afternoon.

"How do you know there won't be anyone else there?" she asked, pouting just a little.

"I'll deal with that when I get there," I said. "But you know how Griffen is about affection in public – and I don't want to just look at him all afternoon." I smiled at her and she, of course, understood. "But we will do something with you and Ben soon, I promise."

I had been selfish with our alone time, and it was time for us to start doing things with other couples. Everyone was going to our regular spots Saturday night – maybe we'd do that together. I'd like to show him off anyway. Maybe we could do that after the work party.

Griffen arrived, and I met him downstairs. We drove to the barn and caught the horses. Even though or perhaps because it was Friday afternoon, few people were at the barn, but we weren't completely alone. *Perfect.*

"Don't bother saddling them," I said. "We'll be riding bareback."

The best swimming pond was not too far from the barn, but it was out of sight. I walked out in just my swimsuit and a cover-up, for now, and his jaw dropped. He got the message, grabbed his swimsuit, and lost the jeans. He didn't bother to keep his shirt on – thank you God for *that* vision!

He swung up on Jet, and I did the same with Viva. We walked, then cantered easily to the pond. When we got there, I tossed my cover up and Griffen grinned appreciatively. Panzer picked it up and pranced around with it, and we both laughed.

"Come and get it," I said, and Viva and I plunged into the lake.

Griffen, Jet, and Panzer were right behind us, then beside us, then ahead of us as they stretched out across the pond. The horses pulled us beside them in the cool water, and we climbed onto their backs when their feet touched bottom on the other side.

"That was unbelievable," Griffen said. "I've never done anything like that before. Why haven't you told me about swimming horses?"

"I have to keep a few surprises for you, dear," I smiled and stood on Viva's back, trying hard not to stare at Griffen's perfect…everything.

"You are breathtaking," he said as I looked down at him.

I dived into the water, letting Viva enjoy her cool spot as she flipped her lower lip just below the surface. We played this game all the time, and the worst thing that could happen would be that she would leave me here to ride back double with Griffen on Jet. Panzer swam out to investigate what we were doing, then left to look for more interesting creatures on the bank.

Jet started when I popped up next to Griffen, but he didn't go anywhere. Griffen slid down and wrapped his gorgeous arms around me and pulled me to his magnificent, oh so bare, chest. He kissed me hard on the lips, and in spite of the cool water, I felt like I was being consumed by fire. I wanted to stay here with him and the horses until time stopped.

After a few minutes, he stopped kissing me and looked deeply into my eyes. His eyes were glowing, but his smile vanished.

"You, here, like this…is over the top," he said. "I want to keep doing this, but you really are going to have to be careful. Don't say I didn't warn you if I gallop away from you with no explanation. You can't possibly know what you are doing to me, or you'd be running for your…well…you'd be running."

"I trust you, Griffen," I said weakly and ran my fingers down his arms. His face and magnificent body were inches from mine, and I kept my eyes locked on his. I could feel the heat emanating from his skin.

"You shouldn't," he whispered. "Not here…not like this."

We stared at each other for what seemed an eternity. My body ached for him, to pull him closer, but I did have the sense to be still and enjoy this feeling – just wanting him, having him, but not. Wanting and waiting, passion and principles, looking into his sparkling green eyes for the lifetime I hoped I'd get to share with him.

He closed the distance, very slowly, with a soft, so sensual kiss. He wrapped me in his arms then lifted me, cradling me like a baby in the water. Jet turned around to see what he was doing, and we both laughed.

I kicked away and swam up on Viva. We chased each other around the lake letting the horses pull us through the cool water and racing each other across the pond. Finally, we rode back to the barn for a sunset picnic.

It was late when he brought me back to the sorority house. We had made plans to help William in the morning then be back in time to go out with everyone. He kissed me softly goodnight, and I staggered to my room. I had just enough energy to shower and collapse into a boneless sleep.

The work party started at 8:00 am. We convinced William to push it back from 7:00 am so we could at least get one more hour of sleep. Griffen drove while Ben, Addy, and I slept. When we got there, William wasted no time and began barking orders. Sylvia, his lovely wife, brought us cinnamon rolls and orange juice to get us started – bless her.

Bo and Bob were working on the tractor and several other members cleaned the hunt house. Lydia was not here, thank goodness, so I wouldn't have to deal with her. Most of the members had sent money, and Griffen was mad that I had not given him that option.

Griffen, Ben, Addy, and I were assigned coop, or jump duty. We were to repair seven coops, and all the boards were pre-cut and ready to be screwed into place. Our job was to clear the branches with limb-loppers, replace old boards, and repaint each coop's name. Members paid a premium for the privilege of naming a coop, and that project paid for all the jumps and their upkeep, as long as some of us volunteered our labor.

"I still don't see why he won't hire this out," Griffen said. "I really don't like doing this. We had to drive over an hour, we'll break our necks doing this; I need to be studying – this is ridiculous."

"At least you're with me," I said and looked up at him underneath my lashes pouring on my most alluring, cheer-you-up charm.

"Oh boy. With you, Ben, *and* Addy," he said not loud enough for them to hear.

"Quit being such a grouch," I teased. "Manual labor will not kill you."

"This *and* law school *and* partying all night all the time with you will, though," he snapped.

"Ben, let's get this started," Griffen said. "I don't want to be here all day."

"Easy Griffen, it's not even 8:30," he said and got in the farm truck.

"Thanks again for the breakfast, Mrs. Sylvia!" Addy said as we pulled away.

We piled on to the truck's huge bench seat laughing at how Ben managed to hit every bump, but once we reached the first coop, everything went downhill. Griffen stayed irritated, and I tried to ignore him. Ben and Addy did, too, but I could tell they were uncomfortable. It started to get embarrassing, but I did what I could to make the most of things and hopefully, get the job done quickly so we could leave faster.

"Elliott, hand me the drill," Griffen said when he had the board and screw lined up on the frame.

When I walked over to him, I accidentally bumped the board. It landed with a crash on his hand, and he roared in frustration.

"What is *wrong* with you, Elliott?" he yelled. "Watch what you're doing!"

He'd done it again. This time, Ben and Addy didn't miss it. They were in on the whole conversation. Thankfully, they looked away to give me some privacy. I straightened up, walked over to Griffen, leaned in close to his ear and whispered with great clarity into his angry face.

"If you *ever* speak to me like that again, Griffen, I will go so far away from you that you will never be able to find me. Apologize right now, so I don't have a reason to drive away and leave Ben and Addy here stranded," I hissed. "Don't think for a moment that I won't."

He glared at me, and I glared right back. He had the drill in his hand, but I had a hammer, and it felt good…solid. For a moment, I considered using it to drive home my point.

"I have the key," he said.

"Give it to me."

"No way," he said, eyes still boring into mine.

I didn't think he really had the key; after all, this was William's farm truck and not his. And why would he have removed the key when there's no one around to steal anything? On a whim, I whirled on my heels, walked back to the truck, got in the driver's seat, and saw the key in the ignition.

"Ben, Addy, I'll send someone back for you," I said and drove away.

My heart was pounding as I drove back to the hunt house. *What would I say to William? Was I overreacting? Ben and Addy are going to kill me.*

I started shaking and wanted to cry.

"Honey, you are doing the right thing," Grand said. "You can't let him get away with treating you badly; especially in public. If it doesn't work and he doesn't learn, then you have to be strong enough to walk away. I love you, honey. You are too good to let him talk to you like that."

By the time I reached the hunt house, I had made my decision. I had to go all the way through with this or it would not work. This was going to inconvenience so many people, though, and it was embarrassing. I would take his truck. I knew where he kept the extra key.

When I pulled in, Sylvia was sitting on the porch. There was no one else around, and I was glad.

"Elliott, honey," she said. "Do you need something?"

Her sweet, pleading eyes were too much. I couldn't speak, and she saw the look on my face.

"What happened; are you all right?" she reached out to me and pulled me into a hug. "Is it Griffen?"

"Yes…ma'am," I stammered. And then I told her everything. She assessed the situation and immediately took charge.

"I'm taking you to Oxford, dear. Leave Griffen's truck where it is. I'll send William to pick them up…in a little while," she smiled, and her eyes twinkled.

"You know I love that boy like a son, Elliott, but you are right to not put up with such nonsense, and this is the only way they learn," she said. "They can be just like children – the ones you care about. You have to love them and yourself enough to teach them how you expect them to behave towards you. He's a good boy, but he needs guidance. Now's the time to see if he's teachable. Most of them are, but if they're not, then…you're better off moving on."

"Thank you, Mrs. Sylvia," I said, feeling much better after another round of orange juice and cinnamon rolls. "You really don't have to do this, though."

"Please dear, let me in on the drama!" she said. "Do you know how long it's been since we've had something like this in our little foxhunting family? I hope this works, but if it doesn't, there *will* be other boys for you, young lady. And really, teachable is all you're looking for, certainly not perfect. I've been training William for more than fifty years, and he's still got a ways to go!"

That remark about other boys gave me no comfort, for I seriously doubted that, but I did not say so. I wanted Griffen or no one. I'd just go back to Viva and stay happy alone like Griffen said he had planned to do in the first place – before we met. I could do that, too. I had done it for so long and used to be happy, well, content at least. That thought didn't help, either.

My cell phone buzzed – 615. I ignored it. Then the text.

> Please call me as soon as possible. I can explain some things. Griffen

What is that? Did he have that message on quick text or something?

Sylvia returned, a smug look on her face.

"William is going to pick them up right now and tell them that I drove you to Oxford. We'll let him sit on that for the rest of the morning. I'm sure he's not going to like what William has to say to him," she chuckled to herself.

"I'm glad you are on *my* side," I said. "I want you on my team from now on!"

We had a great ride to Oxford, and I enjoyed so much getting to know her better. She was as tough as could be with a heart that loved people in her world more than most. She knew all about Griffen's background, and it was comforting to talk to someone so freely about him without feeling like I had to guard his secrets.

Neither of us was concerned that Griffen would really be like his father, but we agreed that he may not know how to behave towards people he loves because of how he was raised. We knew, though, that only he could change that. Sylvia was glad to hear me say that to her. *I just hoped I could be strong enough to break things off with him if he* didn't *change. Leaving him would be like pulling my heart out of my chest and flinging it on the ground.* I kept those thoughts to myself.

She pulled up to the sorority house, and I was not ready yet for her to leave. She, too, had been in my sorority many years ago, so I invited her in to see the renovations. We admired the grand piano in the lobby, and she played a few songs for me before she left.

"Chin up, dear," she said, and I could hear my own Grand in her voice and all the other Southernmothers that kept me company through the twists and turns of my life. "I believe he'll come around. You two look like you were created for each other. God, with His wonderful sense of humor, makes us finish ourselves, so it will be up to Griffen to rise to the challenge of you…the best gift ever that God has put before him. Just see to it that you don't lower *your* standards, dear. That is never the Lord's intent for any of His beloved."

"Thank you, Mrs. Sylvia," I said, and gave her a huge, grateful hug. *What a grand lady. I hope I can be like her some day.*

I walked back up to my room, and my cell phone buzzed again – text – from Addy.

> Don't respond to this. Griffen is watching my phone. He's in a rage, but Ben has things under control. William picked us up and we are on our way home. Wait in your room for me. Love you.

Raindrops. Maybe I overreacted and turned the raindrop into a hurricane…again. No, I did the right thing. But it feels so wrong, and I hurt so much. I buried my head into my pillow and cried myself to sleep.

Addy woke me when she came in. I told her everything, except the part about Griffen's history, and the whole picture from Nashville to now made much more sense. She was such a great friend. She never judged, just listened and empathized more than I realized. I learned that she and Ben had plenty of storms, too, but I would have never known it.

"You should have seen Ben when Griffen got so unreasonably mad at you," she said. "I thought they were going to fight each other right then and there. If I didn't know Ben loved me, I'd be worried!"

"He does love you, Addy," I said. "He loves me like a sister."

She looked at me a little askew.

"*I promise*," I said. "He's never even tried to kiss me."

"That makes me feel better, then," she said. "Not that I don't *know* he loves me. But you should have seen Griffen's reaction to William! Now, that was a surprise. William took him aside, said some things to him, and Griffen just deflated. He was still mad, but much more in control. I could *feel* him, Elliott. He filled the whole car up with his anger. It was like he internalized it, though."

"I guess I'm on my own tonight," I said.

"He needs a day or two to calm down," Addy said.

"Well, I'm going out. Without a date," I said. "I'm not sulking around in this room acting scared. *He's* the one who was a jerk, and *he's* the one who owes *me* an apology."

"Warn me when that's going down, and I'll sell tickets," she smiled. "We'll be able to fund our formal this year with that show!"

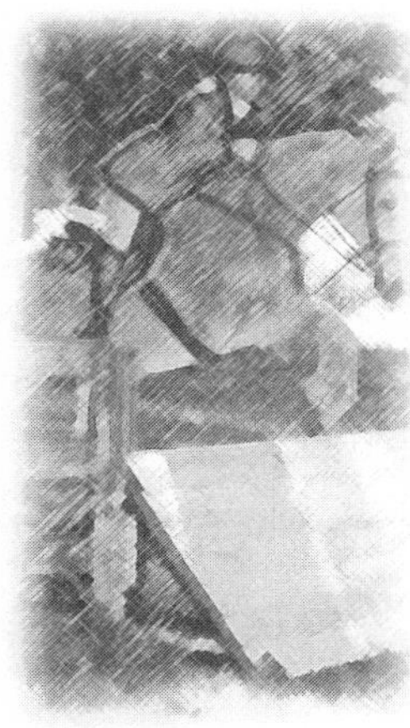

GAMES

Chapter 12

Not the fastest horse can catch a word spoken in anger.

~ *Chinese Proverb*

Griffen did not try to call but one more time. I ignored him and didn't check my voice mail…until around 3:00 pm. By then, I couldn't stand it and had to know what he wanted to say.

"Elliott, call me, please." No remorse in his voice. Just a command. Not calling him.

"Elliott, stop playing games and call me." No remorse and angry now. Not returning that one, either.

I didn't want to saddle Addy with me tonight, so I asked Elaine if I could go out with her and Shannon. There was no home game this weekend, so we'd just go to the regular hangouts and make it a low-key night. I needed a night without Griffen for a change.

We settled on a big table and ordered some food. Ben and Addy had Sam with them, and they joined us.

"Have you talked to Griffen?" Ben asked me.

"No," I said and shot him a look that clearly said to change the subject.

Sam was sitting next to me and started telling stories about his high school days in small town Alabama. He had us laughing in minutes, and I was delighted Ben had brought him. He had transferred this year from Alabama for a girl, but she had left him for a *girl* and that made us all laugh uproariously at the unjust nature of life.

Elaine said her water-ski boyfriend was the best she'd ever seen on a slalom course and that they had conned her into jumping…as in…over a ramp…earlier that afternoon.

"I was so brave watching everyone else do it," she laughed. "But when I lined up with the ramp, it looked like a mountain with a fountain on top! Then it got bigger…and bigger…and I remembered that I was going to go *up* that mountain on *water-skis* and *land*, somewhere – hopefully upright and not face first, hoping my swimsuit stayed on! I did it, but it still hurts to sit! The best part is…I *never* have to do that again!"

"Where is the ramp?" I asked. "Is it in the same area as the slalom course?"

I felt Shannon's elbow punch my rib.

"Ouch! Shannon! What are you…?" and there he was. Griffen walked in with two guys I didn't know. They sat at a table in another part of the restaurant. I didn't think he had seen me, and I was glad. My heart felt like it had been squeezed, and my stomach fluttered madly… I was behaving like a little girl with a crush…again.

I tried to act like nothing had happened, and we had a pretty good time laughing and cutting up with each other. After a while, I asked for the check, for I was ready to go. Shannon and Elaine agreed to drive me home, but they planned to come back. After all, table dancing had yet to begin, and that was always great entertainment.

When the waiter returned, he said our tabs had been paid… everyone's at my table…but he wouldn't say who did it. He didn't have to, and that made me even angrier. *What an arrogant jerk! Thinking he can buy me…and all my friends. I'm still not calling him.*

To leave, we would have to walk by Griffen's table, and I dreaded having to ignore him. Thankfully, when we got there, he was gone. The other guys were there, but they didn't seem to notice us. I walked by, heart pounding, and fuming at thoughts of Griffen being even more under my skin.

When we finally made it to Elaine's car, Griffen was waiting.

Although I was still angry, seeing him unexpectedly caught me off guard. He looked like a statue – like someone I didn't know, and it hurt. My anger softened…I was really tired, and this whole thing was making me sad.

"Elliott, would you mind if I spoke to you for a moment?" he asked. When I looked doubtful, he added, "Only a moment. If Elaine and Shannon don't mind waiting."

I looked at them, and they nodded. He indicated a spot a few feet away, and I walked with him.

"Elliott, I owe you another apology," he said, stiffly. "I should not have spoken to you like I did, and I hope you will forgive me." His words were flat, rehearsed, and his eyes cold.

"Ok," I said.

"Ok?" he asked, a little surprised.

"Yes," I said. "Goodnight."

I turned quickly to leave with Elaine and Shannon. I felt like I was running away, and I guess I was. This was just not right. They dropped me off at the house, and I went up to my room and cried myself to sleep.

The next morning was Sunday, but I woke at 6:00 am – unable to sleep. I pulled on my riding pants quietly so I would not wake Leslie and left to see Viva. I had plenty of time to ride before church, and I was desperate to get away and think. What did I want? What was wrong, and why was I so sad? Griffen had apologized, but I felt empty inside, like this whole incident had shot a hole in my heart.

I drove in silence and let the wind blow my hair. The early morning air was balmy but so much cooler than the night before. Viva and the other horses were grazing, and they looked up when they heard my truck. In the woods behind the horses, the few first signs of fall tints barely revealed themselves through the lush, green overcoat that shrouded the woods.

Viva was glad to come into her stall, knowing she'd get an early morning treat. She was filthy, so I brushed her, then let her eat while I gathered her tack. I heard another truck and was surprised. *Who else would possibly be riding this early? It was probably someone coming to fix something, but on a Sunday morning? What if…?* I shook my head to clear it and kept putting on Viva's tack.

I stepped out of the stall right into Griffen's path. He was leading Jet into the barn.

"Good morning, Elliott," he said, and the smile was back in his eyes, but he was wary and guarded…and gorgeous. "I didn't expect to see you here this early."

Jet nickered to Viva and pulled on his lead for Griffen to take him to his stall and feed him, too. I wanted to crash into Griffen's arms, for him to hold me, and for everything to be instantly back to normal… all the ridiculousness of the day before forgotten. But I didn't. I gripped the brush tighter to keep at least one of my hands from flying around Griffen's neck. There was that elephant in the room – the way he'd snapped at me in front of everyone – and his strange apology the night before had not yet cleared the air.

I did not know what to say or do, so I stood there. Like an idiot. Hand gripping a brush, the other one dangling by my side. Jet kept pulling on the lead rope, so Griffen turned to the stall closest to him and let him in. That gave me a reason to get the rest of my gear – my helmet, gloves, and bridle…and a peppermint just in case – and walk back to Viva's stall.

"Do you want to ride with me?" I asked, desperately trying to disguise my nerves and sound casual. My voice sounded too loud and strained, and the question hung in the air for what seemed like an eternity. He didn't answer, and I didn't know if he had heard me. Surely he had. I put Viva's bridle on, tightened her girth, and waited… but trying to look like I was still busy getting ready.

I felt him appear in the stall doorway. When I looked up, he looked at me, guarded. Then he walked toward me and my whole body tensed in anticipation of his embrace. Instead, he reached in front of me and stroked Viva's neck, his arm passing so close and his body so near I shuddered.

Viva nuzzled him looking for a treat, and he gave one to her. Watching her nuzzle his hands made me long for that easy, simple affection. He looked at me then, and gently ran his fingers along my cheek and under my chin. So soft, gentle. My body was useless when he was near, and he was so very, very close to me now. I kept watching his eyes and they too, were soft but…sad.

"I want *you* back," he said, almost in a whisper. "I want to fix what I so thoughtlessly smashed yesterday, but I don't know how, or even *if* I should try."

At that remark, my heart clenched. The thought of him not trying hurt worse than anything.

"Please don't say that," I said.

"What part?" he asked.

"The *not trying* part," I said, my voice cracking a little with the combination of his presence making my throat go dry and for not having used it much yet this morning.

"I love you, Elliott," he said. "But that's not enough. I don't want to ever hurt you, and yesterday I did it so fast without thinking over nothing, and now we're here. How much more will I hurt you by not thinking over who knows what? What if I do more than just hurt you with words? There's a *real* monster inside me – I see it clearly now. My feelings for you are so raw, and that monster waits pounce – on you of all people – any time I'm in the least bit agitated. And I don't even have to be mad at you. I've already done this once before, and I went right back to it yesterday. I'm not strong enough for this. Being here near you has clarified that. This can't work."

Oh no. What was he saying? I did not want to hear this…I would rather him justify himself and fight back. "This is all up to you," I said. "You know I love you…so very…very much."

"I know that," he said and stepped closer to me. "But that's not enough to make this work…without someone…you especially…getting hurt. I'm not willing to hurt you any more just to have you love me. You…

you don't...know...what I've seen...what someone like me who supposedly loves someone can...and will...do to them."

He was so close. I started to tremble. His eyes were glowing again, and I could see he wanted me to hear what he was saying but ignore it. He was warning me, but I was drawn to him like a moth to a flame – when he was near me, I was helpless...and I didn't care.

Viva nuzzled him again, but he ignored her. He stroked my chin with his finger and tilted my face to his. "You are so very, very lovely, Elliott. Such a treasure."

I leaned toward him, ever so slightly, and closed my eyes. I could smell him, but he was just far enough away that I could not quite feel the warmth of his body, but I could imagine it...anticipate it pressing against mine...him pulling me close. His delicate, tentative touch on my face made me dizzy on top of the shivers charging up and down my spine.

He moved back, and when I opened my eyes, he had left. He finished tacking up Jet and led him outside. After the initial shock that he had walked away, I recovered, gathered Viva's reins, and led her outside. I mounted her and rode over to him and Jet. Distance from him definitely cleared my head.

"You never answered my question," I said looking down at him from Viva.

"What question?" he asked. He turned to swing up on Jet.

"Are you going with me?"

"Like I have a choice," he said, as he sat up on his magnificent horse. "You'd have to outrun me, and that's not likely...on foot for sure... much less, now that I'm on the *superior* horse." The old, maddening, and oh so wonderful cockiness was back in his voice.

"Well then, come and *get* it. We'll see about Jet's *speed*," I teased and galloped away from him like my life depended on it.

We outran our demons for an hour and finally returned to the barn, exhausted, this time, from doing something we both really really loved. I felt whole again and ready to see what Griffen would do with us next. I did not want to think, though, about us – just wanted to enjoy being with him now, doing the things I loved the most with my best friend.

"Will you let me take you to church and lunch?" he asked, as I walked by his stall carrying Viva's tack. He stopped me and collected my gear in his arms.

"Yes, that would be great," I said. "10:00?"

"I'll be there," he grinned.

He put the tack away and met me in the doorway…again. This time, he gathered me up in his arms and kissed me. I kissed him back like I'd been depraved for a lifetime of his kisses, and he stopped for a moment, surprised, grinned down at me, and pressed me close.

"That's my *Elliott*," he growled into my neck. "I like it when you kiss back like…that."

"Why'd you stop me, then, if you like it so much?" I asked, reaching up and stopping short barely an inch from his perfect lips.

"Church, Elliott. Remember we have a date? Keep that up, and we'll skip."

"Oh no," I said. "Then you'd miss lunch, and I'd be stuck here with you hungry and grumpy all afternoon. No thanks."

With an impressive show of willpower for me under these conditions, I pulled away and walked to my truck. After all, I'd see him again in no time. So strange that he had all but broken up with me an hour or so ago and now we were going to church...like nothing ever happened. I was not sure what to make of that and pushed that thought, too, back in the far reaches of my mind.

The five little ladies greeted us, and this time had enough candy for me, too. They were delighted to get the full force of Griffen's smiles and winked at me every time I caught their eyes.

Shannon and Leslie were surprised when we arrived together, for Leslie had already left our room when I returned from my ride. Their looks demanded an explanation – later – of course. Lunch was great, although Griffen and I didn't get much of a chance to talk there either, with so many people coming and going and stopping by our table to say "hello." Griffen was new flesh, so every girl I remotely knew feigned deep friendship with me and hoped I would introduce him to them. It amused me to watch them gawk when I made the obligatory introductions.

At last, we were alone and heading exactly where, I did not know. He had his iPod hooked to his truck playing the Blues. *Excellent Sunday afternoon choice.*

"I have to study this afternoon, Elliott, so I'm taking you home... your home," he said, disappointed, but resolved. *I guess that answered my question.*

"How are your classes?" I asked. "You've never mentioned studying to me before. Are they that much harder?"

"I don't know yet, since we haven't had any tests, but there's a great deal of material that I'm supposed to absorb. It's a lot more intense than college already. For the first time, I'm a little intimidated about the volume," he said.

I contemplated that for a minute and made a mental note to pursue another field of post-graduate study if law intimidated *him*. My concentration must have translated to disapproval, although I did not really intend to prevent him from studying.

"I tell you what," he said after a few moments. "If I get finished earlier than I expect, I'll call you. How's that? That'll give me that much more incentive to focus." He looked over at me and pulled my hand to his lips. I shuddered, as always, at his touch.

"I think you need to change your focus to another field," I said. "So you can study me on Sunday afternoons, rather than law."

"Tempting. So very, very tempting…" he said. "You are going to be my nemesis, yet, if I don't keep you at bay."

"So, are we hunting Saturday?"

"Yes. What time? I don't have a fixture card yet."

"Early – 6:00 am. He's only doing that for a few weekends, then changing to 8:00 am sometime in October."

"He's been throwing around wanting me to hunt the hounds," he said. "Did you know that?"

"Griffen, no, but that's quite an honor!" I said, pleased that William was so glad to have him back.

"Yes, but such a responsibility. I would love to, but I don't know how much time I can give to him being so far away and not knowing how much time law school, and you, will require."

"Count anything hunting and with me *as* me," I said. "I think you'd be a great huntsman. You have a sixth sense about what game is going to do and which hounds do what."

"Elliott, when I'm with you, you make me feel invincible," he said. "There's just something about you…" he trailed off as he picked up my hand and brought my fingers back to his lips. "But now, I'm returning you to your castle. I've got to study if I'm to support you some day."

He walked me to the door, kissed me softly, and left me alone to face the barrage of questions sure to follow about us when I went upstairs. Uncertain of my answers to these questions, I opted to escape for a little while longer into remembering a wonderful day. I went to my truck, grabbed my journal, put my iPod earbuds in, and hid in the courtyard to write. I selected the classical category, settled into a comfortable spot, and wrote down every wonderful memory I could think of about Griffen.

Somehow, I couldn't shake the feeling that my days with him like these were numbered, but I didn't want to think about *that part* now, at least. Write these memories now to be cherished *forever…*

PRESSURE

Chapter 13

Young hot colts being raged do rage the more.

~ *William Shakespeare*

King Richard II, Act II, Scene 1

Fall flew by as always. The early part of foxhunting season, or cub-hunting, is hard work on the staff getting the puppies ready and other riders getting young or new horses introduced to all associated with the chase.

William had placed more responsibility on Griffen and asked him to ride with him more often than not, hoping he would be willing to take the pack someday. Occasionally, Griffen hunted the pack under William's careful guidance. This added a new dimension for me to hunting, for on the days that Griffen hunted the hounds, he was particularly edgy. I was cautiously optimistic that he would learn to control his temper and prayed every day that he would be able to do just that. I knew I couldn't change him, and I never brought it up, but

I also didn't want to have to live without him.

Law school had him studying harder than he ever had to in college, plus I kept him busy with all our sorority social functions. I loved to parade him around, and he never showed any signs of jealousy – other than that one incident with the actor. Of course, my being so obviously besotted with him couldn't have hurt things, either.

Since my college workload was manageable, I agreed to help with more of the Opening Meet plans this year. The Cantata Hounds and its laughing and energetic kids had made a strong impression on me, so I wanted to see more people my age and younger riding. Since I started hunting, I noticed most hunts had aging memberships. Also, I noticed that even in the South, many horse people were not connected with the natural world, especially those that rented or leased horses at the big barns. Until I foxhunted, I had been one of those people. Until foxhunting, I had never experienced the joy of riding in vast, unfenced spaces. Getting more people to participate in this timeless, centuries old activity that pitted horse and hounds against the elements as well as their quarry was a way that I thought I could give back to the sport that gave so much to me.

So, like the well-bred church and sorority girl I was, I formed a committee. With my whipping-in responsibilities, I couldn't ride with guests myself, so we built a network of like-minded members who were willing to bring along new people both young and old. We added an award at Opening Meet for the barn with the most people that attended – mounted or otherwise. This already promised to be a hit all around due to their naturally competitive natures, and tickets were selling like hotcakes. For the spectators, we would decorate a kid-friendly tally-ho wagon complete with a team of mules, soft drinks, and snacks. We also encouraged each barn to decorate not only a wagon of their own, but also braid their horses' manes with their barn colors, relaxing the tradition that only members with their hunt colors could braid colors in their horses' manes.

Each barn was allowed to set up a table at the silent auction with information about boarding and riding lessons. One of our members agreed to give free half-day foxhunting seminars at the barns on fox-hunting traditions, attire, and how to ride cross-country most effectively. In turn, barns donated lessons to our silent auction.

Things were going so well with Opening Meet plans, but I still had the unsettling feeling that mine and Griffen's perfect world was coming to an end. This weekend, Griffen was going to be hunting the hounds alone, and I considered going home for a rare visit with my parents. William had to be out of town and would not even be around for back up if the hounds got out of control. Of course, my Grand would hear nothing of that and convinced me to stay and let this thing go as it may.

"Better to find out all about him now, than when you've got three kids by him and are stuck raisin' 'em and livin' on eggshells 'till they're grown!" she chided.

We decided to take two trailers this day, but I never told Griffen the real reason. I let him think it was a good idea for him to go up the night before and stay at the hunt house, and that I would come up the next morning. I promised to follow Ben and Addy, so he wouldn't worry about me driving alone in the dark.

I hated to be thinking these thoughts; it was almost like I was predicting disaster. But I had found that with Griffen, I still couldn't make rational decisions around him. I had to do all my thinking when he was out of sight. Brains, not hormones, made better life decisions, and my decision about Griffen was fraught with uncertainty – on his side and mine. The trouble with his side was that it was all up to him. And that made me crazy.

My cell phone rang – home. Mother must have told Daddy I was driving my trailer in the dark…unescorted.

"Hi Daddy!" I said brightly, knowing Mother would never be awake at this hour.

"Hello Elliott, dear," he said. "Just checking on you. How's my most precious little girl?"

"Fine – and right behind Ben and Addy. I can see their taillights. We're about thirty minutes from the hunt," I said, hoping to spare him having to ask the things he wanted to know, without putting him through the ordeal of cell phone questioning.

"Well, you drive carefully," he said. "And have fun. Let your mother know when you're coming home, or when we can come up to see you."

"Yes sir, Daddy," I said. "I love you."

"Love you, too, dear. Bye," he said.

I smiled thinking I have the best Daddy in the world. I did want to see them, but I didn't know when I could make that happen before Christmas. Mother was coming up for Opening Meet, but Daddy…

My cell phone rang again – my favorite 615 number this time – still using that one I noticed…

"Hello, my dear," I said, glad to hear from him so I could stop thinking ominous thoughts.

"Where are you?" he asked with a distinct edge in his voice.

"About thirty minutes away," I said, ignoring the tension and thinking I had not exchanged a protective father for a protective boyfriend, I'd just collected two people to harass me into staying safe.

"Ok. When you get here, make sure Ben lets Addy take first flight. I need both of you to whip-in today. Lydia and Stephen are coming, but not any of the others," he said, tension already building in his voice. "And Eilene is going to be late. She's not planning to ride. Her horse is lame."

Eilene Watson was one the Masters of Foxhounds, or the people who actually ran the hunt. William was a Master and the huntsman. There were two other Masters, but they did not ride as often as Eilene and William. Eilene usually led one of the groups or whipped-in when she hunted.

"I will tell Addy," I said. "And Griffen?"

"What?" he snapped.

"You're going to do great."

"We'll see," he said a little softer. "Just get here, but don't drive too fast." The line went dead, and I smiled. He was so predictable. I just hope he holds it together today…for *our* sake.

After pulling in and parking, I walked over to give Ben and Addy Griffen's message.

"I'm fine with taking first flight," Addy said. "Unless Jane shows up. Then I'll let her take the lead if she wants to."

"I'll take care of Griffen, Elliott," Ben said. "Everything will be fine. If he starts acting stupid with you, I'll punch him."

"Thanks a lot Ben," I said. "That'll help things – having you at each other's throats."

"We'd be fine, Elliott," he said. "But he'd think twice about what he said to you in front of people. Look at it this way, I'd save you tons of money on marriage counseling!"

"That's enough, Ben!" Addy snapped. "You need to keep your nose out of her business."

"Look who's being the public grump now!" Ben smiled.

"You two are too much," I said. "This day will go well, in every way. We'll make sure of it."

"Hey guys!" Christopher said, riding up on his big bay warmblood mare, Magic.

"Oh Christopher," I said, relieved to see him. "Griffen will be so glad you're here!"

"Yeah, he called me last night and begged that I help today," he said. "I have to be in a wedding tonight, but he twisted my arm. He'll owe me big for this one!"

"Just drink a lot of caffeine…you'll be fine," I said. "I'm glad you're here, too. This is going to be fun. Let's go get our radios."

We moved to the kennel, and I saw that Jet was already tacked up and chomping hay contentedly from his net. We had about thirty minutes until cast time, so we needed to pick up the pace. We found Griffen pulling out the radios and extra hound collars.

"Elliot, do this," he snapped, as he handed the radio box to me. "Make sure anyone who can whip-in does and knows where they need to be. Where have you been?"

I ignored the edge in his voice, slipped him a slice of a hot breakfast ham and cheese roll wrapped in a napkin that I had stolen from the cabin, and remained calm trying to sooth him with my voice like he always did to me. "Christopher, Ben, Stephen, and Lydia are all here," I said softly and steadily. "And, me, of course. We've got your back, front, and sides. You just hold it together here," I said as I reached up to put his face in my hands.

That was *not* the thing to do in front of everyone, and I knew it right before I touched him, but it was too late. He straightened slightly, and I felt the reprimand. Nobody else would have noticed, but I got the message. *I'd have to be a little more careful.*

"Honey, no! You be yourself and let him deal with the consequences! No eggshells, just Elliott!" Grand started screeching.

"The radios," he said quietly, but his eyes were not angry, just determined and focused…and gorgeous.

"Got it," I said, and turned to deliver them.

"Christopher, you and Stephen put the collars on the hounds once Elliott gets them to you. Here's the list," he said and handed it to Stephen. "Lydia, I need you to take the east side but ride with Christopher and me until we cast. I'm going to keep him with me."

"Why Christopher?" she asked. Her acerbic tone unmistakably challenged his authority. "I'm the senior whipper-in here today and know the country much better than he does. He's just a guest. You're going to need all the help you can get."

Her remark rang as everyone stopped what they were doing and stared at Griffen. She was way out of line, and we all knew it.

"Just do what you are told, Lydia or leave," Griffen said.

"Don't *start* with me, Griffen," Lydia hissed, "it ends right here."

Lydia was inches from his face. She exuded impertinence and enjoyed putting him on the spot…and in his place. Knowing her as I did, I expected she'd been planning this.

"Give me your radio, Lydia," Griffen responded in a low rumble. "I will not be needing you today."

"I'll speak to the Masters about this," she spat and tossed her radio at me. I barely caught it before it smacked me in the forehead.

She flipped her long blonde mane in defiance, motioned for Stephen to follow her, and stalked to her truck.

Without skipping a beat, Griffen continued. "Elliott, you take the east side, Stephen, you take the north, and I'll put Ben on the west side. Addy and the field can help us cover the south should we need help there. Please be sure she gets a radio, Elliott. There should be enough."

Pretending the exchange never occurred, the rest of us checked the radios, and I left to get Viva. Stephen had not followed Lydia, and that made me smile. As I walked past Addy, I gave her Griffen's instructions.

"Good luck!" I said and winked at her. "Check your radio. You can talk and listen on channel one, but only listen on two. Keep it on two unless you need to report anything. Don't speak unless spoken to…or have something important to say. Oh, and if you see something, make sure it is the hunted game before you 'tally-ho'. When you do see something that's being hunted, be sure to say in which direction it is running."

She looked nervous, but Harley was calm, so I knew they would be fine.

"You can probably get Fox News if you play with that radio long enough," I said and was rewarded with her nervous smile.

"Thanks. Looks like I'll be the leader today," she beamed. "Jane's not coming. No pressure…"

"You'll be fine," I assured her.

Viva was ready to go. She had finished her hay and was looking for Jet. About ten riders were here beside the small number of staff, but the weather was perfect. The humidity had dropped the night before, and I was not sure what that would do for scenting or even where Griffen planned to hunt. Opening Meet was next weekend…I hoped nothing happened to the hounds.

William had instructed Griffen to take the older, slower pack for his first solo hunt. We had only five couple, or ten hounds, to watch today. Christopher would let them out when Griffen gave the signal. All of us, with the exception of Lydia, were ready.

Griffen had everyone bow their heads for a silent prayer of thanks for the privilege of riding to hounds. He ended with "Go in Peace, Return in Safety…Amen," and his calm, confident voice gave me goose bumps. *Magnificent way to start a hunt. Focus…you have a job, Elliott! And… he definitely needs you to be* on *today!*

Griffen blew the horn, and the pack pranced around him in perfect formation. I trotted next to him and winked. He flashed me his brilliant, glorious, smile. I could barely resist riding over and planting a big kiss on his fabulous face, but thought better of it…for now. *Being on Jet must have calmed him – he looks like he does this all the time.* Jet tried to pull up beside us, but Griffen slowed him imperceptibly back in place.

He and Jet were a picture like none I had ever seen. Jet's ebony coat glistened with his new clip, and Griffen had been able to keep his mane and tail black in spite of the less-than-glorious accommodations in Oxford. He did have him on the "up in the day, out at night routine," and I had agreed to put Viva through that, too, just to keep Jet company. She had been a little more spirited than usual this season, but I didn't mind.

A few of the hounds acted confused since they didn't know Jet as their huntsman's horse, nor Griffen as their huntsman. They milled around looking for William, but we were able to contain them. Sounder, however, lagged back. He was timid, so I knew he would come along, but Addy didn't.

"Get *to* him!" Addy snapped and cracked her whip trying to be helpful. Unfortunately, she hit him, and Sounder howled like he'd been shot.

"Damn it, Addy! *Never* put a whip on the hounds!" Griffen shouted...in front of the whole hunt.

Silence – the former hum of conversation ceased.

The only sounds were the horses' rhythmic clops as they moved with the pack and Sounder's nervous whimper.

Addy's face flushed scarlet, and I could tell she was about to cry. Griffen had humiliated her in front of everyone, and all she had been trying to do was help. Anger flared in me, and I felt my blood boil. It took everything I had not to strike Griffen with *my* whip for doing that to her. Only the strict foxhunting hierarchy that Lydia had so flippantly breached contained my outburst.

I tried to put my mind elsewhere to keep from succumbing to that anger, so I could focus on my job. In foxhunting, the Master is just that, the master. What he or she says goes, particularly in the field. It has to be that way to ensure the safety of the hounds, horses, and riders….in that order.

Although Griffen was not a Master, he was the huntsman for the day. And, especially with no Master riding, Griffen was in charge. That is why he had to send Lydia home. She had challenged his authority in front of everyone, and that would *not* do. Her empty threat to speak to the Masters was just that. They would back Griffen. In fact, she could probably lose the privilege of wearing the hunt's colors for her insubordination, but that was not likely, since she was staff, and overall a big help to the hunt. That, too, is why Stephen did not leave with her.

He knew she was in the wrong. I smiled again at the thought of what he had to deal with when he faced her.

"Elliott," Griffen barked, snapping me back into action.

"I'm going," I said through clenched teeth and galloped to the east.

"Casting here to the north, then plan to move east at the Rattle Trap," he said over the radio. "Report what you see, but no chatter."

I was still so angry with him, that there was no danger of chatter from me. Murder perhaps, but no chatter. *Poor Addy.*

Sounder must have recovered, for his was the first voice I heard. The others joined him, and they headed toward Stephen – straight north.

"Hope you have your big boy pants on, Stephen. The whole pack's coming your way," Ben cracked, ignoring Griffen's "no chatter" command, and I was glad. I liked chatter. Especially today. The mood definitely needed to be lightened. I still wanted to smack Griffen.

Viva and I bolted north – the pack was in full cry now. Glorious glorious galloping! I love this horse and this sport! Three coops and two long, straight pasture gallops later, they checked.

"Careful Elliott," Griffen said. "We're getting close to the road. Turn any game you see. Keep the hounds off the highway."

"10-4," I said, not being able to say "Yes, sir," like I usually did under these circumstances. What I wanted to say to him would have to be censored.

Griffen's mind, as usual, was right on target. The hounds started my way and a gray fox popped out of the covert underneath our noses. Viva snorted, and I turned her toward him so we could try to send him back onto our country. Miraculously, he turned, and Sounder was the first to appear. I was delighted to see Sounder at last growing into his job and leading the pack. As far as I knew, this was a first for him.

"Tally ho, gray fox!" I called triumphantly. "Sounder, Rufus, Solo all heading west."

Seconds later, a huge coyote bounded across the field moving too fast for me to get in front of it and attempt to turn it away from the highway. We tried, but to no avail. As we were galloping, I reported to Griffen. So far, no hounds on him.

"Make sure nothing follows that coyote – whatever you do – keep them all on the fox!" he barked.

My heart was racing. I had only seen half the pack come out on the fox. I hoped the rest had honored Sounder. Then, my heart sank as three hounds popped out on the coyote.

"No! Leave it! No!" I screamed and cracked my whip.

"Valiant, Victor, and Saber on the coyote heading east – not stopping!" I reported as we galloped ahead of them.

"Come on, Elliott! Get *to* them and stop them! What were you doing? Don't let them get on that road!" Griffen raged. I turned off my radio to keep from saying things a lady should never think, much less say to the huntsman on the air.

"Leave it!" I screamed, whip cracking, *well, sort-of*, hounds still ignoring. The ground was flying past as Viva stretched to her full, glorious, length planeing out like a racing boat at her top speed in no time. We were fast approaching the highway, and the coyote was still ahead – there was no way that we were gong to be able to catch him in time. Hounds were fifty yards behind, so I was going to have to do something drastic.

Ever so slightly, I sat back in the saddle and turned Viva, positioning her between the coyote and the hounds. The whole time I was screaming "Leave it!" at the top of my lungs. Hounds were coming on strong –

I was being ignored. We were so close to the highway that I could feel cars and worse, trucks, roaring...I had no choice –

Galloping straight into the hounds directly on the coyote's line, I ran over Valiant, and he yelped when we rolled him. Victor paused, and Saber froze.

"Leave it!" I screamed and jumped off Viva to grab Valiant. He did not move far, for he was holding up his hind leg and yelping pitifully. I let him go and snapped a couple strap to Victor and Saber as they trotted over to investigate, wrapped my belt around Viva's forelegs, then bent to check on Valiant. I approached him slowly, hoping he wouldn't bite, for his leg was clearly broken. He was in pain, but his eyes were soft and trusting. *Why? I could not imagine. What a sweet hound.*

I turned my radio back on in time to hear Griffen calling, or rather yelling, at me.

"Elliott! What is going on with my hounds?"

"I have the three that were on the coyote; they're stopped. But I need a truck. Valiant's leg is broken, and we're right next to the highway," I said.

"Are you hurt?" Griffen asked.

"No," I said.

"Then why weren't you answering your radio?" he roared.

"I've been busy," I snapped back.

"I'm bringing the truck," Eilene said.

"We're near the tractor shed," I said.

I made a mental note to ride in the field or visit my parents the next time Griffen hunted the hounds. I was glad that Eilene had arrived; she was one of the Masters and would, hopefully, lend some balance to Griffen's raging. All in all, he had done well, right up to when I nearly killed a hound. *Oh well, I'm sure I'd hear all about it.* And I was too angry, sad, tired, and disappointed in who Griffen was letting himself become to care. After all, this was supposed to be fun. And Daddy was worried about me pulling a horse trailer in the dark. *I'm so glad he did not know the things I did on a horse. Or the kind of guy I had fallen in love with.*

I cradled Valiant in my lap holding his head gently and stroking his big, floppy ears. I tied my stock tie around his muzzle so he wouldn't snap at anyone when we had to move him. He didn't protest, too badly. I ran my hands along his silky coat and somehow, this calmed me.

Griffen appeared in all his raging glory with Addy and the field. He glared down at me like a Lord to a serf. I looked up and met his green, glowering, eyes and was pierced with a sadness that I couldn't suppress. All the anger toward him had sunken to pity…and that was far worse. I was losing him…to his choices. He was letting his temper rule him in something as insignificant as a hunt field. *How would he react to real pressures life will throw him? And who would be the one who would bear the brunt of all that anger?* My heart would never recover from what had to be done…

"What happened?" he barked.

"He broke his leg," I said.

"How?" he asked.

Before I could answer, Eilene pulled up and saved me the trouble. She took Jet's bridle and motioned for Griffen to lift the hound into the seat of her truck. I uncoupled the other hounds, retrieved my belt, and swung up on Viva. I took a quick count of the hounds and noticed they were all here before I rode over to check on Addy.

"How was it?" I asked, trying to sound brighter than I felt.

"Great!" she said a little too cheerfully.

Christopher met my eyes, nodded in acknowledgement, and looked away. Ben was not here, and Stephen was just now trotting over to join us. I wondered if Ben was going to kill Griffen. He had not heard his remark to Addy, but everyone else had, and I knew Ben well enough that it was only a matter of time before Griffen would pay for that. It made me sad that I didn't care at the moment that the one I supposedly, well, *did* love, was in grave danger and probably didn't even know it. It's one thing for him to be rude to me...entirely another for him to embarrass Addy. Part of me wanted Ben to deck him; most of me just wanted Ben to punch out the bad and leave me the good. I was definitely getting delirious.

Thankfully, the hounds gave us no trouble on the way in. I rode in front of the pack, so I wouldn't have to look at Griffen. I knew I needed to leave quickly or my resolve not to give in to him would vanish. I couldn't act like nothing had happened and let him use his charisma and charm to keep me addicted to him. We, or rather I, needed some space...some distance...from Griffen Case.

When we got back to the trailers, I didn't want Griffen to notice how upset I was, so I collected the radios as instructed, put them in the box, and returned them to their proper place. Everyone was congratulating him on a spectacular first solo hunt and Eilene had her arm around him, praising him for standing up to Lydia. Slipping stealthily through the jubilant crowd, I noticed that neither Ben nor Addy was around. After I made the obligatory pass at the food and mingled for an acceptable amount of time, I slipped out, unnoticed.

I drove in silence, the distance from Griffen giving me courage as the road pulled at my thoughts. It would be hard to find a way without him now that I had fallen in love, but I knew it had to be done. We had been balancing this since he moved here in August, and it was now toward the end of November. We had been in the same city for almost four months now. So far, he was not making any attempt to control his anger, and there was nothing that I could do, except put some distance between us and date other people, that might possibly get him to see what he was doing or motivate him to change.

Cell phone buzzed – 615. This will be interesting.

"Hello," I said.

"Where are you?" he said. "I've been looking everywhere."

"About thirty minutes from the barn," I said.

"What barn?"

"Oxford."

"Oxford? Why? What's wrong?" he asked.

"Because you're having to ask, everything," I said and did what I could to steady my voice. It was starting to quiver, and the last thing I needed was him on my doorstep…today.

"What kind of cryptic answer is that?" he demanded.

"The truth," I said, keeping my responses short so he would not know I was crying.

"I'm coming to get you," he said, much softer. "I was hard on you today, Elliott, and I'm sorry."

"No, I'm going home for a few days," I said. "I'll be back Tuesday."

"Please don't leave before I can see you," he said. "Something's wrong, I can hear it. You don't need to drive to Canton today. At least let me take you if you need to go."

"Thanks, but I'm fine. Goodbye," I said and hung up the phone.

I felt the tears come, so I pulled over to the side of the highway.

For fifteen minutes, tears streamed from my eyes. Body heaving in sobs, I crouched over the steering wheel and let the pain surge through me. I had to be strong to do this, so I needed to cry all this out.

Why had I not just ended this before I had fallen in love? But when was I not in love with Griffen? He hit me like a bolt from the start. Why won't he see what he's throwing away? God, why don't you *change him? What am I doing yelling at God over a guy, even if it* is *Griffen? Surely I'll be struck down now. Old Testament retribution…moving into modern times.*

I was starting to think crazy thoughts, so the worst, for now, must be over. I pulled back onto the highway and continued to the barn. By the time I turned Viva into her paddock and put her tack away, Griffen's truck roared into the driveway…no horse trailer. He'd left Jet in Memphis and driven – no telling how fast – to find me. *This was not good…because my other side rejoiced.*

HURRICANE

Chapter 14

Great riders quietly guide, not force, their horses to learn.

I resisted the urge to run, but I knew instantly that is exactly what I should have done. As soon as I saw him, so worried, so anxious, so magnificent, my anger and pity vanished, and all that was left was the longing. *Longing…not leaving…wins every time.*

He locked his gaze on me and once again, I was paralyzed. Before I could move or protest, he swept me up in his arms and kissed me. My knees buckled, and my bones went soft.

"Elliott, Elliott," he whispered kissing my neck and throat. "My Elliott, where do you think you're going?"

"Away, for a while," I stammered.

"Not without saying goodbye, I hope," he said and moved back up to my lips.

"I said goodbye, on the phone," I muttered.

He released me and looked into my eyes, searching for answers I did not want to give. Another car pulled up – someone coming for lessons – and he stepped back to a respectable distance.

"Come inside," he commanded, not asking, and pulled me into the barn. "Talk to me."

"Griffen, I…" I tried to form the words, but this was not the place. "Let's find somewhere a little more…public."

"I don't like the sound of that at all," he said and rubbed his finger along my jaw. "But if that's what you want, I'll follow you outside."

We walked to the big tree and sat on the picnic table beneath it. Kids poured out of the van for their afternoon lessons, and it was hard to believe that it was only noon. It seemed like this day had lasted an eternity.

"I cannot accept you like you were today," I said, at last. "You were not the Griffen I love. I don't know what you did with him, but he wasn't there."

"You are right, Elliott," he said, immediately. "I thought about what you said all the way here, and the way I behaved was wrong."

"Why did you do it then?" I asked.

"No excuse, but I will tell you this, so maybe you can understand, and…help me," he said.

My heart fluttered at that thought – the thought that he was admitting that he needed help. This was too good to be true.

"I wanted everything to be perfect, to do a good job for William, and I was way too nervous. Just like those hunting harpy women we hate so much, I was right in there with them, snapping at the people I love the most. By the way, I apologized to Addy in front of the whole party *before* Ben found me. He punched me anyway, but I deserved it and let him live," he said and grinned at the memory.

Guys are so strange. Would I ever understand their logic?

"Do I have to apologize for running off Lydia?" he asked, amused.

"No way, that was great!" I said and smiled for the first time in a while.

"There's my Elliott," he said and pushed a loose strand of hair behind my ear. I shuddered and tried to remain focused.

"And, just so you'll know," he announced, "I was not mad at you about Valiant's leg. I was *worried* about you! You had the strangest look on your face, almost like you were in shock. I thought you had fallen from Viva until I saw you had her hobbled."

"I thought you were mad," I said. "And it made me sad that you had run away with the Griffen I loved."

He leaned in very close. Then, in spite of the public spot, he kissed me gently. "Dear, dear Elliott, I love you so much," he whispered.

I closed my eyes and knew he'd won. And was glad. Hope restored again...*Please dear Lord, let this last, let this be real.*

The week flew by with last minute preparations for Opening Meet. I was only able to see Griffen a little, for he was swamped with studying trying to get ahead, so he could spend two days in Memphis.

It looked like we were going to have one of the largest crowds ever, for our outreach program to the barns had worked better than any of us could have expected for several reasons. This was a home and night game weekend for Ole Miss, so people were not traveling and had the morning free. There were no horse shows scheduled in the area, the weather promised to be spectacular, and the barns could not resist our competition.

I had agreed to get Jet ready for Griffen, so I pulled into the barn at an insanely early hour to braid his and Viva's manes and tails. This job was best done the morning of the events, for keeping the tiny plaits in their hair damaged it. The air was cold, and I dreaded how numb my fingers were about to be. They heard me arrive and poked their pretty heads out of the stall looking for breakfast.

"Hey babies," I said as they blinked the sleep out of their eyes. "Good morning. You ready for this?" I handed Viva an apple, and Jet nickered in protest. "Here's yours, silly, just hang on."

To keep their heads still, I refilled the hayracks and fed them. I then walked back to get my braiding kit…black yarn, scissors, mane comb, rubber bands, hair clips, hair gel, and brushes, and packed what I needed in an apron that hung from my neck much like a chef's apron. This helped me contain everything I needed within reach. I grabbed a stool and stepped in Jet's stall.

To my horror, he had a huge gash behind his left leg that was going to prevent him from hunting for a while. Blood was everywhere, but it looked like the wound had stopped bleeding. He was stiff, but it didn't look like he had any permanent damage. *Griffen will go through the roof.*

I immediately went into task triage mode. It was too early to call the vet, and this was not life threatening. I would get Ashley to handle this – she didn't have to be in Memphis as early as we did since she wasn't riding. William had a new horse that he wanted us to ride for him…now was as good as ever. I'd get him to bring that one for Griffen. Maybe I could get up there in time to braid it, too.

I led Jet out of his stall to clean his mess and get a better look at the damage. He protested mostly because I pulled him away from his food. I bathed the wound in warm water causing it to bleed a little, washed it with betadine, and returned him to his stall. It was not in a place that I could bandage, and it was definitely going to need stitches. I decided to tie him to make sure he did not roll and infect the area worse.

I sent Ashley a text, since I knew she was probably not awake yet. I knew William and Sylvia would be up at this crazy hour, so I called their house. No one answered. I left a message that Griffen would need Rocket if he was still available and to call me as soon as one of them got the message. Between us, we really did need another horse, but I certainly could not afford the upkeep on another one. It was a miracle that we had not had to do this before now. We had been lucky that Viva and Jet were never lame as often and as hard as they were ridden. *Oh well, so much for that.*

I braided Viva, wiped down my tack once more, and loaded everything in Griffen's trailer. William said he would have one of the barn girls there get Rocket ready and braided for Griffen, and I breathed a sigh of relief. That was one extra hour I did not have that he just saved me. Griffen didn't take the news well, as expected, but he appeared on time with a toasted English muffin and sausage for me.

"Thank you for handling all that this morning," Griffen said after he had inspected Jet's leg. "I'm glad it's not worse, but I hate not to have him for this weekend. Who knows what Rocket will do? Opening Meet is not exactly the best time to start a young horse."

"Ah, just more of a challenge for you, darling," I said and kissed his cheek. "You can ride anything."

"And I'm sure we'll have to ride separately," he said ignoring my compliment. "With all the world coming because of your recruiting efforts, everyone will be scrambling."

"Don't you just *love* a challenge?" I said and winked at him. "It will make it all the more sweet when we're alone…"

"Yeah, when? Next week?" he snarled and pulled me close for

another round of glorious kisses.

"We have *got* to go," I said and stood up.

The big stone house and elegant grounds were already abuzz with activity when we arrived. I unloaded Viva and got her settled with a hay net in her place for the morning and tacked her up. Griffen left to check on Rocket, and I inspected the kid tally-ho wagon. Everything was in order there, so I left to see if Griffen needed help.

I heard him before I saw him. There was a loud bang in the barn followed by a shout that sounded more like a roar. When I got there, Griffen was furious.

"He just tried to kick me!" Griffen barked. "Nutcase hit the stall door instead."

Rocket's chocolate eyes blazed, and he glared at us, sides heaving, nostrils flaring, ears twitching. He shook his head and stalked in large circles around the stall. He looked terrified, angry…and beautiful. The tiny braids accentuated his snake-like neck, and he held his tail high, even confined in this tiny spot.

"He's magnificent," I said under my breath.

"The color of nutmeg…the heat of ginger…all air and fire – not a bit of earth and water," Griffen said sardonically under his breath. "Looks like Shakespeare's words will follow me to my grave."

"At least you'll look good," I said.

"Easy for you to say. I'm the one who has to ride him," he snarled. "And he just took his best shot at killing me."

"Maybe it's the braids," I said.

"They're staying in. He'll have to deal with them."

The grounds were filing up quickly…beautiful horses floated across the lawn, riders were resplendent in their best attire, and spectators everywhere admired the scene. November hickories and their golden branches embraced the reds and browns of other, less colorful trees. The dark green evergreens stood alongside as if their purpose this season was to accentuate the spectacle of the surrounding hardwoods.

Ashley said the vet would be out to take care of Jet that afternoon, and I was relieved. Mother *and* Daddy had come with Ben's parents since they were all going to the football game in Oxford that night, and we had a brief, but very nice visit. Mother and Carolyn bid on everything in sight. This was their favorite place to start their Christmas shopping, and I was glad they chose to spend their money for our hounds.

All the planning and preparing paid off, and I admired the scene from Viva as the priest began the beautiful blessing chant. One lady on a spectacular gray rode sidesaddle, and their elegance took my breath away. Children on ponies surrounded her, and I made a note to myself to meet her and learn how she does that. *Some day…*

Everyone was quiet and their horses still, except a few errant ponies, a new horse or two…and Griffen. Rocket looked like he did this morning in the stall, except he had now been released with a rider, and neither seemed pleased with their lot.

Watching Griffen ride a horse like that truly revealed his gift. He remained calm, almost motionless, in the saddle, while Rocket exploded any time the smallest irritation provoked him. He shimmered with energy, his bright chestnut coat gleaming with golden highlights that sparkled with his constant movement. Griffen had him walking, slowly, steadily, keeping Rocket's feet moving forward rather than up or out. His reins were loose, almost slack, and Rocket chomped at the metal between his jaws in protest. His mouth was foaming, and that was a good sign, I hoped. Specks of white lather appeared under his breastplate in spite of the brisk morning air. *This was going to be a long day for both of them.*

Spice, one of the hounds, wandered toward Griffen before Susan could stop her. Griffen quickly turned Rocket to face Spice, so he would not be able to kick her and dropped the thong of his whip to warn Spice to get back. Rocket reared in protest, but Griffen remained calm. Spice hesitated, then returned to the safety of the pack.

Lydia could hardly contain her glee at Griffen's predicament. She was back, in spite of the Masters having supported Griffen's decision to run her off last weekend, and she was as bitter as ever toward Griffen and me. I did not understand why someone as nice as Stephen put up with her. Then I thought about how Griffen could be and decided to keep my thoughts to myself. *I really hope Griffen is past all that.*

"Elliott, Susan, and Stephen, please ride ahead to your positions," William said. "Find us a coyote, for Griffen's sake!"

"Nice horse, William," Griffen snapped.

"Yeah, well, you two deserve each other," William said. "Don't you hurt my horse."

"Not until he throws the first punch," Griffen said. "Then its legal for me to kill him."

"You don't want to have to buy that one," William said.

"We'll see," Griffen barked. "It might be the best money I spend all year."

After that exchange, we were so busy that I hardly had time to speak. The hounds struck immediately on a bobcat, which was the worst thing that could happen to Griffen. We got all worked up and galloped to the creek, but the hounds circled on the cat for thirty minutes.

Staff had nowhere to go, and the field stood and watched. It was great for watching hound work but difficult on fractious horses. I could only imagine how Rocket was handling this.

Finally, they put the cat to "ground" in a deep hole underneath some roots along the big ditch. William cheered the hounds for their success, lifted them away from the angry bobcat's lair, and cast them to the east. Susan viewed a coyote, and the pack burst from the covert right behind him. The coyote took us across the entire property in minutes. Members of the field were exhilarated, covered in mud, and overjoyed. Some were still mounted, but a few were scattered about the countryside.

Most of the hounds were in, but a few escaped Susan, and we gathered the tracking equipment and two large dog boxes so we could collect them. Stephen had unhooked his truck and Lydia, William, and I piled in with him to help. Griffen and Susan were trying to stay with the remaining pack.

"Where are you, Griffen?" William asked.

"By the graveyard," he said. "They're still on the coyote."

Stephen sped to the spot, but they had moved north by the time we arrived. They were quiet now, and we set up the tracker to see which way they were going. William blew his horn. I had the hound list and read out which hounds were showing up on the signal.

"Griffen, go east," I said. "I'm getting several signals that way. It looks like Spice and Servant."

"Servant is not one of ours," Griffen barked.

"He's on the list," I said.

"That's a misprint," William said to me. "It's Seven."

"Are you going east?" I asked Griffen over the radio.

"Yes, Elliott!" he snapped way too forcefully.

Lydia beamed. "Nice," she mumbled to me and grinned.

I felt my face flush. *Not again. Not in front of* her *of all people.* I stayed off the radio but tried to look like his remark was no big deal. William looked at me, but I looked away before he met my eyes and pretended not to notice.

We finally collected the hounds and gathered them in the truck. Susan rode up, but still no Griffen. Since I had not attempted to call Griffen, William did.

"Griffen, where are you?" William asked. "We have all the hounds."

"I'm going back to the barn," he said. "I'm closer to the house than to you."

When we returned, most everyone was gone. A few people were left picking up trash and folding up all the chairs. We put the hounds in the kennel and met Griffen as we were leaving.

He looked all wrong, and I moved toward him to put my arm on his. As I reached out to him, he pulled abruptly away and left the room. Lydia and William looked at me and I stood there, mouth agape. *Not again. This is so embarrassing. He is acting like a spoiled child.*

"I'll talk to him," William said and followed him out the door.

This left me alone with Lydia. *Oh joy.*

She turned on me, eyes glinting with malice.

"You know, I've never liked you, Elliott," she hissed. "But now, I just pity you. If he treats you like this in front of us, I can only imagine what he says to you when you're alone. You're a disgrace…following him around slobbering after him while he just steps on you and twists his toe to crush you in the dirt…you know, like you do when you step on a roach. I'm looking forward to hearing you 'pop'. I just wonder how long it'll take."

"You're sick," I spat, for that was all I could think to say. Her words hit home way better than she'd intended, and I had to get away from her before she could see my reaction. I would not give her the satisfaction of watching me 'pop' as she had so eloquently stated. I wanted to be sick but certainly not in front of her.

All my Southernmother training prevented me from saying or doing anything unladylike to her, but unfortunately, nothing clever had come to mind that I could have done anyway. That, in itself, was depressing. When it came down to it, I was embarrassed...and could think of nothing to say. What Lydia said was too true.

Griffen was quiet as we rode back to the barn in Oxford. He didn't say much about Rocket except that he would ride him tomorrow. I didn't want to fight with him, so I sat quietly in the truck. We listened to his music in our own little worlds. The vet had done a good job on Jet, and Griffen spent a good deal of time in the stall with him.

I let them have some privacy and started taking out Viva's braids. After a little while, he joined me in her stall, wrapped his arms around me from behind, and whispered into my neck, "you looked beautiful today, as always," he said.

I leaned back into him, enjoying the comfort of his arms and letting his presence surround me. I had not forgotten today, but I had no energy left for fighting. It would go no good. That was becoming clear the more time I spent with him in stressful situations. I fought back the tears that wanted to burst from within me. This wasn't going to last, but I didn't want to end it until the weekend was over. I would enjoy every precious moment I had in the eye of the hurricane with Griffen, this Griffen, the one I loved, and treasure the good memories forever.

AFTERMATH

Chapter 15

Four things greater than all things are –
Women and Horses and Power and War.

~ *Rudyard Kipling, "The Ballad of the King's Jest"*

He picked me up at the sorority house 6:00 pm, and we drove back to Memphis. Ashley had planned the evening party, and I knew it would be fabulous. She promised me there would be a place to dance under the stars, and I could not wait to see.

"I've been thinking about this morning, Elliott," Griffen said as we listened to jazz music in his truck. "I let things get a little out of hand again, and I'm sorry."

"Griffen, I really don't want to talk about this morning right now," I said gently. "You had a lot to have to deal with riding Rocket. I want to dance with you and enjoy this night and forget everything about this morning."

He looked at me curiously but did not press. He lifted my hand to his lips and kissed my fingers gently. For the first time ever, nothing happened – no pounding heart when he did that, but I closed my eyes anyway and leaned my head back on the seat. *I'm going to enjoy this weekend with him, my best friend, no matter what.*

We pulled into the restaurant and walked to the back where Ashley and her committee had reserved a huge room for us to play. There was a tiny spiral staircase that looked like it led to the roof – that would be perfect for dancing under the stars. The band was just setting up, and food was everywhere.

"Elliott! You and Griffen have *got* to go see the view from the roof," she said. "That's what sealed the deal for me."

"Let's go," Griffen said and pulled me with him. I felt like I was in the wake of a ski boat.

The tiny stairs would be interesting after the party got going, and I smiled at what merriment it would provide later. Griffen stopped at the top, smiling satisfactorily that we were actually alone.

"I love you," he said and pulled me close, then kissed me gently.

I kissed him back, but there was no hunger in my response. The morning's events had definitely left their marks. I hoped he wouldn't notice, but he did. He looked at me, eyes guarded, and stepped away. "Let's see what Ashley found for us to eat," he said.

My heart tugged and started to ache. I wanted him to stay this Griffen all the time. My predictable, hungry, gorgeous Griffen.

More people had arrived and as the evening went on, the room was almost impossible to negotiate. The band played great music ranging from country to rock to blues and even 40's swing band tunes – and all the songs kept me dancing. As usual, I didn't dance with Griffen on fast songs; that was not his style. He found me, though, every time the music slowed and wrapped me in his arms.

"You smell wonderful," he said into my neck, a rare treat for him to show affection in such a public place, and I shivered…*at last.*

"Watch it, Griffen," I teased, "Or I'll have you thrown out to where it's a little more private."

He grinned and relaxed, seeing the spark return in my eyes. I was glad, too, and wanted badly now to return to the roof.

"Let's go to the roof," he said, reading my mind.

"Lead the way," I said and followed him.

Addy knew what we were up to and winked at me as we passed. Everyone else was engrossed in their food, conversations, or dancing and didn't notice us leave. We passed Lydia and Stephen on the way, and she flashed us a big grin.

"What's gotten in to her I wonder?" Griffen asked.

I didn't respond, but my euphoric feelings vanished. *So fragile now, these feelings.*

"Let's get something to eat before we go," I said.

Griffen stopped, not pleased, but turned back toward the food tables. "Whatever you want," he said, but his tone was flat and disappointed. "I'll get some drinks." He left me with the food, and I turned when I heard someone call my name.

"Elliott!" Susan said. "I want you to meet someone. This is my friend Daniel, Daniel Peters. He's the new vet that will be working in Memphis with Dr. Halliday. Elliot is another one of our whippers-in, and she goes to Ole Miss."

"Hello Elliott," Daniel said. His voice was soft, but his eyes were astounding. They were pale blue and seemed to stand out from his otherwise plain face. And they were taking all of me in with great appreciation.

I worried a little about that, but it was…nice.

"Nice, to meet you, too," I stammered, surprised that I found myself smiling back at him a little more than I usually do and blushed. He noticed. I looked down. *No ring on his finger. Oh my, not safe.*

"Susan," Griffen said as he approached with our drinks.

"Hello Griffen," Susan said and grinned up at him. "I was just introducing Daniel to Elliott. He's a vet here in Memphis. Daniel Peters, this is Griffen Case. He's also a whipper-in for us and a law student."

"Ah, I remember those *student* days," Daniel said, clearly making the point that he was no longer one of us. "It is nice to have a little income, at last, to better be able to appreciate the finer things in life."

He looked at me when he said that, and I blushed…again. Griffen did not miss my blush or his undertones and stiffened.

"Fortunately, I'm not attracted to ladies who require me to purchase their presence," he said. "Elliott?" He lifted his arm to me in the unmistakable gesture that would require me to put my hand on his arm and walk away with him, the victor. *Boys and their games. Trees again – marking territory. Ridiculous.*

I filled my plate when we reached the table even though my appetite was gone. There was so much going on in my heart, and I wanted it all to go away. The music was too loud for talking, so we ate and watched everyone dance and visit and generally have a raucously good time. Even the reserved William and Sylvia were dancing, and that was a funny sight.

"To the roof," Griffen said, noticing I had finally cleaned my plate. He pulled me along, and we negotiated the staircase with ease.

The music had slowed, and there were no other couples on the roof. Stars were doing their best to shine in spite of the suburban glow, and they twinkled down on us congratulating Griffen in his effort to get me alone. He looked at me and said nothing, just stared intently into my eyes. It worked, and my body went limp again. Feeling my tension vanish, he kissed me and pulled me tightly to him – much tighter than usual in such a public place – and I felt my head spin.

The music changed to something much faster, but he kept holding me and kissing me, and I wanted this to last forever even though I knew it could not. I pushed those thoughts as far away as I could and ran my fingers through his soft hair and down his iron arms lightly touching his velvet skin.

"Time to go, Elliott," he whispered.

"Where?" I said, blinking to clear my thought.

"Somewhere more public," he smiled. "Or home. You tell me."

"Let's stay here a little while longer," I said. "I don't want to hurt Ashley's feelings."

We remained for one more dance, but soon he guided me to the stairs. With each step downwards, I felt like I was being lowered back to earth, and my heart resisted. I wanted to stay with him on that rooftop forever – in his arms – just like that – no complications. It was not going to happen.

When we returned, the first face I saw was Lydia's, and she threw another evil grin at me. Griffin didn't notice that time. The music picked up even more, so I left Griffen to dance with Christopher while Griffen went to finalize the plans for tomorrow with William. Christopher and I danced around everyone, and I loved playing with these great friends, dancing like crazy, and letting the music take us away.

The song changed and suddenly Daniel stepped between Christopher and me.

"Do you mind?" Daniel asked Christopher.

"No, sure," he said looking at me.

"Daniel, this is Christopher James, another whipper-in and a graduate student at Ole Miss," I said. "Christopher, this is Dr. Daniel Peters. He works with Dr. Halliday."

"Nice to meet you," Christopher said. "I hope not to be needing you any time soon, though." He smiled, claimed another willing partner, and left us.

The music was loud, so it was hard to talk. We had to lean into each other and yell to be heard.

"How long have you been riding?" Daniel shouted.

"Only a few years," I shouted back. "Do you ride?"

"Some," he said. "I'm coming tomorrow with Susan."

The music changed to a slow tune, and before I could turn back to the food table, he'd put his arms around my waist. I was surprised, but his touch was casual, nothing overt in spite of it being at my waist rather than my arm, so I decided to dance this one out. The gesture made me uncomfortable, but I tried not to show it.

"Do you have a horse?" I asked, immediately thinking that surely he did if he was a horse vet and how stupid that must have sounded.

"A few," he said. "But I've only foxhunted twice. So, I'm not sure what will happen tomorrow."

"Susan will take good care of you," I said. "Will you be riding with her?"

"I don't think so. She said I'll be in first flight with some guy named Ben," he said.

"Ben is one of my best friends," I said. "He'll make sure you have fun."

"I see you have a lot of guys for friends," he said, locking his blue eyes on mine. I could feel him subtly pushing the envelope with his grip on my waist and wasn't sure exactly what he meant by that comment. The music was ending, and I was glad. I certainly did not need *this* tonight. I looked up to see Griffen approach.

"Care to dance?" Griffen said as he approached us.

"Now I *think*, Griffen," Daniel said, "that it is up to the lady to end the dance."

"Two songs," Griffen said. "More monopolizes her. Basic dance manners, Dr. Peters."

"Thank you, Daniel," I said over my shoulder as I gratefully took Grifen's hand.

He spun me away and over to the band. I smiled at his gesture, but it was a little over the top.

"*You've* danced with me for a lot more than two dances," I said, trying to lighten his brooding mood.

"Not in a row," he said. "And I brought you here. But technically, that doesn't matter in a place like this. It's not exactly a place to exercise proper dance etiquette. Like *that guy* would know anything about it."

"And you would?" I asked, curious.

"Of course," he said deviously. "My mother forced me to take formal dance lessons when I was fourteen. It was awful, but I've just now found it useful."

We made one more trip to the roof. Others had discovered its magic, so we were not alone. It was still lovely, though, just having him hold me next to him under the stars. Like I had hoped, the party was magical…memories of those rooftop dances would stay with me for a lifetime.

On Sunday, we had a full staff and a lot of members and guests, and I could hardly wait to see what the day would hold. William said we could whip-in together today, and I was delighted. It would be fun to see how Griffen rode the fireball.

Daniel did show up with Susan, and he was riding with Ben and Addy, as I had expected. He and his horse fit perfectly, although the horse looked a little over-excited to be in such a charged atmosphere. He was a handsome bay with two white socks on his hind legs and a broad blaze down his face. His coat shimmered with good health and grooming – well kept. *Must be nice to belong to a vet.*

Griffen and I were covering the east side, Bob and Susan were going north, Stephen was covering the west, Bo was in the south, and Lydia had been asked to ride with William, I was sure, to let her know he still supported her. William was gifted at ensuring everyone got along. It was probably harder to keep *us* in order than the hounds.

William sent us on hoping to keep Rocket from kicking any hounds. He, too, shimmered in the November light and was mesmerizing to watch at all his paces. He held his tail high, as if he knew it made people notice him, and his head and neck were arched, balancing his frame perfectly. He'd already thrown about six bucks at Griffen who took it all in stride.

"Why don't you smack him when he does that?" I asked.

"A hunt's not the place for smacking horses, Elliott. That would be like cursing in front of ladies. Here we ride," he said and grinned.

I noticed that Griffen seemed to do more riding than teaching, at least, to my untrained eye. He was an incredible horseman. Most riders I knew concentrated on making horses do their bidding but not Griffen.

He rode all of them differently, letting them be the individuals they were, and the result was magical. Even the oldest plodder pranced when he carried him. It was hard to explain, but I hoped to emulate it someday.

I let Viva get too close, and Rocket let fly with a menacing kick that nearly dislodged me. Griffen growled his disapproval at Rocket and spurred him into a gallop. He bucked twice before he reached top speed, and we followed at a much safer distance. Two runs later, it was time to call it a day. Rocket was heaving, but he was much more manageable. It looked like he was finally relaxing into his job. We kept our distance, but Griffen was beginning to lose his patience…again.

"Jet needs to get better, soon," he said. "I can't get *near* you on this horse for fear of him getting you or Viva. What's the point of getting to be alone with you all day when I have to deal with this idiot?"

"You'll get your turn," I said. "You have me all the time."

My smile did not reach my eyes, though, for I knew the weekend was coming to a close. The day had been magical, but then again, it was a *perfect* day. *How many days are perfect in the real world?*

Griffen rode Rocket to the hunt house barn and asked me to be sure to let Panzer out of my trailer for him when I got there. I assured him I would and headed back to my trailer with Viva. Daniel was already there waiting for me, his horse tied to his trailer that was parked not too far away.

"You have a lovely horse," he said.

"Thanks," I said. "You, too. How was your day?"

"I'll be back, if that's what you mean," he said. "This is a great hunt, and Ben was a lot of fun to ride behind. He kept us right up with William the whole time, and Addy made me laugh all morning."

"That's no surprise," I said and smiled at the thought.

He held Viva's reins while I dismounted and untacked her.

"What's her name?" he asked, as he stroked her head and neck.

"Viva," I said, pleased that he had thought to ask.

"You ride her well," he said.

"Thanks," I said and blushed. "Um, have you had breakfast?"

"No, I am hungry, though," he said. "I'll walk with you. Will you make sure I don't mess up any of their names? Susan introduced me earlier, but I'd appreciate a guide. She's still out with the hounds."

"No, I'll be glad to," I said. "Just give me a second to change."

I replaced my hard hat with my brown waxed cotton one and exchanged my filthy, heavy red coat for a clean tweed…manners training overriding my raging appetite. Grand would start fussing if I showed up filthy around the food. When we walked into the hunt house, I made sure to reacquaint him with several others before I went to check on Griffen. I turned to leave right as Griffen walked in and marched straight over to me, eyes blazing.

"You forgot Panzer," he said, jaws clenched. "You *said* you'd let him out for me."

"Oh, sorry," I said, and felt Daniel's eyes on me. My face flushed at the realization that he had overheard Griffen talk to me like that, even if it was barely audible. His anger was mercurial and so out of place and out of proportion.

"What were you doing?" he snapped.

"I just forgot, Griffen," I said.

"It was my fault," Daniel said, and Griffen looked up in surprise. "I distracted her."

"Oh, really?" he asked, eyes glinting like a rattler's realizing a mouse had just approached.

"She was nice enough to agree to help me navigate this sea of sharks," he said. "It's embarrassing for me to admit that I have a hard time with names."

"I am sorry to have to relieve you of your able captain," he said. "But we were just leaving."

He walked me to the truck, and I knew the time had come for me to end this charade. He could refrain from smacking a crazy horse in public, but he had no problem snapping at me. Never cursing, but spewing such venom when he was irritated…to me that was worse.

Even though I knew I had to do this, I still couldn't do it – not now. I would wait until we got to the barn – after we checked on Jet. No, I'd have to wait until right before I got in my car. If he had the chance to touch me, or even worse, hold me, alone, I'd never have the willpower to resist him. But I could not, *would not*, do this over the phone. The House…I'll make up some reason for him to come to the sorority house, and I'll tell him in the courtyard.

We rolled the windows down and headed south, the cool wind blowing our hair and music blaring. I laid my head back on the seat dreading the next few hours. At the barn, Jet looked fine, and we put Viva next to him to keep him company. He would not be turned out until the next day, so I made her stay up.

"Griffen, I've got something for you at the House. Will you come by there before you go home?" I asked casually.

"Why don't you just bring it to my house," he asked. "I'm ready to have you to myself for a while."

"I thought you had to study," I said, my stomach clenching with each carefully planned word.

"It can wait," he said and pulled me to him. "I really need you right now." He bent to kiss me, but a car was pulling up, and we backed away from each other looking innocent.

"I'll see you at the house," I said before he could protest and drove away.

Tears were trying to well up, but I forced them back. Grand was with me, speaking softly, and giving me courage.

"Just make this easy, Elliott. Tell him you need space, just for a while, and be gentle. You can't change him yourself, so this is the only hope you have for him to ever really change. If this does not do it, nothing will. This is your only chance to save what you have with him."

He was following me, thank goodness. My heart was pounding, and I hoped Grand was right. This would hurt, but this gave me hope. And it was up to me alone to make this happen – for us.

He parked beside me in the parking lot, and I was surprised to find that there were no other people around. *This may actually be a better place than the courtyard where we were likely to be bombarded with inquiring eyes.*

"Griffen, come over here and sit down," I said, indicating a large tree that was behind the parking area. There were no people nearby, and the ground around it was cool and soft. But, it was public enough that I did not have to worry about him affecting me like he always did when we were alone.

"Remember, the whole point of this is to get him back. You are doing this because you love him," Grand said.

By now, Griffen could tell something was wrong. He said nothing and sat by the tree. I sat beside him at a safe distance and pushed a stick through the pine straw.

"What's on your mind, Elliott?" he asked, his eyes wary and gorgeous. I looked into them, then looked away and continued playing with the stick.

"It is not fair for me to ask you to be anyone else than who you are," I said, carefully choosing my words knowing each contained the power to build or break our relationship forever. "I love you more than anyone in this world, Griffen, but there is a part in you that I will not choose to spend the rest of my life fearing."

I paused and swallowed, trying to collect my thoughts. Griffen was motionless.

"I need some space, Griffen. I love everything about you but the part I cannot change, and it is not my place to do that. I can't continue to date only you when that part of you keeps coming back," I said, astounded that my voice held steady.

Griffen didn't move. I could feel him looking at me, but I did not dare meet his eyes. One look, and I knew I would melt. I kept playing with the stick and avoiding his gaze. After a few moments – moments that seemed like an eternity – he spoke.

"Elliott," he said. "I told you I love you, and that I would leave you if I could not be the person you needed…someone you would choose to spend the rest of your life with. So, I will do just that. Starting today."

My heart stopped beating, and the world around me started to spin. I looked up at his eyes and wanted to reach out and hold him and take it all back. I wanted him to be wrapped around me, swimming in the lake with me, kissing me…but he was leaving me…and it was my idea.

He reached over and touched my chin with his fingertip. "I do love you, Elliott. Never forget it."

He walked to his truck and drove away.

SEPARATION

Chapter 16

It is not enough for a man to know how to ride; he must know how to fall.

~ Mexican Proverb

There was nothing left for me to do that day but crawl in my bed and cry. After several hours of sobbing, I decided to get lost in Michener's descriptive passages and read about wild horses.

I tossed the book aside when I reached the part about gentleman riders and picked up the new Mitch Rapp book, then tossed it, too, for he was as angry as Griffen. Justifiably, of course, at terrorists, but it was too close to home.

Leslie and I didn't have a television in our room, and I was not ready to venture out and risk encountering company, so I tried something unrelated to horses *or* men and dug out *Watership Down*. Rabbits. That will keep me occupied. I reached the place where the male rabbits started looking for does – only my depressed mind could read romance in a children's book about rabbits, and grabbed my favorite Elizabeth Peters book, *The Curse of the Pharaohs.* That one was perfect; my thoughts were redirected, and I considered the benefits of wielding a parasol…oh no, Emerson has too many Griffen tendencies…find another book…Ah, *The Prizoner of Azkaban*…no…it has Sirius Black…*Cemetary Dance*… surely that will be safe…Leslie said that was a great book…

My cell phone buzzed – not the 615 number – the barn.

"Hello?" I said.

"Elliott, I just checked on the horses and Viva is a little off on her right fore. I don't think it is anything big, but I thought I'd let you know," Janie, the owner of the barn, said.

"Thanks, Janie. I'll take a look at her after class in the morning," I said. "How is Jet?"

"He's fine," she said. "Tell Griffen I'll let him out tomorrow for him if he gets tied up with studying."

"I will," I lied. "Thanks again, Janie."

I plunged back into the book and read about kite fighting – and I could see Griffen and me doing that together like the two Afgan boys. Keeping thoughts of him at bay was going to be harder than I thought.

Leslie returned, and I had to relive the whole ordeal. Thankfully, she agreed to tell the others so I would not have to be put through it all time and again. She helped me hole up in our room telling everyone that I had girl problems and needed to rest.

Mother's inquiries, however, required a personal touch. I told her most of the story, and she insisted that I had done the right thing and that I should come play with her and my sisters over the Thanksgiving and Christmas holidays rather than hunt in Memphis the whole time. She had a point, and I made a note to clear it with William.

Leslie had an even better idea.

"Elliott, I have tickets to the Vanderbilt game next weekend. Why don't we go? A friend of mine set me up on a blind date, and I'm sure she can get you one, too – no pressure – just one date. What do you think?" she asked, eyes gleaming.

"I think that is the *last* thing I want to do, but the best idea I've heard. I know Griffen won't be at a football game, I don't think he'll have any reason to be in Nashville, and I need to get away from here," I said. "I'm all yours. And thanks, Leslie."

The next day, I went to the barn to check on Viva after class. She was definitely off, so I called Dr. Smith. He said he would be there in thirty minutes, so I took the time to clean my tack and brush her. Jet nudged me for treats, since he was also up for the day. I patted him, and it pained me like I knew it would to see him.

Cleaning leather was a peaceful, mindless, heartbreaking task. It was too early for anyone else to be at the barn, and my mind was left to wander and think about Griffen. Knowing Griffen could be here, though, made me jump every time I heard anything that could resemble crunching gravel. No Griffen. At last, Dr. Smith's truck drove up, and he came over to examine Viva's foot. There was no specific sore spot on her hoof, but she was definitely in pain. He told me that it was probably just an abscess and gave me detailed instructions to soak it, wrap it, and watch it carefully daily until it drained. He said to call him daily with her condition, which I gladly agreed to do. While he was there, he looked at his handiwork on Jet and asked me to give Griffen his regards. I was relieved that Griffen never appeared but still very sad.

When I returned to the house, Leslie was bouncing around the room. "I've got a date for you," she said. "He's a football player named Brandon and my date, Jimmy, says he's really nice – a great guy!"

"Great," I said, not at all excited about going on a date, but glad to be leaving. "What's the plan?"

"We leave Saturday morning and return on Sunday," she said. "No big deal. There's a party Saturday night somewhere off campus, and we're staying on campus with my friend, Bethany, in the sorority house. She has room for both of us."

"Good, that gives me time to make sure Viva's all right," I said under my breath.

"What's wrong with Viva?" Leslie asked.

"She has an abscess, but it should be fine by the weekend," I said. "I don't think it is a big deal, but I have to soak it every day."

No sooner than I got the words out of my mouth than Ashley, Shannon, and Elaine burst into the room with three other squealing girls.

"Elliott! The movie! It's coming out December 5! We've all been invited to come see it on December 1 in Virginia! Can you *believe* that??? It's a special party for the crew and everyone who helped! They sent Shannon and me enough tickets for two other people, so you and Elaine can come with us!!!" Ashley squealed and hopped around the room – so unlike her normal behavior that we laughed uproariously at her.

"Take Leslie," I said and smiled. "I'm not up for that for sure."

"But Elliott, you are *crazy!"* Ashley protested. "This is a ONCE IN A LIFETIME chance to meet the actors! How cool will THAT be? You've *got* to GO!"

"Take Leslie," I repeated. "Leslie, do you want to go?" I asked.

"Of course!" she said.

"Then go," I said. "I promise you *all* will have more fun without me."

None of them knew what I did about Griffen having replaced Sean in the movie, but they understood why I didn't want to see Sean's horse racing around being ridden by Griffen. Mercifully, they backed off and left after not too long, so I could finish my homework and read my cares away.

Two days passed, and Viva wasn't improving. Dr. Smith suggested that I take her to Memphis for an x-ray. He was not set up for that, so he gave me some bute, or horse aspirin, and I made arrangements to take her to Dr. Halliday's clinic after class on Friday morning.

Daniel met me in the driveway of the clinic and showed me where to take Viva. He examined her, x-rayed her foot, and asked if I could wait a moment for him to study the shots. I told him that I had all the time in the world for Viva, and that made him smile.

The office was clean but crowded. I was surprised that a horse clinic had so many come to them, rather than the vets visiting on-site like Dr. Smith did. I guessed they had some out on farm calls, too. Although I had never met Dr. Halliday, I had heard a lot of good things about him, so I was glad that I chose to drive here. Everyone kept telling me that this was no big deal, and I hoped they were right.

Daniel returned, concern obvious in his expression.

"What's wrong with her?" I asked, fighting down a wave of panic that tried to burst from my throat.

"Viva's injury is in a place where it is hard to reach, and really, too deep to dig. In fact, I'm not sure what caused this. Typically, abscesses come right on out but this is not behaving typically, and it is not near any surfaces that are easily penetrable. I've drawn some blood, and we will have preliminary results after lunch," he said in his pleasant soft voice. His blue eyes showed real concern, and I appreciated him so much for that.

"Will I be able to take her back to Oxford with me today?" I asked.

"I think it would be best if you kept her here over the weekend so I can watch her," he said. "I'll have a better idea of what's going on in there, though, after lunch, when we have some results on part of the blood work."

"That will be better for me, too," I said. "I'm going to Nashville this weekend, and I was concerned about who would take care of her. In fact, I was about to cancel that trip if you thought I needed to."

"She'll be fine here," he said. "Now, about lunch. Would you let me take you to get something to eat? You look like you could use it," he said, and his blue eyes brightened.

"Sure," I said. I had no polite way to refuse him since I just told him I had all day for Viva. Besides, what harm was there in lunch?

He drove a beautiful deep blue Lexus convertible, and I was self-conscious about getting it dirty with my boots and dusty jeans. He took me downtown to The Rendezvous for what he said were the best ribs in the country, and I had to agree. Afterwards, we drove to the Mississippi River with the top down. It was unseasonably warm, so the wind felt wonderful. He played Led Zeppelin on his great stereo and before too long we were back at the clinic.

"Now, you wait here and let me check Viva's report," he said. *I really liked that he remembered her name.*

He returned too soon, face grave.

"What is it?"

"She's picked up a nasty infection," he said. "I'll start her on antibiotics immediately and make sure she gets plenty of stimulation on her leg to keep the blood flowing."

He sat down beside me at a respectable distance but looked me directly in the eyes. "Elliott, I am not going to tell you that this is not a big deal," he said. "An infection of this kind could be bad. She actually could die. I need to know how much you're willing to spend on Viva, so I will know what course to take for treatment."

I stared at him blankly. This I had never considered. Or expected. Just an abscess…no big deal. This could not be happening. Not to my Viva. My world.

"Elliott, are you all right?" he asked.

"Just…please…just give me a minute," I said, my voice shaky, and I got up and walked outside. I was trying to keep tears from exploding and making even more of a mess of things.

He followed me outside and put his hand on my shoulder. "Take all the time you need, Elliott. I'll be inside. You can talk to me or any of my assistants whenever you are ready," he said and thankfully, left me alone to think.

I walked out to my car and retrieved my cell phone. I took a deep breath and hit my 'Daddy' button on speed dial.

"Hello dear!" he boomed on the first ring. "How's my favorite baby girl?"

"Oh Daddy," I said, trying to keep my voice from shaking. "I'm not doing very well. I'm in Memphis with Viva and the doctor says she has a really bad infection in her foot. He wants to know how much we're willing to pay to get her well. Daddy…she could…die from this."

"Sounds like ransom to me," Daddy barked. "Let me talk to him!"

"No, Daddy, it's not like that…at all," I said. "They, well, Dr. Halliday is well-respected. They just need to know what we can spend to get her better, so we don't go over budget."

"You tell those birds to get your horse well, no matter what it costs!" he said.

"Daddy, are you sure?" I asked, relieved.

"Honey, we've got the money to take care of our animals, or we wouldn't have them," he said. "Now, you go tell them to get her better so you can bring her home and ride for me. I like to see you smile when you ride that horse."

"Thanks, Daddy," I said. "I love you."

"Keep me posted," he said. "I love you, too."

I gave Daniel's secretary the message and asked her to thank him for lunch since he had gone into surgery. I walked back to see Viva and give her another apple. As she reached for the last bit, I wrapped my arms around her and filled my soul with her smell.

"You'll be fine here, Viva," I said into her neck, releasing a few tears, and running my fingers over her silky coat like a harpist to calm myself. "I'll call and check on you every day. I'm going to Nashville on a blind date this weekend. Hope it's fun, but I don't want to go. The last thing I want is a date. But it seems to be a package deal. I'll come see you on my way home on Sunday if Daniel will let me. I love you so much. You are my whole world now."

"Just let me know when you want to be here, and I'll meet you anytime," Daniel said, and I jumped.

"Oh, thanks," I said, disconcerted and a little piqued that he'd been listening to me sob to my horse.

He noticed and turned away. "I'll call you tomorrow and let you know how she's doing," he said. "And, I enjoyed lunch."

"Me, too," I stammered, "about the lunch. Thanks."

How idiotic I must seem to him. Can't even speak in coherent sentences and crying to my horse. *How embarrassing.*

Viva's condition stabilized but did not improve, so I left for Nashville with a heavy heart. Leslie had a great selection of audio books that she borrowed from Elaine, and we settled on Michael Crichton's *Congo.* We got so absorbed in the book that she almost ran off the road when the crazy apes appeared.

We dressed for the game in Bethany's room, but Leslie and I noticed right away that her room was not on campus and that it was in a duplex with boys on one side and girls on the other. This was news to us and somewhat disconcerting, but we were willing to go forward with the plan.

Bethany proudly displayed a football program with my date's picture, and he was handsome, if you liked the Cape Buffalo look. It boasted his height, weight, and all sorts of other statistics that I neither understood nor cared to know. They were impressed with themselves that they had set me up with a linebacker. I just hoped he did not expect any romantic participation from me. I was not sure that my 5'0" 100 pound frame would have much to say about it if I was disinclined to acquiesce to his requests.

We dressed for the game like Mississippi, and especially Ole Miss girls know how to do so well and pranced to our places in the stadium. Lots of heads turned, and we loved being the cause. Mr. Buffalo and Bethany's football player boyfriend were supposed to pick all of us up at Bethany's place in a Yukon after the game, but Leslie planned to take her car, just in case. She told Jimmy that she would follow him in her car, and that he could ride with her if he liked. I thought that was an excellent plan.

The boys arrived on schedule, and I almost backed out when I saw just how big a 243-pound linebacker was. He had a generous smile and kind eyes, so I faced my fears and left with him to parts unknown with two other people I had never met. *At least I had my cell phone, and Leslie had her car.*

The band was great, and I was delighted to find that Mr. Buffalo liked to dance…with a pitcher of beer in one hand and me in the other, but he did like to dance, so we had something to do that did not involve conversation or being alone all night. It disturbed him that I only wanted Coke, so I let him buy me wine coolers and poured them out little by little when he wasn't looking. That way I avoided screaming the finer points of the legality or morality of underage drinking over the blaring band. I was sure that would fall upon his rapidly deafening ears.

He swilled from his pitcher and swung me around, inspecting my drink and buying more when the last drops I splashed onto the floor disappeared. I felt like Bugs Bunny in the arms of the Abominable Snow Man. Any minute I expected him to say "Ahh my vewy own wabbit, and I will name him George, and I will hug him and pet him…"

We danced next to Leslie, and I saw the concern on her face. Jimmy was getting overly affectionate for her, too, and I gave her *the look*. We did not want to embarrass Bethany, but we both knew we were getting in over our heads, literally, for me, of course. My feet had not hit the dance floor in ten minutes. This monster was squeezing the breath out of me.

Thankfully, he and Bethany agreed to let me drive, and we started back to Bethany's house. Leslie and Jimmy followed. Things did not improve once we returned to the suite. Everyone started pairing up, and I could tell that was exactly as Bethany had planned. Leslie seemed all right with it too, but I was not interested in any alone time with the Buffalo. He sat next to me on the sofa in the den and put his arm around me. I smiled politely but stared at the television hoping he'd have some sense of propriety. After all, there were at least two other boys and a girl in the dark room with us.

I was not so lucky. He turned his bulk toward me, and I felt like I was going to be consumed, or flattened, as the case may be. He kissed me hard on the mouth, and I tried to pull back, but my protests were ignored. That was not acceptable. I had just signaled, clearly, that he was to stop, and my anger flared. He tried to pin me down with one hand and his enormous bulk and was almost successful. Adrenaline shot through me like electricity, and I gouged his eyes with my fingers jamming them as hard as I could into his rock-like face. He jumped back in surprise, and I bolted.

Once outside, I found Leslie locked in Jimmy's arms against her car, and I slammed into them.

"Keys! Leslie, I need the keys! Get in!" I gasped. "He's coming!"

"What?" she slurred, but she handed me the keys. I knocked her back and jumped into the car, snatched her inside with me, locked the doors, and sped away, sure that Mr. Buffalo would make a mess of her windshield if he connected with her car. The last thing I saw in the rear view mirror was Jimmy's mouth hanging open and a monster of a guy charging outside looking for me.

I pulled into the nearest gas station, leaned over the steering wheel, and took three deep, long, breaths. Leslie was hysterical and mad that I had pulled her away from Jimmy. She could not fathom why I made such a big deal about dashing away. Our purses were back at the house, too, with my pepper spray. I was too afraid to go back, but didn't have a choice. We had no money, just our phones.

"Call Bethany," I said.

"What for?" she snapped.

"I'm not going back there until Mr. Buffalo and company are gone," I said.

"We can't order people out of her house, Elliott!"

"Of course we can if they are…attacking people!"

"Calm down, Elliott. You're overreacting. He probably just wanted to kiss you."

"He *did*, Leslie!" I yelled. "Don't you get it? He *attacked* me!"

"I don't think a kiss is an assault," she said sardonically.

"Leslie, I have the sense to know when a guy's intentions are NOT honorable, and his were NOT!"

"But you were in a room full of people," she said.

"He DID NOT CARE!" I yelled. "I had to FIGHT him off me! This was not just about kissing!"

Finally my adrenaline dissipated, and I started to tremble. I felt nauseous and hideously dirty.

"You're not joking, are you?" she asked, softly.

"No, Leslie, I'm not," I said fighting the nausea that threatened to mess up Leslie's pretty car.

"Ok. I'll talk to Bethany."

After an hour, Bethany called us and said the beast had retreated. He had raged around looking for me on foot for thirty minutes and never realized I had left in Leslie's car, thank goodness. She apologized and said it was safe for us to come back.

I still felt dirty and did not want to go back to her place, but wanted to collect my bag. I convinced Leslie to take me to a hotel, and told her I would rent a car early in the morning and drive home. She thought I was overreacting, but I didn't want to ruin her weekend any more than I had already and insisted.

The hotel staff had a car for me at 6:00 am, gassed and ready. It had cost me, or rather, Daddy, to get this done, but it was money well spent. For this reason, Daddy would have probably been fine if I'd chartered a helicopter to take me home.

I sped to Memphis and hesitated to call Daniel. I had the clinic number and his cell phone, but I hated to disturb him so early on a Sunday morning. I waited until 8:30 to call.

"Hello," he said, voice a little sleepy, but hopefully already awake.

"Daniel, it's Elliott," I said. "I am so sorry to call you this early, but I'm almost in Memphis and thought I'd see if you could get the people that feed the animals at your clinic to let me visit Viva this morning."

"Sure, no…I mean…I'll meet you there," he stammered. "Where are you?"

I told him, and he said he would be glad to let me in. *Now I'll really owe him. Oh dear. But I have to see my horse.*

He met me at 9:30. Viva looked like she had when I left her, and she was glad to see me. I had an apple from the hotel for her, and she chomped it eagerly.

"She has not improved as much as I would like," Daniel said. "Let me keep her here another week – through Thanksgiving," he said. "If she's better by Friday, you can come get her."

"Thanks," I said. "I was planning to go home over Thanksgiving, so keeping her here will be for the best."

It was only 10:00 am, and I decided that I badly wanted to go to church. Any church…anywhere…just as long as no one knew me, and I could worship quietly in a pretty sanctuary.

"When did you get a car?" Daniel asked.

"Oh, that's a rental. Long story," I said. "Would you mind if I changed in the bathroom? I won't be long."

"No problem, take your time," he said.

I retrieved my suitcase and put on the dress I had worn to the football game. When I returned, he looked me over appraisingly.

"You look…very nice," he said. "Where are you going?"

"To church," I said.

"What church?" he asked.

"I'm not sure yet," I said.

He looked at me quizzically.

"No more questions," I said, but smiled at him politely. "I really have to go."

"Ok," he said. "I'll take care of your girl."

"Thanks, Daniel," I said. "For everything."

SANCTUARY

Chapter 17

Courage is getting back on…no matter how far you were thrown.

I found an Episcopal church downtown that I had admired from Daniel's car and slipped inside. The ceilings were supported with flying buttresses and the stained-glass windows took my breath away.

My soul ached and had taken such a beating in the past few weeks that I longed to kneel, pray, and let the music lift me and encourage me as if God Himself were wrapping me in His arms. The people were friendly, but not overly so, and I was grateful. In my home churches, a visitor like me would have been assaulted by five people by now, been asked to complete forms in triplicate, and placed on a committee. Thinking about that and my five little church lady cheerleaders made me smile.

The sermon drew me above my daily troubles and brought my focus back on eternal, lasting thoughts. For the hour, I did not think once about Viva, the Buffalo, or Griffen, in that order. I felt the wonderful peace of knowing I was loved unconditionally – no matter what.

Afterwards, I drove through Wendy's for a chicken sandwich combo and headed to Oxford, thoroughly relaxed. My phone buzzed – Leslie.

"Hey Leslie," I said. "Where are you?"

"I'm about to leave Nashville," she said. "Bethany wants to talk to you."

"Ok," I said.

"Elliott, I am *so* sorry about last night. I had no idea Brandon would act like that. Please forgive me. I *do* hope you'll come back another weekend. I'll do better next time," she gushed.

"Thank you, Bethany, and don't worry, I'm not mad at all," I said. "Just feed Mr. Buffalo some rat poison for me ok?" I said and laughed.

"Deal!" she said. "That's the least I can do!"

"Elliott, where are you?" Leslie asked.

"Almost home," I said. "I went to church in Memphis and stopped by to see Viva."

"How is she?" she asked.

"The same. I'll see you tonight," I said and hung up.

My visit home over Thanksgiving was exactly what I needed. Everyone at the Woodland Hunt already knew about Viva's situation and offered me horses to ride any time I wanted to visit.

Daniel called every day to give me a report on her progress, but Viva was not getting better. I could hear the concern in his voice. He was watching her carefully now for signs of too much strain on her good leg that could cause her healthy foot to founder. Should that happen, she would not only be unable to stand, she would be in great pain and would have difficulty recovering. Since she wasn't coming home after Thanksgiving, I made plans to go see her on Friday – a random visit – so Daniel would not be expecting me and ask me out. I had no desire to be alone with a guy under the age of 80 right now. Even then, I'd want an escort.

William needed me to help him on Saturday if possible, and he discreetly mentioned that Griffen was going to be out-of-town. He offered a room at the hunt house and Rocket, and I agreed to both. I planned to try Rocket Friday afternoon to make sure he wouldn't kill me at Saturday's hunt.

It had been two weeks, and I had neither heard from, nor seen, Griffen. I wanted badly to tell him about Viva, but I was sure he had heard about her injury already. Or maybe he hadn't. The urge to call him nearly overwhelmed me, but Grand put a stop to that.

"Honey, to see a rainbow, you have to tolerate the rain," she whispered.

Friday came, and I sped to Memphis to see my horse. Viva was the same, and I was beginning to fear the worst. As I expected, Daniel offered to take me to dinner, but I told him I already had plans. They were with Rocket, but he didn't have to know the details. He said he was hunting Saturday, so I knew I'd have to come up with something to do that evening, too, or I'd likely be trapped into a date.

It was so good to be back on a horse, albeit a crazy one, and we flew around the country like a comet hurled across the sky. Hunting in our home country on Rocket made me ache for Griffen, but I did what I could to focus on the hounds. Rocket took the jumps expertly even though he was young, but he and I did not communicate well in the woods. My knees hit more than one tree, and I was sure there would be plenty of bruises. Thank goodness this was not the 'shorts' time of year.

At the hunt breakfast, Ben and Addy asked too many questions about Viva, and I tried to find a reason to escape. Ashley, of all people, came to my rescue, but I understood, too late, what she wanted to talk about. Their plans for the Virginia trip were coming together, and she had heard that all the stars would be there. She gushed on about what they were wearing and how they were going to get pictures with Matthew and Sean and on and on and on.

At last, I caught Sylvia's eye, and she came to my rescue. "Elliott, dear, could you help me with this soup?"

"My pleasure," I said and gave her a hug when we got into the kitchen. "Thank you so much for letting me stay with you. I really appreciate it. I'll be in touch."

"You are so welcome, dear, any time," she said and kissed me on the cheek.

Two things happened simultaneously by the next weekend. Griffen hit the media, and Viva's whole leg started to swell.

I had already heard from Ashley that Griffen was the new improved Sean. I was not as shocked as she had expected, but what I was not prepared for was the media coverage the world was giving this random movie. Mercifully, I watched little television, but his face was on billboards and in magazines, and movie trailer spots were blasted on the radio and all over the Internet. He was now a teen idol, and I was not at all prepared for that. His face was even on pillowcases at Wal-Mart! He'd become an action figure within a matter of weeks. Still no word, letter, text message, or even a "hi" through someone else from him.

Viva's injury had gone way beyond anything anyone expected. The hideous infection was not backing down no matter what they tried. I visited her every other day, and my heart was breaking. Daniel was concerned about her other legs being able to bear the strain of holding her up for so long. He assured me she was not in pain, so I told him to keep trying to get her better.

Exams occupied my mind, thank goodness, and Sylvia told me Griffen would be gone every weekend, so I could hunt Rocket anytime I liked. He was making progress and was actually a horse I looked forward to seeing. So far, Daniel had not pursued another date with me, and for that, I was glad. I think he was embarrassed that Viva's treatment had not gone as expected, but I certainly didn't blame him.

At last, I was able to leave Oxford to spend Christmas at home. Mother had planned a host of parties, and Ashley was even throwing a New Year's Eve party at her house. They schemed to keep me busy since the attempt to get away from Griffen was futile. The whole thing was so unfair. He did not have to see *me* plastered everywhere he went. *Oh, the injustice of it!*

Christopher and Ben were worse than my girlfriends about trying to get me to go out with people, but they didn't know about the Nashville incident, either. I was afraid they'd try to take the linebacker down and even though I would like to have seen him poisoned, I did not want my friends to get hurt messing with the Buffalo. I just wanted those memories erased.

Daniel called daily to give me a report on Viva. I felt so grateful to him for taking care of her and bad about continuing to have other plans when he tried to take me out, that I invited him to come to our Christmas party Friday night and hunt the next day.

Everyone was surprised when he showed up as my date. Daniel was a delight to be around now that he felt like he could treat this like a date. He made me laugh, he was nice to my friends, and even Ben and Christopher approved. I had made arrangements with Robin for two horses for the hunt, and he was looking forward to meeting the members of the Woodland Hunt. When he left, he did not make any untoward moves, and I was relieved. He gave me a friendly hug and agreed to meet me at the hunt the next morning.

Christmas day had come and gone with no word from Griffen. Not a card, no phone call, and nothing from any of our mutual friends. I knew by now he was in South America, but that did not help. My heart was still aching, and I dreaded hunting the next day for fear that all those memories with him would come flooding back, as usual. In my room among my favorite books, I dug around until I found something that would send me off into another world, so I could sleep without Griffen or Viva on my mind. I read five chapters of *Anne of Green Gables* and fell into a dreamless sleep.

Hunting with the Woodland Hunt was not nearly as bad as I had expected. Daniel and I had fun on our horses, Shaker and Spin, two new thoroughbreds that Robin had acquired. They jumped everything and were willing to go anywhere. I had a little trouble stopping Shaker, so Daniel let me bump into Spin anytime the runs got crazy.

Ben, Christopher, and Addy had returned to Memphis to help William, but I chose to stay in Canton as long as I could. They were coming back for Ashley's party on New Year's Eve, but were ready to return to Oxford and their own horses.

At the hunt breakfast, Daniel left to take an emergency call. *The life of a vet must be really crazy. All kinds of nutty women to appease at all hours.* He was really nice and had not tried to attack me, thank goodness.

"Elliott, come with me," he said appearing from nowhere. His face was grave, and my euphoric mood vanished.

"No..." I said, knowing what he was going to say.

"She's down, Elliott," he said, and my heart fluttered faintly in my chest. "This is what we were afraid of. That she'd founder."

I collapsed into a bench outside the hunt cabin. When I looked up, he was staring at me, waiting...waiting for what?

"I need to know what you want me to do," he said.

"What?" I asked, not comprehending.

"She's in pain," he said carefully. "But I will take you to her if you like."

"Can you...can they...give her something...so she won't hurt..." I asked, breathing in quickly to squelch the tight knot of my own pain threatening to thwart any intelligible words, "until I...can get there?"

"Yes, of course," he said, and he left.

I was all alone...outside. My world was crumbling around me me and not one of my close friends was here. I bowed my head and prayed... for courage, for peace, for strength, for wisdom, for grace, for patience, and for anything else God thought I would need to get me through the next decision. I felt the cool wind caress my face, my hands, my neck, and thanked Him for touching me...like that...right now. I had felt so alone but not anymore. A nice thing to remember...He is always there...waiting for me to reach out to Him, and I felt His peace and presence.

Daniel returned, and I stood. "I'm going to Memphis now, so I can get back here tomorrow," I said.

"We can be back here tonight, if that is what you want," he said, and I wanted to hug him for that.

"No, Daniel, I'll take my car," I said. "It won't be necessary for you to shuttle me all over the South. I am sure you have plenty of other things to do with your time."

"Actually, Elliott, I don't," he said. "And I can assure you from a professional standpoint that you will be in no condition to drive."

After returning the horses to Robin's we made it to Memphis in record time. He said he had connections with the highway patrol because everyone had animals they loved. That actually made me laugh. He did all he could to keep my mind off the horrible task at hand and for that, too, I would be eternally grateful.

Suddenly, we were at the clinic. Although I had a marvelous blanket of peace around me, I dreaded the next few minutes. Daniel's hand gently touched my elbow as he guided me to Viva's stall. One look at her broke my heart.

She was lying on her side relaxed but sprawled unnaturally across the soft shavings like she was trying to take a nap. I went into the stall, lifted her beautiful head onto my lap, and stroked it gently. Daniel left us alone, and I burst into silent tears. I watched them splash on her face, brushing them away drop by drop. I laid my head on her soft gray neck and felt her move slightly beneath me. Her liquid eyes showed no recognition – they were looking far away and already seemed empty.

I knew she was not in pain, but that it would return, and I didn't want to prolong this any longer than necessary. Even so, I didn't want to let her go. This whole thing was so hard to believe. I rubbed her long legs, ran my fingers through her black mane, and gave her one last big hug. When I looked back, Daniel had walked by to check on us.

"Are you ready?"

"Yes," I said. "I want to hold her, but I don't want to watch."

Daniel slipped in behind me and gave my sweet Viva a painless injection that took her away from me until the day I would see her again in heaven.

We drove all the way to Grenada before he spoke. I cried the whole time but was calmer now. At first it was strange to be crying like this with him, a stranger, but I got over it when my sobs would let me keep them at bay no longer.

"Let me get you something to eat," he said, gently.

The last thing I wanted was food, but I was sure he was hungry, so I agreed to let him stop. We ate at Jake and Rip's and thankfully, he didn't try to make small talk. I swallowed a few chicken tenders, and he had steak. There is definitely something to be said for being in the presence of a professional in times like these.

The food made me feel better, but I was exhausted and wanted nothing more than my pillow and a full day to sleep. We pulled into my parents' driveway, and he got out to walk me to the door.

"If you will let me, Elliott, I'd like to take you to lunch tomorrow," he said. "But only if you feel up to it."

"Ok," I said, unable to form any other words.

"I'll call before I come in case you change your mind," he said and leaned in to give me a gentle hug.

"Thanks, Daniel," I said and went inside.

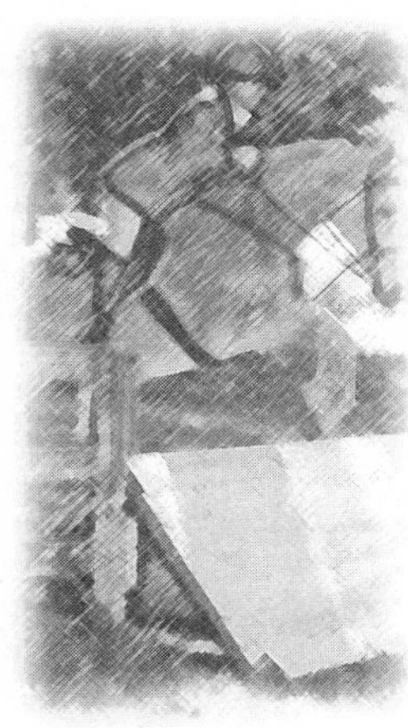

AIRBORNE

Chapter 18

Who shall declare the joy of the running!
Who shall tell of the pleasures of flight?
Springing and spurning the tuft of wild heather,
Sweeping, wide-winged, through the blued dome of light.
Everything mortal has moments immortal,
Swift and God-gifted, immeasurably bright.

~ *Amy Lowell from "A Winter Ride"*

Church with my parents was a special treat. Kimberly and Jessica, my sisters, had returned to their homes, and I was glad not to have them around while I worked to heal from losing Viva. It was good to have my cheeks pinched and myself squeezed from my grandmother's and mother's friends and some of the friends I had that were home for the holidays.

Only a few made Griffen comments, for most were redirected by Mother before anyone said anything to me about him. No one at church knew about Viva, and I was thankful. I lost myself in the wonderful, soul-filling hymns, and felt a new infusion of the love and comfort I craved.

Mother and Daddy dropped me off at home to wait on my lunch date. He had not specified where we were going when he called to confirm that I was willing to crawl out of my hole to have lunch with him, so I stayed in my dress, but exchanged the pretty, impractical pumps for dress boots. He arrived on time, and we had lunch at a little café in Canton on The Square. I introduced him to everyone that walked in.

"Do you know *everyone* in this town?" he asked, impressed.

"No, but they know me," I said, grinning and tossing my head. *That was the first time I had flirted with anyone in weeks.*

"Will you let me take you somewhere after lunch?" he asked, pausing to sign something at the register that the waitress presented to him when he mentioned his name.

This place didn't take reservations, and I wondered what it was that he was signing, but I kept my thoughts to myself. "That depends on what you plan to do with me when you get there," I said, but made sure not to sound too forward. He was fun, but there were no sparks radiating from him like there were when I was around Griffen. Nice, but nothing else…so far. Then again, I was not looking for anything else either, and I still felt numb and disoriented.

"Let's just say it will knock you off your feet," he said, and I started to get a little worried.

"Daniel, I'm not that kind of girl," I teased, but hoped he'd get the message.

"You have a filthy mind," he said, and we both laughed.

The waitress brought an appetizer that obviously Daniel had ordered in advance, and I was impressed at his foresight. It was a huge pile of delicious homemade fries. She took our drink orders and gave us menus.

"So, did you already order my meal, too?" I teased, but I was painfully reminded that I loved when Griffen did that for me and hoped Daniel didn't already order.

"I wouldn't begin to assume what you wanted to eat," Daniel said. "At least not in your own town at a restaurant that you know much better than I do."

"What were you signing?"

"Oh, that was nothing. They wanted my signature. I did that to make sure we wouldn't have trouble getting a table. So what's good here?"

I told him all the food was great, but the pizza was the best. He ordered a large pizza with pepperoni, sausage, ham, mushrooms, onions, green peppers, banana peppers, and black olives. Once it arrived, we were quiet for a while, enjoying the pizza, and I found my thoughts drifting from Griffen, to Viva, and my mood began to darken.

"Hey," he said gently. "You sure you're ok?"

"Yes, and no," I said. "One minute yes, then just as suddenly, no."

"Let's go," he said, and he shot out the door with the last piece of pizza so fast I had to jog to keep up.

"I hope you paid the bill!" I yelled at him playfully.

"They don't know who I am, remember, but they *all* know you," he said. "I think *you* better be worried!"

He slammed the door almost on my leg and leapt to the other side of his car like an overjoyed kid. My mood lightened instantly, and he reached over and took my hand playfully.

"My dear Elliott," he said magnanimously. "Let it be known that today is the first day...of the rest of your life!"

He looked at me; I looked back at him wondering what he expected me to stay to that, and we both laughed uproariously at his ridiculously trite inspiration.

We drove south for a while, and he turned into the small Madison airport. Now he had my attention.

"Daniel, am I going to need a passport?" I teased, but wondered what in the world he had planned for the afternoon.

"No," he said. "But you will need to trust me."

That, I did not like to hear. Too painful. Too close to home. Too much like Griffen. He saw my reaction to his words and changed the subject.

"Ok then, maybe not trust, just blindly follow!" he said, and I had to laugh. *Perceptive.*

We walked to a little building where he really was getting keys to an…airplane. He made some notes, spoke to a few people, and called someone on a radio. Then, he turned to me and indicated that I was to step outside.

We walked over to a small, *way too small*, car sized machine with a propeller in the front.

"Here are your headsets, ma'am," he said.

"What are these for?"

"All the better to hear you with."

"Aren't you forgetting something?"

"No, whatever do you have in mind?"

"The pilot," I said. "Who is going to fly this?"

"That will be you," he said. My jaw dropped.

"Oh no…no way. What…are you *totally* insane? I'm not getting into that! Not without a pilot!"

"What about *with* a pilot?" he asked. "Promise me you'll go if I find a pilot."

I knew he was up to something, but I decided to play along. "Ok.

I'll go if you find a pilot."

He grinned widely and opened the tiny door for me. "Get in."

"I'm supposed to believe *you'll* be flying this plane?" I asked.

"Yes. Or, if you prefer, we can fly that twin engine over there or perhaps a jet, if you want, but that will have to be another time, for it took me a while to arrange this one. I imagine it would take more than a day to get the others lined up. But I will, if you insist," he said, backing away from the tiny craft.

"Showoff," I said, but I was impressed. For the moment, all my cares were behind me.

They stayed behind me for three hours as we soared, dipped, dived, and played all over the skies. There were moments that I was painfully aware of just how much flying felt like riding Viva, and a few tears escaped. If Daniel noticed, he did not comment. He let me fly, and it was glorious. I was definitely hooked. I needed this more than he knew, or maybe he did know, and that was why he had brought me here.

He drove me home with the top down and even though the late December air was cold, it felt great. It started to rain, so he had to put the top up and for a moment, the car felt small, quiet, and too intimate. He turned the music down and changed the station to jazz, making me think about listening to jazz with Griffen…*Griffen, who hadn't even bothered to call…and who I had not, until then, thought about all day, for once.*

"Elliot, this may not be the time, but I'm going to mention it to you anyway," he said, and I was instantly nervous. *Here we go. Brace yourself. Please don't let him do something stupid and noble like ask my* permission *to kiss me…*

"One of my clients has a horse, a very nice young horse, that needs a home," he said. "He is four, fractious, and too fragile looking for me.

He looks like a lady's horse. Would you like to try him?"

"I'd like to see him sometime, yes," I said, grateful and surprised. "How much is he?"

"Leave that to me," he said. "Like I said, my client needs to find a home for him."

We were pulling into my driveway, and I was nervous again. After a day like today, I hoped he wouldn't try to kiss me, but I was sure he would. If not, then I would know that either he was not interested in me romantically, which I doubted, they always seemed to be to some extent, or that he was truly a nice guy that knew that what I needed the most right now was a friend…and lots of distractions.

He walked me to the door and stopped.

"I had a great time with you today, Elliott," he said. "I know you hurt, and you can call me any time you want to talk…or fly." He chuckled softly, for there was no hiding that I had been impressed.

I laughed, too, and looked up at him. His bright blue, intense eyes met mine briefly, and he kissed me softly before I could react. *No thunderbolt, but very nice.*

"Thanks, Daniel," I said and went inside. *I guess that answered my question.*

The next day, he called late in the afternoon. He asked me to dinner for the next evening, and I agreed. He wanted to pick me up at 5:00, which I thought was a bit early, but I agreed to that as well. Then, he told me to wear my riding clothes, and I was instantly suspicious.

I liked Daniel, but I *loved* Griffen. And I was not planning to let Griffen go regardless of what Griffen was doing…or not doing…by ignoring me. I still held out hope that he would come back, have his temper managed, and sweep me off my feet…again. Grand was holding onto that hope, too, even though I had not heard from him in more than a month. She, too, had been quiet, but I had attributed that to my mother's presence pounding the same sensible things into my head daily.

Mother liked Daniel, of course, but she, too, held out hope that Griffen would come around. I told her Daniel was taking me out on Wednesday, and she raised her eyebrows.

"That boy, or man, rather, is quite interested in you, dear," she said. "Be careful that you don't give him the wrong impression."

"I won't Mother, but I do owe him at least one real date," I said. "Especially after all he's done for me, and for Viva."

"You don't *owe* him anything," Mother said. "But you certainly can go out with whomever you please. Just keep your head about you."

"That's the problem, Mother. With him, I do. With Griffen, it was impossible, but so *perfect*," I groaned.

"No dear, it was not," she reminded me. "That is why you have not heard from him in a month."

"Stop it," I said. "That was below the belt."

"I'm just so proud of you, Elliott," she said. "You really *do* have a wonderful head on your shoulders. If Griffen is to come around, he will. You just watch."

"I'm certainly *waiting*," I moaned.

"A month is no time," she smiled. "Hang in there, honey. And don't ever let Griffen think you are just hanging around waiting on him. You stay busy."

Daniel picked me up promptly at 5:00 Wednesday afternoon and drove me straight to the barn. I was impressed that he remembered the way so well. *Must be a vet thing.*

He walked me inside, and I dreaded what we were probably going to do…go riding…and I would be reminded painfully of Viva and Griffen and…

"Come this way," he redirected me when I turned toward the stalls for the rental horses.

"Daniel, I think I know the way around my own barn," I said.

"Yes, I'm sure you do," he said. "But you don't know what I've set up for our afternoon."

He was a different, much more confident Daniel than what I'd seen before. We entered the owners' barn and all the familiar and not so familiar faces peered at us from their stall doors. He led me up to a stall where a bright bay with a narrow blaze and white star on his nose looked eagerly for handouts. He was breathtakingly beautiful… it was love at first sight.

"Masterpiece, meet Elliott Marks," he said, and Grand started shouting.

"*Oh no, no no no you don't young lady. You never accept gifts like that from any man other than your husband. And even then, you'd better be able to pay the price. Tell him 'no' right now!*"

"Holy heavens, Daniel! He's gorgeous," I said.

"He's all yours," he said leaning in closer, much closer, to me. Grand was shouting so loudly, that I could not hear myself think.

"I…can't," I said weakly, with absolutely no conviction. "I can't accept this, from you," I said. "It's…too much, Daniel." *But I've got to have that horse. He's…perfect. Hush Grand! Daniel just wants to be friends…he understands…*

"Don't be ridiculous, Elliott," he said. "You'll be doing my client a big favor if you take him. He was going to have me put him down because he can't pay for him any more, and no one he knew could ride him. Masterpiece's not exactly a gentleman…yet. You may not even like him."

"I like him," I said. "And if you're sure I'll be saving his life, I'll take him."

"Let's ride, then, and see what you think," he said.

We tacked him up and took him to the arena. At first he was jumpy, but I loved the way he moved beneath me. He felt like paddling a canoe without a keel, but we'd fix that in time I was sure. I let him trot for twenty minutes to see how he felt once he relaxed, and around the nineteenth minute, he finally did.

"Wow Elliott…you two look great," Daniel said.

A few other people were watching us now and admiring Masterpiece, as he picked up a canter on the perfect lead the first time.

"I never could get him to do that for me," Daniel said. "How did you do that?"

"I just do it, but I have a hard time putting it into words," I called back to Daniel. "Robin can tell you better than I can. She says something complicated like feeling when one foot hits the ground somewhere, but I can just *feel* it. I can't describe it."

"Well, when you can write it down let me know, and I'll make you a millionaire. Every rider would like to know how you *just feel* that every time," he said.

We rode figure eights, and Masterpiece even did a few flying lead changes. I was totally amazed and once again, in love with a horse. He was certainly no Viva, but he was a very acceptable substitute and a real project.

"Take him over the jumps," Daniel said.

"Has he jumped before?"

"Yes. Go ahead," he said.

And jump we did. We jumped everything in the arena many times, and he acted like he enjoyed it. It was getting late now, and almost everyone had left but us. I cooled him down, and led him back to his stall. By now, everyone had left, and we had the whole place to ourselves. I had not been paying attention to that, but Daniel had.

Daniel removed Masterpiece's tack and returned my saddle to his car. I brushed Masterpiece, and the first signs of hope that I would actually survive losing Viva were creeping through my head. I had not noticed that Daniel had returned until he was behind me, very close, and in *the* space. I dared not turn for fear that he was going to kiss me here, in this very private place. Way way way too private. *Oh no!*

He reached around and spun me to him, and I was so shocked at how suddenly his whole manner changed that I didn't react. His kiss was strong, but soft, and I felt my body respond. Not a lightning bolt, but not unpleasant either.

"Elliott, you look magnificent on that horse, and here, right now, too," he said and kissed me again.

I pulled back, surprised at his bold assessment of me all of a sudden, and bumped into Masterpiece. He leaned towards me and moved in cautiously but very close to my face.

"I'm no college boy, Elliott," he said in a very silky, but highly possessive voice. "I can buy you anything you want, take care of you," he said. "I'm not a gamble, and I'm crazy about you."

He bent down and kissed me again, and I felt myself respond in a way that I was not at all ready to respond to anyone. I pushed him back gently, but firmly, but he pressed on, and everything about his actions said he planned to travel much further down this path – right now – than I intended to go. *Not again!*

"No! Daniel!" I gasped, louder than I intended. "I'm sorry…no."

He sat back like I'd slapped him, but unlike the Buffalo, I didn't have to hurt him, *thank goodness*. But his eyes turned dark with anger.

"What is *wrong*, Elliott?" he snapped. "You *want* to kiss me, I can feel it!"

I was embarrassed that he actually called me on this. He felt my reaction to him – there was no denying that. How could I tell him that I didn't want this? He'll never believe me. I felt like a trashy tease and could find nothing to say.

"I'm…sorry, Daniel," I stammered. "It's not…you…I promise."

"Are you still hung up on Griffen Case?"

"No," I lied. "It's just that…well, I'm not, I don't want to, no, I'm, its not like that, well…it's not what you think," I stammered.

"That's ok, Elliott," he said, but smiled knowingly now and moved closer. "I can wait. You're right. This is not the place. I have a room…"

"No!" I said, shocked at his assumption. "Daniel, no. I mean, I'm not going to *go* there, right now…with you…I mean…with anyone...to a *room*, you know, like *that*, until I, we're, I mean until…I'm…married." *At last, it was out. Barely, but it was out.*

"No way!" he scoffed. "You've *got* to be kidding. This is just my luck. No wonder Griffen dumped you. I was wondering how I was able to move in on you so easily without having to deal with him. I bet he's getting a real kick at *this* right now!"

Laughing! He was laughing at me.

I felt my face flush and my trusty anger was right behind it along with the humiliation, disappointment, hurt, and everything else left inside me wanting to explode…all boiled up like lava about to spew forth venom on this…this…fiend who had the nerve to *laugh* at me after all we had been through! His words about Griffen hurt, too. Maybe he *had* found himself some starlets. I'm sure that's why he's not calling me. Our little romance must have changed his mind about no other woman for him but me – how could I be so stupid, so blind, so arrogant!

"Take me home right now!" I fumed. "Before I kill you *and* your horse. And by the way, I don't *want* that horse. You take him back by tomorrow morning, or I'll have him hauled off…by the…the police!"

"Elliott, Elliott, calm down," Daniel said trying hard to contain his laughter. "It's me, Daniel. I'm not going to hurt you, or *kiss* you. You're safe, I promise. No need to kill the horse because you're mad at me. I've not been the gentleman you expected me to be, and I apologize. You *did* surprise me, though. The only thing I fear in all the world right now is meeting a real lady. *I'm* the one who should be running!"

"That's ridiculous! You're just sucking up now," I spat. "I meant every word I said and still do! Take me home now!"

"Calm down, we're going. Oh, if only I *wanted* to get married any time soon I'd have to snap you up right now," he said still laughing in my fuming face. "You really are too good to be true. I read your signals wrong, but, hey, I'm not perfect. Look, I'm sure Griffen is having his fun among the starlets, but you, Elliott, are the best I've ever seen!"

I was shaking and really wanted him to quit talking. How dare he even hint that this was partly my fault! If I had my pepper spray, he would have felt the full force of *that* signal for *days.*

He drove me home, but I jumped out and refused to let him walk me to the door. He tried to argue, but I told him I'd scream for my daddy if his door so much as cracked open. That really made him laugh, and I considered screaming to spite him, but thought better of it, spun on my heels, and stormed back into my house.

Once inside, I remembered he had my saddle. Oh well, I'll just have to buy another one. What's a $2000 saddle among friends? I winced thinking about the cost, or worse, having to break in a new one, but refused to chase him down the street or call him…

SOLO AGAIN

Chapter 19

To expect to ride without encountering difficulties and worries, as well as risks and dangers, is only to look for something that cannot possibly be attained.

~ *Riding for Ladies 1887*

Thursday morning I drove straight to the airport. I had picked up a business card when I was there with Daniel and intended to see if I could rent a plane myself and learn to fly.

I would give him this; he had shown me something that I would probably never have done had he not come into my life, and as angry as I was at him, I was grateful. Our friendship would probably survive, but I didn't want to think about that right now. That incident happened way too close behind Mr. Buffalo, and I had not seen the force of Daniel's intentions coming…at all. I would have to be so much more careful around all guys. Right now, trust in all of them was deteriorating rapidly, and the single life sounded far more appealing.

When I entered the flight building, there were three people inside.

They looked up in surprise. One had been there the day before, but the others I had never seen.

"May I help you?" an elderly lady, probably the receptionist, inquired.

"I'm Elliott Marks, and I would like to have a…flying lesson," I said.

"Would you like to make an appointment?" she asked.

"Mmmm, yes, ma'am," I said, realizing too late, that I should have called.

"When would be a convenient time for you?" she asked, raising a perfectly plucked eyebrow and looking at me much like my mother did when she knew I was up to something.

"How about…now?" I asked, and the voices behind me laughed. *Why did the whole world find me so amusing this week?*

"Miss Marks," one of the men behind me stood and extended his hand. "I'm Dale Upshaw, the flight instructor. This is Ricky Lind; he's an instructor, too."

"I remember you, Ricky," I said, and he blushed. "You were here Sunday when Daniel brought me in."

"Yes ma'am," Ricky stuttered. "I…it was nice to meet you; I mean, it's nice to see you again."

"You said you wanted a flying lesson, now?" Mr. Upshaw asked.

"Yes, sir," I said. "When can we go?"

"Now's as good as any time," he said and grinned widely. "I'll get things set up."

"How much?" I asked.

We completed the necessary paperwork for him to get paid and for me to sign my life away and were in the air in no time. Of course, we spent thirty minutes going over all the particulars, but I was focused solely on feeling the air beneath my wings and leaving my cares on the ground.

The hour passed way too quickly, and we soon returned to earth. I had to go back to school but promised I would keep in touch with him and let him know the next time I came home. He gave me the name of an instructor in Oxford, and I knew this new hobby was going to be trouble, but that it was just what I needed. And this was one new thing in my life that did not make me think about Griffen.

The next hunt was New Year's Eve, and I planned to ride. Addy was coming to stay with me overnight for the party, but she and Ben were not going to be down in time to hunt. So, I made arrangements to rent Shaker for myself for the day. I couldn't wait to see my friends and tell them all the crazy things that had happened to me in the past week.

The New Year's Eve hunt was on a Saturday, so it brought out a ton of guests planning to celebrate a long weekend. The Woodland Hunt was doing well, and I was glad to see that the membership had nearly doubled.

Janice asked me to whip-in with her, and I was delighted to get to learn from someone who had been doing this much longer than I had. Shaker wasn't comfortable away from the field, but once he settled, we enjoyed day in spite of the uncomfortable rental saddle Robin let me use. I would have to figure out a way to get mine back, but I would think about that later. No way would I really buy another one. Maybe I'd get up the nerve to call Daniel next week.

There was not much game moving, but we were able to coax a coyote to give us a run for the last thirty minutes. As usual, the hunt breakfast food was excellent, and we gathered around the clubhouse's pot-bellied stove and ate soup, drank apple cider, and swapped hunt stories. Janice, thankfully, did not ask me about Griffen, nor did anyone else. I discreetly thanked Bonnie, the hunt secretary, in person for the flowers they had sent me when Viva died. It made a huge impression on me, and I wanted her to relay my feelings to the members.

Ashley came to the breakfast with her cute new Memphis physician boyfriend and invited everyone to her house that evening to ring in the New Year. Ben and Christopher kept picking on me to take them flying, and I promised that we'd go when we got back to Oxford. We agreed to meet at Ashley's later and Christopher said he'd pick Leslie and me up. I hated to ride with Ben and Addy and mess up their time together, even if we were just next door.

Ashley's parents' house overlooked a lake. By the time we arrived, it was dark, and the neighborhood lights' reflections sparkled like a million stars on the water. For a moment, the pain of Griffen's absence shot through me, and I turned away from the sight. *Why had he not called? I meant for him to give us some space, and for us, or rather, me, to date other people as well as him, not for him to vanish. How could I know how we would be as a couple if we never spent time together? It takes more than this obnoxious physical attraction to make a life with someone. This was my idea. I miss him so much it hurts. Time is not helping things.*

The room was rapidly filling with people, and the food was going fast. Around 9:00 the band started to play, and Christopher spun me to the dance floor. I jumped around and danced with everyone, then the music slowed. I was *not* dancing a slow dance with Christopher, or *anyone*, I decided. Keep it light, and I would be fine. No more romantic complications.

As I turned to leave, I felt his arm come around me and pull me close to him. *Oh no, not Christopher. Why do they always have to go and ruin a good friendship? And now, he's starting to smell like Griffen. Not fair…*

I turned to face him, annoyed that he was pulling me so close, but the eyes that met mine were not Christopher's brown ones, but my favorite green, ever so piercing, glittering with mischief Griffen eyes. My knees buckled, and he really *did* have to hold me up this time.

By now, people wanting autographs surrounded us. Two men I did not know backed them off, but we were still in the center of attention. In spite of their stares, he held me close, so very very close, to him.

"I hope you've had enough of your *space*," he said in his wonderful growl grinning widely at me, "because I'm hungry to see you and talk to you and hold you. I've had all the space I can stand."

I opened my mouth to speak, but nothing would come out. I felt like a beached fish gasping for breath, and the image of me as a fish facing Griffen after all this time made me laugh out loud.

"What's so damn funny?" he barked but kept smiling nonetheless.

"Where should I begin?" I asked, not really knowing what to say. I wanted to pull him away from here and never ever ever let him out of my sight. But words would not form.

"Tell me the biggest thing that has happened to you since you ran me off," he said, still grinning. "We'll start there."

My face fell, and he knew he'd said something terribly wrong. In spite of the crowd, he put his arms around me and guided me outside in the cold, but I was warm in his arms. Random people followed us; he turned to the two refrigerator-sized men I did not know.

"Guys, please get us some privacy," he said. "Be nice though; these are her friends, and mine, too. Tell them I need some time with her, then I'll talk to them."

He cradled my face in his hands, and I melted into his touch. Tears started streaming down my face, and no matter how I tried, I couldn't stop them. He pulled me close and rocked me to his chest, stroking my hair with his gentle hands. At last I could relax in the comfort of his arms, where I belonged.

"Shhhh," he whispered into my hair, "I'm here, dear Elliott. I'm here now, just relax."

He held me until my sobs quieted, then cradled my face again with his hands. He brushed the tears from my cheeks, kissed them softly, and my stomach contracted with longing. I had absolutely no resistance in me toward him, but I felt perfectly safe.

"Now, tell me," he said. "Or, don't. Whatever you want, my brave little vixen. I had no idea you were hurting…like this."

"Viva," I started to say, and the sobs began again.

"Oh, no…not Viva," he said, and he pulled me closer to him. "Why didn't you…" but he stopped short.

"Why didn't *you*?" I asked, but I knew the answer before I finished the sentence.

He sat back then and opened his mouth to speak. I could see him weighing his words. *Definitely an improvement.*

"You said you needed space, Elliott. And the last words I said to you were never to forget that I love you," he said carefully, watching my eyes.

"Did you come here to pick a fight?" I asked, glaring back at him through a fresh tunnel of pain.

"No, no, no," he said. "I don't want to go there with you, at least not now. I have too many things I want to tell you…to show you. If you're going to run me off again, at least wait until the end of the night."

"It's cold," I said.

He pulled me closer to him. "Do you want to get in my car?"

"Yes," I said. "Car?"

"I have a car…and a truck," he said. "Gas mileage, you know."

He walked me to the passenger door of a bottle-green Jaguar and my jaw dropped.

"You like this?" he asked with a grin.

"If I *had* to drive a car, this would be what I would want," I gaped. "Wow."

He cranked the heat, leaned over to my side of the car, and kissed me softly. "Not exactly the best place for this, but I want to hear… everything, or anything about you since…November, and I want to tell you all about Argentina, and the movie, and…other things. You first."

I took a deep breath. "We've covered Viva; her abscess was much more than that. I took her to Memphis, and they did all they could, but she foundered on her good leg before her infection could heal."

"Like Barbaro," he said. "Oh my dear, I'm so very very sorry I was not here with you. Have you hunted any…since, well…have you?"

"Actually, yes. Rocket did all right after a while, and I rented Shaker from Robin and rode one of Daniel's client's horses named Masterpiece. I did not hunt him, but I may want to buy him," I said a little too quickly.

"Daniel, that *vet* Daniel?" he bristled. "He's a piece of work. I wouldn't trust him as far as *you* could throw him."

"I like the horse, so I may try to get him," I said, switching away from the topic of Daniel. "How's Jet?"

"He has a scar, but it looks good on him," he said. "Makes him look like a tough guy."

"I flew an airplane yesterday," I added and smiled at his reaction.

"You did? Now, *that* tops the charts," he said. "Being with you banishes boring, that's for sure. What was it like?"

"Riding Viva."

"Will you take me?"

"Absolutely. But you'll have to stand in line behind Christopher and Ben," I teased. "Tell me about Argentina!"

"We wrapped everything up there, for now, at least my end of it, and the kids were great. I will take you there with me someday – it's a beautiful place. I don't want to have to leave you for that long, ever again. Please don't send me away like that, Elliott."

"I didn't tell you to go away," I said. "I said I needed space, and that I loved every part about you except the part that treats me terribly and other people that you love terribly when you lose your temper. But *that* I can't change, you have to, if you want to," I said way too quickly.

"Did you see the movie?" he asked, changing the subject.

"Of *course* not," I said. "It was *killing* me not to hear from you and to see you plastered all over every billboard and magazine in the modern world!"

"Killing you?" he asked. *So much for remaining aloof.*

"Of course!" I snapped. "Do you hear *anything* that I say to you?"

"It's time to go inside. They're going to wonder what happened to us," he said. "And I'm ready to see everyone, too."

We returned to the party, and Griffen spent the next half-hour signing autographs while I danced with anyone who could keep up. Griffen appeared like clockwork during the slow songs, but he left me when the music picked up.

The night flew by, and I was so glad to have him here popping in and out, holding me one minute and letting me play the next. I felt whole again and ridiculously happy, at peace. I so badly hoped things would work out with him and that time would show that he truly would change the only thing that kept me from committing to him for a lifetime. His carefully chosen words earlier in the evening were a promising start, and so was his demeanor with his…bouncers or whatever they were. I guessed he had even more women than Lydia flinging themselves at him now, but I couldn't care less. That part about him I wasn't worried about…anymore.

I felt him wrap his arms around me from behind, and I leaned back into his magnificent chest. He kissed the top of my head and sent shivers down my spine. This time, though, my knees held. I was prepared. The clock was getting dangerously close to midnight, and I knew he wouldn't kiss me like I liked in such a public place. When he steered me outside, goose bumps covered my body.

"This is much better," he said, as he pulled me into the shadows. "Are you warm enough?" he asked, his voice mesmerizing me completely.

"Yes," I said and tilted my head back, exposing my throat.

He leaned down and kissed my jaw line, my throat, my collarbone, then pulled me up and covered my lips with his. I let him consume me, and my whole body went limp in his arms.

"It's not midnight yet," he whispered as his lips brushed my neck.

"Practice run," I said. "Do it again."

He did, over and over until I was delirious. I wished we'd started this hours ago and left off all that crazy talking. I wanted this more than anything – all the time – every other moment was a waste of time when it wasn't spent sharing breaths with him.

The crowd started to count inside, and he gazed at me with his hypnotic eyes.

3, 2, 1 – Happy New Year!!!!

He kissed me again, so soft, so gentle and so very, very perfect. When the uproar died, he dropped to his knee.

"Elliott, my brave little vixen," he said. "Marry me."

EARTHQUAKE

Chapter 20

There is nothing in which a horse's power is better revealed than in a neat, clean stop.

~ Michel D. Montaigne

Through the shock of it all, my eyes focused on one clear thing. He was putting a spectacular ruby ring on my left hand and smiling brighter than I'd ever seen him smile.

Anger rose up in me like bile.

"Elliott?" he asked, comprehension that something was wrong finally sinking in. For the second time tonight, things were going very very wrong.

"Griffen Case!" I hissed through clenched teeth. "What part of showing me you've changed the only part I can't tolerate about you did you miss? I thought I made that very clear to you in November. Then you disappear for two months, put a ring on my finger, and expect me to believe you've changed? You are the most *arrogant* insulting, infuriating…person…I have ever heard of! No one compares to you, Griffen!"

I took one quick breath and continued, tears threatening to expose the frustration I was feeling at wanting him so badly but knowing I had to refuse him. "How *dare* you assume – something I want more than life itself – but you can't just expect me to believe. You have to *show me*!!! That was your idea in the first place, from the day you first kissed me – and now you do *this*?"

By now, he was on his feet. I had wrenched the ring off my finger and put it firmly back in his hand.

"You take that back and show me, Griffen Case, *prove* to me that you've changed, and we'll see," I said, spatting the words at him like an angry cat.

"What's more, Griffen, I *will* be dating other people while you show me whether or not you can hold your end of the bargain," I said.

"That's *not* going to happen," he said jaw clenched. "And it looks to me like *you're* the one having problems with your temper."

"I'm not yelling this from the mountaintops, Griffen, I'm trying to get this through your beautiful, thick skull, so you'll *do* something about this so I *can* marry you!" I said, still steaming.

"Don't you see? I *don't* want to date anyone else, but you are *giving me no choice!* This whole thing can be stopped, but by you alone. You have to show me that you treasure me and will protect me in public as well as in private."

My breathing was coming a little more regularly, and I weighed my words carefully, for his sake now, hoping he would hear me.

"You may have been raised with a father who spoke derisively to your mother in public, but that stops now. With you. You *will not* carry that forward if you want to spend the rest of your life with me," I said quietly.

"I present you with my grandmother's ruby and you don't think that is enough to show you how much I love you," he said quietly back at me.

"It's not about what you give me, Griffen. You can give me all the gold, and now fame, that you have, and it wouldn't be enough. You have to show me," I said.

"And you will not let me show you while you wear this ring?" he asked, quietly.

"No."

"I'll not tolerate you dating other people. I *will not* share you," he said, and his eyes bore into mine.

"Then you will not date me," I said. "Because I will not marry you like this. We've already tried it your way. I will not close off my options completely until I'm convinced you really will do this…for us."

Impasse…again.

I turned to leave.

"We're not finished here," he growled.

"I believe we've said all that there is to be said," I replied. "Now you have to show me."

"You're not dating anyone else. I don't share," he said.

"Exactly what is it that you think you'll be sharing, Griffen?" I asked, infuriated at his suggestion that I'd be sharing anything…especially anything physical…with random men like some cheap whatever…*he* of all people knew better than that…so why is he being so unreasonable?

"If you date anyone else, I'm keeping the ring," he said.

"I don't want it…not now…not yet," I said, turning my back on him; I had to escape, so I headed to the dance floor to find Christopher. I had had way too much of this, and I knew I had to get away from him before I lost my resolve and caved in to his most tempting proposal.

Christopher saw me coming, and I motioned for him to take me home. Leslie was with him, so that was one less person we had to corral.

"Christopher, please take me home," I said. "Now."

"Is everything all right? I thought you and Griffen…" he trailed off when I interrupted him.

"We've had a disagreement, and I'd like to leave now, please, Christopher," I begged.

"You're not hurt?" he asked, noticing my brimming tears as we headed to the front door.

"No, nothing like that," I said. "Where's Leslie?"

"She wants to stay. I'm coming back to get her," he said.

"Thanks, Christopher, really," I said. "I owe you big."

We were almost to the car when Griffen caught up to us and spun me around to face him. Christopher turned just in time to see Griffen pull me to him and kiss me hard on the lips. I gasped, furious that he'd done that, now, of all times, in front of Christopher, and pulled away from him before my body collapsed.

Having dealt with horses so much in the past few years, I knew that a punch to his face would break my knuckles and just make him laugh. So I flattened my hand trying to remember how to hit a black belt without killing him or getting killed, swung my arm in a wide arc, and slapped him on the face with as much force as I could muster. My hand blazed with pain like I'd hit a cinderblock, and Griffen roared.

Christopher, God bless him, stepped between us.

"Christopher, move away," Griffen said. "I don't want to hurt you."

"She wants me to take her home, Griffin, and that's what I'm going to do. Or I'll go down trying," he said, and he stepped toward

Griffen to prove he meant it.

I didn't answer my phone that night. Despite my raging hormones, exhaustion finally overcame me. I let my pillow, the cool sheets, and the thick blankets swallow me to sleep.

The smell of bacon woke me at 8:00 am. I was going back to school today, but I had one last wonderful morning's breakfast beckoning from Mother's kitchen.

In spite of the covers fighting to trap me in bed, my stomach took over and led me downstairs into the kitchen. Comfort dictated compromise, so I had wrapped a fleece blanket around me before I left my room. Passing by my sister's room, I saw Addy still burrowed under her blankets. I never heard her come in last night, so I was sure she and Ben were not in a hurry to get back to Oxford. I stumbled into my chair in the breakfast room and embraced the warm mug of hot tea Mother placed before me.

"Good morning, sweetheart," she crooned. "I hope I didn't wake you."

"You know you did," I said. "But I'm glad. I couldn't resist the bacon."

"How did Ashley's party go?" she asked. "Did you meet any interesting people?"

I paused a minute for dramatic effect, a trick I learned from her.

"Yes, I did," I said and sipped my tea.

"Male or female?" she inquired raising an eyebrow.

"Two dark males," I said. "I think they were bodyguards or something." I watched her take that in and took another sip. The tea felt good, and I started to wake a little and warm up.

"Why would there be bodyguards at the Woods's house?" she asked and looked directly at me, game over.

"They were protecting Griffen," I said mischievously. "Can you believe he has two goons following him around now? Like a black belt needs protection. That'll probably be in today's paper."

"Griffen was there?" she scowled. "Why does he just show up and not call, Elliott? What is *with* that boy? Did he explain himself?"

"He, of course, blames it on me," I said. "He said I was the one who sent him away."

"He has a point," she said. "What else did he say?"

"Come sit, Mother," I said.

"Let me fix your plate first," she said. She set a platter full of bacon, eggs, toast, and grits in front of me with a tall glass of milk, and I feasted while the food steamed. I drank most of the cold milk in one long gulp.

Mother sat across from me at full attention. I was so lucky to have her, and I really needed her wisdom right now.

"He asked…no, he told me to marry him," I said. "And put the biggest, most beautiful ruby on my finger that had belonged to his grandmother."

"So, where it is?" Mother asked calmly. She was much more calm than I expected.

"I gave it back to him," I said.

"What exactly, did you say to him, dear?" she asked, hands patiently folded around her own mug of tea.

"Well, I said that he was unbelievably arrogant and thick-headed or something like that because the whole reason I asked him for space was for him to prove to me that he was willing to get control of his temper, for our sake," I said, scooping up the last of the hot grits.

"How did that go?" she asked.

"Not well," I said.

"Oh dear," she said. "My, Elliott, you certainly picked a good one for keeping things interesting."

"And I told him I would date other people until he showed me that he really would stop getting overly angry and unpleasant," I said.

"Does he ever scare you?" Mother asked.

"No, why?" I said.

"Because, you are walking a thin line with him here, and you should not be walking it at all if you have any doubt in your mind whether or not he would ever physically hurt you," she said.

"I'm not worried about that," I said. "In fact, I feel the safest when I'm with him. It is just that he gets so angry and lets hurtful words fly out of his mouth in public," I said. "That is so embarrassing. I don't want to fear his reactions to things and have to always walk on eggshells."

"Of course not," Mother said. "Sometimes what you are describing is covering up deeper problems. You are wise to proceed with caution with him. I am just so sorry for your sake that he *is* so gorgeous, that you are *already* so in love with him, and that he is now so *famous*."

"No kidding," I sighed. "What's a girl to do?"

We both laughed at the irony and finished our tea.

"Just remember what a prize you are, dear, and don't compromise for the sake of a gorgeous face," she said. "You have a lifetime to work this out. Don't let him or anyone else pressure you. You decide in your own time."

"I'm going to head back to Oxford in a little while," I said. "I need to get things ready before classes start. And, I want to check out the airport."

"You are too much, honey. Another expensive hobby is not exactly what you need right now!" she laughed.

"Flying lessons don't cost half as much as my sisters' wardrobes," I said. And, they *do* keep my mind off Griffen. There are no billboards with his face on them in the sky and the radio talk up there, at least in the little planes I'm flying, is not exactly Fox News."

Daddy came in then, and Mother put a cup of black coffee in his hands and kissed his sleepy, rumpled cheek. *Out of all the hopes and dreams I had, that one, most of all, was the one I now wanted the most. To be able to do that simple act of love for Griffen, someday, in our own house…in front of our children's adoring eyes.*

AFTERSHOCK

Chapter 21

In my opinion, a horse is the animal to have. Eleven-hundred pounds of raw muscle, power, grace, and sweat between your legs – it's something you just can't get from a hamster.

~ Author Unknown

My cell phone buzzed – 615. I looked at it for a moment and considered answering. I supposed that I needed to answer the phone now, or I'd be dealing with him in person later. I opted for the phone.

"Hello," I said.

"Elliott," Griffen said sounding surprised. "I expected your voice mail."

"Do you want me to hang up?" I asked.

"No, of course not," he said. "Where are you?"

"On my way to Oxford," I said. "Grenada."

"You got up early," he said.

I started to wonder why he bothered to call. The line was quiet, and I thought maybe that I'd dropped his call.

"Are you still there?" I asked.

"Yes," he said. "I wanted to apologize for last night. In front of Christopher."

"Accepted. Anything else?" I asked.

"That's about it," he snapped.

"Ok, then. Bye," I said.

"Elliott," he said before I disconnected.

"What?" I said.

"The offer still stands, you know."

"I thought you retracted it when I told you my terms."

"I did."

"My terms are the same," I said. "I want proof, not promises."

"That's not acceptable."

"Then you'd better put that ring back in its box," I said. "I'm not accepting your terms."

"I thought you'd might be stubborn like that."

"So why did you call?"

"To see if you could resist my charms," he said. "I see that you've perfected the retreat."

My face flushed, and I felt the anger flare again. "You're not building your side of the case very well right now," I said. "Still the angry arrogant unpredictable animal you promised you would fight everything in you not to be. Why don't you get on your knees and get some real help rather than pull me into this storm with you?"

"I don't need you preaching to me about how and when to pray," Griffen said calmly, but with a good dose of tension in his voice. "And for the last five minutes, *you've* been the angry one."

"Yeah, well, angry I am," I said. "Because I love you and cannot stand to be away from you and knowing I have to, to make you prove to me that you will be willing to step up and be the person that I can make coffee for in the morning." His words stung, and I was babbling because I knew I was out of line bringing in prayer – that was below the belt. *Maybe he's right about me being the problem.*

"Elliott," he said quietly.

"What?" I snapped.

"I don't drink coffee."

"Oh, well, then."

"What are you doing this afternoon?"

"I don't know yet. I may go to the airport," I said. "But I need to get things ready for class tomorrow, too."

"I thought we could go look at Masterpiece," he said. "Then, would you like to go to a movie?"

"Let me think about it and see what the state of my affairs are at home," I said. "Call me later."

"You'll answer?"

"Maybe."

"I love you little vixen," he said, the smile clear in his voice, and the line went dead.

The long stretch of highway soothed me, and I switched the station to classical music. Griffen's mentioning Masterpiece made me think that was exactly what I needed, a horse to love again. And that horse needed me as much as I needed him.

I wasn't sure I was ready to see Daniel yet, especially with Griffen in tow. And if Griffen picked up that we had spent so much time together outside of his clinic, he might kill him on the spot. Then again, it may be a good test. Testing and proof of his attitude were the very things I needed.

I made up my mind and called him back.

"Hello," Griffen said, his voice wonderful in my ears.

"I want to go get Masterpiece," I said. "And then see your movie."

"That was fast. Are you sure, about the horse, I mean?"

"Definitely," I said. "What time can you meet me at the barn?"

"I can be there in an hour, say, around noon."

"We'll take my truck and trailer," I said. "Everything will be ready when you get there. You're going to love this horse!"

"See you in an hour," he said. "You've lost your mind."

Detecting the smile in his voice, I was not sure if this was a good idea, but I pushed that thought away…for the moment. I was trembling at the thought of actually getting a horse. I forgot for a while my carefully choreographed steps concerning Griffen and was glad that we'd be doing something together that we both loved – nothing more. I kept telling myself that. Truce, for now, with him.

Daniel was glad that I called. He did not mention our disastrous incident, and I was relieved.

"I want to buy Masterpiece," I said. "Do you have time today for me to come get him?

"He's not for sale," Daniel said.

My heart sank. I had so hoped to fill my empty Viva void with him, today.

"Oh, well, then," I said, my voice trying to quake. "Let me know if you hear of any others like him."

"You can *have* Masterpiece, Elliott, but I won't let you buy him," he said. "I told you he was given to me."

"Oh!" I exclaimed. "Then I can come get him today? Will you let me?"

"Yes, of course," he said with a distinct smile in his voice. "What time will you be here?"

"Around 2:00, if that will work for you, maybe a little earlier," I said. "But I *am* buying him. I don't care what you say."

"Your money is no good with me," Daniel said. "I will not accept it."

"Griffen is coming with me," I said, just to make sure he was clear about my intentions.

"So movie boy is back?" he chided. "You still can't buy Masterpiece."

"We'll see about that," I said. "I'll be there at 2:00."

"I look forward to seeing you both," he said. I heard the sardonic smile whether or not that was his intent.

I blew through my room throwing my luggage on the bed and changing into riding clothes that would double as movie attire. The weather was bitter cold, so I wore jeans, my cowboy boots, a pink turtleneck, a pale gray sweater, and my Barbour jacket. My chaps were at the barn and they were designed to fit over my cowboy boots. They would enable me to go from barn to movie without a drastic change of clothes.

I tossed my waxed cotton hat in my truck in case my hair didn't recover from being in a hard hat. My hair, for now, was in a ponytail, and I left it that way. My class schedule looked in order, and I had all the books I needed. A few more notebooks and supplies remained, but I could pick them up sometime later today at a drug store if I remembered, or borrow from Leslie if I didn't.

Mission accomplished, I sped to the barn to collect my trailer.

Griffen would be there in minutes, so I hastily hooked up everything and gathered my halter and lead rope. But when I opened the trailer door, my body froze. The sight and smell of all my gear, all Viva's gear, punctured my newfound giddy anticipation of getting another horse. I collapsed against the trailer as a wave a grief suddenly crashed over me.

I let the tears fall freely, considering them a tribute to the gifts Viva had given me. Mourning her was so hard, because few people understood the depth of my feelings. It was also unpredictable. One minute I was going along as usual, then something as small as a peppermint would trigger a memory, and I would fall to pieces. So much about her I could not put into words. She was such a big part of me and every step I took where we'd trod brought back stabs of loss with their memories.

Griffen pulled up then, and I stood to close the tack room door. I walked over to my truck to repair my face and went to the barn. Jet was in his stall, begging to be acknowledged. I dug in my pockets for his peppermint and walked over to rub his nose. A giant gray horse I didn't know was next to him, and I offered him a peppermint as well. He gobbled it eagerly. Finding nothing left but my fingers, he went back to his hay.

"Who's the gray?" I asked as I met Griffen at my truck.

"Oh, that's Churchill," Griffen said, "Jet's friend. He's a Percheron cross that I picked up in Virginia. I thought he'd make a good back-up horse for me, or anyone else that wanted to hunt. He loves jumping, and he's not complicated."

"He's gorgeous. But…let's go get Masterpiece!" I said, hardly able to contain my excitement.

"Hold on a minute," he said, and pulled me close. "I want to try this again." He leaned down and kissed me gently on the lips. His arms did not release me, but he pulled back after a long, blissful moment and looked deep into my eyes. "No retribution for that one?" he asked, his voice so low and soothing, and cautious.

"I…you," I stammered. "Well…that was just…fine," I said and blinked up at him.

He kissed me again, harder this time, and I melted into him, letting him pull me back, away from the truck, back to the barn, and into a stall piled high with fresh shavings. Jet nickered for attention when he saw us, and Griffen chuckled but kept kissing me as he pulled me down beside him.

Time stopped. It was midday on New Year's Day and no one was at the barn, right now at least. We were so wonderfully alone after all this time, and my carefully plotted moves and countermoves concerning him were forgotten. I let myself go completely and relished his arms, his lips, his hands pulling me near him – the smell of sweet shavings and his presence surrounding me and filling all the places in me he'd neglected for so long. The places only he could fill; being able to trust him completely was such a pleasant and wonderful relief.

He stopped kissing me for a moment and propped up on an elbow, his hand stroking my face and what little of my neck that was exposed. We were fully clothed, of course, but his touch, wherever he touched me, sent shocks all through me that reverberated through my soul.

"We have a horse to collect, dear Elliott," he said reluctantly. "And I promised to be your driver."

Daniel met us at the clinic, for he had brought Masterpiece over from his house. He was outside rearranging buckets and making a space for us to circle the trailer when we pulled up. The clinic was closed, so we had little trouble negotiating the parking lot.

"Hello Elliott, Griffen," Daniel said. "Good to see you. Masterpiece is right in here." He shook Griffen's hand and indicated for us to follow him into the main barn, which we were able to access from outside.

"Tell me about this horse," Griffen said as Daniel opened the stall door and clipped a lead rope to his leather halter.

"He's young and a little bit crazy," Daniel said. "A lot like Elliott."

I stiffened and looked incredulously at Daniel, careful to be out of Griffen's line of sight, but he wouldn't meet my eye. I could swear he smirked, though, because he had to sense I was gaping at him.

Griffen did not smile. "Define crazy," Griffen said, face expressionless.

"He's not good at standing still; he bucks, he rears, he kicks, he occasionally bites when his girth is tightened, and he's been known to bolt. When he does that, he's almost impossible to stop. He's never been hunted as far as I know, but he jumps nicely in the arena," he said.

"So what makes you think this horse could possibly be suitable for Elliott?" he said, his patience visibly sifting away with each word Daniel said about Masterpiece.

"She looks good on him," he said smugly. "He's completely sound, the price is right, and he's too fine boned for me."

I hoped that Griffen missed that Daniel had seen me ride Masterpiece. I was not ready to explain that one. He did not make a comment, just focused on getting more information about Masterpiece.

"Daniel, I don't know what you are trying to pull, but we're not interested in this horse," he snapped. "Elliott, let's go."

"Just a minute, Griffen," I said. "He's going with us."

Daniel's eyes glinted, and he raised his eyebrows at me behind Griffen's back.

"No, he's not," Griffen said under his breath to me and out of Daniel's earshot. "Elliott, life is too short to ride bad horses. There are too many good ones out there. You can have any horse you want. You know the money does not matter if that is what you're worried about. I can get you any horse you want. And if you won't let me buy you one, then you can pay me back."

"This one's a gift," I said softly. "From Daniel. He really feels bad about Viva. But he said the guy that has him can't keep him and will have to put him down if they don't find him a home. I love him, Griffen, and he was wonderful when I rode him. We can't let them put that beautiful creature down. Not now…not after I've ridden him and know I love him. He works…with me."

"You can't accept it as a gift," Griffen barked under his breath. "That's not right."

"I know, I'm working on that part," I said.

"Where do you want Masterpiece to go, Elliott?" Daniel asked.

"In my trailer," I said, and he grinned.

"Daniel, if this horse hurts her, you'll pay," Griffen growled.

"Griffen, settle down, this horse will be fine. It is my gift to her," he said, grinning maliciously. "I'll give you two a minute while I put Elliot's saddle in her trailer."

I looked at Griffen hoping he didn't catch what Daniel had just said about my saddle…no reaction. When Daniel returned, Griffen handed Masterpiece's lead rope back to Daniel.

"She's paying for him," Griffen said.

"That won't be necessary," Daniel said lightly as he led Masterpiece down the isle. "She's already done that, Griffen. As a matter of fact, I quite enjoyed spending time with her over the past few weeks while you were off chasing starlets."

Silence. Daniel stood directly in front of Griffen now and neither moved.

I could have heard a mouse running across the floor. My world stopped, and I hoped the ground would swallow me immediately. *How could Daniel do this to me?*

Daniel glared, and I watched Griffen hold his anger inside with each breath. But Daniel was not finished, and he continued in a voice that got more forceful with each word.

"Someone had to look after her while her heart was breaking bit by bit each day, knowing her horse was dying and that there was nothing that she could do. Masterpiece is the *least* I can offer her to compensate for all her pain. Certainly you must know what it feels like to lose something that you love deeply regardless of what you do to try to save them!"

Griffen opened his mouth to speak, but Daniel continued. "Where were *you* when she had to make the decision on how to best take care of Viva? Where were *you* when she held her horse and decided which breath would be her last? And, Mr. Griffen Case, if you do not know already what a treasure she is, then you are a *fool.* A fool to leave her here to suffer alone, and a fool not to do a better job of taking care of her!"

I waited for the aftershock, but it never came. He looked at Daniel appraisingly and said, "Thank you, Daniel, for taking care of her when I…couldn't," he said. "You are right; she is a treasure, and *I…know… that.*" Griffen's voice was soft, but menacing. He extended his hand to Daniel and Daniel shook it, then handed Masterpiece to Griffen to load in my trailer.

"By the way Daniel, I'm still coming after you if she gets hurt," he said, unmistakable malice in his tone as he opened the door for me to get in my truck.

"Back atcha, Griffen," Daniel said keeping his gaze steadily on Griffen as we drove away.

THE BIG SCREEN

Chapter 22

Riding an elegant horse is an emotional experience…one even the most gifted writers cannot describe.

Griffen reluctantly agreed that Masterpiece was a beautiful horse, but he made no promises about his opinion of him for me in the hunt field.

We rode quietly to get him used to his new home and to Jet, and I used a simple snaffle bit to gauge his reaction to me. His stride was longer than Viva's, but not quite as fluid. He hardly responded at all to my legs, but time together would solve that. Griffen rode him, and I watched, mesmerized, at how after only a matter of minutes, they looked like they had been together for years. *Uncanny. I want to be able to do that.*

"He's nice and not too nervous now," Griffen said. "If William will let us ride together, I'll let you take him next week."

"*Let* me?" I smiled. "Since when do you tell me when, what, and where to ride?" I liked that, but I did not want him to know.

"Since you brought home a nutcase," he said. "I'll ride him if we have to go separately."

"Why you and not me?" I protested.

"Elliott, you're a fine rider, but you don't have anywhere near the experience I have with horses," he said. "Don't argue…for once… about this."

"Yes, sir," I said, but grinned. "I'm ready to see you on the big screen. Let's go."

The movie theater was crowded since it was New Year's Day. Griffen blended in perfectly with the other Ole Miss boys in his white button down shirt, jeans, and Sperry's…even in January. He had exchanged his Barbour for a sweater, and we hoped he'd be able to attend without much ado.

"I liked being your wardrobe consultant," I said as we approached the theater. "This is funny having to think about making you blend in with everyone. Where are your bodyguards?"

"They show up only when needed," he said.

"Have they been following us?" I asked, the thought of us in the stall earlier causing me to blush crimson.

"No, it's not like that," he said, chuckling at my alarmed expression. "They only show up when there are crowds. They're more like polite, proactive, police. That way, they're the bad guys, and I don't have to go around slugging people that bother me."

"Yeah, but I bet you'd like that; a license to punch people," I joked.

"You know I don't, and remember, it is illegal for me to do that unless they start it," he smiled and brought my hand to his lips. *In public! He is losing it!*

"Two for *The Chase*", he said as we approached the ticket counter. The agent never looked up, and we grinned at each other. So far, so good. He put his arm around me and leaned down to whisper in my ear, "You are excellent cover, my dear. No one suspects us. Just around the corner," he said and his breath on my ear sent sudden shivers down my spine. It occurred to me then, that this was the first time he'd ever taken me to a movie.

As we were about to enter the theater, something flashed, and I was blinded.

"Hey!" Griffen barked, "What do you think you are doing?" he growled and lunged for the kid's camera, but the boy was too fast. We did not want to make a scene, so we went in to find our seats. A few heads turned our way after the cameraman scurried away, but Griffen flashed his perfect smile and said, "Hazards of dating a beautiful woman, they all want her picture."

They smiled politely and ignored us. Just another college boy and his girlfriend on a date.

We nestled in to watch the trailers for upcoming movies. It was exceptionally nice to be so close to him in the dark and to have him holding my hand. Such a simple pleasure. I offered to get popcorn if he wanted it, so he could stay hidden. We laughed at the absurdity of that, but he sent me anyway with cash, unable to resist the delicacies offered at movie theaters.

The movie kept me on the edge of my seat. The horse scenes frightened me tenfold, for the one I loved the most in the whole world was in the middle of every scene. I could not believe he had not been killed, and I understood clearly why stunt doubles made so much money.

But, when Griffen played his character, I fell in love with a whole new side of him. He was nothing like my Griffen but irresistible nonetheless. He was a softer version of himself, and when he kissed Keira Knightly, I felt the passion of the characters, and not of Griffen toward another woman. It was spellbinding that he could transform who he was just like that. None of the mannerisms that I was so familiar with transferred to these scenes. He never cupped her face in his hands or gently stroked her chin or her hair. Their attraction was believable, but it certainly was not ours.

Griffen watched me the whole time. I could feel his eyes on me while his character kissed on screen, and I smiled. I knew he wanted to kiss me now but would not because we were in the theater – and not on the back row. Why, I did not know. Perhaps we thought we had outgrown that. *Pity.*

When the movie was over, I was so desperate to kiss him I could hardly concentrate. I felt the electricity pulsing through my skin longing to connect with his. My guess was that he was in the same frame, too, for he was unusually tense and in a hurry to get to his truck.

As soon as we stepped into the light, we were blinded with flashes. Someone else had recognized him and spread the word that he was in Oxford. For a minute we were paralyzed, uncertain of what to do. Then, he took my hand and bolted back into the theater and out the fire escape doors. We dashed to his truck laughing at our narrow escape.

His telephone buzzed as soon as we were safely inside.

"We're fine," he said. "Thanks for watching. I had it in the truck, not with me. I'll be more careful next time. Yes, you better send someone. I don't know what will happen with class tomorrow."

"Your buffoons?" I asked.

"Oh yes. It looks like you'll be seeing a lot of all of us now," he said, not smiling. "I guess it was going to happen sooner or later. They tried to tell me, but I figured I could blend in here."

"Griffen, you could not blend in anywhere; you know that," I said.

"You stand out among everyone no matter what you do. You are a beacon of light, irresistible, especially to me."

I crossed the seat and was beside him in an instant, covering him with kisses. He pulled the truck over immediately and responded in kind.

"Now, then, young lady," he said and set me back on my side of the truck. "I am taking you back to my house, just for a little while, to finish that very kiss…properly. Then, I am taking you back to your house, so we can rest and be responsible students in the morning."

He noticed a few reporters following us but lost them. I was sure that it would matter, though, because there would have to be throngs of them at his house. When we arrived, no reporters.

"Where are all the reporters?" I asked, surprised that we really did have privacy.

"They don't know where I live. This house is not in my name, so there's no way to find me in the traditional manner. My agents set all this up. You, however, may be a problem. They did what they could with you, but you may have to be moved. And in a small town, well, it's only a matter of time."

A light bulb then went off in my head. "Griffen, this is perfect!" I said. "Look, I told you that I was going to date other people…under protest…remember?" I added when his jaw clenched.

"Listen to me. Break up with me. Publicly. Then I won't matter, and they'll leave me alone," I said.

"I'm not following you," he said. But I knew he knew exactly what I was talking about.

"After we finish in here, make a big deal at the sorority house about dumping me, or I will," I said. "I'll still see you, of course, but no one will know. And, it will give us time to see if you, and if I, can handle this. If we can handle this together."

"I'd rather you be wearing my grandmother's ring," he snarled.

"It can't be like that, Griffen Case, not yet. And you *know* that," I said. "Remember our first kiss? *You* are the one who told me you have to beat this…and it is up to you to do that. To admit we need help and let God give you the power to lift us both through this… above this."

"Get us there, Griffen, I trust you, and I *know* you can do this," I said softly to him, hoping he'd listen better when I whispered. "*You* are what I want more than anything else in this world...you forever… us as a team…taking on life and all its challenges together. Maybe this is the perfect way to test all of this now."

Once we got to his house, he took me inside, and kissed me softly on the lips like he was telling me goodbye. I wasn't having any of that, so I kissed him back like a consuming tigress and pulled him down on the couch.

"Griffen, remember this and fight for me," I said and kissed his neck, his jaw, his forehead. I ran my fingers through his dark hair and pulled his face into mine, kissing and holding him until my head swam.

When it was finally time to go, he drove me back to the sorority house. Just like we had thought, cameras were camped out in the parking lot ready to record what was soon to be our very public finale. He made me promise to let him handle this, and I agreed, but with great reservation.

Cameras flashed in all directions, and I looked at Griffen's face. He smiled at them all, and my heart constricted with love and longing for him. I so hoped that this would work and that we were not really saying goodbye.

"Evening, guys, ladies," he smiled, and acknowledged each one. "So nice of you to join me at the door, as I take this lovely lady home."

They laughed and started shouting questions at him.

"Is she your girlfriend?" a woman asked.

"Well, she was, but not anymore," he said. "She doesn't want to put herself and her family through this."

"Hey miss! How do you feel about breaking up with Griffen Case?" she shouted.

"No comment," I said and started to cry. This was all too much and too very real. *How could I possibly hold on to him anymore when he had the whole world at his fingertips – plenty of women who could care less how he treated them and would not put so much pressure on him. Or rather in his case, plenty to do now that he was a star – plenty of people to take care of him if he decided just to be a bachelor the rest of his life like he always planned to do…no distractions. What he could do for these kids now that he was well on his way to being famous and in great demand! He doesn't need me any more. Someone like me would just hold him back. Who am I kidding?*

Tears streamed down my face uncontrollably, and he started to look concerned as we crossed the street. Miraculously, they had also silenced the reporters. Maybe they were human after all.

He led me to the door, cameras clicking. I looked up at him blinking back tears, and he looked down at me. He brushed the tears softly from my cheek and pulled me closer to him.

"Goodbye, Elliott," he said. He bent down and kissed the top of my head gently, then left.

I ran upstairs to my neglected room. By the time I flopped down on my bed, my favorite 615 number flashed across the screen.

"You should get an Academy Award for that!" I said, smiling now, giddy with the release of all those tears and such close proximity to the cameras.

"Elliott, are you all right?" he asked urgently. "I can't believe I walked away from you crying like that. *You* are the one who will win awards if that was not real."

"Oh, the tears were real all right," I said. "All I had to do was think that you were really telling me goodbye."

"I'm not; *you* are," he growled.

"This is only a test," I said. "Remember? I'm going to go out-of-town next weekend hunting somewhere, so you do something like take someone else out, too, and make this look real."

"I'm not interested in going out with anyone else, and I wish you wouldn't either," he said through his teeth. "You've trapped me, you know."

"Black widow – but I don't plan to be a widow," I said.

"You're well on your way; you're killing me."

"I love you, Griffen Case, superstar," I said. "Goodnight."

"Elliott," Griffen said before I could hang up.

"Yes?"

"The ring is yours, whenever you're ready for it."

TRIALS

Chapter 23

Impetuous Thoroughbreds require more time and patience from their riders. But more often than not, they are well worth it.

Ashley, Addy, and I made plans to travel to a hunt in Alabama for the upcoming weekend. No one knew Griffen kept a horse in Oxford, so the barn was still a sanctuary – no media assaults. We knew, however, it would only be a matter of time before things there and in the hunt field were likely to change.

We were itching for a girls' weekend and went to work picking out outfits, cleaning tack, and grooming horses until they gleamed. I was taking Masterpiece on his first hunt much to everyone's disapproval. Since I had no staff duties, and I just *knew* he'd be good, I didn't budge on my decision.

We left Friday afternoon and started the five-hour trek to the hunt. The horses were staying at the place that we were hunting on Saturday, but we were sleeping at a hotel, preferring real beds and bathrooms whenever possible for hunting and party weekends. Ben had called

Addy three times already, and Griffen was almost as bad. My friends knew about our strange arrangement complete with the impending ruby, but they were sworn to secrecy and loved being "in" on the clandestine love life of the most sought after male in the country.

Ashley updated us on her latest beau, the Memphis physician, who sounded like a jerk. She was blinded by the promise of his fortunes, and I started to get concerned. She noticed and stopped talking about him deftly changing the subject back to Masterpiece…and Daniel.

"Leslie told me that Daniel raised all kinds of a stink with Griffen when he got the news of your's and Griffen's break up this morning," Ashley laughed. "I'm surprised Griffen let him say those things to him without driving up to Memphis and killing him."

"All part of the act," I smiled. I had forgotten about Daniel's promise but remembered it now. "How did you hear about that?"

"Griffen must have said something to Ben. He told Addy and she told Leslie," she said and Addy blushed.

"I hope you don't care," Addy said.

"Of course not, Addy," I said.

"So, would you really go out with someone else, Elliott?" Addy asked, and it caught me by surprise. She usually did not pry. That was Ashley's specialty.

"Of course she wouldn't!" Ashley said for me. "She'd be an idiot to let Griffen get away. This is just her ploy to keep him hooked. I think the horse-crazy girl can teach us all a lot about guys!"

"That's not all true, Ashley," I laughed. "You make me sound like a genius, but it's not like that. I really *don't* know if I'll marry him."

"I know you will because I'll knock you in the head if you don't," Ashley said. "What's the big deal? You love him, he loves you…you live happily ever after, and now it looks like you'll have great fortunes to spend as well! With this one, you'll never have to work a day in your life if you don't want to."

"Ashley, it's not that simple," I said.

"It worked for my parents," she insisted. "You're just looking for reasons – there will never be a perfect guy – you have to take what you can get and hope for the best."

I decided not to argue. Neither of them had any idea of what kind of past Griffen had; like me, they had parents that loved each other and were not at each other's throats all the time. They had no idea what kinds of darkness lurked behind closed doors and neither did I, really. Griffen's past was something I intended to keep to myself, but I had to constantly consider it when planning a future. I wish I had found someone for which things did not have to be so complicated, but I hadn't. So, no matter how much I didn't want to, I was determined to keep all my options for future prospects open.

The Alabama hunt, Wild Run Hounds, was open to guests, and William said they were a fun, rowdy bunch. The Masters of this hunt found land then started a hunt, and he said the galloping and views here were better than any in the country. When we arrived, everyone welcomed us with open arms. Ashley came along on this trip for the parties, and because we had heard that people could ride with their wheel whippers-in who were like our mounted whippers-in. These guys used trucks rather than horses to assist in monitoring their hounds. She also heard that they often saw the most action. All of us needed a change of scenery.

We arrived in the dark. Thankfully, someone was on hand to direct us to a paddock where Harley and Masterpiece would stay. This group hunted on both Saturdays and Sundays because their members traveled so far to get to their glorious galloping country. We were in for both days and hoped our horses were up to the challenge.

The hunt house was rocking when we arrived. We brought plenty of food to share, and we ate, drank, and swapped stories. Soon I felt like I'd known these people all my life. There were more guys at this hunt than usual, and that was a pleasant surprise. Most were married to hard-riding very likeable women, but a few, we noticed, were single and definitely noticing us. *Ah, the pleasures of being the new girls in town.*

They fluttered around Ashley, and she worked them like Scarlet O'Hara under the Twelve Oaks pecans. I loved to watch her in action and was glad to see she kept her options open in spite of the goofy physician boyfriend. I was content to pick up her strays, as usual, for it had worked well enough for me over the years for my requisite football and sorority function dates. Although I had never found anyone that could come close to Griffen, I reminded myself that I had to hold out some hope in case this desperate scheme of mine didn't work. Addy was devoted to Ben and made it clear that she was being polite only, no possibilities surrounding her. She was a dead end, to several of the guys' dismay.

Eventually we moved to the den and gathered around the fireplace. Every room was decorated with fox/coyote/bobcat and horse/hound accents. Next to the fireplace, a huge plaque had brass nameplates with what looked like hunt members' names and the dates engraved on them. At the top, it said "Gone to Ground." Since there were so many, I hoped it was not a list of the members that had died. Upon closer inspection, I saw that many had the same name…so that couldn't be the reason.

"I see you've noticed our wall of fame," Jennifer Muse, an elegant brunette in her early 50's said.

"What do the names mean?" I asked.

"Henry has a crazy tradition here that makes us a little different than most hunts," she said with a mischievous glint in her dark eyes. "When foxhunting began in this country, is was a far more competitive sport than you see today. You could say he revived that old spirit and came up with another way to help pay for hound food, jumps, and anything else the hunt needs from time to time."

"Each member, guest, or even car-follower that gets to the game first, whether it is bayed, goes to ground, or happens to get caught, gets a nameplate, but also gets to donate $100 to the hunt," she said.

"But, how does that work?" I asked. "Why is the name not always just one of the whippers-in or field masters?"

"Once we get on a run here, field hierarchy is relaxed. Of course, no one is to ever run over or get ahead of the hounds, but you are free to pass the field master and take your own line – but only when they are on a run. That means you can dash away on your own if you see the game take off or know where the game is likely to go. We have so much room here that it works great. But, we also require that everyone carry a compass and encourage them to also take their cell phones."

"It looks like you've accounted for a lot of game over the years," I said, impressed.

"Oh, we have. We have so many coyotes here it is hard not to view every time we hunt."

"Every time?" Addy and Ashley asked in unison. As they said it, I looked closer – that large plaque was only for this season. Unbelievable.

"We have a great place here."

"That's awesome," I said, my long dormant competitive juices stirring. If only I had Viva, my name would be on that plaque this weekend I was sure. With Masterpiece, I started to worry that this bunch would rile him up so much, that I would be lucky to return in one piece.

One talkative, cute guy started showing some interest in me, and I appraised him like I would examine a nice horse. He was not much taller than I was, had a great build, and was probably my age or slightly older. He had short blonde hair that looked like it would be soft and dark brown eyes. He said he was at Alabama and planned to graduate the next spring. He'd been a jockey before and had foxhunted off and on most of his life. I think his name was Scott, but I couldn't remember.

"I just thought of something," he said, and he addressed the three of us. "I bet you know that guy, that Case guy that's in the movie now. My sister said he usually hunts in the Memphis area and that they discovered him when he was hunting in Nashville. Hired as a stunt rider then got to be the star. You know who I'm talking about. Don't ya'll know him? I bet you do because it was all over the news today that he dumped his girlfriend. I don't blame him. Why would he hang on to a hometown honey when he's got the world chasing after him? That would be the life – all because of a foxhunt!"

Silence.

A very pregnant pause that he and the others did not seem to notice. They would soon, though, unless someone slayed it. I could not find the words.

"Yeah, we know him," Ashley said. Addy was too stunned to speak.

"Really? Can he ride for real?" he said.

"Oh yes," Ashley said. "For real."

"How do you know? Does he hunt with ya'll?" he pressed.

"Yes," I said. *Might as well shoot the elephant in the room now.* "I'm the one he dumped…hence, the girl trip."

That stopped the conversation. He looked at me like he'd been kicked in the stomach, and I actually felt sorry for him. The rest of the members and guests looked at us like we had been elevated to star status. Most had heard about this in the morning papers, and I registered that they were trying to remember my face and see if it matched what they had seen or heard from friends. Griffen, it seemed, was even bigger news in the small foxhunting world. I would definitely have to spend more time flying if I had to resort to broadening my social horizons.

"Oh, no… I'm really really sorry that I brought that up," he stammered.

"It's fine, really," I said and smiled at him. He looked devastated. "Really."

"Well, at least now I know you'll let me take you to dinner tomorrow, maybe? Since you, well, you know, and if you're interested," he said, and it was touching. He *was* cute. And it looked like he would probably do all the talking.

"We'll see," I said. "I have to see how you ride."

He grinned.

"Well Scott, that was fast!" another guy named Chip, I think, said. "And we've all just been hovering around them. Now you're going to swoop in and take one out tomorrow night!" He laughed and put everyone at ease.

"Hold on, now, I have not said yes to Scott," I stated firmly. "Let this be a challenge. Let's have a race at the end of the day with a jump off or something – you said you have jumps outside. We can use those if that's ok with Henry. May the best rider who so wants to wine and dine Ashley or me tomorrow evening to assuage my broken heart and attempt to win hers, win!"

Henry Williams, the Master and huntsman, came over to address his raucous guys. "I might add, dear, that in the interest of your safety and propriety among these young men whom I know so well, that we propose that the two winners get a candlelight dinner here at the hunt house with you two – well-chaperoned, of course," he beamed. "And attended by the losers. Mostly because the nearest restaurant is an hour away, and I feel quite certain that none of these upstanding gentlemen will be fit to drive anywhere after having hunted all day and a dinner date with either of you."

Ashley looked at me, very impressed. Addy thought I'd lost my mind and so did I, in fact. *Where did* that *come from?*

"Furthermore, the challenge will be held *after* the hounds are all returned safely to the kennels, and we will have a two part test. First in the race will dine with Miss Elliott and first in the jump-off will dine with Miss Ashley. Do we have any that wish to compete?"

Five guys including Scott and Chip lifted their drinks in the air and cheered. *Oh dear.* The sixth and seventh ones were married, and their wives good-naturedly poked them in the ribs.

"All right then," William continued. "We'll have a short race then a jump-off, both held right out here in front of the hunt house at 4:00. That is only, however, *if* the hounds are all in. If not, then my wife and I will have dinner with both of you while they are scouring the country for the beasts they lost. And, if the same person wins both…he gets you both to himself."

Everyone laughed and cheered at this pronouncement and obviously, with this group, a good time was always had by all.

"Also," he said, "William and I are close friends, and he threatened me with my life if I let anything happen to his girls," he smiled. "Dinner at 6:00 here in the main room and outside by the fire, and we'll have the private dining area set up in the den. Welcome to Wild Run."

I was really beginning to like this bunch.

We woke at 6:00 am to the sounds of our cell phones. Ashley's blared *I'm Here for the Party* and Addy's an old fashioned telephone ringing. Mine jumped in with *Walk this Way*. We had stayed up way past our regular hunting bedtimes laughing and talking by the fire. It was so much fun swapping stories with new foxhunters, but we finally left for our hotel and fell asleep before our heads hit the pillows.

After a quick continental breakfast, we drove back to the hunt house. Addy left to feed the horses and check their water, and Ashley headed to the kitchen to whip up some breakfast for whomever was staying in the hunt house. I hooked up the trailer, organized our gear, and finished getting dressed. Just as I was pulling on my boots, Addy came running over to the trailer, breathless.

"Masterpiece is gone! I guess Harley and he didn't get along and Harley ran him out of the paddock. There aren't any boards broken, so he must have jumped out!" she gasped.

I threw on a coat and ran to the paddocks. No Masterpiece. My heart raced – *Was there a highway nearby? Would he try to run back to Oxford? How long has he been gone?* My head spun and stomach flipped. *Where would I even begin to look? And where was everyone?*

It looked like everyone that stayed in the hunt house was either still in bed or had left for the kennels. I hated to wake anyone and had no idea where the kennels were. *This is so embarrassing.* Finally, I saw one of the ladies feeding her horse, Cynthia, I think…

"Ms. Cynthia? I'm Elliott, Elliott Marks. And I seem to be missing my horse. Can you tell me if there's a highway nearby or how to call the police?"

"Oh dear. You shouldn't need to do that. Just wait a minute, and I'll call Henry. We can get one of the hound trucks and go look for him. This place has cows on it, so there are plenty of pastures to contain him. We'll find him, don't worry," she said and fished for her cell phone.

"Elliott!" Addy yelled, and I looked back toward the hunt house. Someone had Masterpiece and was leading him to the paddocks.

I ran over to them, stopping short enough not to spook Masterpiece… just in case. It was Chip, the very cute guy who seemed to have more than a passing interest in Ashley.

"Thank you so much, Chip!" I beamed. "You saved my weekend!"

"He was at the kennels ready to hunt," he said. "How did he get out?"

"We think Harley, Addy's horse, chased him out of the paddock. There weren't any boards broken, so he must have jumped."

"That's impressive. I'll take him if you get tired of him. With scope like that, he'd make a good jumper. That is, if I can get him past Henry. He tried to steal him already since he came straight to the hounds when he escaped. Henry likes that in a horse!"

His smile was mesmerizing, and I thought I'd have to flirt a little more with this one if Ashley discarded him. Right now, though, I was hoping he'd get her mind off that doctor-guy.

"You can ride with me if you want, Elliott," Chip said, and I blinked, caught off guard by his invitation.

"Thanks, Chip," I said. "Masterpiece hasn't, well, I haven't hunted him…yet, so I'd better ride in the field." I dropped my gaze, embarrassed that this horse was completely new to hunting. I now felt ridiculous that I had brought him at all.

"You sure? The field can be harder on a horse than whipping-in," he said. No reprimand, just a polite way of letting me save face.

"Thanks, really," I said. "But I would appreciate your retrieving him if we get separated."

"Absolutely," he said, smiling impressively…again. *What a smile…*

Henry's voice cracked orders over Chip's radio, so he wished me luck, as he jogged back to the kennels. "See you tonight at dinner then!" he yelled over his shoulder when he was within earshot of all the other guys.

I laughed and hurried away to get ready.

Henry invited Addy and me to ride with him, for most everyone else either whipped-in or rode as hilltoppers. This wide-open country required as many whippers-in as possible, so all hands helped, including riders in the field and two wheel whippers-in.

I was nervous about riding so close to the hounds with Masterpiece and rightfully so, but I certainly did not want to hilltop, or ride in the slower group. He leapt and bucked for the first twenty minutes causing me much embarrassment. Addy offered to ride back to the hilltoppers or the hunt house with me, but I was determined to stay out until he flung me off. He never tried to kick the hounds, but he was a twitching wreck for the first hour. After some long gallops in the deep, soft, mud, he was much more manageable. The Pelham would replace the snaffle, tomorrow, though, for it had much better stopping leverage. Ben and Griffen would be gloating that they had been right about the bit I should have used.

The day was overcast, and I noticed that everything, the woods, ground, and sky, was gray. The bright coats stood out like red marks on newsprint and the black jackets, too, were easy to spot. I could see for miles here, and I thought that if I ever whipped-in in country like this, I would want binoculars to tell which hound was doing what.

Masterpiece had settled and began to relax behind Harley, as he expertly negotiated the ditches, muddy banks, and limbs scattered along the way. He did not understand how to sit back on his haunches in the turns, and we slipped several times. I hoped the Pelham in his mouth tomorrow would help with that, too. All in all, though, he had a soft mouth and was really flexible. He just needed to flex *with* me when and where *I* wanted and not on sporadic, panicky, whims.

Occasionally we saw the other riders, and they were all beautifully turned out and sat their horses well. Only a few slouched, but most of those were guests or new to the sport. All the contenders for the afternoon competition made sure to ride by us, and I loved the attention and the eye-candy. Addy rolled her eyes.

"They probably will not even do it," I said. "That was just hyped-up testosterone-fueled drunken banter. We've seen that before."

"I don't think so, Elliott," she said. "These guys are itching for competition, and this is right up their alley. You may have started a new sport."

"We've only revived a very old one," I said. "The tournament. We just have two princess's hands for which they can vie. Three if you weren't so impossibly devoted to Ben."

"Yeah, well, impossibly devoted I am. And don't you forget it!"

"No possible way to forget it when you two are together. He's just as bad as you are," I said and winked at her. She blushed and positively glowed thinking about him.

Hounds were milling about around us now, and Henry cheered them on. Masterpiece would not stand, so I circled him in place quietly staying as far back as possible to give the hounds room. Finally, one hound spoke, the others honored, and we were off!

The three of us crashed through underbrush, splashed through swampy hollows, and leapt fallen logs following the pack's uproarious cry. At one log, Harley jumped so high that Addy's stirrup came off her saddle, but she was able to keep it on her foot before the whole thing hit the ground. She snatched the leather and slung it over her head never slowing from her pell-mell gallop. I was astounded at how well she was riding, and was doing all I could to contain Masterpiece and keep him from banging my knees into trees.

"Tally ho!" Henry cried, and we saw the coyote right in front of the pack splashing through the swamp. Almost instantly, the pack was on him and the coyote went under. Henry rode to the coyote, plunged into the now waist-deep water, and Addy grabbed his horse's reins.

"There he goes!" I called as the coyote surfaced, scrambled onto the bank, and dashed away.

Meanwhile, Henry mounted his horse. Although Addy didn't have time to reattach her stirrup leather, she bolted after him with the pack. Within fifty yards, they bayed him in a huge log. Henry dismounted again, blew gone to ground, and Addy handed me Harley's reins as she jumped down to photograph the very angry and wet, but safe coyote.

The rest of the field and staff gathered around to see the coyote, then Henry called them away to find another. He bellowed his praise at Addy and me for not only being right with him, but also at Addy for having the presence of mind to photograph the moment. He loved it when she showed him she'd only had one stirrup for that run.

"Send me those pictures, and I'll sponsor the plaque for you, young lady!" he shouted with a hearty laugh.

Several other members had joined the group, and the field had now grown to more than fifteen riders.

"How's that horse doing?" Chip called to me.

"I'm still on!" I said. "He's finally settling down, so maybe I'll keep him."

"Hey, I've got dibs if you change your mind," Scott said. "A clean jumper with speed and good luck. He's all mine!"

"Get back to your places, boys," Henry said. "We're just getting started. The ladies and I have coyotes to chase. Jessica, glad you could make it! You and Alex can take first flight…if you can contain these enthusiastic guests. "

I was disappointed that we now had to ride behind a field master since we had enjoyed riding with Henry. Although I had not spent a lot of my brief foxhunting career in the field, I remembered that field masters can make or break a hunt, and I hoped these were as good with the first flight as Ben. Some stayed too far away to feel a part of the hunt, and we had just had a blast being right up with the action. I hoped Jessica and Alex were the exception and made sure we stayed with hounds and got to jump some as well.

Six other riders joined our flight, and we made brief introductions. This group had been delayed with trailer trouble, but was ready to roll now that they had found their hounds. I was glad to meet these riders, but Masterpiece started giving me much more trouble with the addition of new horses. I moved him to the back of the group, which made things worse.

"Addy, can you ride in front of me?" I asked quietly, when we had a break in the action. "Masterpiece is being a nut, and I may need Harley's behind for brakes."

"I've got you, Elliott," Addy said.

Henry cast the hounds in the woods, and we jumped two coops set over barbed wire fences to get closer to them. I was relieved that Jessica and Alex certainly knew how to entertain their field. Masterpiece started hopping and jerking his head, and I began to have real trouble containing him. When the hounds struck, I barely had time to settle him before he leapt straight up and bolted. I grabbed his breastplate in one hand, held the reins in the other, dug my heels as deep down as I could manage, and prayed.

Our flight catapulted across two pastures, down a narrow trail through the woods, and up a hill. The whole time, I strained to keep my balance and prepared to haul harder on Masterpiece's reins. When we reached the top, I saw a lake on our right, and to my horror, we approached the dam at what I thought was top speed. Little did I know, Masterpiece was just getting started.

The coyote darted out of the woods in plain sight, and I knew I would not be long for this world should someone fly by me. And fly by they did. The field and Addy, formerly my brakes, charged after the coyote, and I did what I could to hold on.

Henry was way in front, but we were narrowing the gap at a terrifying pace. Masterpiece bolted past Addy and Harley and the rest of the field – including the field masters. At this point, I knew I would not be invited back, for I had broken every rule of order even for this hunt. I was doing my best now to survive and keep from hurting others with this maniacal runaway. I had no idea where the coyote had gone – I was riding for my life.

Masterpiece ignored my efforts to slow him, and there was no room to circle – lake on the right and steep drop on the left. At the spillway, we clattered over the concrete, and my heart flipped hoping he would not slip and kill us both.

"Incoming!" I screamed, hoping Henry would move so I would not catapult into him from behind.

Thankfully, Henry turned left, but there was no turning Masterpiece at that speed – even the usual pony club pulley rein action having long been ignored. I kept him on the gravel road, but it, too, had no space for turning a speeding horse. Both sides were lined with barbed wire fences, and there was a blind bend three hundred yards ahead. I took a deep breath trying to calm myself while this fifteen hundred pounds of madness thundered beneath, each desperate tug on the reins causing him to thrust his jaw harder against my efforts and plunge faster.

If a car comes around this corner, Masterpiece and I will go through the windshield. That will kill the driver and maybe the passengers. It is one thing for me to die, but I'm not going to let this crazy beast hurt anyone else. I've got to stop – what can I do at this speed? Dear God, please help me think!

Finally, the fence disappeared on the left leaving thick woods as my only option. *If I could get him to turn into the woods – maybe he would stop. At the very least, maybe he would hit a tree.* I leaned back slightly putting my knees up in "dashboard" position, bent my head, braced myself, and turned Masterpiece into the woods. He responded slightly, and I prepared for the worst.

Dear God, please protect me. I hope my guardian angels are on alert!

Branches ripped me off the saddle, and time stood still. It felt like a hundred hands lifted me off the saddle, held me airborne for several minutes, and set me on the ground. Actually, limbs and vines snatched my jacket, ripping it and my face in several places before slamming me to the ground behind Masterpiece. A large oak tree stopped him, and I had never been so thankful to be on the ground.

I sprang up, grabbed his reins, and kicked him as hard as I could manage in the ribs and stomach, screaming incoherently at the top of my lungs. Angry, terrified, exhausted, and now dizzy, I pulled the reins over his head and collapsed on the ground beside him. His nose was bloody from smashing into the tree, but I saw no other injuries. Once I realized we had survived, the world started to spin, and I put my head between my knees. Then, my body began to shake.

"Elliott!" a strange female voice yelled from a very long way away.

I stood up, unsteadily, to show her I was not dead, waved, then sat back down as the world continued to spin. As far as I could tell, I had not hit my head, but I was ever so dizzy.

The field master, Jessica, galloped up to me and wrapped her arms around my shoulders.

"Hey girl, are you all right?" she asked softly.

"I think so," I said after a few minutes. "Nothing's broken, but my pride." *And my foot from kicking the stuffing out of my horse, but I didn't tell her that.*

"Don't worry about that," she said squeezing my shoulders gently. "I'm just glad you are alive."

"Is that Elliott?" a male voice asked.

"Yes. She's fine. And that's a miracle," Jessica said.

I looked up to see Scott. He had galloped from the bend in the gravel road back to where we were sitting. I glanced at him to be polite then looked down again; no words would form, and I was so very dizzy.

"I saw you come across the dam – then head down the road," he said, hesitantly. "That's when I knew you weren't after the coyote… and were in trouble. So I galloped to the highway to stop traffic in case you couldn't stop your horse in time. You would have had room to circle on the other side, but you didn't have any way to know that."

"Thanks," was all I could manage. I looked up when he finished talking.

"That was quite a ride. You want to switch horses?"

"No, thanks. I'll just be sure to toss this snaffle bit. I'll be all right as long as I don't let him get away from me again. He just caught me off guard."

Jessica helped me back on Masterpiece after a few moments, and Scott radioed to Henry that everyone was fine, and that he was back in position. I still felt weak, nauseous, and embarrassed but said nothing. Addy's eyes were wide when she saw me, but she didn't say anything. She smiled, grateful that we were in one piece.

"Henry, sir, I apologize," I said when we caught up with him. "I will retire immediately if you can point me to the hunt house."

"Nonsense, young lady, that is, unless you want to retire," he barked with a smile. "If you're up to staying out, don't give that a thought. Most of us have had that happen to us at least once in our lives; I'm just glad you weren't hurt. And, thanks for the warning when you hit the spillway. That horse sounded like he was revving up for a shuttle launch!"

Despite my humiliation and embarrassment, I forced myself to smile, and Addy gave me a "thumbs up." Masterpiece was in big trouble.

The more I thought about the incident, the angrier I got. This hunt may be getting a good horse cheap.

As if he could read my thoughts, Masterpiece behaved perfectly for the next thirty minutes. Perhaps the bloody nose served its purpose. Henry cast the hounds near a creek bottom hoping to find another coyote. I rode right in Addy's pocket letting Harley's calm presence keep Masterpiece settled. In this area, there was plenty of room, so we rode beside first flight rather than behind them. Masterpiece could see Henry and the hounds and settled; although he would still be getting new headgear the next day.

Hounds struck again, and we raced after them. Masterpiece was more subdued, but I fought a wave of panic when he tried to pass Harley. I had already galloped way past the line between exhilaration and terror once today, and I did not feel up to crossing it again any time soon. Five deep breaths later, I had his head firmly planted behind Harley, and we galloped at a sane pace after the hounds.

Two coyotes later, Henry called it a day. These escaped, but the staff was able to view them many times and report their direction and descriptions. Henry said they were out in force since the cows were calving this time of year.

"So, how does this hunt compare with yours?" Cynthia asked. She had been riding with the hilltoppers, but joined us on her big, pretty gray since we were roading the hounds back to the kennels.

"Much more open," Addy said. "And a lot more coyotes! This place is unbelievable!"

"I was glad to have the action, too, since this horse is so new," I said. "He'll be wearing much more bit tomorrow and hobbles tonight for sure."

"We have an extra paddock you can put him in tonight," Cynthia said. "The Browns aren't hunting tomorrow, and they were right next to your other horse's paddock."

"Thanks. I'll still put hobbles on him just in case," I said.

"We usually see a lot of game, but rarely do we get to bay a coyote. Most of the time they escape in the culverts. That was a surprise. Be sure to send me the pictures, Addy," Cynthia said. "You two brought us luck today in spite of your little incident, Elliott. By the way, that was quite impressive – the part we could actually see. I'm glad you're all right. I hope visitors' viewing luck holds for tomorrow, too!"

I was right about the competition – the guys were all fired up about this, and ten competed, including two thirteen-year-old boys, Turner Crews and Will Morrison, who were being given great grief about their willingness to participate. They didn't care for which hand they fought; they just wanted to win. We were *old* to them, anyway, but they reveled in the competition.

We laughed and cheered and decided that the next time we came, we'd reverse roles and let the girls compete for the guys, and we'd supply the girls. In the end, the teenagers beat all the others hands down. They may not have necessarily had the best horses, but they rode fearlessly. They beat the other guys by at least two lengths in the race, and their horses both would have jumped the redwood forest clean. They played rock-paper-scissors to see who dined with whom, for to them, either of us would do just fine. Scott was not happybeaten so soundly by his young cousins, but he agreed to be headwaiter for the dining rooms.

More people came to the Saturday dinner and party than had hunted that morning. About thirty people, many of them landowners, came by to hear tales of the day. After I had been "wined" and dined by my cute victor and kissed him on the cheek, I went outside to sit by the fire ring. Scott sat beside me, his dark eyes glowing in the firelight.

"Elliott, I really am sorry about what I said last night," he said. "And, I would like to take you to dinner some time…in a restaurant, not the hunt house den. If, of course, you thought that I looked good enough for you on a horse." He smiled his easy smile, for he knew he had passed *that* test.

"That would be nice," I said. "I'll keep it in mind. Call me if you are ever in Oxford." *I knew he was just being nice and trying to make me feel better after what he said about Griffen. He'd never come all that way for a date with, well, me, but it was nice to flirt harmlessly with guys I would probably never see again.*

"I may be there sooner than you think."

Sunday's hunt started at 8:00 am so we were on the road to Oxford by noon. Masterpiece had been perfect, and I hoped that now I had the right combination of bit and balance going for us to start making real progress together.

We did not view that day and not as many riders hunted, but I saw lots of deer, ducks, and even a few raccoons. Jessica and Alex made sure we jumped plenty of coops and ditches in spite of the slow game day. Henry said they were going to incorporate the lady tournament for all their guests to encourage more women to hunt with them. He invited us to come back any time, and we promised to do just that.

Ashley gushed on and on about Chip, and I hoped that would get her mind off the Memphis doctor. Her cell phone buzzed, and she took the call. When she hung up, she was angry.

"What's the matter?" I asked.

"John's mad that I will not be back in time to go out tonight," she said. "I *told* him we'd be gone all weekend."

"We'll be back in plenty of time," I said.

"Yes, but I don't want to do anything except blob," she said. "I'm not *up* to him tonight."

"Are you sure you want to date him, Ashley, really?" I asked.

"I don't, actually, but my parents get mad if I'm not dating *someone*," she said. "They think it is better for me to have one boyfriend at a time than date around."

"Really?" I asked. I had never known that. That explained a lot about her.

"Yes, so I have to keep him around until I find something else," she groaned.

"So you liked Chip?" I asked, not wanting to pry unless she wanted to talk about it.

"Oh yes, so far," she smiled. "But he lives so far away. I'm sure nothing will ever come of it."

We rode for a while in silence as I let her think about Chip and continue if she wanted to talk about him. We were friends, but not so close that we shared a lot of intimate girl talk, mostly just jabber. But what she said earlier made me wonder about Ben and why they broke up. As far as I knew, she hadn't had anyone else in the wings when that happened, and there had not been a lot of drama surrounding it. And, they were still such good friends. I wondered if Griffen and I would be like that if we really had to break up – for good. I shivered at the thought.

Since Addy was snoring softly, I felt safe in asking Ashley more about Ben. "If you are supposed to always have someone around, then why, or how did you and Ben break up?"

"He was never that interested in me, Elliott," she whispered. "I never could get him to *see* me. He really is more like a big brother, and that suits me fine. Besides, all he ever talked about was foxhunting. Kind of like someone else I know." She rolled her eyes at me and smiled.

"It looks like he sees Addy, though," I said. "Don't you think? They click."

"Yes, they're perfect for each other," Ashley said. "I'm really happy for them. They seem to have it so easy."

"And you are still such good friends," I said.

"That is why I knew we were not right for each other. He always treated me more like a sister than a girlfriend. Very much the gentleman, but almost too much of one…if you know what I mean," she said.

I wasn't sure exactly what she meant, but before I could ask, my phone buzzed. That wonderful 615 number.

"I am in one piece and on my way home," I said, delighted that he was calling to check on me.

"Good," Griffen said. "Call me when you are thirty minutes from the barn, and I'll meet you. Oh, and we have an open day next Saturday. William has to be out of town, and I promised my uncle I'd duck hunt with him as soon as an open weekend came up. See if Addy and Ashley would like to come to my duck camp. I'll invite Ben, and Ashley can bring that doctor guy. He told me he likes to duck hunt when I met him at her party."

"That sounds like fun," I said. "How's the neighbor situation?"

"I don't really know, but we can discuss that with my uncle when we get there," he said. "How was Masterpiece?"

"A handful, but much better today," I said. I did not want to tell him about the runaway incident...not yet. He and Ben both would be unmerciful about my not using the right bit...taking a green horse to a visiting hunt...and on and on, and I was not ready to deal with that over the phone.

"The people were great; you'd love them! That is a *wild* crowd," I said, directing the conversation away from Masterpiece. "They're almost all guys. Oh, and in case you find out from someone else, I had a date...with a thirteen-year-old."

"Poor kid, I guess I'm going to have to kill him," he growled. "Maybe if you date around with guys *that* age I'll be able to handle this."

"You have all the cards," I said.

"Oh, *right*," he said. "See you at the barn. And clear everyone else out, please. I'd like some *us* time."

I shivered and resisted the urge to accelerate. "I'm thirty minutes out now. Come and get it."

THE CAMP

Chapter 24

Feel your horse as you ride him,
Learn from the rhythm of his strides.
It's something no book can teach you,
No teacher can give you,
These treasured lessons, the magical rides.

When we pulled into the barn, Griffen was not there. I hid my disappointment, for I had been ready to see him and tell him about Masterpiece. We unloaded the horses, brushed them, and turned them out.

Masterpiece was on the same turnout schedule as Griffen's horses and he was glad to be free. Jet and Churchill whinnied in protest that their stable mate was already given the run of the place. We had put up our gear and cleaned it by the time Griffen arrived. I told Addy to take my truck and that I'd be riding with Griffen. She winked at me, collected Ashley, and left. A few more people mingled around the barn, but they were getting ready to leave, too.

"Do you want to come to my duck camp next weekend?" he asked the girls as they drove by.

"We're in!" they said in unison, and they left.

"Sorry I'm late," he said. "Tell me about that horse."

I filled him in leaving out the bucks and kicks, but telling him most of the truth. The runaway part he took surprisingly well, chastising me, like I knew he would about being foolish enough to hunt him in a snaffle the first time out and allowing him to gallop. I helped him turn out Jet and Churchill, and we walked to the pasture, away from the barn's activity. It was getting cold, but I didn't care. I was just glad to be near Griffen.

We sat on a slope overlooking the horses grazing below, their teeth cropping rhythmically as they nibbled at the barren winter ground. Jet rolled in the soft dirt, then trotted over to claim the treats he knew Griffen had for him. Masterpiece followed but was not brave enough to steal anything around Jet's menacing hindquarters. I stood up and walked to him, hand extended with a peppermint. Jet tried to follow, but Griffen stopped him, wrapping his gorgeous arms around Jet's neck.

Masterpiece raised his head, snorted, and acted as if he'd whirl away at any second. His body trembled, but he fixed his wild eyes on my extended hand. I spoke low, approached cautiously, then stopped. He relaxed and lowered his beautiful head, then shook it from side to side. I backed up, and he took a step in my direction. When I stopped, he reached his lips to my hands and took the candy.

I moved closer, rubbed him behind the ears, stroked his soft neck, then turned back to Griffen.

"He's coming around," Griffen said. "You are so lovely, Elliott. Especially with your new battle scars. I guess I have that crazy horse to thank for that."

He wrapped his arms around me then and pulled me close. Jet bumped us both, and Griffen reached back to push him away as he bent to kiss me. I played with the fine hairs behind his ears, tickled my fingers down his neck, and tried to remember to breathe as he kept kissing me. Standing became impossible, so he eased me down gently beside him in the sparse grass by the tree, his arms surrounding and swallowing me completely. I rolled onto my back and pulled him beside me feeling his wonderful warmth everywhere. My arms gripped his shoulders, and I kissed him, reaching up as he held himself over me just slightly so my lungs were not pinned.

"I missed you," he said into my neck as he kissed up and down my jaw and back to my lips.

"Me, too," I said as I closed my eyes and let him brush soft kisses all along my neck.

We stayed there watching the horses and each other for what was left of the afternoon. The sunset glowed on the horizon and stars started to sparkle behind us. The horses had long since wandered off, and night fell around us like a blanket.

"I'm hungry," he said. "Come home with me, and I'll cook you a steak."

"Feed me, I'm yours."

The week went by fast, and Griffen was able to attend classes without too much hassle. Scott said he wanted to come to Oxford this weekend, but I told him that I had already made out-of-town plans. I was surprised that he called, and my stomach lurched any time I thought about going out with anyone beside Griffen.

Griffen's acquiescence to the dating plan did not mean he approved. I was beginning to think he was playing this game to his advantage by preventing me from having time for anyone or anything else beside him. I didn't know how he was keeping up with his studies, but I didn't ask. He was masterful at keeping me out-of-sight, so I had had no more flash camera surprises.

Friday finally arrived, and we left for the duck camp. I was overjoyed about going again, especially on a hunt where we could stay out longer. It was funny watching Griffen get ready – I think there were as many logistical considerations for this event as there were for foxhunts.

The girls and I were staying at the Hale's camp next door to Griffen's. We would have the run of their place, for they weren't going to be hunting that weekend. We would all travel together from Oxford but in two cars. Ashley said John would meet us at the Madidi Room at 6:00 for dinner. Our plan was to duck hunt Saturday morning then return to Oxford. Griffen and I were considering hunting for two days, but that had not yet been decided.

I loved the drive through the dark cypress bottomland once we crossed the Mississippi River levee. We were safe from prying eyes here, because access was limited at all these river clubs. Only members and their guests could come or go. That was strange to me, but very convenient now that I was clandestinely involved with an international superstar. I smiled to myself at the absurdity.

"Now what?" Griffen asked.

"Oh, nothing…just thinking about you and your paparazzi," I said.

"What about it?" he asked warily.

"You're handling it well, but I'm glad to have some privacy from the world's prying eyes this weekend," I said.

"Me, too," he said. "I can focus on feasting my eyes upon you rather than dodging cameras and well-wishers."

"Where are the goons?" I asked.

"Not necessary here, thank goodness."

We unpacked everything and Panzer positively exploded with delight being back in his true element. I was sad that he had not been able to go duck hunting as much this year, but hopefully tomorrow would make up for it. Griffen's uncle was so happy to have all of us invade his world, but he declined our invitation to dinner, preferring an early evening alone with his steak. We promised him we'd frolic at the Hale's when we returned from dinner so we would not interrupt him.

John was waiting for us when we arrived at the Madidi Room. He had already been seated and had ordered sweet tea for us all. I noticed that in addition to his tea, he had already started on what looked like gin. His efficient and easy manner was admirable, but something about him disturbed me. I had not been around him and Ashley much, and what I saw made me nervous.

The hostess recognized Griffen at once but was discreet. After all, her boss was Morgan Freeman, so I'm sure she was accustomed to stars popping in unannounced. Still, Griffen was a sight to behold, and she went out of her way to be gracious. He returned the favor and autographed everything she placed before him, even consenting to a photograph with her and the other staff.

I returned to watching John's and Ashley's interaction. John seemed edgy, but I did not know why. Ben and Addy hadn't noticed, but Griffen had. He met my eyes and raised his eyebrows when John started getting pushy with the staff. John was trying to sound jovial and casual, but he had an edge to his tone.

"Hey, do you think y'all could stop stargazing and take our orders now?" he snapped. "We've got some hungry people here wanting some service."

Ashley ignored that and acted like nothing happened. Ben and Griffen let it go, but I was sure that would be strike one. I hoped John had the sense not to test either of them, for I didn't want to be around for that showdown.

We placed our appetizer and dinner orders at the same time along with more drinks. Griffen had been here many times before, and we let him guide us all with the menu. His reputation for excellent culinary taste preceded him among all of us except John. He made his own choices.

"So, girls, tell us about last weekend at Wild Run," Griffen said to get some conversation going about something other than John's tedious movie inquiries. "All Elliott would tell me was that there were more guys than girls, and that you and she had dates with thirteen-year-old boys."

Everyone laughed except John. He bristled. Griffen noticed, and so did I.

"Elliott is insane," Addy said. "But you all know that. It seemed that the people there had already heard about your very public break-up with her, and they were all tripping over themselves to ask her out. Then she whipped those poor boys up into a frenzy by suggesting they compete for the privilege of wining and dining them. It was very proper and appropriate of course. William made sure that their Master, Henry, kept his boys on a short leash. The vanquished had to serve the victors. I thought it was priceless that the teenagers beat the older ones in the competition so badly."

"Why didn't you have a thirteen-year-old at your feet, Addy?" John asked, coldly.

"I'm way to shy to do something like that," she said. "Besides, Ben's not too fond of sharing."

"Well, neither am I," John growled. "I think that was highly inappropriate."

"It was a game, John," I said. "Ashley and I were playing around. She helped me, so I would not look ridiculous being the only one involved as the *prize*."

"Yes, but you *are* the only one that needed to save face," he snapped. "I don't know why you had to drag Ashley into that…spectacle."

"John…it was a game," Griffen said. "And I hardly think you or I need to feel threatened by little boys, or any boys, for that matter." He smiled conspiratorially at John, hoping to diffuse this bomb politely.

It worked. *Thank you, God. Thank you – there is hope for Griffen yet. Bright shining hope.*

"You're right, Case," he said, and his mood abruptly changed. "This little missy is way too much for any child," he said and pulled her to him. "She breaks hearts everywhere she goes. I guess I'll never get used to it."

Once the food arrived, the rest of the evening was delightful. John told fascinating stories about his duck hunting days in the Delta. He was a few years older than we were, but he related to us all in the universal language of the hunt. He ordered whatever drink that was that I noticed earlier four more times, and his speech became more and more animated. Fortunately, when we left, he didn't argue when Ashley offered to drive.

"Ah, beautiful and responsible is she," John proclaimed. "What more can a gentleman ask?"

"Here here to all three of them," Ben said as he raised his glass to us.

Back at camp, the guys decided to hang out with us for a little while longer at the Hale's place since it was late, and none of us was tired. We were keyed up from dinner and John's funny stories. John got everyone to play cards except me, since I had no idea how to play poker. I watched him take all Griffen's money first. Then the others fell to his skillful maneuvers. Even my untrained eye was impressed at how quickly he vanquished his foes.

Addy was getting tired, but we were not ready for the guys to leave, so she put in *Napoleon Dynamite*. The later we stayed up, the funnier the movie got, and we laughed at each other's reaction to the scenes until our sides hurt. After a while, we noticed that John and Ashley had disappeared.

"They're on the porch," Griffen said. "I saw them leave a few minutes ago."

The four of us were nestled on the couch. Griffen had his arm around me, and I reflected, again, on the simple pleasure of being in his arms so casually, so comfortably, and inhaling him. I leaned my head back and savored the feeling. It was nice, too, to be able to enjoy him in public for a change. I liked to see how he reacted to my friends and their mini-dramas.

Ben got up and walked toward the porch where John and Ashley had gone. Seconds later, he came briskly back into our room then left – out onto the porch. Griffen sat up when he saw how quickly Ben went outside.

"Stay here, Elliott," he said in a low, careful voice. "You too, Addy."

I immediately heard Barry shouting…at Ben.

"Get off me," John slurred. "This is not your business."

Addy and I bolted off the couch and ran to the porch.

"Get back inside," Griffen growled.

I heard Ashley crying, so I ignored Griffen and ran to her. As soon as I rounded the corner, John's bulk slammed into me knocking me over the porch rail. I fell for a long time before my body smashed into something very hard, then everything went blank.

PRESENT PAST

Chapter 25

No philosophers so thoroughly comprehend us as dogs and horses. They see through us at a glance.

~ *Herman Melville*

When I opened my eyes, it was cold. Griffen was leaning over me, but I still had on all my clothes. *Not in a hospital then this time, but where am I?*

"Elliott, can you hear me?" Griffen said softly. He looked so worried.

"Yes," I said and started to sit up.

"Wait, don't move," he said. "You fell a long way. Lie still for a minute, and let's see what hurts."

"Nothing hurts, Griffen, I'm fine," I said impatiently. "Where's Ashley?"

"In the cabin," Griffen said. "Don't worry about her; she's not hurt, but you may be."

"I'm fine," I said, wiggling my fingers and toes just in case. "All my parts are working…let me up."

"Go slowly," he said. "Make sure your neck's ok – can you move it?"

"Yes, see?" I said, as I raised myself up ever so slightly and slowly.

"You hit your head hard enough to black out," he said. "Just for a minute, but you were definitely out. I thought you were dead. We all did."

I slowly sat up and touched his pale face. "I'm fine. See? Watch this."

Carefully, I stood up as he helped me. Then I stretched up to his face and kissed him gently. "I'm fine."

The color had returned to his cheeks, and he bent down to kiss me so harshly on the lips that I gasped in surprise. When he pulled me to him I gasped again, but this time in pain.

"Ouch! That won't work." I stifled the scream that wanted to explode from my lips from the pain slicing through my side. "My ribs may not have been so lucky."

"We're going to Clarksdale," he snapped. "Come on, I'll help you get in my truck."

"I want to see Ashley first," I said.

"Here I am," she said weakly, stepping into my line of sight.

"What happened?"

Ashley smiled ruefully. "Ben beat the stuffing out of John. You just happened to get in the way of him being flung off of me."

"Did he hurt you?" I asked, horrified.

"No, but he was shaking me pretty hard when Ben rounded the corner," she said. "But not for long. It happened so fast. Ben was there, then Griffen; then Ben grabbed John and threw him off me. He slammed into you and you went flying..." she trailed off and looked away.

"I'm so sorry...I...I didn't see it coming...I had no idea he'd do that...that I'd made him so angry...and he'd had more to drink than I thought..." she said, her eyes glistening with tears that spilled over her burning cheeks.

"It was not your fault, Ashley," I said. "And I'm fine."

"And stupid," Griffen snapped. "I told you to stay inside. At least Addy didn't follow you."

"Ashley, I'm taking her to the hospital," he said. "You and Addy go to bed. I don't have any idea how long this will take, but I'm having her head checked. Set your alarms for whatever time you need to be ready at 7:00. We'll go a little later tomorrow morning, but that shouldn't matter. The ducks fly all day where we're going."

Griffen helped me into his truck. My ribs were really hurting now.

"So, where's Ben? And what did you do to John?" I asked.

"John will not be joining us tomorrow. Ben drove him to the gate. He had to unlock it to get him out of here," Griffen said.

"What did you *do* to him?" I repeated, hoping that jerk would suffer for what he did to Ashley, but hoping Griffen didn't kill him.

"He's not pretty anymore, but I had nothing to do with his condition. That handiwork was all Ben. When he caught him shaking Ashley, he tossed him…into you…then you went over the rail before I could do a thing. I ran to you, and Ben wailed on John until he couldn't get up. I had to stop Ben, or he would have killed him. And I really wanted him to." He waited a moment and then continued.

"But I didn't. I *know* what kind of scum he is. I recognized it, because I could see it in his eyes. It was all too familiar," he said, and his knuckles turned white, as he gripped the steering wheel.

When he slammed his fist on the wheel in frustration I jumped, and my ribs ached in protest.

"Elliott, I recognized it, because he is *me*! *That* is what I understand happens to beautiful, innocent girls like you when they're exposed to monsters!" His jaw clenched, and he stared angrily into the cold, black night.

"Look at you now," he hissed. "You're on your way to the hospital because that guy lost it. You! Do you see how out-of-hand this gets? If you'd tried to help her, he'd have turned on you, too. He just couldn't get away with it with Ben in the picture. He's twice his size and was angry as a lion."

"You are overreacting, Griffen," I said quietly and winced when he hit a bump. "*You* didn't do anything."

"But some day, what if I did that to you?" he growled. "It takes one to know one, Elliott. I knew what was going to happen, but I was in denial, and I almost let it get too far. At least Ben saw too and acted."

"Griffen, you are *not* that monster. You recognized the evil in him because *that* guy was an insecure jerk – and a drunk one at that. We all saw it coming except, of course, Ashley. Just because you are the son of a monster does not make you a monster!" I said, wincing with the effort to catch my breath.

"You're right not to want to marry me, Elliott," he continued. "I'm not willing to risk hurting you like that if there is *any* possible way I could do that to you. I love you too much. Besides, I know what I'm supposed to be doing with my life…I always have. And it does not involve you. It never has. I have been acting selfishly – well, no more."

His words should have stung, but they didn't. All I heard was that he loved me too much…my ribs were the only thing hurting every time he hit a bump. And, if he did mean anything behind all this, at least he had to deal with me now *and* all day tomorrow. By then, I was sure I could talk some sense into him and at least get him to consider this a lesson, not an ultimatum. He had worked himself into a frustrated rage, and it was time to calm things down.

"Did your father ever have a dog?" I asked.

"What?" Griffen said, looking at me like I had lost my mind.

"Or a horse?"

"No, why?" he said testily. "Wait, we *did* have a dog, but it was my mother's. It never let him near him. What's your point?"

"Have you ever beaten Panzer, or Jet, or anyone or anything else?"

"Of course not, but it is not the same thing," he said.

"No, it isn't. But it is very close. Your animals love you, Griffen. There's no fear of you in their eyes. And they are good judges of character because they don't care who you are. They never flinch around you; they don't look for you to wail on them in anger," I said. "They relax when you're around them."

We were at the gate and pulled up beside Ben's truck.

"Glad you're back among us, Elliott," Ben said, his face, too, a little drained of its regular glow. "You gave us quite a scare. Sorry I flung that jerk at you. I had no idea you were there. He was the one that was supposed to hit the ground."

"I'm fine. I'm glad you rescued Ashley," I said.

"We're going to the hospital to have her checked out," Griffen interrupted impatiently and took the gate keys from Ben. "We'll leave at 7:00 tomorrow morning instead of 6:00."

"Are you sure about that?" Ben asked. "What if they're not up to this…Elliott?"

"I'm fine. And I'm going," I said. "I want the chance to shoot your ducks – payback for tossing me over the rail."

Ben's face twitched, but I could see his smile and him shaking his head as we drove away.

"That wasn't a very nice thing to say to Ben," Griffen said, his voice clipped making him sound angrier than the situation warranted. "This isn't a joke."

We continued to Clarksdale, and I tried not to wince when he hit the bumps.

"How's your head?" he asked breaking the icy silence. He was determined to make more of this incident than I thought he should.

"It's ok. I'm not seeing double or anything," I said.

We rode for a while in silence, Griffen still brooding. Finally, I had to speak, to thaw this ridiculous iceberg. We never had enough time alone, and this was not the way I wanted to start our weekend.

"It's not that I don't *want* to marry you, Griffen. I've chosen to give this, well, us, time. Don't you see? It will take time to prove even to yourself that you are *not* that monster. Yes, you could be, but so could I, so could anyone. You know how to keep it at bay, physically. Your martial arts training taught you that. You choose. You don't get drunk. You don't throw things or hit people. Everyone gets angry, Griffen. You just choose how you react. The only thing you've ever unleashed on me is your tongue. If you can control that, the rest will follow, I'm sure of it," I said. "And I don't even care what you say to me when we're alone, it's normal to argue. Just not in front of other people."

"You'd better be right, Elliott," he said. "You're gambling on me with your life."

I smiled, hoping I was right in sensing the air thaw. "So far, you're doing great. And I really like the part about spending time with you being the only way to know what will happen. That's a definite perk."

"I'm all for you keeping a foot out the door, though. You're right to do it. It kills me, but it *is* the best for you," he said. "As much as I *hate it.*"

"Let's not talk about that," I said and winced when he hit another bump.

There was nothing wrong with me except two slightly cracked ribs. Griffen drove back to the camp, and it was late when we returned. Everyone was asleep. After helping me up the steps, out of my jacket, and into my room, he sat beside me on the bed.

"Do you need help with any of your other clothes?" he asked, hopefully.

"No, sorry," I said, laughing nervously as I blushed and winced at the pain. "Just don't make me laugh."

He leaned over and kissed me carefully. Since I didn't want to see the uncertainty I knew was in his eyes, I closed mine and felt his lips on my neck, his arms gently guiding me back onto the soft bed. He lay beside me, trying not to touch me, but his body being so close to mine was irresistible.

His gentle, careful kisses made me want the rest of him even more, so I closed the distance between us. He reacted by pulling me tightly to his chest – as if this would prevent our inevitable separation. Pain shot through me, and he jumped back as if I'd slapped him.

"I'm leaving," he said hoarsely. "Now. Or I won't be able to. Goodnight."

I stared after him, dazed and disappointed. He stopped at the doorway and turned to look at me.

"I love you, Elliott. You don't have to go in the morning. Just rest."

"I'm going. I *will* need help getting dressed, though. Those waders…."

He grinned. "I'll be back at 6:45," he said, morose mood vanquished. "Goodnight."

Our entourage did not make it to the swamp until well after 9:00, but ducks were everywhere. Not only did it take much longer for me to get dressed, the other girls had trouble with their waders, too. Addy had hunted growing up, but never duck hunted, so waders were a challenge for her.

Griffen's uncle met us as we were heading to the blind, and he let Panzer get in our boat. He'd already shot his six duck limit, but he was looking forward to the entertainment he was sure we'd provide. Ashley and I were not shooting, but Addy was determined to get her ducks. After missing five, she finally connected on two in a row, and we cheered her marksmanship.

I was beginning to understand the appeal of hunting, not only chasing game as we do in foxhunting, but also the process of collecting food in a sportsmanlike, respectful manner from its natural state. The time I spent outdoors now gave me great peace and satisfaction, and I could feel a passion for even more things outdoors growing within me.

Spending time outside was becoming more of a necessity than a luxury and testing the elements was addictive – in its own way. Duck hunting, like foxhunting, involved a great deal of planning and gear, but it, too, was full of artistic splendor and steeped in tradition. And the camaraderie of these friends was the perfect seasoning.

And Panzer…well, he was in perfect form. He brought the lovely ducks back to us, and I admired their distinct beauty. He would only let Griffen take them from him, and each time Panzer brought him a duck, Griffen took it and carefully hung each on a strap looped over a nail inside the blind. If Griffen was shooting or busy with something else, Panzer dropped the duck on the bench by the strap and got back to his spot. Griffen rarely gave Panzer any commands, and I did not understand how that could be. Every dog show I had ever seen had people blaring on whistles, but not Griffen…not ever. He wore a whistle, but I never heard him use it.

Ducks would fly in, circle, fly back, then hover over the decoys. The whole time, Panzer waited, trembling. Once the ducks were down, he waited until all guns were lowered, then shot out of the blind to collect them. If one moved, he switched to that duck and saved the others for later. Once he brought two back at the same time and another time, he went under water after one that dived to escape. It was fascinating, and I had a new appreciation for his discernment and their relationship. This was even more astounding than watching Griffen and Jet…Panzer in paradise.

Addy's ducks were widgeons, a bird I did not know existed until Griffen introduced me to the swamp. The drake had a pale blue beak, and the white splash on his head contrasted brilliantly with the dark green stripe beneath. He was such a striking specimen.

"You should 'frame' him, Addy," Ashley said, beaming at the beautiful bird.

"That's a great idea, I think I will do just that," Addy said, politely stifling a giggle at Ashley's misnomer.

"Framing" actually sounded better than "mounting" so I, too, kept my mouth shut. Griffen and Ben didn't pounce either; since Ashley was still shaky from the prior evening's debacle. I knew, however, that they'd have great sport with this later at her expense – too irresistible for them to drop.

"I'll take care of that for you, Addy," Griffen said. "And send Ben the bill!"

Griffen looked glorious in his element. I was having great difficulty keeping from laughing at all their banter. The pain medicine was wearing off, but I didn't want them to know it. This was too much fun. *What was a little pain anyway to a Southerngirl? I'd danced for hours in shoes that inflicted worse.*

Ashley was more subdued than usual, but she seemed not to have any bruises, except a few she'd told me about on her upper arms, where he'd grabbed her, to show for last night's trauma. Griffen's uncle couldn't believe I had fallen so far and survived.

"Did you see that?" Addy said. "I got another double!"

"Put your gun away," Ben joked. "You've got a limit!"

"I thought it was six!" Addy said in protest.

"Just four for you, since you're a girl," he said.

"Really?" she asked, crestfallen.

"No," Griffen said. "Keep shooting Addy. Ben's just being a game hog."

"She's making us look bad," Ben said. "That's not something we should tolerate."

Griffen responded by bringing down three in two shots with the next volley. They were teal, and he gloated at his marksmanship.

"Speak for yourself, Ben," Griffen said. "*I'm* catching up."

I smelled heavenly bacon, for Griffen's uncle had started breakfast. There was a permanent stove in this blind, and Griffen had brought enough food to feed the five thousand without divine intervention. We ate bacon, eggs, and French toast lightly seasoned with swamp water shaken from Panzer's thick coat, and I was totally hooked on duck hunting now.

Griffen said stove steam attracted the ducks and wasn't kidding. He silenced our chatter with a stern, "Mallards, be still."

Only the bacon hissed. Twenty pairs of wings pierced the silence with their distinctive whistle as they circled the decoys. When they passed overhead, Griffen chattered on his timeless wooden Hambone duck call, and the long string of duck bands around his neck tinkled while he monitored their movement. I peeked up from beneath the brim of my waxed cotton hat and saw them turn back to us, green heads gleaming in the sun.

They approached from the left, and the lead hen hovered over the decoys, trying to find a perfect place to land. She dropped into the decoys bringing the other nineteen in like moths to a flame. Griffen, Addy, and Ben fired at once and five drakes splashed back into the decoys. They all whooped and hollered and slapped their hands in the air, but I just watched, still favoring my ribs. Panzer was swimming back with the last one when another group approached.

"Let's land these," Griffen said.

The group fell into the decoys perfectly, and we watched them as they noticed something was not right and paddled around nervously. Two more groups landed right behind them until we had nearly forty ducks swimming all around us, bacon sizzling in the background. Panzer quivered, but remained otherwise motionless.

"Get up!" Griffen said to our green-headed guests, and they finished the limit on the rapidly escaping drakes.

The swamp glittered this morning, and the bright blue sky was breathtaking. We let a few more groups of ducks come and go as we finished off the breakfast feast. Panzer was used to this routine, but he begged for us to shoot the ducks landing so temptingly close. I had never seen a dog that loved ducks more than bacon, but Panzer would not eat until we were picking up the decoys. Griffen had saved some

French toast and bacon just for him, and he consumed the sandwich in one large snap.

"I still think he looks more like a Grizzly than a dog," I said to Griffen as I scratched Panzer's ears. He leaned into me and whined with pleasure.

"He *is* a bear around you," Griffen said. "A *teddy* bear."

Griffen's uncle left before we did and was already back at the camp when we arrived. Griffen and Ben dropped us off at the camp where the girls were staying and went to put away the gear.

Addy helped me up the stairs and they both had to get me undressed. Their "help" hurt worse because they couldn't stop laughing at me trying to keep from laughing.

"Stop pulling so hard!" I said to Ashley. We were trying unsuccessfully not to laugh at her leaning back with my huge boot in her hand. She fell over backwards when the boot came free and we exploded into giggles.

"You two are NOT helping!" I winced.

Ashley went to her room and came out in a t-shirt. She walked over to Addy and me and showed us where John's hands had grabbed her.

"Can you believe he left bruises like that through my *sweater*?" she said as we gaped at the angry blue marks his hands left on her pale skin. "How could I have been so blind?

"That's why we date, Ashley," I said, "a long time before you decide on getting married. Not everyone was raised in a perfect home…like we were. And even if they were, you just need time to figure everything out."

"But I never expected it from someone, well, so educated. You expect to see it from others, you know, like low class people or something," she said trying not to sound haughty, but failing miserably.

"Evil doesn't follow class structure," I said. "Some of the worse things done in the history of the world were done by the ruling classes, the *gentlemen*, and a lot of it justified by being done 'in the name of the Lord.'"

"You're right. But you have it so easy with Griffen. He may be a little moody, but he's a guy. What do you expect? Who wants one that bows and scrapes to your every whim anyway? At least you know he'd never *hurt* you…like this. It's so hard to believe it happened to me," she said, her unplanned jumble of comments crashing into me with more pain that she could realize.

"Have you heard from Chip?" I asked, changing the subject before my face gave me away.

"Yes. He's coming next week," she said and paused thoughtfully. "And he says Scott wants to come with him, to take you out."

My stomach clenched. I didn't want to think about that either, not right now at least.

Too late – my face gave me away and she snorted. "Are you really going through with this dating other people charade? I hardly think that's fair…especially to Scott. He's seems like a nice guy. And he is more than a little interested in you."

I was silent for a moment too long and Ashley glared at me for an answer.

"Yes," I said. "It really is for the best. Trust me on this. But I still want to spend time with Griffen – a lot of time."

"Oh, I'll just bet you do. You and every other female from fourteen to forty!" Ashley mocked. "I'm not so sure he's going to have a whole lot of time for you, Elliott. Pull your horse-crazy head out of the sand for once and think about this. He's got a chance most of us only dream about with this movie stuff. You weren't so sure he loved you so much when he vanished for so long because you needed some 'space.' Then, you punch him for proposing! Don't be sure he won't be gone for good the next time you pull something like that. He's crazy about you, and you're just tossing it all to the wind! I'm working so hard to find what you and Addy both have with Griffen and Ben – and you don't even appreciate it! Careful you don't torment him to the point where someone else a lot less demanding moves in and saves you the trouble of making up your picky unrealistic mind about him, Miss Cocky he-loves-me-forever-I-know-it!"

Addy stormed back into the room when Ashley spat the last part of her speech. She gaped at us wide-eyed as I flung a stream of pillows past her head at Ashley and threatened them both with their lives if they tried to defend themselves. I could not contain my laughter because I was trying so hard not to laugh at Addy's face when the pillows started whizzing past her. All three of us then doubled over with laughter, but I started to cry – in pain. Addy finally pulled Ashley off me just in time to save my screaming ribs.

Addy and Ashley finished packing their things and cleaning up the camp. They were riding with Ben to Oxford, but Griffen and I planned to stay another day since his uncle was staying for the whole weekend, and he wanted to spend some time with him.

Ben arrived to collect Ashley and Addy, and Griffen and I followed them to the gate to let them out. As we drove back to camp, we reflected on the great morning and relished the day ahead that we could spend together while his uncle was napping – just us at last. But when Griffen and I pulled into his uncle's cabin, he met us at the door.

"Are you two alone?" he said, face unreadable.

"Yes, what's wrong?" Griffen said immediately sensing his uncle's drastic mood change.

"Come sit over here," he said. "I have some news. Elliott honey, you, too. You need to hear this."

My thoughts immediately went to Addy, Ashley, and Ben, but we'd just that second seen them. *Surely not them. What else? Not Jet, we just saw him outside – where's Panzer?*

"It's Jackson," he said to Griffen.

I relaxed. "Your agent? I asked.

"Yes," Griffen said.

Relief washed over me. At least this was not about any of our friends, or anything that really mattered.

Not yet.

"I hope he's got another summer job lined up," Griffen said. "That last job looks like it is going to pay off better than we expected."

"Unfortunately, no…not hardly. This one's more involved," Mr. Hinton said. "It's for a year. But the contract is, well, quite lucrative. In fact, it is what an actor would jump at that had been in demand for quite some time, so this is somewhat of a surprise. It seems that your talents in this particular case demand a high price. In exchange, you would not be allowed to commute, and you would also be bound entirely by their schedule for the duration. They wanted your answer now, but I stalled them. You would start next week."

"Next week?" Griffen asked. And then he understood. "You mean, I would have to agree to be owned by them for a whole year?"

"Yes."

The word sat, suspended in the air like it contained a bottled genie, something we were afraid to touch and afraid not to grasp for fear of what possibilities would forever be missed should it disappear. Griffen's uncle watched him, and so did I.

"There's more," he said. "They need your answer today."

So many emotions roiled within me…and Ashley's words about not getting another chance with Griffen rocketed into my mind. I stifled these thoughts, doing what I could to help him make this decision without influencing him.

"I'll give you two some time to talk about this," Mr. Hinton said.

"You don't need to leave. What would there be to discuss?" Griffen asked.

My heart lurched. He was right, of course. I certainly had no claim on him…now. I had forgone that on New Years' Eve. And I had all but shoved him away with my ultimatum, the impasse not yet resolved.

"If you and Jackson think it is a good idea, I do, too. You said I'll be compensated handsomely for this, and they'll give me the details ahead of time on what exactly I'll be doing," he said with such confidence that I could feel the blood draining from my face.

"The money's more than generous, he's made sure Panzer and Jet can come with you, and the contract sounded like a perfect opportunity to us both – given your strict parameters," Mr. Hinton said, eyes glinting. "Jackson was about to explode he was so enthusiastic."

Griffen looked at me, and I steeled myself. "Elliott?"

"Sounds like it's too good to refuse," I said. "What have you got to lose?"

"You tell me," he said. "Will this work with your plan?"

Of course not! I wanted to scream. Instead, I blushed, and I think

Mr. Hinton even noticed. *How embarrassing.*

"I think you two better discuss this without me," he said and left before Griffen could protest.

Suddenly we were alone. I waited to hear what Grand would tell me to do, but nothing came. *Silence.*

"I don't see that I have a real choice, Elliott," Griffen said looking at me intently. "You said you need to see other people while you make up your mind about me, and I would prefer that you do that without me being in the same country."

"You're leaving the country?" I gasped before I could stop myself.

"No, not really, I don't think so. That was one of the things I asked that Jackson make sure doesn't happen. And it's only for a year," he said, obviously pleased with himself at my reaction. "I won't be that far away, and it won't make *that* part about you dating other people any easier, but perhaps more bearable. I'll keep in touch with you, but I won't be able to smother you like I'd have to if I remained here."

No words would come. At last, Grand spoke up. *"Elliott, stay aloof. You need to do this for both of you. Give yourself some time away from him. God's watching out for both of you. Take this as the gift it is."*

"You're right. What a chance! This can be a real adventure for you – for both of us. And the timing couldn't be better," I said sounding much more enthusiastic than I felt.

He crossed the room in one giant stride and pulled me against him, kissing me so suddenly that I gasped. My body went limp, but he held me close. He backed away slightly, looking intently into my eyes, but holding me near him…I could feel him breathing…and wanted to stay like this with him forever.

My heart hammered in my chest in spite of the pain in my ribs, and my head was spinning. He was so excited about my false enthusiasm that I was shocked. *Maybe I'm the one that should go into acting.* I tried hard not to let the panic that I had just blown everything show on my face.

"Let's go. I've got calls to make," he said leaving the room already making plans. His sudden disappearance left me feeling very very alone.

I watched him go and knew this was the right thing to do. Not what I wanted at all, but certainly the best for him. After all, I loved him…no doubt there. But I knew love was not the only reason to marry someone. He was happy before I arrived, and all this with us has him so conflicted.

Maybe once he started this chapter of his life, he would save us the trouble of trying to make something happen that couldn't by just losing interest and leaving me alone. I could understand that. He will certainly be well distracted in that environment. The thought made my stomach lurch again.

On the other hand, if we made it through this test…well, we'd be all that much better off with that knowledge. He wasn't going that far away; we would be in touch a lot I was sure; and who knows what doors this new path will open for him…and maybe even for both of us?

Just a year. A lifetime. No time at all.

THE COMPROMISE

Chapter 26

Hast Thou not given the horse strength? Has thou not cloaked his neck with thunder? Canst Thou make him afraid as a grasshopper? The glory of his nostrils is terrible! He paweth in the valley, and rejoiceth in his strength: He goeth on to meet the armed men. He mocketh at fear and is not affrighted, neither turneth he back from the sword.

~ Job 39:19-22

Masterpiece snorted. He could tell I wasn't paying attention and stamped impatiently when I didn't react fast enough to suit him. Riding him still felt like being in a canoe without a keel, or really, in a rocket without rudders – but I was used to his antics by now. Small flecks of foam dripped from his mouth as he chomped his copper Pelham bit. His black mane glistened against his red gold coat as he impatiently raised and lowered his graceful neck.

"Easy boy," I crooned and patted his soft, glossy withers. "We're not supposed to ride out front today. We're to cover the south side."

William was taking the pack away from us, and I watched as he and Chip rode away. He had assigned Scott to ride with Bo, and they had already disappeared to the east. Chip and Scott were over for a weekend visit to see Ashley, but they had also wanted to hunt, and I had made the arrangements. William had offered them the option to ride with our staff since they were staff, too, at their home hunt. Although they would have been fine in first flight with Ben, they accepted William's kind gesture of allowing them to ride with our staff. Ben was being polite to both guys but watching them like a hawk. He knew Chip was over for the weekend to take Ashley out, and Scott was my date for the evening. After Ashley's bad incident, he had taken it upon himself to hover over her, too. He was back in full-fledged "big brother" mode.

Susan was covering the south with me since my ribs were sore from the prior week's incident. She and her palomino mare, Tirade, were riding behind Masterpiece and me, so Masterpiece pranced, anxious to go with the group that was leaving us. I sat him easily and kept trying to get him to settle down as we listened for William and the hounds.

"Have you heard from Griffen?" Susan asked.

My throat clenched, and I hoped my blush was not too obvious. I had been trying hard not to think about Griffen, which was nearly impossible when I hunted. And, out of respect for my upcoming date with Scott, I was trying to push him out of my immediate thoughts. It was hard enough to go through this dating-other-people thing without having to talk about him.

"Steady now, honey. Don't give anything away. Give 'em somethin' else to talk about," Grand whispered.

Susan's question was innocent, casual. Mine and Griffen's public break-up was still big news, but Griffen was, too…the summer success movie giving everyone starry eyes when they were looking for information about him. Susan was asking about him as if we were just great friends that kept in touch…which we were…and more, of course…but no one else knew that. Everyone was curious about his sudden disappearance, but I was sworn to secrecy. I tried to keep my face void of too much emotion when I answered her.

"No, I haven't," I lied. "I'm sure he's hunting somewhere in Nashville on a day like today."

"William's sure going to miss him," she said. "He had big plans for that boy."

"I know. And maybe they'll happen sometime," I said casually. "Who knows with Griffen?"

"The guys from Alabama are nice," she said. "I would like to visit their hunt, too, sometime."

"We had a great time when we visited them and will probably go again. I'll let you know. Maybe we can even have a joint meet," I said, glad to keep the conversation away from Griffen.

Just then, Spice cried out in her clear, piercing voice. Masterpiece lurched up, hopped, and pulled down violently with his mouth nearly unseating me. I smacked him on his withers with the byte, or my extra reins, and growled "no" as he kept trying to bounce out from underneath me. I goaded him into a circle to keep his feet moving forward and not up. If he were not so balanced, I would have been flung into the air with that stunt.

"They're coming this way," Susan whispered.

"I'll hang here – you go to the gap," I said. "They almost always run that way. Don't worry about me. I'll stay here in case they circle."

I had nearly had it with Masterpiece's antics and did not want Susan to see me get after him here. After all, the hunt field was not a place to "train." But, I couldn't let him get away with this, so I gave him a quick "lesson" in obedience. When Susan left, he tried rooting down and hopping a few times, but after a few minutes of circles and corrections, he acquiesced. He was never a horse for tantrums. The boring circles had made their impression, and I could hear the hounds' melodious voices getting closer and closer to Susan.

"Tally ho, William," Susan cracked on the radio. "Bobcat moving southeast along the ditch, Gypsy, Sounder, Rhett and the rest of the pack ten yards behind!"

They were coming right for us! Masterpiece's lesson flew out the window as he rooted into his bit and lurched to go with the pack. My ribs screamed in protest as I directed him to a game crossing nearby to watch the action. We had plenty of room here so far, so all was well.

We stood motionless, a miracle for Masterpiece, as the hounds' voices got louder and louder. Suddenly, the bobcat shot right past us with the pack nearly on top of him.

"Tally ho! Still on here moving southeast…the whole pack right with it!" I reported.

"That's my girls!" William cheered. "Stay with 'em! Watch those ditch banks in case they bay him!"

I could now see William, Chip, and both first and second flights across the ditch galloping hard towards us. Bo and Scott were also across the ditch, but a little ahead of the pack.

"Tally ho!" Bo cried over the radio as the cat sprang across their path and dived into a thicket.

The hounds' booming cries turned into yips as they bayed him at the base of the bushes. William called them off and rewarded them mightily for staying on the bobcat for that long. The run lasted only fifteen minutes, but that was long for this group to stay with a bobcat.

Masterpiece was about to explode beneath me, so I reported to William that I was taking him back to the trailers. My ribs were not up to dealing with an uncooperative horse. Bobcats were my favorite, not Masterpiece's. He preferred long gallops after coyote…and that initial short burst had him way too keyed up to listen to his invalid rider. For the first time in a while, I really missed my Viva and felt unwelcome tears welling up in my eyes. I wanted Griffen to be here…not gone again, and I didn't feel ready to go on a date with anyone, not even Scott. But I couldn't just bail out after he had come so far. And I wanted to hunt, not have to take this crazy horse back to the trailers. *Oh why did I have to be so weak in every way?*

I goaded him into a trot to keep his mind on the ground rather than hopping around in protest. He was convinced we had a purpose in this action, so he stopped giving me trouble. I hated to leave but knew it was for the best. I was hurt; pushing this could get me hurt worse if Masterpiece didn't settle. Today, I had no body to back up my commands.

"Elliott," an unfamiliar, male voice caught me completely off guard, and I jerked in the saddle. Masterpiece had shied when I jumped making my ribs smart with pain again, and I bit my tongue before something unpleasant spewed out.

"Oh, Scott," I said, feeling my face flush with embarrassment. "I didn't expect anyone to be here, back at the trailers I mean, so soon."

"Switch with me," he said, his voice a command, not a request. "Come on, we don't have much time. Shasta's an angel. She won't give you any trouble. If you hurry, we won't miss anything. William said he's taking them somewhere else to find a fox."

"Probably to the Burned Down House covert," I said, trying to recover from my embarrassing tears and hoping he didn't notice. "You go on; I'm fine Scott, really. You didn't come all this way to train a horse, and I'm not up to riding today."

Before he could plead any more, I ducked around my trailer to check my face for mascara rivers and any evidence of recent tears. By the time I returned to wave him off, Scott had switched the saddles; his self-satisfied smile at my shock had me laughing – then smarting in pain.

He ignored me. *Ignored* me.

"Are you hurt?" he asked, noticing my grimace.

"No. Well sort-of. I…fell…last week and hurt my ribs. So don't make me laugh," I said trying to sound firm but laughing nervously again and bracing against the pain. There was something about trying not to laugh that always made it impossible not to. The harder I tried to stay somber, the more hysterical this whole scenario became. Soon we were both laughing; I was aching too hard to get on Shasta unassisted and had to find a mounting block.

"Sure you don't want a leg up?" Scott asked, innocently enough, but that made us both laugh harder when I raised my eyebrows playfully at him, and he blushed. I was flirting, just a little without realizing it; he was so easy to be around and made everything seem so hysterical.

"Just keep her still for me, and I'll do this myself. If I can't get on, I'm staying here and you're going on with the others. I don't want your whole trip ruined because of me," I said, wiping my eyes.

"Elliott, I've laughed more in the last fifteen minutes than I have all week!" Scott said with a wide grin. "You are *not* ruining the hunt. At least, not for me. I want to see if I can manage your crazy horse. I've been looking for a challenge."

I tried not to read the obvious double meaning into his words and concentrate on not laughing. He had moved much closer to us and looked me directly in the eyes when he spoke. His brown eyes were piercing but playful. It felt so good to laugh, except for my ribs – and I really did want to have a good time this weekend. Mostly for Ashley's sake. But I did not want to give him too much encouragement.

Shasta arched her dark neck toward us nudging Scott into *the space* with her impatient shove. Later, I would wonder if that was not something else he'd taught her to do on command. I stepped back, unsettled by our sudden contact. We both had helmets on, so safe – I was pretty sure – for now. Scott acted like nothing had happened and led Shasta to a mounting block.

Awkwardly, I clamored aboard. No sooner had I adjusted myself in the saddle than the hounds started speaking again. Masterpiece started to hop while Scott was getting on and nearly tossed him, too, from the saddle. His face registered such surprise that I burst into laughter again. Bad, bad timing – hounds were on the way.

"Tally ho, fox – moving southeast toward the trailers," Bo cracked. "Pout's on this one, boss!"

My favorite puppy! Attaboy! Masterpiece was jumping all over the place ready to get back into the action. Scott was ready for him this time and rode him with the ease and grace of a lifetime of dealing with errant Thoroughbreds.

"Let's get back in the action," Scott said. He let Masterpiece lead the way, and we galloped towards the symphony of sound.

Shasta felt like riding a cloud, and we flew alongside Scott and Masterpiece until we arrived at the top of hill in a pasture that overlooked the hounds. She responded immediately to my signal to halt even from that glorious gallop – so much like Viva. I hoped she would do that when we were really on a chase. Scott and Masterpiece looked magnificent; it was the first time I had seen him stretched out into a glorious full gallop, and he took my breath away. Scott didn't look bad, either, but I didn't want to spend a whole lot of time thinking about that.

From where we were, we could see the hounds but not their quarry, so we trotted closer to where I thought the action would be. As long as they continued this way, we should have no problems. We had to prevent them from turning due south, so we watched carefully.

"There are two!" Bo cracked. "Tally ho two red foxes! Running together twenty yards ahead of the pack!"

"Careful – watch for a split!" William warned.

And split they did – one red turned south, the other, due north. The pack was coming…south.

"Scott, get to the highway!" I croaked as loud as my ribs would allow. "Masterpiece has plenty of speed! But he's short on brakes!"

"So does Shasta, Elliott! But she'll stop when you need her to. Come on, show me the way!" he said as we galloped south picking up speed.

"I'm on it, William," I cracked. "We're just ahead of the pack in the south."

Speed never worried me. It was brakes that gave me the greatest pause. Especially with cracked ribs, but I didn't want to remind him about that. Too late, I had the tiger by the tail. Shasta knew her mission, and I was relegated to passenger. Masterpiece was long gone, and I prayed that Scott was half the rider everyone said he was.

There was a huge ditch one pasture before the highway, but the best crossing was a quarter of a mile back to the east. Scott charged straight to the ditch hoping to outrun the fox. In an incredible burst of speed, the fox plunged down into the creek right ahead of them. Since I was a little behind, I was able to turn Shasta toward the pack to do what I could to stop them hoping Scott would follow suit and catch those I missed. As I turned, I caught a glimpse of Masterpiece airborne, Scott still on top, as they leapt the ditch and raced to turn the fox, his whip steadily cracking like gunfire once they hit the ground.

My jaw dropped. The ditch was at least twenty feet to the water and ten feet wide. Masterpiece and Scott had just jumped it bank-to-bank. As far as I knew, no one had ever done anything like that before. I was astounded, a little angry, a lot jealous, and well, something else I wasn't sure about, and nearly forgot to stop the pack.

"Whoa hounds! Pout, Rufus, Cora, here here here whoa now! Back to him! Leave it! Back to him!" I shouted as loud as my ribs could stand and cracked my whip. Shasta responded perfectly to my thoughts – so well that I didn't even need to give her commands. The hounds stopped – mostly due to the ditch rather than my pitiful cries and whip cracking skills, and I could see Scott and Masterpiece still flying – but they were heading north now – away from the highway. They had turned the fox!

William rode up, and I recounted the story. He stared at me incredulously for a heartbeat; Chip shook his head knowingly, but William was overjoyed that the fox had been turned regardless of how it had been accomplished and gathered the pack to lay them back on the line. We mortals trotted back to the crossing where William presented them with the scent. Pout immediately shrieked, and the rest of the pack stormed after him. For another forty-five minutes we chased that red fox over-under-around-and-through all kinds of obstacles until he finally gave them the slip back at the big ditch.

"Well now, little missy, what was that we just saw?" Grand asked grinning widely. *"Maybe a little run for Griffen's money? Finally?"*

"Shhh!" I said to Grand. "Not now! I am going to be in so much pain tonight that I'm going to have to call this off…for fear of laughing myself to death…"

"Excellent job everyone!" William cracked. "Only two hours into the hunt and already a bobcat and two red foxes. I'm casting them west now since the wind has shifted once I take them to the poplar thicket. I want everyone to line the east and south sides – I have a good feeling about this spot, but I don't want to cast until everyone is in position. Let's get a Grand Slam today in honor of our visitors!"

As we moved toward the poplars, I watched for Scott. By now, anger was winning. How *dare* he take my horse over such an obstacle? My very *young* horse? What if he had been killed? *My Masterpiece?* I did not want to be in that kind of pain again. How DARE he! Who did he think he was to take such a risk with someone ELSE'S horse? With MY horse!

Scott trotted up to me with a smirk on his face expecting the adulation from me that he'd received from everyone else including, of all people, William the traitor. Admittedly I, too, did feel something akin to that, but I would definitely NOT show him.

When he got close enough for me to speak to him without others hearing, I looked straight at him and growled, "switch with me."

"Is Shasta hurting your ribs?" he asked, feigning ignorance of my venomous request.

"I want Masterpiece back," I said, ignoring his question.

"Fine," he said, looking pleased with himself but asking no more questions. He slid gracefully off his back and unbuckled his saddle in one movement. My dismount wasn't nearly as graceful. I ended up stepping wrong and falling completely backwards in front of the field. Shasta, being the obedient, perfect, horse that she so obviously was, just stared. When I looked up, I met Ben's gaze first and knew from his face exactly how ridiculous I looked. He was trying to contain himself, and it made my anger melt into spasms of laughter. Scott, relieved now, laughed nervously, too, as he switched saddles and helped me back on Masterpiece. His leg up almost sent me across to the ground on the other side.

"That's for not letting me help you earlier," he laughed.

"With help like that…" my voice trailed off as the radio cracked.

"Where's my staff?" William boomed impatiently over the radio.

"On the way, sir. Elliott's having trouble staying on her feet," Ben said, stifling laughter.

"I need her on her horse, not her feet," William snapped. "Spread out, and don't let anything go east or south."

I blushed and made no comment. Scott grinned, and I wanted to smack it off his face even though I, too, saw the humor in the whole thing. Bo hailed Scott back over to him, and Susan and I cantered into position on William's other side. Lydia, Stephen, and the field covered the far side.

No sooner had William cast them than a hound I did not recognize yelped, the pack honored, and a small black coyote exploded from the covert.

"Tally ho heading east – hounds right behind!" Lydia hailed.

"Turn him!" William bellowed.

The hounds were on fire exploding from the brushy sage plot. Suddenly another coyote – large and brown– shot by me heading north. No hounds were on it, yet, but no one had seen him but me. Bo and Scott were busy on the black one – cracking their whips and riding like the wind to get the young coyote to turn. At the last minute, the coyote stopped, twisted, and darted behind Bo and in front of Scott. Shasta pinned her ears and struck at him, momentarily confusing the coyote. The hounds were pressing and the coyote doubled back for a moment, then charged past Shasta and Scott – going east.

"William, I have another coyote over here heading north," I said.

"Stop the pack! We can't go east. Leave the black one! Get them to stop!" William barked.

The wind had started picking up now making it even harder to hear. What had started out as a calm, cloudy day suddenly became cold and very windy.

Bo and Lydia were now on the pack cracking their whips and lifting their heads. They stopped, confused, and William called them to him. By this time, Rufus's clear voice said he'd found the other one and the pack honored him. Before they could get a good start, however, Spice spoke south of us.

"How did she get by?" William cracked. "Someone lift her and get her with the pack before they split again!"

I spun Masterpiece around and flew to Spice. She was moving south and east now, so I decided to get ahead of her rather than risk running over her through the thick bushes. Masterpiece gloried in the gallop and stretched his long neck down and out delighted that we were at last on a coyote mission. I sat back slightly to turn him north – back to Spice – and he responded immediately. My ribs were grateful that he did not make me haul on him to change direction.

"Leave it! Spice, leave it! Get to him!" I called, the sound lost in the howling wind. We slowed slightly to work our way through the young poplars and the wind was not so bad in the thicket. Rounding the turn at a gallop, Masterpiece pricked his ears and planted his front feet. I was almost airborne for the second time today.

"Masterpiece?!" I started to rebuke him, then I saw why he had stopped. A huge ditch loomed ahead just on the other side of the thicket. If we had been going any faster, we could have plunged to the bottom.

Fortunately, there was a way down to the water, but Masterpiece wouldn't budge. I had no energy to force the issue, so I dismounted and led him down, across, and up the other side. Where we scrambled to the top, the bushes were too thick for me to mount, and I worked my way on foot leading him back to the path.

We were moving slowly along a game trail when suddenly, the coyote appeared in the middle of the trail heading right towards us. His golden, laughing eyes gleamed with mischief as he stared. He hesitated slightly to make sure he caught our eye and bolted…right past us! Before either of us could react, Spice and a few other hounds appeared bearing down on him. There was no time to tell William; I reached out to grab Spice as she passed forgetting my injuries. Goboy was with her, and I dropped Masterpiece's reins and grabbed him, too. They were both straining to follow the coyote and killing my ribs. For the moment, Masterpiece stood, bewildered, but not for long.

Radio chatter was crackling through the air…coyotes must be everywhere. It seemed like everyone was talking at once reporting on hounds and coyotes. One was stuck in a fence, but it had broken loose and was running east. Everyone, including the field, was on their own coyote heading in all directions, but I needed to get the couple straps off my saddle before I could report what was happening with me.

I looped my whip in the two hounds' collars and reached for Masterpiece's reins. He backed away, not sure about the tethered hounds and all the others milling around his feet. He was keyed up and wanted to gallop somewhere – everywhere – not stand around dealing with hounds.

"Easy boy, whoa," I crooned. "Easy, easy…"

But he'd had enough. Before I could reach his reins, he whirled and snorted, darting away from the melee. He lifted his tail in defiance as he splashed mud all over me in his departure.

"William, I have Spice and Goboy; they were on a gray coyote. The rest of the pack over here stopped, too. I'm on foot just south of you," I said.

"I need you on your horse, Elliott," William snapped. "Bring those hounds in here so we can gather them up. There are too many coyotes, we're going in once we get them collected."

"Masterpiece is with the field, sir, about a mile from where Elliott is holding hounds," Ben said over the radio. "I'm having him delivered to her as we speak."

I'm going to get him for that. I'll never live this one down.

By the time I got home that afternoon there was already a note from Griffen complete with yellow roses.

> Sounds like you are having difficulty managing that horse again. Join me next weekend in Nashville, and I'll make sure you have better help.

He sent me fresh flowers every other day never signing the cards since that would not help our public break-up story, but this took the cake. I can't believe how fast Ben ratted on me! It wasn't fair that Griffen had multiple layers of spies here, and I had no idea what he was doing or even exactly where he was. I am sure he was *loving* this.

My cell phone buzzed that glorious 615 number…I never added his name to the number just for old times' sake.

"Hello Griffen. Nice note," I said. "How did you hear so fast?"

"Sounds like my little vixen is having trouble with her crazy horse," he said. "Why don't you, Ben, and Addy come hunt with me next weekend in Nashville? I have everything arranged, so I hope you don't already have plans."

"Now what would make you think that, Griffen?" I said. "It seems like you know more about what I'm up to than I do."

"Just protecting my investment," Griffen said smugly.

"Investment? Now, that's romantic," I said, hating having to talk on a cell phone to my favorite actor.

"Jackson's pilot will pick all three of you up in the Sundowner Friday afternoon. I also have horses for Saturday's hunt," he said. "Can you come?"

"I'm in, and I'll check with Addy after I get off the phone with you," I said.

"They're already in," Griffen said. "I'll pick you up at the airport in Nashville Friday afternoon. Ben will be staying with me, and I have you and Addy in a hotel."

I had only been away from him since Monday, but hearing his voice made me ache. Only one more week…and I had a date with someone else in a few hours. My stomach lurched.

"You there?" Griffen asked.

"Yes," I said.

"Everything all right? You're awfully quiet, for you."

"Just tired, I guess. And I miss you…especially when I'm hunting," I said with a little too much gloom.

"I have to leave for a meeting now, but I'll call you tomorrow. Bye little vixen," he said way too soon. "You know I love you."

"I love you, too, Griffen," I said and wanted to come across the phone lines and choke him for being so irresistibly *him*.

REVELATION

Chapter 27

Your horse should never sense in you anger or fear...only confidence.

Dinner was lovely, but I was having a hard time keeping my eyes open. I felt bad about not adding too much to the conversation, so I ordered another Coke. Chip and Ashley hardly noticed – they were having a great time, and I was sorry that I was not being more fun for Scott. We had really had fun hunting, but now that dinner was over, and we had already said everything there was to say about the glorious day, our end of the conversation lagged.

"Let me take you back to the House, Elliott," Scott leaned close to me and said under his breath so Ashley and Chip could not hear. "You've got to be tired after all that you've done today, and I'm sure your ribs are hurting. They're probably ready to get rid of us anyway."

"No, Scott, really, I'm fine," I said, embarrassed that he could read me so well. "Besides, Ashley would kill me. I'd be dead before morning."

"What *are* you, her chaperone?"

"Sort of, but that's another story. Her last boyfriend is the reason I have cracked ribs…but you should see what happened to him," I added when he raised his eyebrows. I used the shift in mood to gather myself.

"I hope you're joking," he said. "You're not exactly the right size for a…bodyguard. Or is there something you're not telling me that will ensure I keep my hands to myself?"

"No, Scott. It's nothing like that," I said. Changing the subject I switched tactics. "Look, let's find a way to give them a little more public privacy and go kill time somewhere else. That way we don't have to sit here and watch them giggle."

"Your town – what do you suggest?" he asked.

Before I could answer, Chip spoke up. "Let's go to a movie," he said. "You two up for that?"

"Sure," I said.

We were in Chip's truck, and the giggling persisted on the way to the theater.

"You never told me what you're going to do when you graduate," I said, trying hard to pay attention and be polite even without Grand's prodding. She was unusually silent tonight. Scott was really cute and so nice and funny. But I was not in a flirty frame of mind, and he had apparently given up. For that, I was grateful. Perceptive…he was that, too.

"That's pretty much set for me," he said. "I'm in the Navy's training program, so they'll pick my path for a few years."

"Really?" I asked, impressed, very surprised, and suddenly awake and interested in his answer. No one had mentioned that to me. This was much more impressive than his very impressive riding abilities. "Was your father in the Navy?"

"Yes, but he's an investment banker now. I plan to do that someday, but he encouraged me to do this first and travel. So, I'll travel the world for a few years then hopefully go to work for him, meet Mrs. Scott Turner, get married, and have 2.4 kids," he said winking at me. In spite of my mood, I blushed. His gregarious nature was infectious.

"Yes, 2.4," he continued when I smiled. "My life is one long 'to-do' list – but that's how I was raised. None of us are ever in doubt about what we're going to do next. To complete your standard list of questions, I have an older sister who is perfect and a younger brother who is the .4 of our two. He's a fourteen-year-old idiot, but I tolerate him," he said, and I was sure that meant he adored him.

"My mother is involved in the school, our church, and everything in which we are interested, to a point. She worships my father and runs things at home. All in all, we're a pretty boring, normal family," he said.

"I doubt you're boring at all," I said. "Where do you live?"

"On a farm outside of Birmingham," he said. "We have horses, dogs, cats, and whatever my little brother drags in from his forays in the woods. Right now he has a turtle and a king snake. He used to have a corn snake, too, but…"

"The king snake ate it?" I asked, smiling wryly.

"How did you know?" he laughed.

"*Everyone* knows that king snakes eat other snakes…" I said.

"You're *not* really talking about snakes, are you Elliott?" Ashley asked in horror.

Thankfully, we pulled into the movie before I could answer, and my thoughts could drift back to Griffen.

All too quickly, the movie was over, and we drove back to the sorority house. Scott and I got out of the car and walked inside the House to give Chip and Ashley some privacy. He settled in at the piano and started playing softly, as it was late. My body tingled as he played… the music mesmerizing and another complete surprise.

I was sitting beside him on the bench watching his fingers drift across the keys. When the song was finished, he looked at me.

He didn't say anything, just looked at me, and I dropped my eyes. His brown eyes were soft, but so deep that I had a hard time holding his gaze. Some things were stirring inside that I didn't want to be stirring, not now, not tonight. His hands were perfect, masculine, smooth. His skin was almost golden and his blonde hair cropped short. Now I understood why it was so very short, and it looked great on him. He had the sleeves rolled up on his button-down shirt and his forearms proved he'd spent a lot of time with horses or some other form of heavy-lifting activity. *How had I not noticed him before? Or had I?* The veins in his arms had me mesmerized as his fingers returned to the keyboard.

At the end of the song, he looked at me again, and I met his eyes this time, bracing myself for their soft, penetrating impact. *Here goes, he's going to try to kiss me…now.*

He was still watching me, not moving. He looked down then and traced magic fingers of his right hand along my left arm. When he looked up, he caught me watching him, and I felt myself blush.

"I had a great time with you today," he said, eyes still soft, hand holding mine now – *when did he do that?*

My throat went dry, and my heart skipped three beats. *Is this really happening to me? With him?* I couldn't find anything to say, so I just kept looking at him. Then I looked down to get away from those eyes.

"Elliott? Have you fallen asleep already?" he said squeezing my hand, eyes twinkling as he flashed his brilliant smile.

"No…not, I…" I stammered, and we both started laughing, my ribs screaming in pain.

He put his arm around me protectively when I winced from laughing and pulled me close. When he did this, I could smell him – so clean and starched, very nice – feel the muscles under his shirt, "Shhhhh, shhhh, don't laugh, I'm sorry," he said, and he brushed a strand of hair from my face. "Really, really sorry."

I looked up at him, and he leaned toward me ever so slightly. I stiffened, and his lips touched my forehead. I relaxed, so relieved, and leaned in to his chest gratefully.

"Thanks," I said, going limp with relief that he was not going to kiss me and hoping he'd understand what I meant without having to say anything.

"Hey, I told you earlier today I was up for a challenge," he said. "I will say, though, you're not putting up much of a fight."

"What do you mean by that little remark?" I straightened and leaned slightly away from him, but he still had his arms around my waist. When I caught his eye, he was starting up that infectious chuckle again.

"I think you know *all too well* what I mean," he said. "And, by the way, you're *not* welcome."

This time, I didn't see it coming…at all. Right here in the piano room of the sorority house, he moved his arm quickly up my back and pulled my face into his, crushing his lips to mine and I…well… I liked it. Really, really liked it. Before I could gather my senses to protest, he stopped, stood up, and turned to leave. No witnesses….

"Today was…something," he said. "Especially just now. A little of that could have a guy rearranging his checklist."

I was dumbstruck and still sitting on the piano bench. When he spoke, I looked at him, narrowing my eyes trying to recover some sense of dignity.

As if on cue, the front door alarm beeped, and Ashley walked in glowing.

"There you are, Scott!" she beamed when she saw us in the piano room. "Chip was wondering what happened to you."

"Yeah, I bet he's been looking everywhere," Scott said, sarcasm dripping in his tone and eyeing me carefully. "Thanks again, Elliott."

"Chip's coming back next weekend, Scott," Ashley said. "Why don't you come, too?"

"We'll see. Goodnight, both of you," he said and left.

Ashley babbled and giggled like a schoolgirl, well, a very young schoolgirl, and I was not in the mood. She finally gave up on me and bounded down to another victim to recount the details of her perfect evening. Leslie, in already from her date with Christopher, immediately noticed something strange in my expression.

"Spill it," she said. "Something wrong with Chip or is Ashley on your nerves again?"

"Neither," I said. "You'll never guess."

"What? Scott kiss you or something?"

"Yes! How did you know?"

"Hmmmm, let me see…he drives all the way over here from Alabama, spends a whole day with you; you both love that insane sport, he takes you to dinner and a movie, plays the piano for you, by the way, yes, we *all* heard that, and you come in like you've seen a ghost or, well, like you do every time Griffen returns you to your roost," she said. "Now, *spill* it!"

"Oh Leslie, I'm so confused! I mean, I *love* Griffen. How could I let Scott kiss me…and like it so much?" I groaned. "I thought only Griffen could do that to me. Maybe he's not the only one for me. It seemed so obvious the way I always react to him. I was hoping that was some kind of heavenly lightning bolt."

"Lightning bolt I'm sure, but who knows from where, silly! Griffen could turn a stump on just by winking at it, that's not anything unusual, Elliott," she laughed. "You're the strange one. All the dates you've had and only two good kissers. I fear you're going to make life-changing decisions based on the way a guy kisses!"

"It's not just that, Leslie! He's really a great guy. I like him," I said, distressed.

"Let me guess…he looks good on a horse," she smiled.

"Of course!"

"Does he have morals, gainful employment lined up? Any murderers in the family?" she asked.

I flinched at the third remark. She didn't know, of course, about Griffen's father, but I still cringed. "I think so, yes, and no, well, I don't think so." *At least, not in his immediate family.*

At least, not in his immediate family.

"He's in the Navy ROTC and seems to come from a really nice family. I think I remember Ashley saying they are both seniors at Alabama."

"Going to put your mother on a background check?" she asked.

"No! This was just a one time thing," and as I said that, I felt a little pang of…what? Regret maybe? "Look, I'm just keeping my options open. Griffen's gone for a whole year and will probably forget me soon enough. Look what he's getting to do and the kind of people he'll be meeting. Sure I interested him before, but that was when he'd only been interested in Panzer, Jet, and foxhunting."

"Right…" she said. "I'll text your mother. By the way, you're eating lunch after church with Elaine. Her cousin's in town, and she promised him a date. Since you're so publicly single, you were nominated."

"What about you?" I accused. I was sure she already knew about the cousin and they were conspiring.

"Oh, today I'm madly in love with Christopher and couldn't possibly stomach even a lunch date with someone else."

"Yes, but Elaine's cousin will be here tomorrow. You and Christopher will be *off* by then.

"Touché. The cousin's still all yours."

"Great. *Thanks*. That's all I need," I snarled.

"Hey, it's a free lunch!"

"That's what they all say…"

Elaine *will* pay.

Not only did she bring him to church, she brought him to our Sunday school class. I was looking forward to catching up with my teacher and concentrating on the lesson but no, Elaine trotted that cousin in, and I had to pay attention to my manners and dodge him all morning. Grand was laughing at me the whole time. His very one-sided conversation centered on what had to be how I answered his "top ten questions to ask a prospective spouse" list, ogled me at church, insisted we pray over the main course and dessert – way too loudly and publicly – and practically proposed over an ice cream sundae after lunch. I guess I answered his questions too well.

"What does that guy *do*, Elaine? Church hop for girls?" I asked when he finally gave me a minute to myself, really annoyed at her but trying to be polite.

"You could do worse, Elliott," she laughed. "He's the sole heir to the family fortune. Too bad we're not siblings, just cousins. His grandfather bought out my grandfather years ago and went on to make millions. So I'm left with trying to earn or marry a living or win the lottery like the rest of the world."

"Oh please, Elaine."

"Surely he's not that bad," Elaine said. "I know you love Griffen, and I do, too, not like you of course, but you had the bright idea of running him off so you can at least go on a few token dates. You know I'd do the same for you."

"I am, and I know. Thanks, Elaine."

When I got back to my room, I looked around and suddenly felt stifled. Griffen's yellow roses mocked me. I had forgotten to call Ashley and Ben about next weekend!

After changing into jeans, I called William first to make sure he would have enough staff for Saturday, and he assured me that he did. He was glad to hear that I was going to hunt in Nashville again and asked me to take good notes on how their kennel was arranged. He wanted me to take pictures of the supplies area if I had time. Griffen's pictures only showed the runs.

Addy was delighted to get to go back and assured me that both she and Ben were already packing. I told her that all was cleared with William, and she said she would let Ben know.

"Hey, you never said how your date with Scott went last night," Addy said.

"Great," I said trying to figure out a way to get off that topic. "I think Chip is smitten with Ashley, and that he's finally the right type for her and all of us to tolerate!"

"I'm so glad," she said. "Ashley's too trusting, but that last incident freaked her out. I'm glad she had fun. But you didn't answer my question."

I hate having perceptive friends.

"He's nice. I had fun," I hedged.

"Ben said the guy was drooling over you. He was embarrassed for him," she laughed.

"Ben's getting tiresomely overprotective," I said. "Can't you rein him in a little and get him to relax?"

"Oh sure. I'll get right on that one. I missed riding with everyone yesterday, but my brother is now happily married and living in Texas," she said. "I'm ready to ride! You would know that I would miss our first Grand Slam."

As we talked, I checked my text messages and missed call list. One more from Griffen, but nothing from Scott. A mystery. I'm sure they've almost made it back to Alabama by now.

"Elliott!" a female voice called from the hall. "Someone's here to see you!"

"Addy, I've got to go. I have a visitor," I said.

"Ok, bye!" she said.

Who in the world would just drop by without calling or texting? Probably Griffen. He's always keeping me off balance. I hoped it was him, and my heart fluttered at the thought. I didn't bother with shoes and just padded down the steps. *Oh yeah, it's probably that leather repair guy. He likes any excuse to come inside the sorority house.* When I rounded the last turn, he was standing by the piano right where I had left him the night before.

"Thank goodness you'd at least painted your toenails!" Grand hissed approvingly.

"Hey Elliott," he said, smiling nervously.

My heart did a little flip; I couldn't believe I had not noticed just how cute he was before, well, now.

"Scott!" I said in surprise. "I thought you'd be in Alabama by now."

"Yeah well, me too. Chip's just gotten back with Ashley – they had a really long lunch," he said and smiled ruefully.

"Oh?"

"He's outside, and we're about to leave," he continued. He stepped a little closer to me and looked into my eyes – searching for something – what?

"I had fun yesterday and last night," he moved into *the space*, but I stayed put…waiting to see what in the world he thought he was doing.

"Scott, I…"

He stayed in place looking at me. I could smell the wonderful, clean starched scent he'd surrounded me with last night, and my heart jumped again. But I didn't move. My mouth went dry. What was he waiting for? Looking for? Did he want me to close the distance between us? *No way*. I didn't have to have Grand to tell me not to do that. I could see little gold flecks in his dark brown eyes…soft eyes…making me melt. *Where was everyone? This had to be the first time in history no one was charging around the sorority house on a Sunday afternoon. No way was I going to do any kissing here, now, with him…was I?*

"I see," he said narrowing his eyes ever so slightly. He backed away a few steps and smiled, but the smile stopped short of his eyes…or did it? He had moved too far for me to tell. "Thanks again. I'll see you around."

The door beeped, and he disappeared.

What was that? I shook my head to clear the fog and sat down on the steps. Something buzzed in my pocket…my phone…*615.* I let it go to voice mail, ran upstairs to put on my cowboy boots, and drove to the barn. It was way past time to see my horse.

Griffen didn't call again, not his style. But Addy did – she wouldn't let it go to voice mail. She sent a text –

Well, who was it?

I ignored both of them. By now, it had started to rain, and I was glad. I needed a day to groom Masterpiece and clean tack. On pretty days, I couldn't resist a ride, and I had only allotted two hours for this. Elaine's adventure had seriously cut into today's playtime, and now I was all mixed up about Scott and Griffen. I also had a Chemistry test on Tuesday that was starting to ring my responsibility bells.

When I got to the gate, Masterpiece was waiting. Like a loyal puppy, he recognized my truck and ran across the pasture to greet me. My thoughts were so muggy today that I'd missed watching him gallop to his spot and saw him only when I got to the gate.

"Hello my one true love," I crooned, pulling two carrots and an apple from my bag. He ate them greedily, as I broke the carrots and gave them to him section by section. We shared the apple. I opened the gate, and he walked to his stall and shook the rain off his russet coat. Fresh hay was in his rack and he snatched a few strands before turning to me to get his ears rubbed. I filled his bucket with feed, gathered my tack, and sat down to clean it and ponder my life to the music of crunching oats.

Ok, Grand, I need to hear you now. Nothing spoke to me at church today, so I guess I'm not too far out of line. I could use some company, though.

Silence…in my head. My cell phone buzzed. Mother. *Perfect timing.*

"Hi Mother," I said. "Perfect timing – I need a Motherspeech."

"Oh dear, what have you done?" she asked, concerned.

"No, not like that, only some of the infinite wisdom you've gleaned about boys from all the years you've worked on your perfect marriage and my boy-crazy sisters."

"Well sure, dear, let me turn off the stove," she said delighted to be of assistance. Her antenna was up. "Leslie already put me on to Scott. I was calling to report that so far, there's no dirt on him and he seems to come from a nice family."

I laughed. It was so good to hear her voice. "That's good, but I miss Griffen. Really miss him."

"Where are you right now?" she asked.

"With Masterpiece."

"That figures. That's why you miss Griffen. You should've gone flying."

"Not enough time today. I have to study later and needed time to think and brush my horse. And I'm out of money this week since I loaned Shannon all I had to buy a sweater that was on sale."

"I don't even *want* to know. So, what's got you so worried that you have to brush it out?"

"I had a great time with Scott, but I miss Griffen and, well, was surprised at how much fun I had with Scott. I don't want to see anyone but Griffen, but, well, you know. I'm not sure about the rest of him. But I would die if he went out with someone else…and felt, well, like I did about someone else, you know."

"Now now, Elliott, you can't have your cake and eat it, too, honey. Be glad Griffen's not there – you can see him when you can see him. He's busy and so are you. You're doing just right for this stage of your life. You both are," Mother crooned.

"I know, but it's not fair. He has spies everywhere. He's going to know about Scott," I whined. "And I'm going to see him next weekend. What if he can tell I've kissed someone else…and *liked* it?"

"He won't be able to tell – don't be so paranoid! And *so what* if he knows you had a date with someone else that was more interesting than just someone who paid for your food?" she laughed. "He'll just be that more motivated to become who he needs to be to share a life with you. And at least you don't have the press stalking you. He will not be able to as much as sneeze without the whole world knowing. Remember that."

"Oh, Jackson and his goons will be able to keep him out of the limelight. Griffen's not stupid, and he's definitely not a publicity hog," I said.

"That may be the case when he's in Oxford, but it is in Mr. Jennings's best interest to keep up the hype surrounding him. As Griffen's success goes, so do all those people backing him and his projects. The movie world is nothing but a huge marketing/pr business. You know that. But you're not worried about that. What's really bothering you?"

"Mother, if I love Griffen, and he's who God wants me to date, why did I have those feelings for Scott?"

"Elliott, remember feeling and loving are not the same thing! You can…yes, even *you* we know now…can have feelings for lots of people. That's why you have to be smart about who you pick to love. That's why God gives you a choice, and that's why you've got to date around," she said.

"That doesn't make any sense. It's all so unromantic."

"Sure it makes sense, honey. It is a big deal, but not really in the big picture. We only go around once on this earth, and it really is only for a little while…just temporarily. Have fun, date around, keep doing what God directs you to do, and enjoy your brief wonderful life here doing what you were put here to do," she said.

"Relax. Just brush that pretty horse, and go home and make plans to see your handsome movie star next weekend. Take it as it comes and enjoy this for however long it lasts. Don't get too caught up in all the drama. Focus more on your purpose – let God pull you toward His goals for you. Only you know what that is…besides the boy stuff. That will all work itself out. Now, go dive into your studies, be the friend someone needs today, do whatever it is God tells you to do and do it. Live! Don't worry. Do the best you can each day. And…Grand will be in your head to make sure you behave!"

I smiled to myself wondering what Griffen would do if a mysterious magic broom hit him over the head. What would he think about my talking regularly to Grand? He'd probably have me committed.

"I love you, Mother. I feel so much better. Thanks."

"You sound better," she said. "Now, I called to check on you. Is everything else all right?"

"Perfect," I said. "Thanks so much for calling, and tell Daddy I love him, too."

"Goodbye sweetheart. Keep me posted…on Scott, too!"

"I will. Love you."

Masterpiece reached over his stall door and nudged my head as I finished cleaning his girth and my saddle. I rummaged in my tack box for a currycomb and body brush and walked inside to work on his coat. I started making large smooth clockwise circles with the currycomb, sweeping the hair back and lifting up with the body brush. This flicked the dirt out and away from his silky coat. He liked me to brush much harder than Viva would tolerate. I started at his rump and worked my way up his neck on both sides. He shined like a new penny and my arms tingled with the exercise when I was finished. *Wish someone would do this to me.* This was such a peaceful sanctuary, and I started to feel much better.

I was prepared now to check my messages to see what Griffen wanted and call Addy back and tell her about Scott. What was that visit of his all about anyway? I forgot to ask Mother about that. Maybe Ben would know, but I better leave him out of this. Maybe Chip will say something about it to Ashley.

This dating business that had now taken over most all my thoughts needed to be just background noise in my life right now, nothing over which I should get really worried, just like Mother said. That Chemistry test on Tuesday, though, could be a life-changer if I wasn't prepared. I groaned inwardly at that thought. Boys are much more easily managed than teachers. Especially old battleaxes like Mrs. Boxx. She was an unforgiving genius of a woman, and I wanted to do well in her class.

Chemistry under her strict tutelage was fun, and I considered changing my major when she explained the interesting things that can be done with that degree. I wanted to make a difference as well as earn a living. We were learning about things that could help people live better lives. Unlike Ashley, I was not counting on some rich husband or the lottery to secure my future. But Tuesday's test could decide this fate for me if I didn't hit the books and focus.

When I finished Masterpiece's coat and started on his mane, I heard Grand moving around in my head.

What now? Do you have some wisdom to add to my conversation with Mother?

"How 'bout that piano player? Now that was some kiss!" Grand cackled.

"Aaaaaghhhh, Grand, go away! You're not supposed to be around for things like that!" I said, mentally throwing a currycomb at her as she disappeared, laughing back to her private boudoir in my mind.

ACKNOWLEDGMENTS

Thanks to all storytellers and writers, but a special thanks to the exceptional authors Carolyn Haines, Jan Neuharth, and Jim Ritchie who keep helping me along and never fail to encourage this fledgling novelist.

The a-team Debbie Adams, Leigh Bailey, Lind Bussey, Anna Lin Conner, Luz Huesca, Megan Kernop, Taylor McCullough, Amanda Morales, Kate Morrison, Alanna Nunez, Lila Sessums, Robert Sessums, John Taylor Schaffhauser, Daniel Smith, Susan Walker MFH, and Susan Williams for helping me land the plane…even if this one is only a touch 'n go.

The beautiful and talented Alison Martin for yet another perfect cover and book design.

My brother, Nolen Grogan, for taking pictures of Chase and me that actually looked good in broad daylight *without* Photoshop.

My teenage sons – Jake for introducing me to Three Doors Down's song, *Here Without You*, that fits this story perfectly, and Turner for coming up with the title, *Impasse.*

Memories of my larger-than-life mother, Nancy Grogan, who was the best Southernmother a girl could ever want, and my Southerngrandmothers, Granny, Mother, Granny Crews, and Mama who weigh in heavily with their opinions regardless of how "grown up" I think I've become.

My very Southerninlaws, Elaine and Jimmy, for their constant encouragement and my Daddy, Bill Grogan, for a lifetime example of living the Christian life to the fullest, taking me hunting with him when I was a little girl, and encouraging me to spread my wings and fly…from the moment I took my first step.

IMPASSE CHARACTERS

IN ORDER OF APPEARANCE – also listed under their hunts

1. Elliott Marks – narrator, this is her life
2. William Greene – Master of Foxhounds and huntsman, Big River Hunt
3. Griffen Case – whipper-in with Cantata Hounds and Big River Hunt
4. Grand – Elliott's deceased maternal grandmother
5. Addison (Addy) Falls – Elliott's foxhunting friend and sorority sister
6. Ben Allen – Elliott's neighbor in Canton and friend
7. Lydia Wright – whipper-in for Big River Hunt
8. Stephen Smith – whipper-in for Big River Hunt
9. Susan Walters – whipper-in for Big River Hunt
10. Ashley Woods – Elliott's high school friend and sorority sister
11. Leslie White – Elliott's roommate at Ole Miss, high school friend, sorority sister
12. Jim Black – sporting clays instructor
13. Charles Johnson – sporting clays instructor
14. Tracy Sullivan, Missy Cole – in Elliott's sorority
15. Elaine Melton – Elliott's high school friend and sorority sister
16. The five little church ladies
17. Shannon Kraft – Elliott's high school friend and sorority sister
18. Raphael Lavalle – barn manager, Nashville barn
19. Ron Jenkins – first flight field master, Cantata Hounds
20. Bob Richards – Master of Foxhounds and huntsman, Cantata Hounds
21. Meredith Stanley – Cantata Hounds member
22. Jill Peters – Cantata Hounds member
23. Carol – Cantata Hounds member
24. Ginger Richards – Cantata Hounds whipper-in, Bob Richards's wife
25. Eleanor Turnipseed – Master of Foxhounds, Cantata Hounds
26. Pamela, Jennifer, Melissa, Chrissy – Riding Camp girls
27. Morgan Freeman – the actor from Clarksdale, Mississippi
28. Sean Reed – actor
29. Harold Hinton – Griffen's uncle
30. Christopher James – Ben's high school friend, graduate student at Ole Miss
31. Sam King – Ben's friend
32. Jackson Jennings – Griffen's agent
33. Sylvia Greene – William's wife
34. Bo and Bob – whippers-in for Big River
35. Jim Marks – Elliott's father
36. Eilene Watson – Master of Foxhounds, Big River
37. Jane Rings – member, Big River
38. Lisa Marks – Elliott's mother
39. Daniel Peters – veterinarian

40. Janie Windham – owner of Oxford barn
41. Dr. Harland Smith – veterinarian
42. Brandon and Jimmy – miscellaneous Vanderbilt guys
43. Bethany – Leslie's friend at Vanderbilt
44. Dale Upshaw – flight instructor
45. Ricky Lind – flight instructor
46. Janice Black – whipper-in – Woodland Hunt – student at Millsaps
47. Jennifer Muse – Wild Run member
48. Scott Turner – whipper-in, Wild Run
49. Chip Harris – whipper-in, Wild Run
50. Henry Williams – Master of Foxhounds and huntsman, Wild Run
51. Cynthia, Jessica, Alex – members, Wild Run
52. Will Morrison and Turner Crews – junior members, Wild Rum
53. John – Ashley's doctor boyfriend

THE WOODLAND HUNT

Janice Black – whipper-in
Bonnie Walters – hunt secretary

BIG RIVER HUNT

Bob Allen – whipper-in (not related to Ben)
William Greene – Master of Foxhounds and huntsman
Sylvia Greene – his wife
Mrs. Harrison – member
Jane Rings – second flight field master
Stephen Smith – whipper-in
Susan Walters – whipper-in
Bo Whittington – whipper-in
Lydia Wright – whipper-in

THE CANTATA HOUNDS

Carol – member
Ron Jenkins – first flight field master
Jill Peters – member
Bob Richards – Master of Foxhounds and huntsman
Ginger Richards – whipper-in
Meredith Stanley – member
Eleanor Turnipseed – Master of Foxhounds

IMPASSE CHARACTERS

THE WILD RUN HOUNDS

Cynthia, Jessica, Alex – members, Wild Run
Turner Crews – Wild Run junior member
Chip Harris – whipper-in, Wild Run
Will Morrison – Wild Run junior member
Jennifer Muse – Wild Run member
Scott Turner – whipper-in, Wild Run
Henry Williams – Master of Foxhounds and huntsman, Wild Run

PLACES

Canton, Mississippi – Elliott's hometown
Hale's Duck Camp – in the Delta behind the Mississippi River Levee
Hickory Hill Stables – barn where Elliott rides in Oxford
Hinton's Duck Camp – Griffen's uncle's camp
The Levee – vast wilderness area between the Mississippi River and its huge levee that runs from Vicksburg, Mississippi to Memphis, Tennessee
Mentone, Alabama – summer camp
River Run Farm – barn where Elliott rides in Canton
The University of Mississippi – Ole Miss, Elliott's college
Virginia – steeplechase set, etc.

HOUNDS – Big River Hunt

Cora
Goboy
Gypsy – likes to chase bobcats
Pout – puppy, young entry
Rufus
Rhett
Saber
Seven
Solo
Sounder – not usually a strike hound
Spice
Valiant
Victor

IMPASSE CHARACTERS

HORSES

Appleseed, DeSoto, Trigger, Jeremiah – Camp Horses
Blazer – Ben's chestnut Appendix Quarter Horse gelding
Churchill –gray warmblood, a Percheron cross
Harley – Addy's black Quarter Horse gelding
Jet – Griffen's black Thoroughbred gelding
Magic – Chritopher's bay warmblood mare
Masterpiece – Elliott's bay Thoroughbred gelding
Rocket – William's extra horse, bright chestnut Thoroughbred
Shaker – Rental horse at River Run Farm
Shasta – Scott's dark bay mare
Spin – Rental horse at River Run Farm
Tirade – Susan's palomino mare
Viva – Elliott's gray Thoroughbred mare

OTHER CHARACTERS

Mr. and Mrs. Benjamin Allen – Ben's parents
Mr. and Mrs. Griffen Case – Griffen's parents
Dr. Halliday – Memphis Veterinarian
Jessica and Kimberly Marks – Elliott's older sisters
Panzer – Griffen's Chesapeake Bay Retriever

- Account for – (v) When the hunted quarry escapes to a place where it cannot be reached by the hounds, is bayed, or caught by the pack.
- Away – The game has "gone away" when is has left covert. Hounds are "away" when they have left covert on the line of their quarry.
- Babble – (v) To give tongue on scent other than fox, on no scent at all, or on a scent too faint to follow. Not a desirable trait.
- Bling – (n) Never appropriate in the hunt field. No excessive jewelry allowed. Wedding rings and tiny stud earrings are permissable. Stock pins should be plain.
- Breastplate – (n) Part of the horse's gear that keeps the saddle from slipping out of place and gives the rider another place to grab in case of emergencies.
- Bridle path – (n) The area of the horse's mane shaved right behind the ears. Usually no longer than an inch or two.
- Button – (n) See hunt button.
- Canter – (v) A three-beat comfortable rocking gait. Usually faster than the trot and slower than the gallop.
- Cap – (n) Riding helmet (v or n) Fee. Visitors pay a "capping fee" for the privilege of riding to hounds.
- Cast – (n) A planned move by the huntsman to guide the hounds to a lost line. (v) Or, the hounds my cast themselves.
- Check – (n) A halt in the run caused by hounds losing the line. (v) Hounds check when they lose the line temporarily. At these times, the field must refrain from excessive chatter.
- Colors – (n) The colors on the collar of the scarlet (gentlemen) or black (ladies) coat that distinguish the uniform of one hunt from another. (Some hunts have coats other than scarlet.) To be awarded colors by the Master is to be given the right to wear them and the hunt button.
- Coop – (n) Short for chicken coop. An inviting, a-frame, wooden jump set over wire fences. Usually around three-feet high.
- Couple(s) – (n) Two hounds, (any gender), for convenience in counting. (n) Usually a leather device used to keep two hounds joined to each other for convenience in control or training. (v) To attach two hounds together by use of couples.
- Covert – (n) (pronounced "cover") A patch of woods or dense growth where the quarry might be found.
- Crop – (n) The stick part of the hunting whip.
- Cry – (n) The sound given by hounds when they are on a line.
- Cubhunting – Early hunting before the formal season.

- Field – (n) The group of people riding to hounds, excluding the Master and staff. There are usually two or more fields in hunting.
- Field Master – (n) The person chosen by the Master to control the field.
- Fixture – (n) The place that the hunt meets.
- Fixture Card – (n) The mailed or e-mailed list of dates and times that is sent to hunt members indicating when and where the hunts will take place. Receiving a fixture card is equivalent to being invited to hunt.
- Gaited Horse – (n) One of many breeds who have more "gears" than walk, trot, canter, and gallop. Usually thought of as show or trail riding horses, some make excellent foxhunters.
- Grand Slam – (n) Successfully accounting for a fox, coyote, and bobcat in a day's hunt. Cause for great excitement.
- Ground – (n) "Go to ground." To take shelter.
- Hair Net – (n) Essential part of a lady's attire. Should either be black or match the color of the lady's hair. Never should hair be seen billowing around. Most unbecoming. In some hunts, a lady may be sent home for the infraction. Exception: junior girls' pigtails are welcome and encouraged.
- Hand – (n) Measurement used for horses. One hand equals four inches.
- Harpie – See Hunting Harpie.
- Hilltoppers – (n) Riders who do not plan to jump and move at a leisurely pace after the hounds. The group usually rides to the ability of the least capable of the group. With the right field master, they often see the most game.
- Honor – (v) A hound honors when he speaks on a line that another hound has been hunting.
- Hounds – (n) Foxhounds are hounds, not dogs, and they are counted in couples. Male hounds are "dogs" and females are "bitches". All other canines are referred to as "curs" regardless of their breeding.
- Hunt Breakfast – (n) Meal served any time of the day after the hunt for the members, staff, and guests. Typically around noon but can be later. Sometimes catered by the host, but more often potluck. If potluck, then attendees are expected to bring a dish and beverages to share.
- Hunt Button – (n) Black or brass button with the hunt's special logo engraved upon it. Members with colors are allowed to wear the hunt buttons.
- Hunt Country – (n) The most critical component of the sport, this is the land over which foxhunters ride. Most hunts need a minimum of 3000 acres to show good sport and more if regularly hunting coyotes.
- Hunting Crop – (n) See hunting whip.

- Hunting Harpie – (n) Usually a female without manners who is over mounted and overexcited enough to shout and snap at those around her who cause her distress during the hunt. Occasionally seen in males, too.
- Hunting Whip – (n) Part of the attire of a foxhunter, these have either a wooden knob or stag handle, a leather thong, and silk popper. The whip is used to open gates, control hounds (only when asked by staff), or to lend to a staff member who has lost or broken theirs.
- Huntsman – (n) Person who hunts the hounds.
- Joint Meet – (n) Planned joint hunts with two or more hunts participating.
- Lark – (v) Jump fences unnecessarily. Typically frowned upon, but occasionally allowed by field masters on slow hunting days.
- Lash – (n) The part of the hunting whip that cracks. Usually made of silk.
- Lead – (n) The leg that is in front during the canter. Horses cantering in a circle to the left would typically do so on the left lead.
- Leg up – (n) The act of helping another person on to their horse by the person on the ground cupping their hands for the rider's knee. The rider is then lifted to a height where he or she can easily put the other leg over the saddle.
- Line – (n) The trail of the quarry.
- Master – (n) The Master of Foxhounds. The person in command of the hunt in the field and kennels.
- Meet – (n or v) Where the hunt takes place. "The meet tomorrow is at. . . or "Hounds meet tomorrow at..."
- Open – (v) A hound "opens" when he first speaks upon scenting the quarry.
- Opening Meet – (n) The first formal hunt of the season.
- Panel – (n) The portion of any jumpable fence between two posts. Also, a jumpable portion built into a wire fence. Sometimes used interchangeably with coop.
- Pelham bit – (n) Leverage bit usually ridden with two sets of reins. Can provide extra stopping leverage when riding horses in groups at speed over uncertain terrain.
- Pilot – (n) Rider who takes fences or dangerous spots first to ensure their suitability or safety for the rider(s) behind.
- Point – (n) The distance covered in a run. "That was a six mile point, but twelve miles as hounds ran." Also, the location to which a whipper-in is sent to watch for game to go away.
- Quarry – (n) Coyote, fox, bobcat.
- Radio – (n) Special communication equipment on the same frequency carried by members and staff of hunts who often encounter coyotes.

Only staff speaks on the radio. Should be turned down low or off so as not to disturb the game or sounds of the hounds. (v) To call to staff on the hunt's radio frequency.

- Ratcatcher – Informal hunting attire. Correct for cubhunting and weekday hunts if indicated.
- Release forms – (n) Paperwork to release the hunt from liability should a rider be injured or killed while foxhunting.
- Riot – (n and v) When hounds chase things they are not supposed to chase. Also, the term for inappropriate game.
- Road – (v) Move the hounds as a pack.
- Run – (n) The time that hounds open on a line and lose or account for their quarry. This usually implies a gallop. "That was an excellent run."
- Snaffle bit – (n) Single rein bit that is often ignored by the best-trained horses when it experiences foxhunting for the first time. Often used by riders in the front of the field, huntsmen, or whippers-in who ride alone, but rarely a safe choice by those trying to survive riding en masse in the field.
- Speak – (v) To give tongue when on the quarry.
- Staff – (n) The huntsman, whippers-in, and kennelmen. Paid are professionals; unpaid are honorary.
- Stern – (n) Hound's tail.
- Tack – (n) Riding gear.
- Tack up – (v) Putting on the horse's riding gear.
- Tally ho – A phrase shouted gleefully when one views the hunted game. Can cause much embarrassment for same if inappropriate quarry is identified.
- Thong – (n) The braided leather part of the hunting whip.
- Tongue – See Speak.
- View – (v or n) Seeing the quarry.
- Vixen – (n) Female fox.
- Whip-in – (v) To serve as a whipper-in for a hunt
- Whipper-in – (n) A staff member who assists the huntsman with the hounds.

NEMESIS

AVAILABLE FALL 2011

ALTERNATIVES

Chapter 1

"For what the horse does under compulsion…is done without understanding; and there is no beauty in it either, any more than if one should whip and spur a dancer."

~ Xenophon

Hills. *Right.* To a Mississippi girl, these are mountains. My borrowed horse, Trouble, scrambles up the "hill" like it is just that, but I can see for miles when we reach the top. I know not to look down, but I do it anyway, and my stomach drops.

We're still trotting up the hill – I'm only a few feet behind the rider in front of me on his magnificent black Thoroughbred, Jet. They pick their way with ease like they have done this a thousand times, and they have. Our friends, Ben and Addy, are right behind me on their borrowed horses. I turn back to see the same wonder and amticipation reflected on their faces. The three of us have foxhunted here once before, but we had never been on this very high part of the hunt's property.

"Some hill," Ben said eyes wide. "I'd hate to slip here!"

Griffen turned back to glare at us for talking, for just as Ben opened his mouth, a hound spoke in the distance.

"That's Music," Griffen said under his breath to me.

"You'd better believe it," I said, grinning back at him.

"No, I mean that's the hound, Music," he clarified. "She's a great strike hound. "Something's about to happen here."

Strike hounds are the ones that find the scent first. When they bark, or speak, other hounds listen. Those hounds then trot over to investigate, and if the game is good, they will all honor the strike hound and the chase is on! Foxhounds chase coyote, fox, and bobcat, usually in that order in Mississippi and east Tennessee where I usually hunted. On this property, however, Griffen said there were more foxes.

His radio crackled and someone said, "Tally ho, gray fox, heading southeast to graveyard."

Trouble pranced beneath me as if he understood, and we were off! My heart pounded as Griffen and Jet led the way through a long downhill slide that felt like a roller coaster without rails, over a stone wall that was at least four feet high, across a small pasture that served as a place to gather even more speed, and back into the woods where we dodged and ducked branches and hopped ditches. Hounds had checked, so we paused briefly to listen.

It was late January, and steam rising from the horses's warm bodies and out of their nostrils gave the woods a mystical feel. It was very cold, about thirty degrees, but I was warm in my many layers of hunting clothes. It was much colder in this part of the world, so I donned long underwear and a white turtleneck in addition to my regular clothes.

I was wearing a black wool frock coat with no hunt colors on the collar and silk stock tie that I had just purchased for the occasion. I usually wore my red coat when I hunted, for our huntsman preferred that staff wear scarlet. But not today. Ben had on his red coat, but Addy, too, wore black. Since she only had one formal hunt coat, she wore the colors of our home hunt, Big River, on her collar. Typically, visitors wore black coats with no colors on the collar, but Griffen had secured permission from this hunt for us to wear our colors if we chose to do so.

I was glad for my warm vest and clothes, for once we stopped galloping, I could feel the wind's bite on my cheeks. Being in the woods helped, but it was still very cold. Trouble and Jet both stamped impatiently, and I stroked Trouble's neck to calm us.

The huntsman and his horse trotted by with the stragglers hoping to lay them all at once on the line. I made sure my horse's head was pointed towards them and not his rear. I had been assured that Trouble had impeccable manners, but it would certainly not do to have him kick a hound.

"Find it! Hup, hup, hup get'em up!" the huntsman cheered.

Hounds milled around all fifteen riders paused at the check. We were riding in first flight, or the group that rides closest to the huntsman and hounds. Normally, as guests we would ride in the back of first flight, but we were offered the courtesy of riding up front today as Griffen's guests. A lovely lady named Libby was one of the Masters of Foxhounds, and she led first flight on a big dapple-gray gelding. She was about thirty and could ride like the wind! I was having a ball watching her go. Not a hair was out of place, and her horse gleamed with good grooming.

The others in first flight were kids on ponies and a few regular adult members. The kids idolized Griffen and were delighted to get to ride with him. He had always whipped-in for this hunt since moving here in college and occasionally took some of them with him to teach them about hounds. He was like a pied piper to them, and they were all very interested in watching the three of us ride with him, too.

"Here hounds, find it, hup, hup, hup," the huntsman said again.

Hounds circled and snuffled, tails up, heads down – working their hardest to please their huntsman. I smiled watching them…my favorite sport with my favorite people in the world – but I do miss my own horse.

When I looked over at Griffen, I caught his eye. He winked, and my heart fluttered. I had not seen him for two weeks until yesterday, and it had seemed like two years. He had been in law school in Oxford in the fall where I was a junior at Ole Miss. But brief exposure to the world of acting last summer had landed him a yearlong movie contract that had just begun. Right now, he was working out of Nashville, so he'd flown us up here for a weekend visit.

Scent was spotty, so the huntsman lifted the hounds and trotted to another spot, or covert, that usually contained foxes. Griffen moved Jet beside me and reached out for my hand…a rare and quite public gesture of affection for him.

"Griffen dear," I smiled at him. "Whatever *are* you doing? People could get the wrong idea."

"Remember it is *your* idea that we're not engaged right now," he reminded me.

"Yeah, well, we're not," I said, but didn't let go of his hand. "That's up to you to fix."

"Not hardly! I've done my part."

"You're doing your part," I corrected. "Just keep it up, and we'll see."

"I'm glad you came," he said at the same time another hound spoke.

"Shhh!" I hissed at him more aggressively than necessary but smiled as I did it – just to get him back for doing the same earlier to Ben and me.

He rolled his eyes, dropped my hand, and gathered Jet's reins. Jet was already prancing in anticipation.

"Who was that?" I asked.

"I think it was Ranger, but I'm not sure," Griffen said. "Music has a deeper voice."

The whole pack was in full cry now, and our group jolted past an old barn, across another field, over three more coops, and down more trails. We had circled back towards the mountain when the pack checked. Trouble was moving along nicely, but he was getting to be hard to stop. My ribs were sore from an accident I had two weeks ago, but they were improving. It still hurt to have to haul on the reins, and I wished I remembered to bring my own bridle like Ben always did. Trouble went in a snaffle bit, but I would have liked to have had better brakes…especially since we were riding in such a jumbled up crowd. For now, Jet's ample backside was serving as a buffer for us.

I looked back to find Addy and Ben – they were coming up right behind now, Addy's horse having refused the first jump…a stone wall. She circled to the back of first flight once he refused, but they got him over, and they were now up with the rest of us.

"You should have seen how high he popped when he finally cleared it!" she said, eyes bright with the memory. "I felt like we were going to hit the moon!"

The three of us had flown over yesterday afternoon after class on Griffen's agent's plane, and I had been allowed to be co-pilot. I had just started taking flying lessons, so it was a real treat to get to fly in a twin-engine airplane. Griffen met us at the airport, settled us into our hotel room, and taken us all to dinner – after he'd sent Ben and Addy off on an errand in his truck so we could spend a little time to ourselves. I blushed thinking about how nice it was to be adored by someone like him. It was unbelievable. And, we'd been able to dodge the media. They had no idea we were here and apparently didn't care. Thank goodness for that…

"Are you here?" Griffen said, and I jumped.

"Yes, of course," I said blushing again. "Where else would I be?"

"You were just staring at nothing and smiling," he said. "Everything ok?"

Before I could answer, hounds struck going straight up the mountain. Griffen collected Jet; I managed to contain Trouble long enough to get my reins in order, and we dashed up the mountain. Addy's horse bolted past me, but she was able to crash him into Jet's solid backside and not kill our friendly field master. Ben was right behind me, and I would soon be very grateful for that. Trouble lurched and pulled himself in great bounds up the mountain. At the top, he accelerated. I remembered the hairpin turn ahead and sat back in my saddle to slow him.

The next few moments were in slow motion. Choreographed by the music of the hounds, Trouble hit the turn way too fast and both back legs went down. At the same time, I was jolted to the right. My saddle spun right, too, and flipped all the way over. For a terrifying moment, my foot hung in the right stirrup beneath his stomach as he hurled me around the precipice like a Biblical slingshot.

"Dear God, I hope you have the angels on alert," I prayed. "This does not feel good…not at all."

I was falling to the right, and Trouble was steady scrambling left at breakneck speed. When I hit the ground, I had the feeling that I was really close to the edge of the mountain.

I was.

For what felt like thirty minutes, my body soared. Finally, I started hitting things, trees maybe…my face…I could feel my skin tearing. My stomach was in my throat…this must be what it feels like to bungee jump…I had never wanted to do that…

And then I hit something hard. The ground. Thank God. I was afraid to move…afraid to look up and see how far I had fallen…afraid I would pass out like I always did in these kinds of situations…So inconvenient… So I stared ahead and concentrated on moving my toes.

"Elliott!" a male voice shouted from way too far above me to be possible. Not looking up –

"Down here!" I said, ribs really hurting now.

"Coming!" he said, and I could hear a body falling a long way to get to me. He must not be falling, just crashing down the mountain.

"Ben! You're nuts! I'm so glad you're here," I said.

"I can't believe you survived that," he said. "Are you hurt? You should see your face…well, maybe not yet."

"I don't think I'm hurt, really," I said. "My fingers and toes work. And I can breathe. What *about* my face?"

"Just scratches. Don't worry, you're still beautiful, neighbor," he said touching my cheek, and his eyes sparkled. He wrapped his big arms around me then and cradled me next to him careful not to squeeze too hard. "Thank God you are alive. That was horrible to watch. You really should be dead."

"Don't sound so disappointed, Ben," I said, but I was starting to feel lightheaded and shaky.

"Everything ok down there?" a young male voice called from way above us.

"Yes, everything is fine. She's not hurt badly," Ben said.

"Just keep going down," he said. "I'll meet you at the turn in the trail with your horse."

Before I could get up, Ben pulled me close to him again, and it felt so reassuring to have him here beside me, anchoring me. I needed that...the mountain started to move, spin actually, and I felt beads of sweat break out on my forehead.

"Oh, Ben," I said. "This isn't good."

"What? I'm just so glad you're alive," he whispered into the top of my head and pulled me closer to him.

"Ben, this can't be happening, not now," I stammered.

He leaned back to get a better look at my face. What he saw there had him quickly pulling away.

"You're green," he said.

I rolled away just in time. My stomach heaved, but I thankfully had time to turn away and miss him. *How humiliating!*

"Here, take this," he said, handing me a handkerchief.

Ok, Grand, where are you now? Where's this in the manners book? Had to be in the 'Helen's Tips on Handling Hangovers' chapter, but I skipped that one. Help!

The only response I was getting was her cackling laughter. She could be so useless at times!

"Can you walk?" he asked, politely averting his eyes. He *is* the perfect guy.

"Yes. Just give me a minute."

"Take all the time you need."

We hobbled down the mountain, for my ankle was sore. He tried to support me by putting his arm around me, but that hurt my already bruised ribs. So, I clung to his arm as we gently picked our way down the mountain.

Seconds later, Griffen and Jet crashed through the underbrush and appeared below us. They looked just like the Headless Horseman of Sleepy Hollow, but of course, with a glorious face and angry/worried green eyes.

"Ben, can't you keep her on her horse? You were supposed to watch my back," Griffen growled and leapt from Jet in one fluid movement. "My turn," he said to Ben possessively collecting me into his arms. I could feel that, for the first time ever, he was going to kiss me – in public. *Ick! No kiss…Nasty mouth! He must really be worried to kiss me here… now…* But before he could do this in front of everyone…well…Ben, Addy, and the helpful boy, I hurriedly turned my cheek.

"Ouch," I said, and he quickly loosened his grip on my ribs.

"Sorry. Oh, and thanks, Ben," he said over his shoulder.

"Any time. Just be glad you didn't see it," he said.

Griffen turned and looked at Ben. "You're right. And I mean it, Ben. Thanks." He took his hand and shook it; then pulled him into a hug. "Thanks, really. I'm just glad she's all right."

"Thank God for that, Griffen," Ben said. "You know how far that was…" he stopped short when he saw my face turning ominously puce again.

Someone had caught Trouble for me. Once I was mounted, Griffen sent the helpful boy, Ben, and Addy back to the others. I assured him that I could ride and wanted to find the hounds, too, but he wouldn't listen.

"I need you to go in with me," Griffen said, knowing I couldn't argue with that. "Looking at you has me too traumatized to hunt.

Wait until you see your face this time! I can't believe Ben didn't take a picture."

"We were…distracted," I stammered, not wanting him to know I'd just thrown up all over the mountain.

"Distracted?"

"Don't ask," I said, feeling the nausea coming back. "I don't want to talk about it."

We rode in silence for a minute…I concentrated hard on Trouble's steady footfalls. Now that the adrenaline had left, I started feeling really weak.

"I need to stop, just for a minute," I muttered.

Griffen turned back looking…worried…or something. I couldn't tell – I didn't care. I just wanted to get off this horse and sit for a few more minutes. He held Trouble's bridle and helped me down. I stumbled over and sat near a rock, putting my head between my knees.

"What's wrong with you?" Griffen asked, a little too testily for me to handle at the moment.

"Oh, I don't know," I said. "I just free-fell about a half-mile through the air and landed on a rock. Can't imagine what could *possibly* be wrong with me."

"You said you were fine."

"I must not be."

"What's wrong?"

"Just…just let me sit here a minute. I don't want to talk."

"Do I need to get Ben?"

"Why?"

"Nevermind."

I leaned my head back and closed my eyes concentrating on

Jet's and Trouble's steady crunching and stomping. What were they chewing? It's January. Leaves?

"Elliott, what's going on with you?" Griffen asked, gently this time.

"I'm just, well…a little dizzy…dazed or something," I muttered. "Just give me a minute, I'll be fine."

We eventually made it back to the hunt breakfast around the same time the others were returning. I felt much better…almost whole…after drinking a Coke and eating a few sandwiches. Ben and Addy came over to check on me and Griffen left to visit with some of his friends.

"Well, I think you just topped Scott's stunt," Ben said.

"What do you mean, his stunt?" I asked, alarmed to be talking about the guy I had a date with last weekend within earshot of Griffen.

"That huge river he jumped your horse over, what else?" Ben asked.

"Oh, that. At least he stayed on," I said. "Did you tell Griffen about that?"

"No, Elliott. I'd rather avoid talking to him about impressive equestrian feats performed by some guy that you happen to have gone on a date with last week, regardless of how innocent you say it is… especially on your horse. That would go over like a squirrel in church," he laughed.

"Can I get you anything else, Elliott?" Addy asked.

"No, thanks."

"Elliott, I'm so very glad you are ok!" Libby, our field master, said. "I have only been hunting here a year since transferring from Huntsville, but I've never heard of anything like that."

"I'm so embarrassed, Libby," I said. "Now everyone will remember me for pulling that stunt."

"We usually lose a few riders at that turn, but we've never had one go all the way over!" she said, and my stomach lurched again at the memory.

"Yes, well…" I stammered.

"Nevermind that; I wanted to see if any of you knew the girl from Oxford that my little brother's fallen in love with," she grinned. "I want to get the run-down on her."

"I'm sure Ben will know any girl in Oxford that's over sixteen," Griffen laughed as he handed me a big glass of sweet iced tea.

"Thanks," I whispered to him.

"Well, he and a friend went over last weekend to hunt with your group, but mostly just take her out. I think he met her when they visited their Alabama hunt, but I am not sure. Anyway, they have a great group, just short on girls his age," she laughed. "I picked on him for traveling a whole state away for a date."

"I know who you're talking about," Ben said smiling widely. "That's Ashley, Ashley Woods. She's a knockout and pretty smitten with him, too. Chip's a good guy. We're glad Ashley finally seems to be settling on someone we like for a change."

"My brother's name is Scott."

COMING SOON